Because of You

ALSO BY KATY TURNER

Let's Just Be Friends
Because Of You

Because of You

KATY TURNER

JOFFE
BOOKS

Joffe Books, London
www.joffebooks.com

First published in Great Britain in 2024

Cover art by Jarmila Takač

ISBN: 978-1-83526-803-2

To F, T and J

PROLOGUE

Skye walked along the coast path and pulled in a deep breath of salt air, the scent of the sea mingling with that of the peaty earth below her. If it were possible, Skye would bottle that scent, and keep it on hand to sniff whenever she needed to be transported to Eastercraig.

Far below the steep cliffs and tumbling rocks came the whoosh of the tide rolling in and out. It was the only sound, save for the occasional high-pitched call of an oystercatcher. Out in the open air, Skye felt freer, better than she had all day. Her jaw unclenched, her shoulders dropped, the fog in her head cleared.

Almost immediately, thoughts of that morning began to press themselves against her hard-fought serenity. She halted, balling up her fingers and toes, forcing all thoughts of what had happened that morning to the back of her mind. She was heading to the rock. Once she was there, she would feel much better.

She began to walk again, more briskly now, her tread light on the grass beneath her shoes. A few more ups and downs of the coast path, and a sharp right turn, and she would be there.

The rock was really rocks, plural, the uppermost point in a collection of huge crags that jagged their way into the sea. When she used to visit Eastercraig as a teenager, this was where Skye would come to shake off the ringing of her father's voice in her ears, the disappointment in his tone. The rock was far away from the troubles of home, a place of safety. At her lowest points, she would stand on it, close her eyes and scream at the ocean. Scream out the frustration, the anger and fear.

Off the main path forked a less well-trodden track, and Skye now took that. It was less beaten underfoot, but she knew every dip in the ground, each stony lump and bump. She slowed her pace as she headed downhill, her body singing with the anticipation of getting there. But as the rock came in sight, she stopped dead.

Somebody was already there.

Skye stared at the man sitting on her rock. *Her* rock. She'd spent so much time on it in years gone by, she considered it almost as her possession. Yet the saying went that possession was nine-tenths of the law (although studying law had taught her this wasn't strictly true), and this man looked unlikely to move.

He was sitting statue-like, almost Rodin's *The Thinker*, with his spine curled over and his chin resting on his fist, taking up her favourite hiding place.

A fierce gust pushed past Skye, whipping her hair up until it stood on end, chilling her face and bringing up goose-bumps on her arms. Not that she cared. Skye didn't come to this spot for the weather. She came here to be alone. She had laced up her trainers and walked over a mile from Eastercraig to enjoy this splendid isolation, where only the most intrepid dog walker, runner or hiker disturbed your solitude.

This guy must have had the same idea and beaten her to it.

Standing watching him felt voyeuristic, and Skye was uncomfortably aware that he had no idea she was there. She wasn't certain how to introduce her presence, or whether if she should at all. He was clearly trying to avoid contact with other people as much as she was. Perhaps it was best if she headed back to town and come back later.

She was already turning, when the man unclenched his hand and moved it up his face so his forehead rested in it, then let out a huge growl, which crescendoed to a roar.

Blimey! The sound echoed in Skye's heart. She tried to take a step back, but she couldn't. She was transfixed. Growl over, the man turned around. His eyes widened briefly, then hardened, and Skye's cheeks burned under his glare.

He stood stock still. Skye had to stop herself from gasping out loud. She was no longer aware of the awkwardness of the situation, distracted in so many ways by the sight of him. Even though his irritation was obvious, he was good-looking to the point of . . . well, distraction.

Tall, and of a slim build, he had a tanned, oval face with an aquiline nose and defined cheekbones. Eyes: an unreal icy-blue. Hair: flaxen. Flaxen? When was the last time she'd used that word? Had she *ever* used that word? And smartly dressed, in dark jeans and a grey henley top, beneath which she could detect the outline of strong shoulders.

She moved her eyes back up to his face, where his scowl snapped her out of her reverie. And yet, she couldn't help but keep staring at him.

'Hi,' she managed, unable to articulate herself further.

He looked at her for a moment longer, the piercing intensity of his gaze making Skye's pulse beat loud and fast — before sidestepping her and storming back towards the coast path.

Frozen to the spot, Skye gaped at the empty space where he had stood.

'Wow,' she whispered.

CHAPTER 1

Driving down the hill into the tiny but perfectly formed coastal town of Eastercraig was like coming home. There was no other place on earth that made Skye's heart sing a sweeter song. She slowed the car to a snail's pace to take in the scene opening up ahead and felt a wash of tranquillity.

It didn't matter that she hadn't been able to scream from the rock. After watching the man disappear back up the coast path, she was too surprised to take her turn and instead gave him a ten-minute head start before returning to where she had parked her car. A good scream would have been immensely cathartic, but her Uncle Hugh was the real reason she was in town. Seeing him would help her far more than yelling from a clifftop.

Before her was the terrace of pastel-painted houses, the little shops dotted along the front, her uncle's veterinary surgery among them, the B&B and a few more white rendered houses beyond. At one end sat the harbourmaster's office, fishing boats bobbing about on the sea in front. Even from here she could make out the flock of rowdy seagulls that lurked in the hope of nabbing a snack from a fresh catch. Down at the other end was the pub, the Anchor, where the giant yellow umbrellas slotted into the outdoor tables, heralded the arrival of summer.

Skye flicked her eyes to the water, a glistering sapphire blue under the June sun. Once she got to Uncle Hugh's house, and apologized profusely for her unplanned appearance, and had a long-overdue catch-up over a cup of Hugh's favourite Earl Grey, she might have a restorative dip. Fresh air and wild swimming being good for the mind and all that.

She paused at the top of the road that led to Hugh's old crofter's cottage, and on an impulse pulled into the town's small car park. After the shock of encountering the angry-handsome man, and seeing him roaring from her rock, an extra few deep breaths of salt air were just what she needed. Plus, she could grab some eclairs from the café. She'd like to arrive on her uncle's doorstep bearing his favourite treat — it was the least she could do for turning up so unexpectedly. She pictured her uncle, recently retired, digging in his veg patch — one of his favourite hobbies — and smiled to herself. He was probably doing it right now, tending to the young plants, or perhaps deadheading the early flowering roses. She could help out with that, just like she used to when she was younger, when Hugh's wife, Skye's Aunt Dorothy, had still been alive. She bet Hugh still used Dorothy's rose snips, the ones with pink handles. Hands in the pockets of her suit trousers, she strolled down towards the front. She crossed the road and leaned against the railings. What was it about the ocean that was so calming? Someone had once told her the lack of a pattern in the movements of the waves forced the brain to relax.

Today the tide was fully in, bringing the sea right up to the front, the colloquial name given to Eastercraig's main road, curving around the harbour in a near-perfect crescent. The water was also as flat as glass. Skye's heart suddenly fell. She felt her tear ducts twitch, which seemed almost impossible. She'd thought she was all cried out.

You're being ridiculous, she told herself. *Just because there aren't any waves to focus on doesn't mean you can't be calm.*

It occurred to her that if she knew how to be calm, she wouldn't be here in Eastercraig, picking over the ruins of her life.

Yet here she was again, hurling unhelpful hyperbole at the situation to boot. No tears came, and she blinked a couple of times, her eyes still feeling a bit raw from the morning.

'Come on, Skye,' she said aloud. She had to stem the lurking panic, force out the fog that was trying to invade her head once more. 'Give yourself some room to breathe, and then you can put yourself back together again. Hugh will know what you should do. He always does.'

Peeling herself from the barrier, she walked briskly to the café.

At the counter, she ordered two eclairs, a doughnut, and a slice of flapjack, plus a couple of enormous lattes to take away. Normally, with such a haul, Skye would be drooling in anticipation. But as she left the shop, she felt her mouth go dry and her chest begin to tighten.

Skye? Skye! Come back! Will's words echoed in her head.

As if she could. As if she would.

It's a misunderstanding. That's all. Come on, Skye. Don't be silly. And it's a big day for you.

The patronizing, condescending liar. She had never felt so brutally wounded in her life. At this moment, she hated the very thought of him.

Climbing back into the car, her stomach grumbled. Using a neatly manicured baby pink nail, and chipping it, Skye unpicked the tape on the box and considered the cakes. None of them now appealed. Will had managed to ruin cake too.

She placed the box on the passenger seat and headed towards Hugh's cottage.

Five minutes later, Skye pulled up in the driveway of a low whitewashed building, with a red door, and little dormer windows poking out of the roof. Pelargoniums spilled over terracotta pots either side of the front steps.

Everything at the cottage looked exactly as it always did: comfort incarnate, welcoming. Even the pelargoniums, shifting on the breeze, seemed to be inviting her in. Skye thought back to when she came here as a teenager, battling with her emotions, but always finding solace in Hugh and Dorothy's open arms, and wisdom in their words.

Her aunt had died three years ago, and while Skye often called Hugh for a catch-up, she hadn't spoken to him properly since the New Year, only sending occasional texts, and she now berated herself for it. A twist of guilt worked its way through her. She had been so focused on work and Will that she had neglected her relationship with Hugh. She would try and make up for it over the next couple of days.

Everything was going to be OK. She was back in her happy place, and Hugh would know exactly what to do.

CHAPTER 2

Famous last words.

Paolo Rossini loved that expression, its portentous air. It was always particularly gratifying when it rang true.

'It feels like nothing bad can happen today. It's so wonderfully tranquil in here,' Holly said, picking up the practice's list for the afternoon. 'And out there too.'

She was asking for it with that. Paolo wondered when it would come and bite them on the backside, like a rabid dog. He hurriedly took that thought back. They'd never had an animal with rabies in, and he didn't want one now.

'Aye,' he said, from where he sat on one of the reception chairs. He straightened out his scrubs. 'I think it's that the spectre of Hugh no longer looms. You don't get shouted at on arrival.'

At the end of the previous year, they had all been amazed when their workaholic former boss, Hugh MacDougal, had finally decided to hand over the practice to Holly. Of course, Holly was of a similarly driven mould, so perhaps that had had something to do with his decision.

Paolo glanced at the sea outside. Holly wasn't wrong. All was especially peaceful about Eastercraig's veterinary surgery

8

today. Spring had turned to summer and the water, with nary a wave in sight, was a shade of lapis beneath a cloudless sky. The sun shone through the windows, warming the reception area like a greenhouse. Like a flower in full bloom, Paolo's face now turned towards it.

'Honestly . . .' Chloe poked her head out from the kitchenette. 'I swear he never took a two-week holiday in all the time I worked with him, and I've been here nearly ten years. Then you come along and he's off.'

'I doubt he felt he could, given it was virtually a second home to him for the last thirty years. But when we encouraged him to take some time away, I didn't expect him to book a month-long cruise.' Holly rearranged her expression to one of someone channelling inner calm, albeit with some effort. She cast her hand over the empty reception area. 'Still, if it continues like this we'll survive.'

During Holly's first year in Eastercraig, Paolo had spent spare moments taking internal bets on whether Hugh MacDougal was going to huff at her, howl at her, or hurl the closest object to hand at her. In fairness, the last one never happened but their every encounter involved a roulette of Hugh's reactions. Eventually, it had turned out Hugh, instead of hating Holly, had wanted to hire her to take his spot, only he'd been struggling with the thought of retiring. They shouldn't have been surprised that 'retiring' in January meant dropping down to two mornings a week, not to mention haunting the corridors on his days off too and offering to help with consultations or operations. What was more surprising was that his unpredictable demeanour of the previous year had all but evaporated.

It took Paolo, Holly and Chloe several more months to nudge him towards taking a break somewhere hot, and Hugh had plumped for the Med, which satisfied everyone. Hugh could indulge his love of the sea, and with mainland Europe and a large body of water between them, it struck Paolo as a decent enough bulwark against any further spontaneous visits.

'Exposure therapy,' suggested Paolo. 'One week wouldn't have cut the mustard. The art of relaxation needs to be learned over time.'

'And a goodly amount of distance. Well, we ought to be OK. I can manage the workload — this morning seemed to go smoothly enough,' said Holly determinedly, as if she was psyching herself up for the rest of June. 'On-calls might be tough, but I've got it.'

Paolo — Anderson and MacDougal's veterinary nurse — interlaced his hands behind his head, crossing one leg over the other, as if he were reclining on a deckchair. Of the three of them, he was the most laid-back, except when it came to his love life. Not that there was much to be excited about on that front. Anyway, somebody had to be a little more chilled, to keep the surgery on an even keel. Chloe, the practice's receptionist, couldn't make it through the day without finding something to worry about. Meanwhile, Holly tended to take on too much — the claim she could manage a month without a second vet a case in point.

'You *can* get a locum, Hols. It's not a sign of weakness. But seriously, guys, we've got fifteen minutes for lunch. Can we manage to enjoy this while it lasts?'

Paolo closed his eyes as Holly went back over the schedule. He'd love to jet off somewhere hot too. His last trip had been to see his family in Glasgow, which wasn't so much a holiday as an exercise in patience. His younger sisters were in and out of his parents' house daily, all three talking nineteen to the dozen, as per usual. Alessandra, his youngest sister spent all week gushing about her new boyfriend, Luisa had moved in with hers a month ago, and Francesca had recently got engaged and could chat about nothing but wedding preparations. At least his parents were so focused on the latter they chose not to delve into Paolo's relationship status at all that week. He'd let the familial chaos wash over him, as he always did, but he had been grateful to return to Eastercraig, and the quiet of his own flat.

A moment later, Chloe's voice whispered in his ear, 'Have you gone to sleep, Paolo?'

'Nah. Just loving how bloody quiet it is.'

'Don't jinx it.'

He opened his eyes and took the tea from her. 'Sorry. Heaven forbid.'

'We need to drink up before Joe MacAllan arrives,' said Holly. 'He's always prompt.'

Holly and Chloe sank back into their respective chairs, clutching their mugs. That postprandial moment before the next cases of the day arrived, when their clothes were still relatively hair-free and the floor still reasonably clean, was always one to be savoured.

And then the door flew open. The panes of glass in it rattled as it crashed on its hinges.

What had he said? It had been less than five minutes since the famous last words.

Paolo stood as a young woman bowled in, then stopped in front of them all. She was wearing a trench coat over a smart suit, and an incongruous pair of slightly muddy sneakers. Her hair was in a shaggy peroxide-blonde bob with a long fringe. Paolo had never seen her before.

The woman looked around, and let out a slow breath, as if trying to calm herself.

Next to him, Chloe was also on her feet, doing a stunned little dance that told Paolo she had no idea who this woman was or why she was groaning in their reception.

Holly gave a small cough. 'Can we help you?'

The woman pulled back the long fringe which had obscured her face. She was visibly pale under a layer of foundation, her eyes rimmed red, remnants of mascara smudged on her cheeks.

'I'm sorry, but is Hugh here? I need to speak to him. I've just been to the cottage, but nobody answered, and I've been calling his mobile but it's gone straight to voicemail. And if he's not here I thought someone might know where he is.'

11

Holly tilted her head to one side, and Paolo knew she was wondering how much to tell this distraught stranger. 'I'm afraid Hugh's not here. Could one of us help instead?'

'Oh God!' the woman said. She slumped into a chair, her head in her palms. 'I really need him right now.'

Was this a new client? Paolo felt a pang of sympathy for Holly. For the past year, people had been wary about seeing her, rather than her predecessor. It was a tight-knit community, and while it welcomed incomers, Hugh had worked in Eastercraig so long he was spoken about in hushed tones verging on reverence. He was considered a living legend by the clients Holly had recently inherited from him. He knew it infuriated Holly that despite her excellent qualifications, and the fact it was her name on the plaque outside the surgery, people still questioned her abilities as a vet.

Holly pursed her lips. Sensing her annoyance, Paolo stepped in. 'Is this about an animal?' he asked.

The stranger looked up, her brow wrinkling. 'What?'

'An animal? Do you have a sick animal, back at home perhaps, that needs our help?' said Paolo. 'This is a veterinary surgery.'

'No. I need Hugh. It *has* to be him,' the woman insisted, a tremor appearing in her voice. 'Is he off on a call? I could wait till he gets back?'

'I'm afraid Hugh's off for the next few weeks. But you're in safe hands with us,' he said in his most soothing tone.

'For a few weeks?' It came out in a squeak, her shock evident. She then let out another long, slow breath though a tiny gap in her lips.

Paolo bit his lip and tried another tack. 'Maybe you can tell us who you are, what's going on, and we can work out what to do.'

For a second time, the woman swept the fringe back, her hands shaking. Paolo looked at her features properly for the first time and couldn't help but stare at her eyes. They were arresting, so blue they were nearly violet. The woman gazed about the room, despair and hope mingling on her face.

Chloe let out a gasp of realization. 'I know who you are. You're Skye, right?'

The woman's eyebrows lifted. 'Yes. But who are . . . ?'

'Chloe. I've worked with your uncle for . . . forever. He talks about you all the time. And I remember you coming up when we were teenagers. You'd go for long walks on the coast path in that long black leather jacket and those chunky Doc Martens — but back then your hair was pink, and . . .'

Chloe tailed off, having caught the face Paolo was making at her. He had been trying to convey 'you sound like a stalker' through his eyes alone, and luckily on this occasion it had worked.

Paolo went and sat next to Skye, with the same tentative movements he usually reserved for terrified pets. He hesitated for a second, then put a hand on the woman's shoulder. 'Listen, duck. Hugh's gone on a cruise for a month. He's let out his house to some ladies from Derbyshire. I think they're here on an artists' retreat.'

'So he *really* isn't here?' Skye's eyes had grown round. 'And the house isn't empty?'

'You were planning on staying with him?'

She nodded. 'I've never known him not to be in Eastercraig.'

Paolo offered her a smile. 'You'd be right. We almost had to book his holiday for him, he was so reluctant to leave.'

'Where did you come from today?' Holly asked.

'Edinburgh.'

'Don't your parents live there?' asked Chloe.

'Yes.' A pained look crossed her face, and she wrapped her arms around her waist, pulling them in tightly. Her voice dropped to a whisper, the tremble returning. 'I can't believe how much of a mess I've made. Oh, gosh. I need some fresh air. Sorry for taking up your time.'

Looking paler than before — if such a thing was possible — Skye got up and walked out of the door, leaving her handbag on the chair.

'You *had* to jinx our peaceful afternoon, Paolo,' hissed Chloe. 'You—'

Through the window they could see Skye weave unsteadily towards the guardrail that separated the road from the drop into the loch below. Now she grabbed the railings, her body hinging over them as she bobbed on the balls of her feet. Beneath them, the tide was in.

'Oh Christ!' Holly sounded panicked, and it usually took a lot to affect her. 'She's going to throw herself over the edge.'

'Och. It's not exactly deep. Worst case, she breaks both legs,' said Paolo, but he had already passed his mug to Chloe. He ran out the door.

Skye was still leaning over the railing as he approached, but at the sound of his footsteps, turned. Her empty expression was far more chilling than if she had looked scared, or determined.

'Hugh doesn't deserve to deal with me either.' She spoke so quietly, her voice seemed to fall into the water below. 'I've ruined everything.'

Paolo raised his hands in a gesture of peace and trod cautiously towards her. Skye didn't move, and he took it as a positive sign.

He inched closer. 'Don't do anything rash, will you, duck?'

'I . . .' Skye stammered. 'I'm sorry . . .'

Paolo got to her and grabbed her hand, giving it what he hoped was a reassuring squeeze. Skye looked for a moment like she might cry, then she vomited all over his shoes.

CHAPTER 3

Skye sat up and blinked, her eyes dry and scratchy. It wasn't surprising. After the initial shocked hollowness, she had cried all the way from Edinburgh. At some points her vision had been so obscured by tears, she needed to pull over for everyone's safety. And between her trips to the rock, the cottage and the surgery, she hadn't thought to have a drink. The lattes from the shop were still in their carrier, untouched, on the passenger seat of the car.

She glanced around the sitting room of the cottage Holly had taken her to. It was light, airy, all blues and whites which mirrored the hues of the sea, which she could see through the window from where she was positioned on the sofa.

Her own little flat in Edinburgh was a maximalist's dream, all colour and clashing patterns, pictures fighting for room on the walls, and trinkets she'd collected from her travels cluttering every space. She had wanted it to have the allure of an antique shop, inviting and cosy, and it was exactly the way she liked it. This place was so neat and neutral, which she didn't mind except it made her feel more disassociated from normal life than she already did.

Skye sighed as she looked down at the white floorboards, and crossed her legs underneath her. She noticed a bucket by her feet too, although she was pretty certain her stomach was empty. She felt a pang of mortification — the latest in a long line of them — at what had happened at the surgery, bringing her own problems into the lives of complete strangers.

If she had known her uncle wasn't going to be around, she would have escaped somewhere else. Her best friend from work, Houda, had two small children, so she couldn't impose on her, but she might have gone to a university friend in London. Or booked a last-minute B&B on one of the less busy Western Isles. Anywhere she could find some peace and quiet to work out what to do next.

Eastercraig had been her first choice though. Hugh had always been her port in a storm, and — heaven knew — she had been in one permanently when she was younger. Less been in, more *been one*. Hurricane Skye, her mum had nick-named her. Whenever she wound up in trouble, worrying her mum and infuriating her father, she had been sent up to Hugh and Dorothy's house for some time out.

'Batten down the hatches,' she'd said to Hugh once, as a sixteen-year-old, as she stepped off the train at Inverness. 'I'm back.'

She had said it with relish, like she was daring Hugh to be angry with her. Really, she had wanted to check he was still on her side.

'The only storms to be weathered are out there.' Hugh had nodded to the sea, as he drove her back to Eastercraig. 'Here you can be just Skye.'

As he'd said it, she'd felt her shoulders release the tension they held. Felt her lungs exhale fully and her mind stop buzzing, the way they always did whenever the pretty harbour town with its rainbow-coloured cottages came into view.

What was it that lifted her spirits in Eastercraig? Perhaps it was the sea air, threading its way into her veins. Or the slower pace of life. There was a leisurely way of doing things here, from the speed at which you got served at the pub, to the unrushed conversations being held in front of you in the queue at the shop. She loved how people wound down car windows to chat to friends on the pavements, holding up the traffic — not that there was ever very much.

Or perhaps it was simply that Eastercraig meant Hugh and Dorothy. Well, just Hugh now. Wonderful, wise Uncle Hugh.

Even though, years ago, Skye had gathered from her mum that Hugh had a reputation for being a little gruff, he had always had time for her. He was patient and kind, lending an ear and a reasoned word of advice. He was her mum's older brother. He and Dorothy had never had children of their own, and Skye's mum said that made their niece even more special to them, and Skye had cherished their close relationship. She had been grateful to have these extra adults in her life.

It made her chest tighten once more, the thought that she had let that relationship fall by the wayside these last few months, especially now that Dorothy was gone. Skye knew she hadn't seen nearly enough of Dorothy either, in her last years. She regretted that bitterly. They had always shown up for her, however much trouble she'd been in.

Now here she was, in trouble once more.

That Hugh wasn't in Eastercraig was probably a sign. She should head back to Edinburgh to tell Tanya Green, the head of Human Resources at her firm, what had happened. Or some of it, at least.

Skye pulled her phone out of her handbag, and checked the display. Eight missed calls, three voicemails, seven texts. With her newly chipped nail, she scrolled though the list. Six calls and two messages from Houda. A call and a voicemail from Tanya. One of each from Will.

There was also a text from her mum. *We are thinking of you today, pet. Let us know how you get on x.* They would be so disappointed. Dismayed. She had let them down. She would hold off replying to that until she could muster the strength to tell them what had happened.

She looked at Will's next.

Call me. W

Skye chose to leave that one as well, and to ignore his voice-mail too. There was no point in talking to someone when you felt nothing but loathing towards them. He had betrayed her so completely, she couldn't have imagined uncovering a worse secret other than maybe Will admitting that instead of heading to rugby on Sunday mornings he was out clubbing baby seals.

And Tanya? She would need to tell Tanya about the exam. Tanya probably knew already. Not the Will thing though. There were rules about dating people in the office. She felt her stomach roil, like the sea when in full fury, unclear if it was a response to the prospect of confronting Tanya or Will. She leaned over the bucket, willing the feeling to pass.

The Will thing started at the Christmas party, in a noisy bar in one of Edinburgh's grander hotels. A Christmas tree towered in the corner, toeing the line between tasteful and gar-ish with its festoons of giant gold bows, and metallic helium balloons stuck to the ceiling, their dangling ribbons brushing people's hair. Wham! and Mariah Carey competed for volume with the increasingly drunk staff of Tilling and Browne, who were determined to drink the tab dry. A wiser person would have recognized it as exactly the kind of atmosphere in which regrettable decisions got made.

Will had approached her, not the other way round. He was dressed down in a shirt and jeans, plus a hideous Christmas tie covered in snowmen. Not the greatest get-up, though it made him look more approachable than he did when suit-ed-up in the office.

Honestly, Skye had always been a little in awe of him. Will Tomlinson rarely lost a case. People often came to the firm and asked for him specifically. Outside of that, she didn't know much about him, although his secretary, Rosie, said he gave the most generous Christmas presents — Diptyque candles, spa vouchers, huge hampers from Harrods — and that beneath the tailored suits which matched his steel-grey eyes, he was 'a pussycat'.

Will said he had noticed her at the office. Very few peo-ple were in the office as early as he was. He had seen her with her head down, completely absorbed in whatever task she was doing. Skye had smiled, and told him she was a paralegal, but taking her exams that summer. Come September, the firm would be employing her as a fully qualified lawyer, a solicitor in the corporate law department.

Will already knew, which surprised Skye as she had never worked with him before. She knew that he, like her, was a lark, but had never realised *he* had noticed *her.*

He handed over a glass of champagne, and Skye accepted, and they carried on chatting. They weren't flirting, not really. In fact, having had a few gin and tonics with Houda before the party, Skye wasn't sure she was on her best form. But Skye had enjoyed talking to Will. She had split up with her previous boyfriend because he behaved like a child half the time, unable to load the dishwasher or handle an argument. Will was fifteen years older, he was interesting, clever and sharp. A grown-up. Eventually, Houda, an eyebrow unsubtly raised, had dragged Skye away to go and dance.

At the end of the night, as the lights went back up and the shattered bartenders refused to pour any more drinks, the crowd started to thin out. At the coat check desk, a hazardously tipsy Skye found herself stood next to Will.

'Skye, I was wondering . . . would you like to go for a drink some time?' His voice was low.

He was charming. And Skye was single, flattered, and propelled by what was undoubtedly a few glasses of fizz too many. She wasn't entirely sure it wasn't against the rules, but he seemed so confident that it was probably fine. It wasn't as if she was working on any cases with him. And she was a lawyer, she could be very discreet when she wanted to be.

For the following six months, their relationship developed — *very* discreetly. Far from the watchful eyes of the office, they skipped in and out of bars, took day trips to the beach at Portobello, spent weekends at Will's cottage in Pittenweem — which Skye loved because it reminded her of Eastercraig — and edged closer and closer.

When Skye finally commandeered a drawer at Will's house, she had reached the joyous conclusion that things were getting serious. Aside from a ring on your finger, wasn't having your own toothbrush at your partner's house the ultimate sign of commitment? Or perhaps that would be confessing to HR you were together.

'I think we ought to come clean to Tanya Green,' Skye had said. 'It's been five months. Or I could tell Norah.'

Gorgeous and chatty Norah was Tanya's assistant and, confession-wise, telling her appealed more than a potentially dicey chat with Tanya.

Sitting across from her in a quiet corner of an upmarket Thai restaurant, Will shifted in his seat, barely suppressing the look of discomfort on his face. 'Skye. You know how much I care about you. You're wonderful. I thank my stars every day I found you. It's risky though. It might backfire.'

Skye understood or, rather, forced herself to understand. He stood to lose a lot, if Tanya decided this relationship wasn't above board. They both did. Skye didn't push him about it.

Besides, she'd had other things on her plate. As well as her normal workload, Skye had internal exams to focus on. It was the culmination of years of work: her law degree, the Diploma in Professional Legal Practice, and then her training contract. She was technically qualified, she just had to pass the paper and have a quick interview with some of the partners. After that, she would at last be a solicitor at Tilling and Browne, one of the top firms in the city.

She could ask Will about telling HR again then.

Bloody exam. Along with her relationship with bloody Will, that had gone down the bloody drain and all. She might leave calling Tanya too.

She looked at Houda's stream of messages. The most recent two said:

Tanya looking for you. Warpath-ing. She's gone so far as to exploit our friendship and ask me where you are. Said you missed the exam. I told her you're sick.

There was a vomiting emoji next to it. Houda must be psychic. She had sent another an hour later.

Call me, S. I am getting a *little* worried. What happened?

What happened? Skye's future, for once so perfectly mapped out it deserved its own page in an atlas, had imploded.

Less than twelve hours ago, she was all prepared to sit down to the paper. She had revised her arse off to the point where she had practically dropped a dress size. Caffeinated, she had gone into the office to deal with incoming emails, a better use of time than staying at home and sweating through the armpits of her shirt while pacing the short length of her flat.

Will was in early too. He always was. And that was when the clinch happened. Skye winced.

The clinch she saw Will in. With another woman.

CHAPTER 4

Now that Skye was safely ensconced at Holly's cottage, and he was wearing a fresh pair of shoes, Paolo was back in his favourite seat in reception. The retro one with the wooden arms. It was even more comfortable since being re-upholstered last year in a remnant of floral fabric. It fitted nicely with the Dutch orange paint he, Holly and Chloe had picked out as part of a decorating project to bring the formerly shabby surgery into the twenty-first century.

Work-wise, the afternoon had been uneventful. Joe MacAllen, the harbourmaster, had arrived punctually with one of his cats, and after that the rest of the list ran smoothly. There had been nothing out of the ordinary, no raisin-eating dogs or cats hell bent on losing one of their nine lives, thank heavens. The day's sucker punch had been Skye. She had lurked at the back of Paolo's mind all day. He was unable to shift the desolate look on her face from his thoughts.

The team at the surgery were well versed when it came to fixing physical issues in animals. Emotional ones in humans? Not so much.

'Well,' said Chloe, from behind the computer. 'Today has been mega weird.'

'Now it's over,' said Holly, from the chair opposite, 'I can admit to you both I was nervous about being busy this week, so the drama was a decent distraction. Does that make me a bad person?'

'Nah. And it's very kind of you, letting her sleep in your cottage,' said Paolo.

'She puked all over your plimsolls,' said Holly. 'You'd done your bit.'

'I have three pairs . . .' Paolo grimaced. 'I once had a dog throw up on some, only for an incontinent cat to wee on my spares. There's mileage to be had in spare spares. I ought to get a fourth pair. What do you reckon happened to her?'

'I don't think it's kind to speculate,' Chloe announced. 'She was very upset, after all.'

Chloe was too empathetic for her own good sometimes, thought Paolo. *Perhaps she would feel differently if it had been her shoes that were covered in vomit.*

'A little light speculation never hurt anyone,' Paolo countered. 'Do you think she's been fired? She could have failed a drug test at work. Hugh always suggested, albeit affectionately, she was on the wild side. Perhaps she's fallen on hard times. Or she's knocked up. Hence the boak . . . Morning sickness.'

'Tear yourself away from the theorizing, Paolo.' Holly stepped in before his imagination took any further twists and turns. 'Look — what can we do to help her?'

'For a start, I'd suggest it's her decision,' Paolo said. 'She's a grown-up. You're talking about her like she's a wee bairn abandoned on our doorstep.'

Holly nodded. 'That's because Hugh generally talks about her like she's still in her teens.'

'I get where you're coming from, Paolo, but Hugh would never forgive us if we turned away his beloved niece in her hour of need.' Chloe made a good point. Hugh would have their head on spikes if they didn't help. Paolo knew he doted on his niece, even though she was probably in her late twenties.

23

Whatever was on Hugh's mind, his face always lit up when he spoke about Skye. Chloe tapped the phone absently. 'I rang Mhairi at the pub, and the B&B. Both fully booked. Actually, I know our project manager has taken one of the rooms in the latter for most of this month so he can come and go. I'd have her up at the farm, but with the builders it's chaos and I'm *still* not getting on with Fiona.'

Chloe let out a heavy sigh as she mentioned her boyfriend's mother, and Holly reached an arm around her shoulders. 'Still no better?'

Chloe lived up at Auchintraid Farm, with her boyfriend Angus, and his mother, Fiona. An extensive building project had begun on the farm, and from what she said, it was causing more arguments than Chloe, who avoided confrontation like the plague, would like.

'It's like she's had a personality transplant. A crap one. We normally get on so well. But as the project isn't going according to plan . . . ' Chloe shook her head quickly and Paolo took that as a cue to change the subject.

'Back to Skye,' he said.

'I'm with you, Paolo,' said Holly, following his lead. 'Our waifs and strays policy doesn't exactly extend to people . . . But Chloe's right. She's Hugh's niece. I could have her stay, but then Greg is back from a work trip tomorrow, which he says has been hideous. He can hardly kick back on the sofa if someone's kipping on it.'

Paolo threw his hands up. 'It's all right. I've got a spare bedroom. She can stay with me.'

'I wasn't volunteering you,' protested Holly.

'You gave me a look,' said Paolo.

'Which look?'

'A pleading one.'

'Me? *I* looked pleading—?'

'Anyway,' Paolo interrupted. 'I'll do it.' He crossed his arms, and looked to the sky. 'Don't all rush to thank me. She's a woman on the edge. I'll be there in her time of need.'

'Awww, Paolo.' Chloe grinned. 'Pretending to be all grouchy. Really you love being a knight in shining armour.'

'It'll play havoc with my dating life,' he said.

'Och . . . When did you last meet a guy who wasn't a complete dead end? You've not taken anyone home in, like, forever. Or been for dinner or a drink with anyone, not that I can think of. And things with Hamish seem to have ground to a halt. You're very much single,' Chloe concluded.

'Please, don't hold back.'

Holly clicked her tongue. 'We're getting off topic. Let's close up and go let her know she can stay with you for a couple of days. Thanks, Paolo.'

Paolo went through to check on the animals out the back, feeling like someone had picked up on the one thing which made him depressed, written it on a poster, photocopied it, and pasted it on every flat surface in town.

Very much single.

With three words, Chloe had pinpointed the root of all his woes.

The previous year hadn't been as bad. Both Chloe and Holly had been single too. There'd been safety in numbers. Paolo hadn't felt as if not having a boyfriend was the end of the world. This year, with Chloe now with Angus, and Holly going out with Greg, he was the last man standing. The trip to Glasgow hadn't helped either. That even Alessandra, his youngest and kookiest sister, had found someone, made him wonder where he was going wrong.

He hadn't been in a serious relationship since his late twenties — and he missed sharing his life with someone. Was that too much to ask?

But finding that someone was proving impossible. As Chloe had pointed out, any potential relationship with Hamish seemed no longer on the cards and so Paolo was forced to admit it was probably time to move on. Recently he'd decided to dip his toe back in the water and been on a few dates. But the dating scene had been like the North Sea in winter. Cold, wet and utterly unappealing.

The door swung open to reveal Chloe.

'Are you all right back here? Thought I'd come and check on you. I'm not sure Holly gave you much of a say in the matter. I'm about to put the kettle on if you fancy a final cuppa.'

'Och, I'm fine, you know? Mulling over "dead end" men and being "very much single", and the fact I've agreed to have a complete stranger to stay.'

Chloe's shoulders dropped. 'I didn't mean to upset you. It was meant to be funny.'

'Funny things make you laugh. Not die inside.'

Chloe looked distraught and threw her arms around him. 'Och, Paolo. I'm *so* sorry. Listen, you're fantastic. You're handsome and clever and kind and . . .'

'Yeah, all right. Enough. I'm fine.'

'But you're not. You look pretty gloomy.'

'You were right, though. Every man I've dated in the last few months has been . . . meh.'

'Don't say "meh", Paolo. You're more sophisticated than that.'

Paolo allowed himself to smile at the compliment. 'So, every guy I've dated has been acceptable, but it's like when you've wanted a poached egg and it's hard-boiled instead. Not exactly awful, but just not what you want.'

Chloe grinned. 'Eccentric analogies! That's more like it.'

'When what you really wanted was something to dip your soldiers into.'

'Jeez, Paolo . . .' Chloe laughed, cuffing him on the arm.

Paolo snickered. 'Couldn't help myself, there.'

'So, if you're finished with the innuendo . . . cup of tea?'

He nodded. 'Please and thank you. You're a peach, MacKenzie-Ling.'

'What are friends for? Apart from occasionally delivering brutal analyses of your love life?'

Paolo gave a genuine laugh as Chloe disappeared back down the corridor, but it petered out quickly.

Sometimes the feeling of loneliness sat at the back of his mind, so quiet he barely noticed it. Other times, it loomed over everything else. He and Hamish had been so close to becoming *something* that Paolo had thought Hamish might be his. That a romantic relationship with Hamish had become *nothing* was unbearably disappointing.

In his spare time, Paolo was a bookworm extraordinaire, and he loved a good romance. He knew his heroes inside out, their broad shoulders, their strong jaws, their deep voices, their other, myriad swoon-worthy qualities. Hamish Glennis — round-faced and ruddy cheeked, with a mop of unruly brown hair, of medium height and with a pretty normal-sounding voice — met none of the criteria. He never wore finely cut suits, or T-shirts that clung to the contours of his chest. Instead, he spent a lot of time outdoors, and wore scruffy forest-green outdoor gear. Sometimes he sported waders. He often had mud on his face. He ticked none of the traditional boxes, none of the clichéd asks Paolo had once put on his shopping list for a future partner. Yet Paolo knew there was something that hovered unspoken in the air between them.

But even though they had spent time together almost every week since the start of the year, nothing had happened. He must have misread Hamish, misread that electricity. Perhaps Hamish hadn't felt it after all, despite the fact Paolo had been sure they both had.

Could you feel bereft of something you never had? Of course you could. It was the basic tenet of unrequited love.

Paolo could go on all the random dates he wanted, and none of the guys would be as right as he thought Hamish had been.

He leaned inside the cage and picked out a rabbit. Sir Hoppity had been sleeping off an anaesthetic and he gave him a quick stroke. Hoppity blinked lazily, eyeing him with suspicion.

'What do you think, Hops? Do I have a chance with Hamish? Or am I doomed to only ever eat hard-boiled eggs? Oh, you deign not to answer that? Thought not.'

CHAPTER 5

A key in the lock clicked, and Skye looked up. Holly, followed by her colleagues, bustled through the door.

Chloe shed her jacket and moved to the kitchen. 'I'll pop the kettle on,' she announced.

'You're awake.' Holly dropped her bag under the coat rack and peered over the bucket with an unembarrassed interest that Skye attributed to her being a vet. 'How are you feeling?'

Skye managed a smile, though the combination of the humiliation over Paolo's shoes and the gratefulness that some-one had shown her such kindness was already causing her to feel wobbly once more.

She wiped her hand down her cheek. 'A little better,' she said, although she felt slightly sick once more when she noticed the make-up smeared across her palm.

Paolo sat next to her. 'Can you eat anything. Slice of dry toast?'

'Maybe that's a good start.'

'I'll pop some bread in,' said Holly, and went to join Chloe in the kitchen.

Paolo watched them go and then looked back at Skye with kind eyes. 'This is kind of a strange situation,' he said. 'I realize

28

you don't know any of us, but we're all concerned about you. And we know how much your uncle loves you. *And* that if we didn't take care of you then he'd come back from Gibraltar and threaten to hurl us all off a cliff. Want to tell us what's wrong?'

Skye looked at Paolo's friendly, open face and felt crushed. The weight which had sat on her shoulders as she'd driven up from Edinburgh came firmly back down.

Paolo gave an encouraging look. 'Sometimes it's easier to talk to people you don't know.'

Maybe owning up would go some way to alleviating the dismay she felt. A problem shared was a problem halved.

Skye took a breath. 'I walked out of my law exam this morning. I got halfway through, then found myself wondering what the point of it all was. And once that set in, I couldn't face it any more. The page was a blur. Or my head was a blur. Noisy and empty all at once.' She thought back to the horrible moment when all she could feel was the tilting ground beneath her feet and her chest becoming so tight that she could hardly breathe. 'And so I just got up and left.'

There it was. The problem might not have been exactly halved but saying it out loud had definitely made her feel lighter. Some of the other secrets Skye was holding flickered through her head. On reflection, they were undoubtedly better kept locked away.

'Sounds like a wee panic attack,' said Paolo.

It had been. Not 'wee', as Paolo had described it, but a whopping one like she had never experienced before.

'Definitely,' said Skye, playing it down. 'I've had them before, and normally I can manage . . . Thing is, my career rather hinges on passing.'

'That you can deal with in a bit.' Paolo placed a hand on her arm. 'Here comes sustenance. Have a few bites.'

Skye glanced down at the immaculate floor, then eyed the toast with suspicion. Having already wrecked Paolo's shoes that morning, she didn't want to burn acidic holes in Holly's floor.

'I'm the surgery's nurse,' said Paolo, seemingly reading her mind. 'I'm pretty swift with a bucket.'

She took a tentative bite. The residual ache in her stomach seemed to vanish. Even her bile-sore throat soothed with a sip of tea. God, she was ravenous. She hadn't eaten any breakfast. Which begged the question how there had been anything in her stomach to hurl up earlier. A wave of nausea rolled through her.

'In here!' Paolo stuck the bucket under her nose.

The urge passed. 'It's fine. My stomach's still a bit sensitive after earlier. And I'd barely woken up before you all arrived, so maybe I'm not ready for food.'

'Go easy,' said Chloe. 'I've got some teacakes in my bag if you'd prefer one of those?'

Paolo grinned. 'Do you always carry snack foods around in case of emergencies?'

Chloe shot him a withering look. 'No. I brought them into the surgery but then forgot to take them out.'

'You know what? I'd really love a teacake,' said Skye. The mention of the gooey meringue-y biscuits encased in chocolate made her mouth water in a way dry toast never could.

'A bit of sugar does wonders for shock. And it sounds like you've had quite the shock today,' said Paolo, passing the pack over.

'Something like that.' She could hardly tell these three the whole truth. She'd barely met them, and they would certainly judge her for diving so stupidly into a relationship with one of the senior partners. Chloe had suggested earlier she remembered Skye as a teenager. One whom Chloe had apparently watched from a distance but had never approached. Skye certainly didn't remember ever having met Chloe. Chloe, who looked nice as pie, in a vintage shirt-dress and hot-pink lipstick, and was the type of person who always had cake to hand. The type of person who would never get herself into the sort of state Skye had got herself into.

As for Holly? Skye knew from talking to her uncle that right before Christmas he had hired this incredibly tall, outlander as a locum, and then passed his beloved surgery to her, so she must be quite something. Holly might be dressed in a far more relaxed way than Chloe, but Hugh said she was 'a brave and assertive young woman', and Skye felt Holly had an air of self-possession which could be intimidating. Not, perhaps, the most sympathetic person when it came to people who got themselves into shambolic circumstances — although she *had* let Skye sleep on her sofa.

Which left Paolo. He seemed approachable. But . . .

'Do you know what you're going to do next?' Paolo asked her, interrupting her thoughts.

Skye shoved the teacake in her mouth in lieu of answering. Her problems were like a collection of threads, knitted together. The exam was only one of them. There was Will. And, perhaps, work in general. Her whole life was on the verge of unravelling.

She knew she would have to go back at some point, but she wasn't at all sure how she was going to face it. But what choice did she have?

Originally, she had intended to talk to Hugh, stay a couple of nights, then drive back down to Edinburgh. Skye swallowed, but before she could say anything, Paolo ploughed ahead.

'Because, if you like, you can stay with me for the next few days,' he said. 'I've got a spare room. Granted, it's not huge, but the bed is comfy. You're not allergic to cats, are you?'

Skye put a hand on her heart, some of her faith in the world restored. 'I'm not, but . . . are you sure? You really don't have to. I'm sure I could just find a B&B somewhere. I wasn't going to be here for long.'

'It's not a problem. Why don't you see if you can take a day or two off. Then you'll have time to work out what to do next.'

'Thank you,' she whispered. She wondered if he was right. Maybe she could take a couple of days off and come up with a plan. She looked around at them all. 'You're all being so kind. I really appreciate it. And I'm *so* sorry again about your shoes, Paolo. Can you please let me buy you a new pair? I can't believe after that you'd risk being within a couple of yards of me.'

'Don't fret about it anymore. We can go over now. Are you parked in the car park? If so, we can get your stuff en route,' said Paolo, and Skye smiled at the boundless goodwill of the man. 'If you're up for it, we could grab a bottle of wine from the shop to have with supper. I know it's only Monday, but it might help you to unwind.'

It was like someone was answering her prayers. While her father would have scolded her for that, and told her the Almighty was unlikely to encourage you to go and drown your sorrows, her mum would have said God created the world, which included pubs, and if he didn't want people to drink then what was he thinking when he gave the go-ahead to change water into wine.

She sided, as she always did, with her mum. 'Sounds great.'

* * *

Paolo led the way home, after another cup of tea. Not much farther along the harbour front, they stopped outside a tall, white rendered building.

'Can I take this?' Paolo stuck out a hand to carry Skye's bag. It was the right thing to do, wasn't it? The woman had obviously had a terrible day.

'Thank you, it's getting heavy,' said Skye, passing him a holdall. 'You know, if it's too much, I can head back to Edinburgh tomorrow. Tonight, even.'

'What can I say? I'm a nice guy.'

He hefted the bag on to his shoulder. Skye had intended to stay a while, judging by the weight of it.

'How long did you pack for?' he asked, panting slightly.

'I was in a rush,' said Skye. 'And you can never accurately predict the weather here. I threw half my wardrobe in. Sorry.'

'No worries,' said Paolo, hoping he didn't topple backwards and crush her. That would be adding insult to injury.

'I'll get the wine in. I'd like to,' she said, following him up the stairs to his first-floor flat. 'I'll nip to the shop in a second.'

'Och, cheers,' he said. He opened the front door, and showed her to the spare room. 'Dump your stuff in here. I'll grab some sheets, and you can make yourself at home. Is there anything else in the car I can fetch?'

'You weren't lying. You really are a nice guy,' Skye turned and smiled at him.

He was, wasn't he? But what did people say? Nice guys finished last. It didn't bode well for him, did it?

CHAPTER 6

The next day, Skye curled up on the snuggler armchair with a book from Paolo's amply stocked shelves. After a walk, and exchanging texts with Houda, she had returned to his flat via the café where she picked up two doughnuts and a coffee. Once back, she had emailed Tanya, explained she had been sick, which was true, and was still feeling slightly unwell — which was also kind of true — and thought it prudent to stay out of the office for forty-eight hours, and said that she would be back on Thursday. Tanya had delegated her request to nice Norah, who had sent a standard response, adding that she hoped Skye felt better soon.

Skye envisioned her orderly desk, the day's paperwork piled high in the in-tray, pens and pencils and notepad lined up, her litre bottle of water and a bag of almonds in case she was snacky. At the thought, it felt like she had swallowed a stone.

How was she going to be able to show her face there again? Not only would she be known as the girl who flunked her test, but Will would be there too, a constant reminder of the hubris she had shown in thinking she had that area of life worked out. Perhaps they would hand her a cardboard box and demand she clear out her belongings.

For a brief moment that wasn't a wholly unpleasant image, but Skye hastily brushed it aside. She had worked hard to get to where she was. There was no space for self-doubt. And even if she did occasionally ponder her suitability for her future role in the corporate department, she would be an idiot not to take it up. Despite working on weekends and holidays all through uni, taking back-to-back shifts in a bar to try to cover the costs of her course, accommodation and living expenses, she had still accrued significant debts she had to pay off. And then there were the other benefits at the firm, which she was fortunate to have, the private healthcare cover, the pension. It was a secure role, with prospects, and besides, it taxed her intellectually, fulfilling her love of research and fine detail. She would be mad to throw it away.

An hour later, with Paolo's cat, Ginger, on her lap, she had shaken off these thoughts and was engrossed in *Pride and Prejudice*. She hadn't read for ages. Or at all.

When it had been assigned to read in school she had dossed around in lessons and never really finished it. Thank heavens for the CliffsNotes. A mine of useful information and a decent shortcut if you hadn't done the work. When she got top grades in her Highers, it also gave her a chance to laugh internally at her father, Robert, who at several points during study leave would recite that part of the Gospel of Matthew, chapter seven, about taking the easy route and being damned.

Once a Religious Education teacher, a role to which he had brought fervent enthusiasm, he had become a headmaster when Skye was ten.

It wasn't only prayers before bedtime with him, or grace at mealtimes, or church on Sunday — most of which Skye recused herself from as she got older — God's will had to be done and his influence permeated her father's every pore. Skye had often wondered if he'd ever had an original thought in his life.

What would her parents make of yesterday's disaster? She still hadn't replied to that text, and the guilt turned her mouth dry.

Not least because her mum, Liz, would be sympathetic. They were close, and her mum's years as a school nurse meant she possessed an unflappability that most people could only dream of. Pupils could be rioting, burning down the school — not Skye in this instance, she was relieved to reflect — and Mum would still address them with the low, calm voice she summoned when someone was having a migraine.

Part of Skye wanted to call her mum and tell her about yesterday. Tell her about Will, and her worries about work, but — even though her mum was never ruffled — Skye didn't want to offload problems on her. Not before she had tried to work through them herself.

Robert Edmonds, though? He would be thoroughly disappointed. Their relationship was so much more stable now, but even after all this time, now as she hurtled towards her thirties, she knew he would react to this in the same way he reacted to the most minor infractions she made as a child: with accusations, recriminations and then blistering silence. Frustration started to course through her body.

She wondered if her mum was right and that the root of their conflict was simply that they were both quite similar. They were both a bit stubborn, intent on ensuring their point of view won out, even though it didn't have to be a competition . . .

She had tried for so long to move onwards and upwards, but the idea that Skye and her father would never quite see eye to eye always hung at the back of her mind, along with the knowledge that she had been far from the perfect teen. And she had reverted to being far from perfect. Perhaps her father was right. Perhaps that was just her.

Once she had rediscovered education — with that initial helping hand from those Highers shortcuts — and found her metier, Skye was unstoppable. She practically lived in the library at uni. She loved diving into her essay topics, often writing double the word count required. Novels, however, she had not quite found her way back to. Today, though, she was taking a step to change that.

She had just turned the page, when the door opened. Skye looked up, and gave Ginger a stroke, before he leapt down from her knees and went to wind himself around Paolo's ankle.

'Hi, Paolo.' She smiled. 'I got you a doughnut. It's in the bag on the side.'

'Ta!' Paolo hung up his satchel and reached down to give Ginger a quick stroke. 'What are you reading?'

He grabbed a plate and the doughnut from the kitchen and sat on the sofa opposite. The cat followed him, curling up into a soft ball of fluff atop a cushion. Skye held the book up in front of her. 'This wondrous classic.'

'Have you read it before?'

'Yes. No. Not really. I mean, I studied it for English, but I skimmed it and mainly watched the films and crammed.'

Paolo gawped at her. 'But it's one of the best books ever written in the English language. How on earth could you have skimmed it?'

Skye felt a funny twist in her gut. Every so often, especially when she was in a low mood, a twinge of guilt ran through her, about how she had wasted so much time acting up, pretending she didn't want to study — or worse, *actually* not studying — and defying her parents at every opportunity.

She gave Paolo a little shrug. 'My friends and I . . . I guess for a while there reading wasn't the done thing.'

'What? *Reading*?' Paolo was aghast.

'Cooperating. Behaving. Learning.' She said it jokingly but felt another ripple of shame.

'Wow. I didn't expect that. Not from someone who's training to be a lawyer.'

Skye managed a half-smile. 'I was a bit of a wild teenager. My final term of school, in which I did said cramming, was a turning point . . .' *After The Event to End All Events* . . . Skye swallowed hard. 'Luckily, my Highers results were significantly better than anyone expected and so, after a couple of gap years, I got into uni. Got a second chance and took it seriously.'

'So you were quite a nightmare?'

'By most people's standards, yeah. A real rebel without a cause — although occasionally I did have a cause. I wanted to stick two fingers up to all the injustice of the world. Like poverty, and war and climate change, or anything to do with animal rights. But I also wasted a lot of time, you know, like, smoking, skiving, partying. Well, some of it was a bit fun,' she said, with a small smile.

'Well, you turned it around, didn't you.'

Skye sighed. 'Really? I've run away from work at a critical juncture. I'm no more together now than I was a decade ago. I've gone back to being impulsive and a little directionless. And . . . well, that's it really.'

She wanted to mention Will, come clean about him too, but the thought of saying his name brought back that flinch in her stomach.

'Being impulsive isn't a bad thing,' Paolo suggested. 'Gut instincts and all that.'

'Yes, but not when it lands you in hot water,' Skye scoffed quietly.

Paolo came over to the snuggler, picked up the Jane Austen and wedged himself next to her. 'I hate the term "snuggler" but this thing is perfect when you need a hug. And you look like you need a hug?'

Skye rested her head on his shoulder. 'Yup. Thanks, Paolo. And thanks for taking me in. I'm taking your kindness as a sign I am supposed to be in Eastercraig.'

'Perhaps it is,' he said.

Skye let out a laugh. 'You know, when I was younger, I used to talk about signs all the time, to wind up my father. The universe would show me the way. I probably put too much emphasis on them, used them to deny my own responsibility, but maybe it doesn't matter. What I'd love right now is a sign telling me what to do about work.'

'Have you called your office yet?' he asked.

Skye made a face. 'I can't even think which greeting to use when picking up the phone. I sent a cowardly email instead.'

'Don't worry, it'll come.' Paolo tactfully changed the subject, 'Did you go for your walk earlier?'

Skye felt herself brighten at this. 'Yes. It was great, but no further encounter with Angry-handsome Man.'

The previous night, after unpacking, she had told Paolo about her trip to the rock, and the man she had seen there. Then, that morning, she had hiked back up, and lain on the rock for an hour, listening to the gulls screeching and enjoying the tickle of the breeze on her skin.

As she had powered purposefully along the coast path, she told herself she was returning there because it was her rock, that she would find some answers there. A puckish voice in her ear, however, told her she also wanted to see if the stranger with the captivating eyes was there again.

A glint appeared in Paolo's eye. 'You realize that he might be *exactly* the kind of distraction you need.'

Skye grimaced internally. Judging from her most recent interaction with the opposite sex, she might benefit from some time off men, as well as work.

'I don't know his name. Anyway, cheap burger. Initially enticing but left a nasty aftertaste.'

Paolo laughed. 'That doesn't matter with distractions. They're to keep you occupied until you get back to your usual day-to-day.'

Skye pushed the focus back on to Paolo, keen not to slip to the subject of Will. 'Do you have a day-to-day?'

Paolo heaved a sigh. 'Nope. You?'

She shook her head. She saw Will again pressed against an auburn-haired beauty, half sprawled across the desk, perhaps in a rehearsal for his evening performance.

All those times he had cancelled last minute, leaving Skye alone at dinner, or wondering whether she still ought to go to the hotel they'd booked. Had those been part of the deception?

Another work crisis, Will would say, full of regret. Or: *There's a client in London, I've said I'll go, seeing as it might be big money.* Or once: *I've been drafted to a meeting at the New York office. It's a couple of days, but I might stay the weekend and catch up with an old friend.*

Skye flared with humiliation once more. Houda had sent Skye a link earlier, accompanied by a content warning, and Skye had opened it, heart hammering. There, looking as glamorous as she did in real life, was The Woman.

Skye scanned her credentials and decided she deserved the capitalization. The Woman was incredible. Head of family law at a firm in London, some noteworthy cases, a top-class show jumper and skier in her teens and early twenties. It made Skye feel sick all over again. All the time Skye thought she was in a committed relationship, Will was having it off with someone whose CV sounded like a work of fiction. Or worse, having it off with her.

Either way, none of Will's sweet nothings held water when he'd probably been whispering the same ones to someone else. It was somehow worse that he was whispering them to a woman Skye could never compete with. When she confessed this to Houda, Houda had replied that Skye had everything going for her apart from dubious taste in men and the tendency to trash talk herself.

'No day-to-day here,' said Skye, finally. 'Shall I go out and get some things and make supper? I can make a decent carbonara.'

Paolo gritted his teeth. 'Alas, no. First, we are going to the pub and we'll grab some supper there. Sun is out and so are we. Second, I'm afraid decent carbonara doesn't cut it. As an Italian, I only eat amazing pasta. Besides, you're my guest and I'm going to look after you.'

'But you barely know me — and I've been an abysmal guest. I basically passed out last night after one glass of wine and an episode of *Eastenders*.'

'Yes. But I now know you were a juvenile delinquent, and you can fill me in with the rest of your life story over a bevvie. Besides, we hugged.'

Skye smiled. 'Reckon I could manage a gin.'

CHAPTER 7

The Anchor, Eastercraig's only pub, was like a second home to Paolo. Sometimes, after a few more pints than the National Health Service would advise, he felt he could curl up on one of the sofas with a blanket and doze off by the warmth of the fire's dying embers. Alas, he never would because Mhairi would make him pay for a room. She was running a business and not a charity.

In winter it was toasty and snug inside, the windows steamed up and people's cheeks were ruddy from their snowy, rainy, sub-zero journeys to get there. Summer, on the other hand, enticed everyone outside. The picnic benches which ran alongside the pub's whitewashed walls were all full, standing groups clustered together, spilling over the pavement and into the road, and some patrons had taken their drinks across the road and were sitting on the harbour wall, legs dangling over the edge.

'There are a number of signifiers summer has arrived,' he said, as they ambled along the front, past the fetchingly painted terraced houses — Holly's included — to the sound of the sea slapping gently against the harbour walls.

'Like ice creams replace potato waffles in the chiller cabinet at the shop,' suggested Skye.

41

Paolo lifted an arm towards the skies, and swept it round expansively. 'Migrating birds change the make-up of the local species.'

'Beer gardens fill up, patio heaters are put inside.'

'And chests are out.' The further north in the United Kingdom you got the lower the temperature was at which people stripped off. On the front at Eastercraig, it couldn't have been higher than twenty degrees Celsius, and yet strappy dresses were on, and — for a number of men — pecs were out.

Skye raised an eyebrow. 'Are you warning me you're about to follow suit?'

'Christ, no,' said Paolo. 'There's warm weather and then there's general decorum. Oh, there's Greg — Holly's boyfriend.'

A very tall man with broad shoulders, and mussed up auburn hair, ducked through the door of the pub and jogged towards them, a bottle of red wine in hand. He clapped Paolo on the shoulder, and pulled him in for a man-hug before stepping back.

'Paolo! How's it going?' he asked. 'And you're Skye?' He turned to her, giving her a broad smile. 'Greg Dunbar. How d'you do?'

'Nice to meet you.' Skye stuck out her hand, and he shook it.

'I'd love to stay and chew the fat, but I'm taking this back to Holly, having negotiated with Mhairi to let me have it at shop price. Not that she's going to have more than a soupçon, seeing as she's on call. Maybe I could water it down for her. Posh Ribena?'

'Criminal.' Paolo laughed. 'She's a mint tea girl at the moment. Feel free to grab some leaves from the terracotta pot outside my flat.'

'I very well might, thanks. And have a lovely time in Eastercraig, Skye. I have a vague recollection of seeing you about when we were younger, but you had pink hair in the old days, no?'

'That was me,' Skye confirmed.

Greg said goodbye, and strolled off down the front towards Holly's. Paolo and Skye hovered outside the Anchor, scanning for seats.

They swooped in as soon as an outside table became free, and Skye went in to buy the first round. Paolo took up one side of the bench, pressing his back against the wall, and put his feet up. His face was already warming up. He whipped his sunglasses out of his back pocket.

In front of him, the harbour hummed with people. Schools weren't out, so it wasn't heaving, but it was noticeably more crowded than it had been the previous month. Tourists who came up once the milder weather appeared had been steadily trickling in, keen to visit picturesque fishing towns like Eastercraig on tick-off-the-sights tours of the Highlands. He often heard the word 'quaint' floating through the air.

'Oh my, what a gorgeous little town,' came a dreadful approximation of an American accent from behind him.

Paolo turned around to see Hamish Glennis standing behind him, faking a jaw drop in disbelief at how picture-book the scene before them was. His heart flipped. Or did it flinch? All the same, he was happy to see Hamish, overall, wasn't he?

'I'm afraid that wasn't very convincing,' said Paolo. 'But points for enthusiasm.'

Hamish smiled. 'I never was very good at accents. You'd think I'd improve, considering I hear them all day long.'

'Plenty of tourists up at the castle?'

'Literal coachloads,' said Hamish. 'I can barely keep up with them. We had a couple of people wander off this week. They wanted to get close to one of the hairy coos for a perfect photo, only the poor thing had a calf with her and got angry. Thank God nobody was hurt.'

Paolo rolled his eyes. 'Honestly. You'd think people would know better.'

'Right? And I need to find a replacement admin assistant. My usual summer temp, Maeve, came in for a week, and went off to look after a sick relative. Mum and Dad try their best, but they're pretty technologically challenged.'

'Agency?'

'Yeah, but they're struggling to find someone who wants to work weird shifts in such a remote place. I'm firefighting.'

'Don't say we need to cancel swimming on Friday?'

For the last few months, they had gone swimming in the leisure centre pool at Cawcross, about twenty-five minutes from Eastercraig, every week without fail. Paolo revelled in the chance to have Hamish to himself for a whole hour during these sessions. The trouble with Eastercraig was you could never turn a corner without seeing someone you knew, all wanting to stop and discuss the weather and the roads, and in his case, their pet's ailments. The pool offered them an uninterrupted slot in which to catch up.

'Och, I don't want to. I'd quite like to be able to do ten lengths of decent front crawl before the month is up. Can I let you know on the day?'

'Sure.' Paolo nodded.

The previous winter, during a storm, Hamish had got into trouble at sea, having set out to rescue his dog. Wolfie, an enormous wolfhound with a love of swimming with the local seals, had been swept out on a strong tide, and when Hamish had followed, in a ramshackle boat, he had ended up falling in. Aside from the waves and the temperature, Hamish was a weak swimmer, and it was a miracle both had survived.

Paolo, keen to help Hamish recover from the ordeal and to be safe in future, had offered to teach him to swim.

While he had attempted to persuade Holly and Chloe that altruism was his primary reason for offering to lend a hand, he eventually admitted that lust came into it too.

He corrected himself. It was more than lust. Lust suggested nothing other than basic instincts, and Paolo's feelings extended far beyond physical desire. He wanted to spend time with Hamish, doing couple-y things. Having brunch, browsing antique shops, curling up on the snuggler — which by very definition cried out to be used that way.

The bloody snuggler. For now, the only person he was going to be snuggling was Skye, who he decided he liked but wasn't really his type. First and foremost because she was a woman.

She emerged from the pub with a pair of gin and tonics, took one look at the table and let out a shriek. 'Hamish Glennis!'

Hamish's face lit up at the very sight of Skye. He flung his arms out wide, and she set the drinks down and threw her arms around him. 'Skye Edmonds. Can it be?'

He pulled her in for a tight hug, ruffling her hair, then stepped back to examine her properly.

'Gosh, given I couldn't make dear old Dorothy's funeral, where we would have crossed paths, I reckon the last time I saw you was your final year at uni — you still had pink hair, I think. And it was that year that my parents expanded corporate event hosting up at the castle. You and I spent half our summer acting as wait staff. Remember those guests whose dinner went on until four in the morning and you had to wake me up when I fell asleep in the pantry?' Hamish chuckled at the memory. 'It's been ages! How the devil are you?'

'I'm well,' Skye said, stepping back. 'Well, not that well. You know I time my visits to Eastercraig with moments of despair. That said, I *did* come of my own accord, rather than being dispatched by my parents.'

Hamish frowned slightly. 'Do I need to worry about you?'

'Not sure. I don't think so,' she said. 'Sorry, I'm guessing you two know each other? Small town that this is.'

'Of course,' said Hamish, seeming to remember Paolo was there. 'Paolo, Skye's an old friend. We used to spend our summers sitting by the burn, going and checking on the hairy coos, and attempting not to make a mess of the silver service. But how do you two know each other?'

Paolo took a glug of his drink, allowing the gin to burn off the whack of envy at Hamish's obvious joy at the sight of Skye and giving himself an excuse not to speak. He chided himself. Jealously was fast becoming an instant reaction of his, and it wasn't becoming.

Paolo was a romantic at heart, even when outward appearances suggested otherwise. The other day he'd told Chloe her baking endless cakes for Angus made him want to puke when, actually, he was delighted for them. He wanted more than anything to have that for himself. He wanted to make other people puke.

He remembered the previous day's dramas and his plimsolls drying on the line, and decided he didn't want any more puke at all. Be careful what you wish for, and all that.

'Skye's staying with me,' Paolo said. 'While Hugh's away. She'd thought she'd come and see him, but he'd neglected to mention his holiday and letting his cottage out.'

Hamish smiled. 'Well, that's grand. You sure you're OK, Skye?'

'Yup. Paolo stepped in when I needed help. He's saved me from uncertainty. It's why this week, all his drinks are on me. Maybe we can grab coffee when you have time, and have a proper catch up . . . ?'

Skye tailed off, staring at the back of a man as he propped a bike up against the railings, slung the helmet over the handlebars and strode towards the Anchor.

'That's him,' she hissed, her head swivelling around to follow him. 'It's Angry-handsome man, who was sat on my rock yesterday. The one who's heading inside.'

'Who? Bear Sinclair?' asked Hamish.

Skye turned back and snorted. 'He's called *what*?'

Paolo leaned in. 'Bear Sinclair. I think it's a nickname, I don't know what for. He's an architect, in charge of turning some derelict outbuildings at Auchintraid Farm into luxury holiday retreats. Chloe was too scared to ask him about it when he arrived at Auchintraid, because she said he's brusque and all business.'

'Certainly the vibe he gave off yesterday. Couldn't wait to get away from me.'

'Apparently, he refused Chloe's carrot cake. Home-made at that,' Paolo continued.

'Further evidence of his joylessness,' said Skye.

'Hot, though,' said Paolo.

'Yeah, he's not bad looking, is he,' Hamish chimed in. 'If noirish Scandinavians are your type, Skye.'

Skye considered this. 'I like Henning Mankell. And IKEA — what's wrong with IKEA, Paolo?' she asked, as Paolo gave a faint wince at this. 'The furniture's good quality and the meatballs are great . . .'

'Nothing, except it's not exactly noirish,' said Paolo. 'And I prefer my furniture from quirky antique shops and my meatballs home-made by my Nonna Maria. Anyway, you were saying?'

'I like a lot of Scandinavian stuff, but first, I don't think he's *that* Scandi, not with a name like Sinclair, and second, based on our first encounter, I'm not sure I like him. Look, here he is.'

Bear Sinclair, who indeed looked noirish in a Scandinavian way, in a roll neck and jeans, his pale blond hair flattened from the helmet, walked briskly over to the harbour side of the street. Drink in hand, he leaned against the railings.

Paolo watched as Bear sipped his pint. Skye and Hamish were eyeing him too.

'This is like stalking,' Hamish whispered.

'We're not stalking him, you twazzock. We were here first,' said Skye.

Hamish chuckled. 'Other stalking, you twazzock. Look at us, we're all keeping our heads low as we stare at him, wondering what he'll do next.'

'Och,' said Paolo. 'I think shooting him and sticking his head on a mount would be a bit extreme.'

Skye laughed out loud, and Bear turned to look at them. His face remained passive as he gave a nod to Paolo, who had encountered Bear up at Auchintraid. When Bear saw Skye though, his brow furrowed, and he turned away.

'Oooh. You were right. He doesn't seem too keen on you,' said Paolo. 'Was that a sneer?'

'I think it was disinterest,' said Hamish.

'Scorn,' Paolo countered. 'Definitely scorn.'

'Detachment,' said Hamish, giving Paolo a grin.

'Utter hatred,' Paolo said, meeting Hamish's eyes, in which Paolo was certain he could discern a twinkle.

'Apathy.'

Skye interrupted. 'Are you two going to spend the next ten minutes swapping single words?'

Paolo looked at Hamish. They exchanged mirthful looks then turned to Skye.

'Apologies,' said Hamish, failing to smother a smile. 'It was a bit of fun.'

Paolo nodded, forcing a serious look. 'Hopefully no offence caused.'

He and Hamish swapped amused glances one last time, before Paolo grinned and looked down. For that brief moment, he had that feeling. The one like when you're cycling down a hill, feet hardly having to pedal, freewheeling at speed, with everything else in the world disappearing for a second.

Surely Hamish felt it too.

CHAPTER 8

'What would you like to do next weekend, darling? We could try that new restaurant over in Glasgow? The one that was awarded the Michelin star last year. Check into a hotel, make a weekend of it?'

Skye rolled over, head still thick from the cocktails they had drunk the night before, a smile forming on her lips. Will met her eyes, and tucked her fringe behind her ear.

'I think that sounds lovely. But don't you have the Gilbert case coming up the week after?' Skye propped herself up on her elbows, which sank into the colossal feather pillows Will had just bought.

'I'm well ahead on that. I think it'll be a pretty easy win. I doubt it'll go to court, and I reckon I can thrash out a settlement with the opposing counsel before end-of-play Friday.'

Will was not the kind of guy she had envisioned herself with. Ten years ago, she would have claimed her ideal man was a shaggy-haired rock star, who travelled to festivals in a camper van, who liked his vodka new and would roll the occasional joint. Funny how much things changed. Shaggy hair no longer held any appeal, and she didn't even touch cigarettes these days, or neat vodka, come to think of it.

Will was the very epitome of establishment, from his polished Oxfords to his politics. Skye had spent so long loathing that kind of person, and now here she was, dating one. It amused her. It would certainly amuse her parents, when they eventually met him. 'In that case, I'd love to.' Skye flopped back down in the downy pillow mountain.

Will leaned down and kissed her. 'Fantastic. I'll get Rosie to book it in.'

Skye laughed and shook her head, her long fringe falling back across her face. 'Can't you do it yourself?'

'I could,' Will said, his lips twitching. 'But I'm far too busy. Cases to win, beautiful girls to keep interested. I mean you, for the avoidance of doubt.'

Had he meant her, though?

Had any of it been real?

* * *

Skye woke up the morning after the Anchor with a buzzing in her head. Was it the thought of Will, memories of whom had kept her awake, and who then plagued her dreams? Or was it the carefree attitude she had adopted towards midweek drinking?

Four gin and tonics had been punchy for a Tuesday night, but each drink had a reason. None of it had been sorrows-drowning and she wasn't self-medicating. She hadn't reached that stage yet, and didn't intend to. The first glass was to thank Paolo for his hospitality. The second was celebratory, having seen Hamish for the first time in years. The third was . . . well, it was a third, and the fourth was when she bumped into Bear at the bar.

Skye had watched Bear, drinking his lonesome pint across the road from them, and felt sorry for him. He was an outsider in Eastercraig, aware that everyone else was on the inside, with enough troubles to need to head to the nearest rock and yell towards the North Sea.

Bear had nursed his drink for a long time. When he took his empty glass back into the pub, Skye excused herself, and followed him in.

She might have told Paolo she wasn't sure she liked him, but she couldn't help but be intrigued.

'Feeling any better now?' she asked, sliding round a stool to stand next to him at the bar.

He fixed her with those piercing eyes. They were the same vivid blue that icebergs looked beneath the surface. 'You.'

Skye ignored the fact he obviously considered this an imposition and was being overtly rude about it. Perhaps he was still feeling low. Someone — Paolo — had come and rescued her in her own hour of need. She could at least try to pass that kindness on. Despite his borderline unapproachable manner.

'Yup. Me again. Her from the rock. I was wondering how you were doing. It's Bear, right?'

He nodded. 'Bear Sinclair.'

He didn't extend a hand or elaborate. Skye refused to be deterred.

'Skye Edmonds. I'm . . .' She paused, musing on how to put it. Not that he seemed overly interested in getting to know her. 'Staying with friends. My uncle lives here, though he's away at the moment. He used to be the vet and has finally retired and gone on a . . . Sorry. I'm wittering.'

The more she had talked the more Bear's right eyebrow lifted. The rest of his expression retained a level of facial immobility tweakments addicts could only dream of.

'It's nice to meet you, Skye.'

Amazing how much his tone was out of step with his words. He managed to make 'nice' sound criminally uninteresting. Skye didn't think she'd ever met anyone who'd liked her less, aside from her father during her bad patch. Still, she would persevere a little longer.

'You're working up at Auchintraid, right? How long are you here for?'

At this, Bear closed his eyes and heaved a sigh. 'Until the project is completed satisfactorily.'

'Not going as smoothly as hoped?'

'I'm not at liberty to discuss. You understand.'

Skye felt slightly affronted, but nodded all the same. 'I'm a lawyer. Not being at liberty to discuss things is an area I excel in.'

At this, his lip curled. A smile beginning to form. Skye forgot his aloofness for a second. The change in expression had transformed his face.

'Then you do understand. Mhairi—' he reached over and passed his glass to the woman behind the bar — 'thank you for that.'

He turned to leave, running a hand through his hair as he did. Could that be exasperation? Or annoyance?

'Nice talking to you,' said Skye.

He gave a curt nod, and without saying goodbye, marched out the door, ducking his head under the frame as he went.

'Wow,' said Skye, to nobody in particular. Bear Sinclair was a ball of misery so big he could block out the sun.

'He's an odd one,' said Mhairi, the publican. 'Cold fish, that man.'

'The guy's basically a walking frozen fishfinger.'

Mhairi, who Skye remembered as being gruff and hard to please, let out a bark of laughter. 'Ain't that the truth. Another one?'

Skye considered the fact she didn't have to go into work tomorrow and, dwelling a fraction longer on her second unsatisfactory encounter with Bear Sinclair, decided she would.

Bear was responsible for her hangover, she concluded.

* * *

Meandering along to the chemist to replace Paolo's paracetamol stores, Skye pulled out her phone and emailed Tanya to request a call. Skye paused before she pressed send. She looked across the harbour at the boats bobbing on the sparkling waters. The calming shush of the waves contrasted with the shrieking of seabirds overhead.

Having permitted herself Tuesday as a day of wallowing, under the guise of a sick bug, she needed to sort out the trail of devastation back in Edinburgh. Once she got back to the flat, she would read more *Pride and Prejudice* and await a phone call from Tanya, who had replied to Skye's email telling her she would ring.

Maybe she could call her mum today too, let her and her father know about the exam. But the last thing she wanted to do was worry them. They ought to be enjoying their well-deserved retirement, not spending it panicking about their grown-up daughter.

Well-deserved. Those words remained in her head as the others faded. Her parents had dedicated their lives to their jobs. Sure, they weren't well-paid roles — the lot of the public sector — but they were worthwhile ones, careers her parents found fulfilling.

When she was younger, Skye had assumed she would work for a charity, or volunteer abroad. The one element of her rebellious youth she never regretted was protesting. She held firm beliefs about social justice; she wanted to fight the good fight for the causes she believed in, and that had never gone away . . . Where did Tilling and Browne fit in with that?

The fear that she had made a major misstep with her career choice crept back into her mind. Who was she? Skye wasn't sure she knew any more. Best not mention *that* to Tanya.

The sun was out again. June in Scotland could be unpredictable, but this was her third day in Eastercraig, and it was still glorious. A sign she was meant to be here, for now, at least.

Across the road, getting off his bicycle, Skye spied Bear Sinclair. As he locked up his bike, he caught her looking, so Skye waved. If three truly was a magic number, then this third meeting ought to be a charm. She enjoyed a challenge, and it was something else to keep her from thinking about Tanya. She grinned at him, picking up her pace.

'We have to stop meeting like this,' she called.

She could see him fighting the urge to roll his eyes. As she got closer, he seemed taller than before, his muscular shoulders broader, and his eyes bluer. Eyes like that could hypnotize you if you weren't careful.

'I was wondering . . .' Skye said.

There she stopped. The sight of him was causing her mind to grind to a halt. She seemed incapable of processing her own thoughts.

She wanted to know what his actual name was. Where he was from. What made him so chronically grumpy. Given last night's exchange, she didn't think she was about to ask him for a drink in the pub or to join her in the café. But there was no time to fret about it, because Skye's pocket began to vibrate.

Fumbling around, she tugged her phone out. Tanya. 'Sorry, I'm going to have to take this.'

'Not at all,' said Bear. He appeared faintly amused, though Skye thought that seemed very unlikely. So far she'd found very little that put Bear in good humour. 'I'll leave you to it.'

He strode into Eastercraig's small but well-stocked shop, and Skye hurried to the nearest bench. It wasn't the most secluded spot, but she had to get this over with.

Don't mention Will, she steeled herself. *Don't hint at your worries about work. Don't say anything that raises any suspicion that everything — aside from the exam palaver — is anything but fine and dandy.*

She cleared her throat and hit the green button. 'Tanya. Hello.'

Tanya, whose delivery was usually so sharp it could slice the toughest of Tilling and Browne employees in two, gave a long sigh. 'Skye. What on earth happened? I got a message from the invigilator saying you walked out part way through your exam, and then your email saying you were sick.'

'Sorry, Tanya. I planned to call you later today. I . . .'

Skye searched frantically for the words. Despite the fact she had been expecting the call, she felt caught out. She'd not yet had a chance to meticulously plan what she wanted to say. Skirting the matter with Will, of course, and the rest.

'Skye . . . ?'

Skye gulped. Showing weakness wasn't ideal. The firm had a reputation for chewing people up and spitting them out if they didn't fit. Skye normally powered through tasks in the office, and proved herself able to get through the dizzying demands of firm life without cracking. Until Monday morning, that was.

One wrong step, and she might wreak more damage. She had already shattered her own illusions she was in control of her life. How could she go about this without shattering anyone else's?

A feeling of angst rose up inside her, clouding her head. 'I had some bad news on Monday morning,' she managed. 'It shook me, and while I thought I could manage the exam it turned out I couldn't.'

'I thought you were sick.'

'Oh . . .' She'd been so frantic about keeping the Will thing quiet she'd forgotten the simplicity of the fib. 'Well, I was sick, after getting the bad news. And wanted to stay off, to be on the safe side.'

And not have to face Will in the office. Or return to the office and let everyone know she'd fled the exam.

'Anything you want to tell me about? You know our conversations are all confidential.' Tanya's voice was suddenly suspicious.

'No,' Skye said. 'Not at the moment.'

At the other end of the line, Tanya clicked her tongue, and Skye felt her heart rate rising. Was Tanya on to her?

'I can arrange a re-sit as soon as you return, or you could postpone until the autumn. Let me know as soon as you do.' Tanya was drumming her sharp nails on the desk, the sound like a hail of bullets.

'I'll let you know as soon as I decide,' said Skye. 'Which will be very shortly, of course.'

Tanya let out a low *hmmmm*. 'I don't actually need you in the office right now, Skye. We have parcelled your work out. So as far as I know, there is nothing urgent on your desk, and I can get cover if you need it. Listen, if you *do* need personal time, we did a review recently, and one outcome was that we decided staff can put in for unpaid time off. It's been my personal project for the last year. We need all our employees to be healthy in body and mind. I was going to send an office-wide email about it next week, in fact.'

Skye was stunned. This wasn't the Tilling and Browne she knew. Even if Tanya was on to her, this was a bonus. '*I* can do that?'

'Absolutely. It's part of a new company policy, which I've fought hard for. Anything from a day to two weeks, or more if necessary, and if you think you can come back fighting fit . . .'

This wasn't the Tanya she knew either. Tanya was offering her a fortnight off, wasn't she? No strings attached.

Tanya clicked her tongue again. 'Scanning the online calendar, you had booked two weeks off at the end of this month. Do you still want those?'

Skye felt her heart contract. She and Will were supposed to fly to the south of Spain, and stay in a glossy hotel in Marbella, read books in the sun, drink cocktails and sleep late. Those plans were surely proof that she hadn't imagined their relationship.

But . . . They hadn't booked anything. Will said to hold on until the last minute, as a big case might land on his desk any moment. Less of the big case, more of the other woman. A sob rose in her throat, and she swallowed it back down.

'Please can I keep that in the diary? I know it's a lot, and it seems like I'm taking the mick, but could I?' she asked.

'You *are* entitled to leave. So, you'll take off a full month?'

She could do that, not see Will for an entire month, get over him and come back as if nothing had happened. Not that an entire month might be enough, but she would certainly give it her best shot. She summoned a steady voice. 'Yes. I'll retake the exam in autumn, and I think this counts as mitigating circumstances if anyone else needs a reason for the time off.'

There was a pause. 'What counts as mitigating circumstances? A forty-eight-hour bug? Or your bad news? I'm still unclear what's happened. Do I need to be worried about you, Skye?'

'Absolutely not,' she said firmly.

'I'll have to run it past a few other people, and I will need a full application in writing by the end of tomorrow. But if you want to take this time, I think it works. In fact, you can return in July, ready to hit the ground running, proof that my new scheme is a good idea. Don't let me down, Skye, and by that, I mean look after yourself.'

'Thanks,' said Skye. A small doubt popped into her mind. 'Tanya, before you go, do you think my reputation will be . . . um . . . tarnished by not being around for a month?'

Tanya took a deep breath. 'No, it shouldn't be. We all need to do the right thing, Tilling and Browne included. Office culture is changing, and we are moving with the times. Don't worry about it.'

They said their goodbyes and hung up. Skye flopped forwards on the bench, resting her head on her knees.

'Don't worry about it,' Skye repeated, aloud. 'Pshhh.'

Skye knew Tanya kept a close eye on all the little seedlings the company was nurturing. The juniors, the trainees, the up-and-comers, all those who wished to grow within the firm and pursue their careers there. While the firm tried to be supportive and fair, play by all the rules and appear a modern workplace, there was a palpable undercurrent of brutality. If you looked like you weren't going to make it, you were weeded out.

She sat back up and inhaled deeply. That could have gone very badly. A whole month off? It could still prove to be a bad idea. That said, she had been granted a stay of execution. Better than that — a whole month off! And — bonus points — she hadn't mentioned Will either.

Will . . . That moment she had seen him with The Woman, it had been as if Will had sliced her open, pulled out her heart and flung it to the floor.

If it hadn't been for him, she wouldn't have skipped out of an exam, wound up camping in a stranger's spare room, and found herself now crying on a public bench in a remote seaside town.

Shoving her phone back in her pocket, she put her hands up to wipe her eyes and dry her damp cheeks. Monday morning, she thought she was about to have it all, and now she had nothing.

Not nothing, she told herself, pulling up her spine and rolling her shoulders back. She had been given a gift. Nearly a month of freedom had fallen in her lap. And a month away from Tilling and Browne was exactly what she needed. A chance to recover. A chance to work out what she was doing with her life . . .

There was a loud splat and she felt something cold run down her neck. 'Shitting hell! I'm trying to be positive.'

She cursed at the passing seagull.

She swiped at her cheek as another couple of tears threatened to drop.

'Arrrgh,' Skye fumed, frightening a nearby pigeon away.

'Are you OK?' came a voice.

Skye turned her head gingerly, and her heart sank.

She dragged herself back from the bird-poo fury which had been threatening to pull her back down. 'Bear Sinclair. The man, the myth, the legend.'

He came to stand in front of her.

'I've only been here a few weeks. I'm not sure I can lay claim to any of those titles.'

'Not even man?'

'Well, obviously I'm a man. I think.'

'Up to you. Feel free to self-identify,' Skye deadpanned. He didn't laugh. 'I'm joking. Deflecting, really.'

'I guessed. What's the matter?' His voice was soft and Skye looked up at him. Sympathy was etched on his face. She must have triggered a long-buried impulse to check up on a weeping woman.

'Plenty. I won't bore you with it.'

'If you're sat on a bench surrounded by sea and sunshine, crying, it can't be that boring. I've got a few minutes before I go back to Auchintraid. Of course, if you don't want to tell me, that's fine. It's not like I've been particularly receptive to your efforts to talk to me.'

Skye paused, uncertain how to answer but surprised by his honesty. She budged up. She looked out at the sea, and shook her head, and took a couple of considered breaths. 'It was just work . . . I was having a work crisis. *Am* having, present tense.'

She stared ahead at the open water, not wanting to meet his eye. Kindness could trigger as many tears as sadness, and she didn't want to start off again.

'Oh, I know all about those,' said Bear, sitting down next to her. He reached into his pocket and pulled out an embroidered cotton handkerchief. 'For your neck. It's clean.'

Skye took it, thanking him, and dabbed the splatter of bird poo off from where it had been threatening to run down her T-shirt.

'But you look like a man who has everything under control. Aside from when you're yelling into the sea. I mean, your clothes are clean, your hair is brushed. You carry handkerchiefs, for crying out loud.'

Bear, who until this point had mirrored her body language, and had been staring out to sea, shifted to look at her.

'A gift from my grandmother. I always keep one on me, although you can keep that one.' Skye could have sworn she heard a smile creeping into his voice.

'As for the yelling — doesn't that tell you something about how under control I have everything? An old adage about judging by appearances?'

Bear looked out across the harbour once more, and Skye looked at his profile, admiring his cheekbones. Those she *would* judge on appearance. Top marks for bone structure.

'I guess so. I'm *really* sorry for intruding on Monday,' she said. 'What's your work crisis, then?'

He shook his head, his lip twitching ever so slightly. 'More deflection? Nice try, Skye.'

'Go on. You show me yours and I'll show you mine,' she joked.

She met his eyes. They definitely had a twinkle in them, the iceberg blue bright.

'Here on this bench? In front of the locals?'

Skye's mouth hitched into an involuntary grin. 'It would be nice to talk about it, but I'd feel more comfortable knowing there was an element of reciprocity if we're talking about our problems. Please?'

He fixed his gaze to hers. 'Och, fine. How about this: I'm here in this town where I'm upsetting the locals with a small project. I've upset the client too, somehow. And if I fail to make it right, I'll upset the architectural practice I work at. And, awkwardly, if I upset said architectural practice, I upset my family. My mother, anyway.'

'What does she have to do with it?'

'She's one of the two partners. Parents. Who'd have them, eh?'

Skye knew that feeling. Still, at least his mum had enough faith in him to employ him. It wasn't clear if Skye's father would have endorsed her given half a chance — or if he'd have warned the authorities.

'Do you fight with her?' Skye pulled herself into a cross-legged position on the bench, wiggling her back into a comfortable space against the wooden slats.

'Occasionally.' Bear stretched his legs out and ran his hands through his hair. Definitely flaxen. It set off those eyes nicely. 'I see my parents once every month or two for a cordial Sunday lunch, and we have a rule not to talk about work. As for in the office? There's the odd blow-up, but more likely a serving of passive-aggression.'

'That's the worst, isn't it? Much better to have everything out in the open. Aggressive-aggression. Good, honest behaviour.'

She realized that she oughtn't be lecturing on honesty, seeing as her secret relationship had nearly brought down her future career. She had always railed against hypocrisy, now here she was thoroughly guilty of it.

'So what's your work crisis? I've shown you mine, so to speak,' Bear said, raising his eyebrow a fraction of an inch.

A frisson ran up Skye's spine, and she fought down a blush.

'I've flunked an exam. One I need to pass to qualify at my firm.' There was no need to tell him about Will.

'How do you know?'

'I think you have to complete more than half of it to stand a chance.'

'Ah.' Bear scratched his head. 'I see.'

He gave her an awkward look, and Skye took a deep breath, preparing for her own moment of truth.

'I was talking to HR before you came out, trying to see what I can salvage and still come out with a shred of credibility.'

'Did you manage it?' Bear asked.

'I think I've kept them at bay for now. Though given what we just talked about, I'm not sure that was the takeaway, was it?'

Bear shifted his body round, and propped his elbow across the back of the bench. 'Do you work for a big firm? Or a cosy family practice?'

'Really big,' Skye said, grimacing.

'One of those places that eats nice people for lunch? You're demonstrating survival skills. It's not as though you've lied under oath. What did you tell the HR department?'

'I said I'd received some bad news.'

Which, as she considered it, was not a lie.

'Standard fudge,' said Bear. 'You've given them something to work with, and they can't get angry about it, and

61

prodding you about any element of truth to it might be to their detriment.'

Skye managed an *Mmm*. Most of the truth would be to her detriment, but she didn't want to interrupt the pleasant flow of sympathy and advice. She explained how somehow her stars had aligned, and she had the month off.

'So you're here until the end of June? Your firm gave you four weeks? Bet that's unheard of.'

Skye nodded. 'Yup.'

'That's when I'm meant to head back too. Where are you? London?'

'Edinburgh,' said Skye.

His expression lightened a little. It was barely a smile, but he looked sunnier. 'Me too. Och, what I wouldn't give to be there right now.'

Skye wrinkled up her nose. 'Really? On a sunny day, there's nowhere as lovely as Eastercraig.'

Bear tilted his head. 'Did you not hear what I said about the project?'

'Does that really take away from the fact this town is perfect? Streets lined with pretty buildings, wild scenery beyond. And you're never more than five minutes from the sea. It's my happy place.'

'Is it?' said Bear. 'If you're that enthused then maybe it's not so bad. I'm yet to see it though. Perhaps at some point you can show me the best bits. Ah — let me see who this is.'

He pulled a phone from his pocket, frowning as he read the number on the screen. He stood up, preparing to answer.

'It's work. I need to take it.'

'I'll leave you to it,' said Skye, in a quiet voice, getting up from the bench. 'Thanks for the chat.'

She turned away and began to walk back to Paolo's flat.

'Skye!' Bear called, making her spin back around. He was holding his hand over the receiver. 'I'll see you around.'

Skye nodded, and gave a small wave. 'I hope so,' she said quietly, but he was already back on his call. It seemed Bear Sinclair continued to make quite the impression.

CHAPTER 9

Friday, and Paolo was out on a routine farm visit with Holly. They'd gone over to disbud calves — remove their horns which was physical work. The sun was high, and Paolo rolled up the sleeves of his overalls, which were acting like a chicken brick and gently roasting him.

He wiped a bead of sweat from his forehead. 'Glad that's all done.'

Holly somehow looked cool and collected, as per usual. She sat down on a bench outside the house with a cup of tea, which the farmer's wife had kindly brought out, along with home-made oatcakes, cheese and chutney. Paolo came and crashed down next to her, his arms aching. A compact gaggle of geese honked their way across the yard in front of them.

'How's Skye getting on? Has she had any luck finding somewhere to stay?' Holly asked.

Paolo, oatcake halfway to his mouth, shook his head. 'Still no openings anywhere. I can tell she's feeling awkward about having been at mine since Monday, but she's clearly not ready to go to Edinburgh yet. Last night she mentioned heading over to Mull or somewhere, and booking a B&B, but I told her there's no rush at all and that she's very welcome.'

'Enjoying the company?'

'Yeah. Reminds me of having flatmates in Glasgow. You know, Eastercraig is the first place I've lived alone. While I loved it for the first six months or so, the novelty's worn off. Plus she's ever so tidy and makes an excellent salad. I don't think I've had to cook or clean since she's arrived.'

Paolo bit into the oatcake. They were one of life's small pleasures, he thought, as it crumbled. He ought to make some at home.

'I'm glad she's not cramping your style.'

'You forget I grew up with three sisters. Having one woman in the house is manageable. Plus, unlike my sisters, she doesn't hog the bathroom, or thieve my cashmere jumpers, or any of that shit. Really, it's a win. The only way she could be a better flatmate was if she was male, and my future husband.'

Holly glanced up and gave him a look which he presumed was supposed to be one of friendly sympathy, but it only succeeded in giving off you're-being-tragic vibes. 'Might you be talking about a certain resident of Glenalmond Castle?'

'No. I'm not doing anything about Hamish,' he headed her off.

Considering even sweet, mild-mannered Chloe could wreak havoc in her live commentary on his relationship status, he didn't want Holly to step in.

'You hang out all the time. You should be using that time to prod it along. Lord knows you've been mooning over him for over six months.'

'It's not hanging out though, is it? When we're in the pool, we're not really talking. We're swimming. I mean, he *does* need to learn.'

'You realize he's only there because he wants to spend time with you. Isn't that obvious?'

'No. Not really.'

Holly smeared chutney on another oatcake, and balanced a wonky wedge of cheese on top, then passed it to Paolo.

'Here. Eat this.' It was the same commanding voice that Holly employed during surgical procedures.

He did as he was told.

'There. Now you can't interrupt me.'

He chewed cautiously, awaiting her assessment.

'Listen, Chloe and I are worried. And Chloe was in a right tizz that she'd offended you the other day. It's time to crack on. If you want Hamish, pull your finger out and make it happen.'

Paolo made an 'mmmph' of protest through closed lips.

'Paolo, you're a veterinary nurse. A fantastic one. You're lots of other things too, all of them good. But you're not a swimming teacher. I've seen you. You're OK, but you splash around a lot, and windmill your arms too much. Hamish might not realize the extent of the flaws in your technique, but he's a non-swimmer, not an idiot.'

Paolo swallowed. He felt a stab of indignation. 'I'm not that bad.'

'Please. The point is he could have got lessons with a professional, but he's gone with you instead.'

'Yeah, well,' he grumbled. 'Hamish probably wants someone he knows for reassurance. It was a terrifying ordeal, and he wants to go slowly. Besides, I'm not out there trying to get him on Team GB — we're learning basic strokes.'

'Like I said, he could do that with anyone. This is a bonding experience.'

'We bond with our friends, as well as lovers,' said Paolo. 'I've definitely been friend-zoned.'

'You're being very pessimistic about this,' said Holly, in a tone which Paolo knew meant there was more to come. 'You need to follow up one of those lessons with a trip to the pub, or for a walk. Get him on his own, when he's not in his trunks worrying if he's going to sink to the bottom of the pool like a stone. It's not like you two even drive there together. You don't even have car chats. There's a missed opportunity if ever there was one.'

Paolo couldn't help but admit she was right on that part. They went, swam and after they would banter back and forth in the leisure centre reception for a wee while, but then they'd go their separate ways. Most Fridays Paolo would have to pop back to the surgery for the afternoon session, then stay to check on any animals that were in overnight, while Hamish would be back at the house to oversee any guest dinners. It hadn't seemed like there was time for anything other than small talk.

'You're right,' he declared. 'Here. What about this?'

He pulled out his phone and typed a message to Hamish. *Want a lift to swimming this afternoon? Save the planet and all that. Hope we're still on. P.* He handed it to Holly for her to peruse.

She scanned the text and gave a nod of approval. 'Perfect. Now you'll have time to talk to him.'

If he says yes, thought Paolo, his inner optimist still struggling to break free.

* * *

But not only did Hamish not cancel their swimming lesson later that afternoon, he accepted the offer of a lift. After the lesson, Paolo drove him home. As they pulled up outside Glenalmond, the castle where Hamish lived, Paolo got out too, crossed his arms on the car roof to take it in.

It was pure baronial, the main tower adorned with turrets and a parapet, all grey stone, like a dark fairy tale. A tad foreboding but magical in summer, almost silver in the light. He had been inside only a few times, including once for a ball last year. It was labyrinthine, all hidden passages and staircases to nowhere, with doors opening into rooms so fantastical that they had to be seen to be believed.

'I think I'm making some headway,' said Hamish, sounding hopeful. 'Do you see much improvement?'

Paolo didn't want to lie, but he also didn't want lose this time spent with Hamish.

'Some. I think if you wanted to go faster, we could. Up the distances, perhaps. Work on breathing.'

'Och. Sounds like a lot of effort. Maybe we carry on as we are. Keep going at a not-too-strenuous pace.'

At a pace slower than a sloth. Paolo wasn't sure what to think. Did Hamish want to learn to swim or not? He wasn't even sure if he actually wanted to teach Hamish how. It was just a good excuse to see each other.

To avoid these thoughts he threw a question across to Hamish.

'Are you up to anything tonight? Only Chloe's cooking dinner. Would you like to come along? Skye's coming too,' he added, to cover his tracks.

Hamish went a little pink and scratched his neck. 'Well . . . I'd love to, only I've got a party arriving later, as per. I need to be there to oversee tonight.'

'Never mind,' Paolo said, quickly. 'Another time.'

'Aye. Sure,' said Hamish. 'I'd better go. I've got to prep for later. Send my love to Chloe. And to Skye too. Gosh, I need to see her while she's here.'

Paolo nodded, and swung himself back into the driver's seat. 'I'll see you next week.'

Hamish waved him off. Paolo, half an eye on the road in front of him, watched as rear-view-mirror Hamish grew smaller and smaller.

Even though Hamish had a reason he couldn't make dinner, he had still said no, and Paolo felt the heat rising up the back of his neck. Had he embarrassed himself? As he played the invitation to dinner, and the rejection, back to himself, he couldn't help but cringe.

67

CHAPTER 10

The Eastercraig bike-hire shop only traded in bikes which could handle the steep hills surrounding the town. Skye, who had thought it might be nice to ditch the car while the weather held, had initially been disappointed that they hadn't furnished her with a graceful Pashley or something similar. But climbing upwards out of town she realized they were on to something. More gears and bigger tyres were definitely better for the undulating Highland roads.

Chloe, who Paolo said was the friendliest person in town, if not the world, had invited them both over for supper, promising home-made pie. She had also texted Skye in advance to apologize for the state of Auchintraid.

And so it was with some trepidation that Skye bumped down the track towards the farm. Bear had made it sound like the project at Auchintraid was a nightmare too, and as she swerved the final potholes before getting into the yard, Skye could see why. The yard was cluttered with scaffolding poles, cement mixers, piles of bricks and random equipment Skye couldn't identify.

'You cycled?' Chloe said, appearing at the door to the farm-house in an apron, a dusting of flour in her hair. 'I thought *I* was the only person mad enough to bike up here.'

'My thighs are burning, but I imagine that's a good thing,' Skye called, as she propped the bike up against a wall. 'I imagine you already know, but Paolo's stuck at the surgery. Someone brought in a last-minute emergency case. He'll be half an hour.'

'Aye,' said Chloe. 'He sent me a text. Doesn't matter. Angus is also somewhere up in the fields. I've tried to get him on the walkie-talkie, but he's not picking up. We'll probably be late eating. Hopefully you're not starving.'

'No. I'm fine. Thanks so much for inviting, me, Chloe. It's really kind of you.'

Chloe gave a broad smile. 'Not at all. And it's nice to have a wee dinner party.' She dropped her voice a little. 'We haven't had much chance lately. Fiona, Angus's mum, has been so prickly over the building work. She was worried about the amount of mess it would be, and she's been proved right. The yard's a state, and there have been delays, so I get it, I do. But she's very tetchy at the minute. Not her usual self. Anyway, she's out tonight at her book group, so I thought it might be fun to host everyone while I can.'

Skye looked around the yard again.

'What exactly's being renovated? I've encountered your architect a few times, but he's never said.'

Chloe bit her lip. 'Bear? You've actually managed to chat to him? He doesn't make small talk with me, that's for sure.' She sighed. 'There are a couple of old buildings over there behind the barns. They've been derelict for ages. We're going to turn them into holiday lets, super-lux ones. And a potential cottage for Fiona nearer the farmhouse, a kind of granny annex. Not that she's going to be a granny any time soon.'

'But that sounds great. What was the sigh for?'

'It's *so* much work. We got planning permission really quickly, which was fab, and then the builders had a job fall through and could fit us in earlier. But there were a lot of grumbles from people in the town. There was a rumour going round that we wanted to sell off loads of land to a developer. And then it turned out that structurally a lot of the buildings were in worse shape than everyone had thought. Making it a very long and more costly job.'

'Often happens,' Skye said sympathetically.

'Come this way.' Chloe motioned towards a corner of the yard. 'I can show you.'

Skye followed Chloe round the back of a shabby barn, to collection of outbuildings. These ones were older, the stonework uneven, but Skye could see they had a folkish charm to them, with their small windows and low doors. Corrugated iron panels, which she presumed had once been roofing, had been removed and stacked up against a wall, as were the old doors and window frames. Despite everything Chloe had said, the potential was obvious.

'You can see, it's all underway. However the pace of work has been unsteady. Bear was sent up from Edinburgh to project manage. I think he's an architect. Either way, he's really quite moody. And I say that as Angus's girlfriend — Angus being famously surly. I've tried to be nice to Bear but he really doesn't want to talk.'

Remembering their conversation earlier in the week, Skye decided not to say anything. 'Maybe he's got other things on his mind.'

'Perhaps, but I hate being on bad terms with anyone. He hardly says more than hello in the morning. He'll talk to the builders if need be, but keeps to himself most of the time.'

It gave Skye a glow inside, like the warmth of a mouthful of hot chocolate, thinking that he had deigned to share a little part of himself with her.

'Look. There he is,' said Skye.

Bear strode into view, from somewhere around the back of one of the buildings. Today he was in mud-spattered indigo jeans, an oatmeal jumper, and a pair of filthy desert boots, hair sticking out at angles, as if he'd been running exasperated hands through it every other minute. He was still, however, rating at the 'worth writing home about' level on the looks scale. She made a note to text Houda about him, then firmly reminded herself she probably shouldn't let her thoughts gallop off like that, given recent events.

'Shite,' whispered Chloe. 'Do you reckon he heard me?'

'No . . . no? No. Probably not.'

But Skye wasn't certain, and her wavering probably hadn't reassured Chloe either. Bear's brow was knitted, and his expression barely changed as he noticed the two of them standing there.

'I think he might have,' Chloe whispered.

'Maybe he's a bit lonely,' said Skye.

She remembered how he looked when he told her he felt as though he was upsetting the locals, and everyone up at the farm. And though he talked to the builders, it didn't mean he was friends with any of them. Then here was Skye, who had barely been in town a week, already being welcomed for a meal at the farmhouse.

'Och. Sod it,' muttered Chloe, before calling out: 'Bear? Will you join us for dinner? Paolo, who Skye's staying with, is also coming.'

Skye was quietly delighted and realized she'd been hoping Chloe would ask him.

Bear raised his eyebrows in surprise. 'Oh, thank you. You really don't have to, though. I wouldn't want to impose.'

'Go on, Bear. It'd be lovely if you could,' Chloe persisted.

Bear produced a brief smile. 'If you're sure, then, yes, please. Can I bring anything? Run to the shop and get some wine?'

'Don't worry. It's all under control,' said Chloe. She checked her watch. 'Apart from needing to check on the pie. Have a look around the buildings, Skye. I don't want you to see me in a flap.'

'I don't mind flapping. Can I help at all?' Skye said. 'I bet you're a veritable Mary Berry in the kitchen anyway.'

Chloe's cheeks went pink. 'She's one of my idols. But still. I'd rather you turned up to a perfectly laid table and didn't see me sweating over the stove. Come back in ten?'

Chloe didn't give Skye any chance to argue, and was already ducking back through the gap in the barns, leaving her alone with Bear.

She looked at him uncertainly. 'Want to show me around?'

'Was that your doing? The invitation, I mean. Are you taking pity on me?' He narrowed his eyes at her.

Skye put her hands up. 'No. Chloe's taking pity on you. I didn't even know you were here.'

'I *am* an object of pity then? You're not denying it.' He looked ready to march up to the farmhouse to rescind his acceptance.

'It was merely a matter of right place, right time. As for the pity stuff, the only person pitying you, is you. And self-pity isn't a good look.'

Skye wondered for just a second whether she was being hypocritical but brushed it off. The time to wallow was well and truly over. Tomorrow she would make plans to fill the rest of the next few weeks. She'd find a cottage to rent on one of the Western Isles, spend the days walking and reading, and reflecting.

Whatever she did for those weeks, she was not going to waste them. She probably wouldn't enjoy a month off again in her life until retirement. A bleak vision of herself keeling over at her desk at Tilling and Browne in forty years crossed her mind.

Skye stepped under a huge, grey stone lintel, through the gap where the door would eventually be. Inside, the room was strung with lights, cables running under her feet. A smell of damp pervaded, mossy, like a forest floor after rain.

'Hey! Come out!' Bear barked.

She jumped as he grabbed her by the arm and pulled her back. 'Why can't I go in?'

'Nobody goes in without one of these.'

Bear tilted his head towards a box of hard hats, and in return, Skye gestured to the pile of corrugated iron with a sweep of her arm.

'There's no roof,' she pointed out.

'Aye, but it's a health and safety issue. It would be a real shame if you'd come up here for a nice supper and then got taken out by a chunk of falling masonry. I might get sued, and you're a lawyer and all.'

Skye picked up one of the helmets and shoved it on her head. Bear reached in and did the same.

'Suits you,' he said, gesturing for her to go first. 'Now you're properly attired.'

Skye walked under the lintel again, this time, she studied the building more closely. Bits of grass and weeds grew out of the cracks in the stones, and the floor was soft underfoot. Above her, large timber beams sprung from the walls, meeting overhead, blue skies visible above.

'How old is all this?' she asked. 'Some of it looks ancient.'

Bear smiled fully, the first time he had. It changed his face completely. Funny, the things that got some people going.

He put a hand on her shoulder and guided her to the middle of the room. 'I'm glad you asked. The rest of the buildings we're working on are a little younger. But this byre's ancient indeed. It's a cruck frame you're seeing, where one large, curved tree is split in two to create a matching pair of timbers which carry the weight of the roof. You'd get several of them in one structure . . .'

He trailed off, and Skye looked at him expectantly. He'd been hitting his rhythm.

'Why did you stop?' she asked.

'Vernacular architecture isn't everyone's cup of tea.' Two dots of pink appeared on his cheeks, and his brows knitted together for a second.

'It's definitely yours,' Skye said. 'Come on. I want to hear more.'

'I'll give you the short version. These are rare, not many around. See, there are cruck holes in some of these stones for more timbers to go in' — he pointed out gaps in the stonework — 'but they will have rotted. You know, there's an example of whale bones being used. Like I said, they had to hold the roof, which would be made of turf or thatch. It was a simple but effective way to build.'

'And you say it's called a cruck frame?'

'Also known as a highland couple.'

'Really? How romantic.'

He brightened again. 'Yes. I think it is. Unfortunately, I've had to pause building work to let Historic Scotland know what I've found, so this one's on hold, while we renovate the newer buildings. It's a minor setback though, and it's pretty exciting. I'm hoping I can adopt some traditional methods for building it. It'd be an interesting direction to take the project in.' He looked down at his watch, frown returning once more. 'We ought to head over, I think.'

He followed Skye out into the open. She dropped her hard hat back in the box and eyed the buildings around the yard again. Yes, she could definitely see the potential. She looked over to Bear who caught her eye.

'It would be the perfect direction,' she said.

She saw a smile flicker across his face. 'Aye. I've got to have courage in my convictions, right. I'll bring it up with Angus and his family.'

Through another gap in the buildings, the land rolled down towards the sea. Skye stopped in her tracks.

'Two seconds,' she said. 'I want to see the view before we head over. Come with me?'

Together they walked through the gap, and the landscape opened-up around them. The sea glistened in the distance. Further up the hill to the right, towards a cluster of pine trees, a herd of cows grazed, a breeze rustling the gorse bushes that edged the fields.

'It'll be perfect when you finish,' she said. 'Picturesque location, buildings full of character. So much potential.'

'Do you think so?' There was a note of doubt in Bear's voice.

'Why wouldn't it be?'

He didn't reply immediately, and a frown appeared on his face. When he did answer, his tone had gone back to being as cool as it had been that night in the Anchor. 'Maybe let's not talk about it now.'

'Sure.' Skye stopped herself from probing further. Maybe it was to do with what he had said on the front yesterday about all the problems with the project. Or perhaps there was more that was bothering Bear than he was letting on.

CHAPTER 11

The farmhouse kitchen was cool, and Paolo was grateful for it. After dropping Hamish home, he had gone and joined Holly at a farm the other side of Eastercraig. He and Holly had sweated their way through a routine tuberculosis testing of a herd of cattle, and it had been sticky work, then rushed to another farm where a cow had fallen into a ditch.

'Montepulciano,' he said, by way of a greeting.

He held out the bottle to Chloe, who popped it next to the cooker.

'Thanks! That looks delicious,' she said, going back to the side, where she was slicing carrots. 'And is Holly OK? I invited her and Greg, but she said she wanted some time for the two of them.'

Paolo leaned against the table. 'Aye. She appears to be coping work-wise, but I think it's impinging on time with Greg. Not that she's admitted it to me yet. That woman is proud as.'

'And how was the Belted Galloway?'

'It's back in the field, as if nothing happened. But we were on our way back to town when the call came in. Sorry I'm so late.'

'These things happen, as we well know. Do you think we can eat outside? It's still warm. Or too midgy?' Chloe left the vegetables and clattered through some drawers in the dresser, dumping piles of cutlery on the table.

'Midgy,' said Paolo. 'Unless you've got some super strength insect repellent. What about the conservatory?'

Chloe's fluster evaporated as she considered the idea. 'Fandabidozi. There's a fold-up-table in there. Would you mind putting it up and chucking this tablecloth over it?'

'Not at all, duck,' said Paolo. 'I'll lay the table too.'

Chloe pulled out a large sheet of pink linen. Paolo carried it through and set up the table. He arranged the tablecloth over it and stood back to appreciate how it looked. Some holes had been darned, others left to fray further. It would give Chloe's impromptu dinner a shabby-chic charm. He was tweaking the corners, when he became aware of movement outside. Glancing up, he saw Skye and Bear walking up through the farmyard, deep in conversation. Bear was gesticulating, and Skye wore a broad smile. Chloe came in behind him, and placed a tray of mismatched crockery and glasses on the table.

'I think there's something in the air,' he said, under his breath, even though it was unlikely they could hear him.

'Oh God! Is it cow muck? Or damp?' Chloe squeaked. 'I think I've got a scented candle in the bathroom.'

'Not that. Them.'

He pointed through the window. Chloe followed his finger and then turned to look at him, a faint look of disapproval in her eyes.

'No, Paolo. You can't live vicariously through others forever. You were doing it last year with me, and with Holly.'

'I'm not. I merely think someone has cracked the hard nut that is Bear Sinclair.'

'Skye, the wildest child ever to grace Eastercraig, and Bear, the man for whom smiling constitutes a Herculean effort? Unlikely.'

'Not necessarily. Opposites attract, after all.'

Chloe's lips became a fine line. 'I'm warning you, Paolo. He's here, on a project which isn't going well, and is rarely anything other than standoffish. She's your famously explosive ex-boss's treasured niece who is going through a personal crisis. Hardly smacks of potential. Mark my words, you're going to end up causing trouble if you stick your nose in.'

'Och, I'm not sticking my nose in anything. Besides, can't you give them a chance?'

'Absolutely not. And you shouldn't either. Focus on your own love life for a bit before getting involved with other people's.'

There was a knock at the farmhouse door. Chloe shot Paolo a warning look as she went to let them in.

He sat down on one of the chairs for a second, and stared out of the window. Aside from the number of men with their tops off, the other thing that dramatically increased in summer — the further north you headed — were the daylight hours. Right now, sunset was barely upon them, and it was not yet eight. The sky had a slight golden tinge, and the scudding clouds had turned a soft peach, and there was still plenty of light flooding the conservatory. It wouldn't be properly dark for another three hours or so.

While the sound of Chloe and Bear chattering drifted in from the kitchen, Skye appeared in the doorway, a smug look on her face. 'I've found out what makes Bear tick,' she said in a low voice.

'Is that why you were looking so happy a minute ago? When you and he were ambling back to the farmhouse.'

Skye looked surprised. 'I didn't think I was looking happy, was I?'

'It's not against the rules. You're allowed to be.'

Skye laughed. 'Turns out our friend likes nothing more than traditional Scottish architecture. He's been telling me all about the buildings in the yard.'

'Horses for courses,' said Paolo. 'Interesting.'

Skye nodded. 'Yes, it is, actually. Ah, talk of the devil. He can tell you all about it.'

Bear came into the room, balancing serving spoons atop a huge dish of greens, and clenching a bottle of wine under his arm. 'My ears are burning. As is this bowl.'

Paolo got up to unburden him. 'Skye says you're into traditional architecture?'

Bear nodded. 'Aye.'

'You ought to head inland. There's an amazing blackhouse they've reconstructed, about an hour away. Sounds like it'd be right up your street.'

'Blackhouse?' Skye asked.

'Like a barn dwelling, with the walls made of stone and earth, with thatch or turf on top,' said Bear, his eyes lighting up. 'You know, I think turf would be a great material to use here. It would mean changing the plans a bit, but it's a traditional way of building. We'd use materials that are local, sustainable. It would be wonderful.'

'What's sustainable? What's wonderful?' asked Chloe. She placed a beautiful pie down on the table, steam rising from the fork-holes in the middle. 'I think we ought to start, Angus is still busy.'

'Local materials,' said Skye, as they all sat down. 'For your project. But I want to hear more about the blackhouse.' She glanced over at Bear, smiling.

'You two should check it out,' said Paolo, ignoring Chloe's glare.

'Let me serve up some pie,' said Chloe, before either of them could answer.

Paolo gave Chloe a mischievous grin as she handed him a plate. She might not want to see it, but he knew a connection when he saw it. And Skye and Bear definitely had a connection.

CHAPTER 12

Skye picked the bike up from the wall, and ran her fingers around the lights, trying to find the button to switch them on. Paolo set off in his car only after she had promised she would cycle back safely and that meant lights. Only there wasn't one, or if there was it wasn't doing anything. She wondered if they were instead connected to the wheels, and so got on the bike and pedalled around the farmyard. Still nothing.

Bear, who had stayed behind to talk to Angus, appeared in the yard. He stopped, and watched her for a second.

'Any reason you're going in circles?' he asked.

'It's the three glasses of wine,' Skye quipped. 'But seriously, I can't work out how to turn the lights on. And lord knows, I'm in no position to be a lawbreaker. Imagine if I ended up passing my exam only to jeopardize my career again by ignoring the Highway Code!'

Bear came to stand next to her. 'I don't want to mansplain anything to you, but could I take a look?'

'Be my guest.'

He crouched down, and after several seconds, he looked back up. 'Think you've got two flat batteries.'

'Shite. And it's twilight.'

She looked up at the heavens, the early stars bright in the pinky-blue sky, and shivered. There was no way she could get home safely without lights.

She could perhaps ask Angus if she could borrow some spares. He must have batteries somewhere on the farm but he and Chloe been so generous already tonight.

Bear jangled a set of car keys and Skye remembered he had opted for elderflower as he was driving. 'Say, Bear, could I cadge a lift? I'm not sure if you're staying in town or not, but I'd really appreciate it. I can text Chloe about the bike and collect it tomorrow.'

His eyes crinkled at the edges, and he stood back up. 'Of course. I'm over here.'

A handful of cars, presumably belonging to Chloe, Angus and Angus's mother Fiona, cluttered up a corner of the yard. Bear led them to a small, battered, red hatchback, and stuck the key in the lock.

'It's not on a fob, but it *does* have central locking,' he joked, dryly.

Skye climbed in. 'I would have expected someone like you to drive something sleeker, more modern. Like a hybrid.'

'My mother has one. She's ever so precious about it. She practically demands hazmat suits if you've been in anything other than dry, fine conditions.'

'But she's a case which illustrates my point. I always think of architects as having swishy cars.'

'While I'm fond of this banger, I'm torn between putting down a part-payment on something newer, and saving up for other things.'

'Like what?'

Bear turned the key, the engine spluttering into life, and they began their journey back up the potholed drive.

'You know. Stuff.'

Skye glanced at him. 'No. I don't know stuff.'

'Och, doesn't matter,' he said, frown back in evidence. 'Really, it's nothing.'

Naturally, Skye's interest was piqued by this. Most people, if they were saving up for a house, or a foreign holiday, would simply say so. Maybe if he was saving for a personal sex dungeon, he wouldn't drop it into casual conversation, but from what she knew of him he didn't seem the type. Then again, you shouldn't go judging by appearances and all that. Bear himself had reminded her of that the other day.

'You're a man of mystery.'

'Hardly.'

He'd returned to the curt answers. Skye had thought she'd started to peel back the outer layers of Bear Sinclair like an onion but, now she considered it, over dinner he hadn't revealed much more about himself. True, he had talked about traditional Scottish building techniques, something Chloe's boyfriend, Angus, had found fascinating and quizzed him on at length. His enthusiasm was infectious. Even Skye had found herself carried along wanting to know more.

She supposed a meal with people you didn't know well wasn't a time for deep dives into the psyche. Especially when you were employed by one of them.

'Come on. I pretty much know nothing about you,' said Skye.

Bear looked at her out the side of his eyes. 'You realize we only met at the start of this week.'

He had a point. 'I guess so,' she conceded.

Bear changed the gears with a clunk, as they headed up a hill through a patch of forest. The car lurched as he did so.

His tone softened. 'Are you really interested?'

Interested in a man who was doing his level best to be of no interest to anyone? You bet. It was like catnip to Skye.

'I am, actually.'

'Fine. You get one question. But not about what I'm saving for. That's off limits.'

'I kinda got that. Right . . .'

While he wasn't laying his cards on the table, he was offering to show her one. She could ask anything. But suddenly it was startlingly obvious what she wanted to know.

'I've got it! I meant to ask you at dinner, then forgot. Bear. Is it your real name?'

'That's what you want to know? When you could have asked anything?'

'Yup.' Skye rubbed her hands together.

The car emerged from the forest, and the stars above them twinkled gently.

He shook his head. 'Disappointing. It's like wasting a wish from a genie, only you don't have two left.'

Skye shrugged. 'I don't mind.'

'Fine. If you're sure. My real name's . . .' He paused for effect. 'Bjorn.'

He pronounced it with the 'or' bit landing somewhere between an 'er' and an 'ur'.

'Which is Swedish for "bear". Not overly complicated, or revealing,' he added.

'But who called you "Bear" in the first place? Was it a name you bestowed upon yourself? I met a guy at uni who introduced himself as Blaze, but was Brian on his birth certificate.'

'Much as I'd love a reinvention story, it was my mum. She thought Bear was cute. It stuck. In fairness, it's easier for people — they tend to mangle Bjorn. My paternal grand-mother — she of the handkerchiefs — is Swedish. My dad's called Sven, although he was born over here, and he wanted to keep that tradition going.'

'That's sweet. And Bear *is* a pretty great name. Personality-wise you can fulfil it in opposing ways. You could be wild and terrifying, or cute and cuddly.'

'I like to think I'm less binary than that.'

'I'm sure you are,' said Skye. 'It's more interesting than Skye, at any rate.'

'Really?'

'My father wanted to name me after a saint — he's very religious, but mum wanted to call me Skye because it's where they went on their honeymoon.'

'Don't tell me you were conceived there.'

83

'I don't think so, thank God. Not sure I could handle the ick factor.' Skye laughed.

Bear pulled up outside Paolo's flat. The car's windows were down, cool air streaming in, and Skye watched as the reflection of the stars wobbled on the rippling sea.

'My turn now,' said Bear.

Skye turned to him. 'There was never any mention of quid pro quo.'

'Don't you throw your Latin legal jargon at me.'

He might have worn a serious expression, but Skye heard the gentle joshing in his words.

'My apologies. I'll try to use laymen's terms for all future conversation. Only one, though. Those are the rules.'

Bear looked at her dead on, and Skye felt her pulse skip a beat. The anticipation of the question, she told herself.

'Why did you walk out of your exam?'

Skye felt a numbness set in. She wasn't ready to talk about this yet. Not with anyone, definitely not with someone she barely knew. Not with the gnawing feeling in her stomach from the knowledge that there was more to her panic attack than just seeing Will's hands all over The Woman, snaking round her waist, playing with her hair. The mushrooming knowledge that her chosen career wasn't necessarily the one for her, cementing the fact that she would never be able to leave her past behind and become a model citizen. Sitting behind that desk, her pen poised above the paper, she had had an epiphany. She didn't want to be sitting in that room in Tilling and Browne. Not in that moment, perhaps not at all, and she wasn't sure how much it had to do with Will, The Woman or anyone else.

'I'm going to use my pass card on that one,' she said. 'Next question?'

It was barely perceptible, but Skye heard him inhale deeply, his lips barely open.

'I'm thinking about going to that house Paolo mentioned, on Sunday. And, if you've got nothing to do, want to come along? It would be nice to have company.'

'Oh!' Skye had prepared herself for a question which plumbed the depths of her soul.

'You can say no. It's not what a lot of people would do with their free time.'

Skye looked at Bear. She had written him off that first time, thinking he was cold, unfriendly. Though burningly attractive. Yet here he was, definitely not cold and perhaps even friendly.

'I'll bring the bug spray.'

'That's a yes?'

'It's a yes. Thanks for the lift.'

Skye got out of the car, waved Bear off, only realizing she was beaming as she turned the key in the lock.

She burst into the flat, ready to share her news with Paolo, only to find he'd gone to bed. A note on the kitchen counter read:

Surgery is open Saturday mornings. I'll probs be out before you're up. Hope you got home OK. P x

Skye, her facial muscles still twitching slightly, poured herself a glass of water and went to take off her make-up. She could tell him all about it tomorrow afternoon.

Shedding her daywear and tugging on her pyjamas, Skye flopped on to the bed and decided to dial Houda. Her friend was a night-owl, who enjoyed binge-watching box sets. It rang a couple of times, then Houda picked up.

'Skye! I was wondering when I'd hear your dulcet tones,' came Houda's cheery voice down the line.

'Sorry,' Skye said. 'I wanted to hole up for a day or so before talking to you. I didn't think I'd be able to manage without crying.'

'I gave Will a dirty look for you, when he passed my desk.'

'Thanks.' Sadness bubbled to the surface. 'I missed so many signs. Or I ignored them. Like never meeting his friends, which he claimed was down to them all having children, or because half of them lived in London and it was a faff to get there. Which, by the way, it's not. And when I mentioned telling Tanya about us, he'd brush it off, and find an excuse. He was always so convincing. Not that that doesn't make me feel like any less of a fool.'

'Older and wiser women have been taken in by men like him,' said Houda. 'Men who want to have their cake and eat it. He already had one on his plate, but couldn't resist a nibble of the pretty fairy bun in the office.'

'Did I confuse smarm and charm?' Skye already knew the answer.

'After a couple of pornstar martinis, haven't we all?'

Skye snorted with laughter, then remembered the exhausted limpness she had felt when she first caught sight of Will and the other woman. She had all but crumpled to the floor of her cubicle. She'd fled, but not before Will had spotted her, locked eyes with her. Called after her.

She had attempted the exam, trying to block out the intrusive thoughts that might distract her, only for them to win out.

'I was literally aching on Monday, Houda. Like seeing them brought on instant love-flu.'

'And now?' Houda asked. 'How are you now?'

'Better,' said Skye. 'I've been out and about. And while Hugh's not here, the rest of the team at the surgery have been lovely.'

'And the exam? What did Tanya say?'

Skye picked off a piece of polish from a nail, her manicure now looking distinctly chipped, its original shine dulling. 'She said she'll sort it out, and not to worry.'

'I'll bet. They don't want superstar Skye slipping the net.'

Skye let out a 'pah' to flick the compliment away. But in truth, until the panic attack struck, there had been nothing in the exam she hadn't been able to answer. In fact, for the first few questions, her pen had flown across the page, almost unable to keep up with the pace her brain was going at. Then, halfway through, she had felt that shot of cortisol course its way through her body.

Was it the discovery of Will's cheating, fuelling the rising panic?

Discovering Will's cheating had lit a fuse, but the sudden desire to flee was fuelled by the culmination of fears she had kept at bay for some time. Fears that Skye had spent all this time trying to become someone who was not the person she wanted to be.

For a second Skye felt the panic take hold all over again. A shiver coursed through her and forced herself to remember that none of this was why she had called Houda in the first place.

'Anyway, the reason I called . . .' Skye trailed off.

She stopped, deciding to keep her weekend plans with Bear to herself. It was far too soon to be thinking about anyone else, especially a man she barely knew from Adam.

'Yes . . . ?' Houda prompted.

'Nothing. I only wanted to hear your voice. And let you know I'm OK. More than OK.'

She could hear Houda smiling down the phone. 'I'm glad to hear it. Oh, Isaac's woken up.'

'I'll let you go. Love you.'

'Love you too. And look after yourself. Now listen, unless you need to, I don't want to hear from you, OK? This is time away from work. By all means, call if you have to, send the odd text. But make sure you switch off, Skye. Recover.'

They said goodbyes and hung up, and Skye settled herself under the covers. She focused on Bear again, on the thought of how he transformed when he talked about the blackhouse. Of how he'd come to her rescue with an unexpected lift.

But then she reminded herself that until just a few days ago, she had been convinced she loved Will and Will loved her.

CHAPTER 13

The following morning, a sunny Saturday, Skye breathed in the sea air as she puttered along the front carrying a too-hot latte from the café. The colours and textures of the town were like nowhere else, the houses every colour of an artist's paint-box. Uneven waves with frothy bubbles hushed in and out of the harbour beach, sea birds swooped and called overhead. Further out, a bob of seals barked contentedly, a couple flopping their sleek bodies up on to a nearby rock. She wondered if Sporran — a seal her uncle had once treated after it had been caught in a net — was one of them.

Did Eastercraig look even more charming than usual? Perhaps her plan to go to Mull next week was making it seem that way. Or did it have something to do with spending the day with Bear tomorrow? She recalled the feelings of the night before, the noticeable thrills she had registered racing round her body. She reminded herself once more that it hadn't been a week since she had broken up with Will. It was far too soon to be thinking about moving on.

She blinked as she repeated her thoughts, a Richter-scale-registering shock jolting her. *Moving on?* She had been in love with Will, she had pictured their future together, decorated imaginary walls in the home they would share, chosen the places they would adventure to. Frankly, it was inappropriate, impossible to think she could be moving on, wasn't it?

Wasn't it?

Well, maybe it wasn't completely against the rules. You couldn't help the way you felt, of course. But she had met Bear a handful of times. He and she clearly had things in common — work crises, tough parents. And he was very handsome, but that was nothing. It was, most likely, a little crush to tide her over following her breakup. Anyway, she shouldn't be considering any men at all, given what happened with the last one.

Skye stopped dead. Forget about the moving on. More to the point, had she broken up with Will? The gusto with which he had been kissing The Woman suggested the end of their relationship was a foregone conclusion, but neither of them had said anything official. She thought about the text and voicemail he'd left earlier in the week. She hadn't opened either of them. Perhaps he had ditched her already after all.

Skye sighed deeply. So, what if she did find Bear attractive? She needn't feel too guilty. If someone cheated on you, you were sort-of a free agent. Right?

She went over to the railings, pondering what counted as suitable attire for hiking to a blackhouse, and whether she ought to read up on them first. She smiled to herself, and carried on along the pavement.

A minute later, she reached the flat, and rooted in her bag for the key. Three more weeks of freedom. Her plan for the day was going to commence with drinking her latte and looking for places to stay. It would be a wrench to leave Eastercraig, but she'd never been to Mull, and while the weather was fine, it would be a good time to explore. Skye didn't want to outstay her welcome at Paolo's, despite loving the book selection, and Ginger's company, and the fact that Paolo was an all-round superstar.

As she put the key in the lock, a deep woofing reverberated through her chest. Skye glanced round and spied Hamish wrestling a large wolfhound. She could see the veins popping in his neck as the dog strained at the leash, trying to make a break for the sea; a seal had slid off the rock, and swum over to say hello. The scar across its face marked it out. It was definitely Sporran. Skye ran over.

'Skye!' Hamish was panting more than the dog. 'How are you?'

Skye went round and grabbed the lead, only to realize she'd entered a tug-of-war with an animal who possessed the combined strength of the Scottish national rugby team.

'Not bad. I'm off work for the rest of the month. You?'

'Fine apart from struggling with this guy. I don't think you've met him before. Wolfie, you idiot canine. Come *on*. Sporran is not your friend.'

Skye turned to look at the seal, who stared at them with twinkling eyes. His wonky muzzle made it seem as though he was giving the dog a goading smile.

'Yeah, pup. He's winding you up,' said Skye, heaving harder.

'I need to get him to his Lyme vaccine. Come on, Wolfie. If I can stop fretting about all the bloody ticks you keep coming in with, it'll be one less thing on my plate.'

Between them, they heaved Wolfie one last time. As luck would have it, a boat came into the harbour at that moment and Sporran swam off to greet it. Wolfie, his bushy eyebrows furrowed, finally acquiesced. The lead slackened and Skye and Hamish collapsed on to the pavement.

'You daft bugger,' said Hamish, as Wolfie came and licked their faces.

'Ugh, gross, Wolfie!' Skye got off the ground, and with her sleeve wiped the slobber from her cheek. 'What else are you worrying about?'

'I've lost Maeve, my admin assistant.' Hamish stood up, and looked to the sky, as if a new assistant might float down, Mary Poppins style. 'She's only four days a week, but she's the one other person in the house who can work a spreadsheet. Mum and Dad try, but Mum oversees tours and can't tell if the computer is broken or simply turned off, and Dad can only type with his index fingers.'

Skye didn't need to think twice. 'I'll take over!'

It was obvious. The B&B on Mull wasn't booked, and she'd still have plenty of time to get some rest and relaxation in. Plus, Hamish was a friend. She'd be glad to help him out.

Hamish drew his chin back. 'Seriously? You'd do that? You want to work Tuesday to Friday on your month off?'

They crossed the road, and walked towards the veterinary clinic, Wolfie sniffing the ground, zigzagging as he went.

'Of course! I always loved going to the castle when I was a kid. You were my first proper friend here in Eastercraig. Your dad taught me how to fish and stalk, and your mum always set an extra place for tea. They made me feel like one of the family. I'd *love* to come and help. Only . . .' Skye couldn't believe she had overlooked it before. 'I don't really have anywhere to stay. I've already been at Paolo's a week now, and I was about to head to Mull. I'd much rather be in Eastercraig though. Maybe if I ask Paolo nicely he'll be OK with my staying longer.' She blew her fringe out of her eyes.

Hamish stopped dead. 'You can come and stay with us. I mean, it's a bloody castle. There's tons of room. We could offer you board in return for you mucking in.'

'Och, Hame! Do you mean it?' Skye threw her arms around Hamish, as he nodded. 'Call me to confirm the details?'

They said their goodbyes and Wolfie tugged Hamish through the door of the surgery. Skye waved at Chloe and Paolo through the window, optimism swelling in her chest, then walked back home.

The universe was offering her a chance to do some good. Getting to stay at Glenalmond was a bit of a bonus.

* * *

Paolo watched as Skye wandered out of sight, moving in a dreamy way as if she walked on clouds, rather than across

91

potholed tarmac. Hamish, too, seemed to have a spring in his step as he shouldered open the surgery door, hauling in a reluctant Wolfie.

Hamish grinned. 'How do?'

'Aye,' said Paolo. 'Good, thanks. Same old, same old.'

He could have done better than that. He was normally more erudite, if he did say so himself. He used the word 'erudite', for heaven's sake.

'Have fun at Chloe's? I was sad to miss it. It's been crazy busy.' Hamish continued, not awaiting an answer. 'But I've found a solution to my staffing issues . . .'

Paolo raised an eyebrow. 'Yes . . . ?'

'Skye's going to come and work for me, until I find a new temp. It gets me through the rest of June, and then schools break up and I can find a local kid or two to take over.'

'Well,' said Paolo. 'It certainly gets you out of a hole, and gives Skye something to do. I mean, I hope she's been happy chilling at mine, but I wouldn't want her to get bored.'

'About that.' Hamish grinned. 'I've offered for her to come and stay at mine. I've got rooms to spare.'

Paolo thought about Glenalmond, about the sitting room, the drawing room, the snug and the library. He loved his flat but it didn't hold a candle to a castle that could sleep twenty people with ease, and not one of them on a roll mat.

Paolo scratched Wolfie's ears, not needing to lean down because the dog's head reached his chest. 'That's kind of you.'

'Hardly. I've got a real soft spot for that girl, you know. We were so close for a while, and then we drifted apart a bit in our twenties, after she went off on her gap year and to uni. It's great to have her back for a bit. I was always very fond of her.'

Holly popped her head out of the door to the consulting room before Paolo had a chance to dwell on what Hamish had said.

'Hi, Wolfie!' she called. 'Bring him over here and we can get this done.'

Paolo followed Hamish into the room, and between the three of them, they persuaded Wolfie to sit down. The dog looked from one to another, eyeing them all with suspicion.

Holly turned her back to Wolfie so he couldn't see her prepare the syringe. 'It's the same as last year, Hamish. Wolfie may be fatigued, or feel a bit sore for the next day or two. He might not be hungry either, which is probably hard to imagine with this guy. But any problems that don't settle down after forty-eight hours, come back with him.'

Holly moved round the table, to the large patch of floor Wolfie sat on. 'It's going in the front left leg. Paolo, stay behind him; Hamish, try to keep him calm. Talk to him for a second . . .' She swiftly injected the vaccine into Wolfie's leg, causing Wolfie to howl briefly. 'All done.'

Hamish scratched Wolfie's ears. 'Good boy. Here, have a treat.'

He produced a biscuit from a sealed pack in his coat pocket. 'I know it seems weird to wrap them up,' he said, looking from Paolo to Holly. 'But he sniffs them out otherwise.'

'Sensible. Dogs like that can eat you out of house and home before you realize.' Holly went over to her computer screen, and updated her records. 'See you soon, Hamish.'

'I'll see you out,' said Paolo.

Hamish thanked Holly, and Paolo returned to reception with him. Chloe, who had been on a phone call, looked up from the desk and smiled. 'That'll be £40, please.'

The phone rang again, and Chloe picked up, simultaneously handing the card machine over to Hamish, and managing to daintily sip from a cup of tea at the same time.

'Tell you what,' said Hamish. 'I have a clear hour this afternoon. Why don't I get Skye out of your hair now? I can help her pack, and she can come straight over. It'll be fantastic. She can settle in, and reacquaint herself with the castle and all its nooks and crannies.'

'Oh. Sure.' This was happening so fast it felt like being on an out-of-control rollercoaster. 'I guess so. Err . . . thanks.'

Hamish, having tapped his card, stuffed it into his pocket. 'Great I'll see you, Paolo.'

He clapped a hand to Paolo's arm. It was such a man-to-man gesture. Still, Paolo tried not to look at where Hamish's hand rested.

'See you later.'

Hamish left, Wolfie trotting along happily after him. Paolo watched him disappear along the front, then stared at the sea out of the window. A nugget of unease proceeded to wend its way through his body, before firmly lodging itself in his brain.

Hamish seemed almost desperate to install Skye at Glenalmond, like a delightful, young chatelaine. It didn't matter she was only going to be there three weeks. Paolo could see the excitement radiating from Hamish as he'd suggested moving Skye in immediately.

'Gosh! Who knew there was such history between the two of them,' Chloe said.

It was not the comforting interruption he needed. Paolo turned around, narrowing his eyes. She narrowed hers back as she took another sip of tea, then winked.

'Are you half bat? How on earth did you get to hear any of that?' He groaned, leaning his elbows on the desk and putting his head in his hands.

'I've perfected the ability to use both ears separately,' said Chloe, with an impish smile.

'That's not a thing,' grouched Paolo. He relented, remembering Chloe was on his side. 'Do you think there's something going on?'

Chloe, who rarely guffawed, stifled one. 'Are you serious, Rossini? They're old friends.'

'He waxed lyrical about her. Like a waxy love song.'

'I didn't hear *that*,' said Chloe. 'Even with my bat ears. You're being paranoid, Paolo.'

'But he's lovely, and obviously cares for her. And she's . . . I don't want to call her a hot mess, because that's offensive.

But she's hot, and she's a mess, and he's relishing the chance to take her under his wing and help her recover, like he did all those years ago.'

'Pah.' Chloe rolled her eyes. 'You're making that up as you go along. Can you stop being so ludicrous?'

'Yes,' he acceded. 'Come on, who's next on the list?'

CHAPTER 14

On Sunday morning, Skye woke up bright and early. It might have been the early light, streaming in through a gap in the curtains where she hadn't drawn them fully. A teensy part of her acknowledged that it might have to do with the prospect of spending the day with Bear.

The night before, she had taken Paolo for a post-work late lunch at the Anchor, as a thank you for having her, before heading to Glenalmond. She and Hamish had chatted over tea in the gardens, she'd cooked dinner and caught up with his parents, David and Moira. After washing up, she turned in reasonably early, wanting to be on form for the trip.

She yawned and picked up her phone from the bedside cabinet. She hadn't looked at it last night — and yet at some point the previous evening Will had called. Twice.

Her stomach wound itself into what felt like a reef knot, that raw feeling of confusion and betrayal returning. Placing the phone back down, Skye looked up at the white plastered ceiling, her eyes tracing the intricate carved oak leaf motif that edged the room.

She could feel the tears coming, and took a shaky breath. She wasn't going to cry over him anymore. Ignoring Will wasn't going to help her consign him to history.

This was it. The moment had come. She had to turn over a new leaf. Which meant confronting him, facing what he had done to her. Was she ready to deal with the feelings that conversation would release? More than anything she wanted to avoid shouting, and crying, and making herself sound hysterical and foolish, which would only let him justify his actions. More than that, she feared that in the moment she might go mute, unable to summon the words to express herself.

It's what used to happen when she was younger. Unable to tell her father how corseted she felt by his views, she had acted out. Perhaps things would have been different between her and her father if she'd been able to express herself better. Then again, maybe not.

Still. That wasn't the matter in hand. Will was.

Skye reached again for the phone, then paused. Was this an impolite time to be calling?

'Come on, Skye,' she said aloud. 'Do you really need to concern yourself with what may or may not inconvenience Will Tomlinson?'

She scrolled through her favourites list, making a mental note to remove Will from that list the moment the call finished, and then pressed the green dial button. It rang a few times, and then Will picked up.

'Skye,' came the familiar voice. 'I'm glad you called.'

A familiar full-body ache threatened to displace the lighter feeling she had enjoyed the last few days.

'You've been ringing me.' She stuck to the facts. They were easier to express than opinions.

'I was calling to see if you were OK. How are you? You've had us all worried.'

Feigned concern was an interesting angle. Any anguish she had been feeling dissipated. Skye felt her blood begin to simmer, but if there was one moment in which she needed to channel nonchalance, this was it.

She ran her fingers over her duvet, letting a pause linger before finally answering. 'Is that so? Including you?'

Will hesitated. 'I'm sorry, Skye. I'd been meaning to tell you.'

'Tell me what?'

She endured a short silence while Will chose his words.

'About my fiancée We've been engaged for a couple of years, and been long-distance for ages, and to be honest I was wondering if it had run its course. I thought it was going to be over.'

Yeah right. Will would have kept both of them going for as long as he could.

'*Going to be over* doesn't justify *over*lap. Besides, it didn't look over from where I was stood,' Skye snapped, noting, with what felt like a sharp kick in the kidneys, that he'd referred to The Woman as 'my fiancée'.

'Are you coming back to Edinburgh soon? I'd like to talk face to face,' he continued, sounding strained.

If he thought Skye so much as wanted to be in the same room as him, let alone be anywhere near his face, he was dead wrong.

'I didn't think you'd . . .'

'What? Find out?'

Skye tried not to feel too foolish in the face of his duplicity, but there was a buzzing in her ears which was part shock and part anger. Perhaps it had only been six months, not truly long-term, but Will had treated Skye like a proper girlfriend. She'd had every reason to believe that the need to keep it hidden was because of the firm's policy.

But — Skye inhaled trying to clear her thoughts — there was no need to make this worse.

'We don't need to talk, Will. There's nothing to say.'

'So you're not going to tell HR?' he asked quickly.

That was the real reason behind the calls. 'You mean inform Tanya, after the fact?'

'We don't need to, do we.'

Will was trying to sound offhand and failing. He was normally so smooth. She had seen him in client meetings, diffusing explosive situations without breaking a sweat.

'Oh. You're worried that I might go to Tanya, let her know, and you'll be in trouble for abusing your position of authority.'

There was a pause.

'Is that it? You think I'm going to do that?' she continued. 'You were never phoning to see if I was OK, or even apologize. You're covering your arse.'

'I'm not. But Skye — are you going to say anything?'

It was hard to say who would come out worse in a disciplinary, they both knew it. Older male members of staff hooking up with their secretaries was never a good look, but Will was one of Tilling and Browne's top earners. They wouldn't want to lose him. Skye would end up being collateral.

She levelled her tone. 'We were both guilty of it, weren't we. Both guilty of letting what started as a flirtation at the Christmas party spin out of control, when it clearly shouldn't have.'

That much was true.

'You're not going to tell Tanya, then? Or Norah?' The relief in Will's voice was palpable.

'You'll live to fight another case.' Skye was careful not to say 'no'.

'Thanks, Skye. I appreciate that. I hear you're back at the end of June.'

Skye made a grunt of agreement.

'And . . .' Will continued '. . . I'm sorry about what happened with the exam. I feel responsible for throwing you off your game.'

'Right,' Skye said. She did not want to reflect on that again, and definitely not with Will. 'I think we're done here. Aren't we? I guess I'll see you.'

'Yeah. See you. And Skye . . . I liked you. I did.'

'Bye, Will.'

'Bye, Skye. And good luck.'

With that, she hung up. Skye suddenly felt light-headed, tunnel vision narrowing her line of sight.

Good luck? She had spent six months with a man who wished her luck, after *he* had cheated on her. The casual arrogance must be the reason he drifted through life on a cloud of untouchability. Give him ten years and he would undoubtedly pop up in parliament.

She flopped back into her pillows, and gave a huff.

Positive mental attitude, she rallied, swinging her legs over the side of the bed. The only way was up. And, right now, that meant getting up.

***

There are some days by the sea when glorious sunshine can reign all day, and yet as soon as you head inland, clouds envelope the hills in a damp fuzz. Sunday — the day of the trip — was one of those days, but even when shrouded by drizzle, Skye found the dramatic Highlands beautiful, and thanked her stars she had them to escape to.

'Apologies for the weather,' said Bear, lines appearing on his forehead as he took in the skies ahead of them.

'I do hold you personally responsible,' Skye joked, pleased to see his brow relax at her tone. 'I rather like it, you know?'

Something about feeling the cool, wet air on her face grounded her, like walking shoeless on grass. As she and Bear drove out of Eastercraig and inland, towards the grey mist that hung in the air and swallowed the scenery, she was tempted to lean out of the window like a dog, hoping to get her fill of it.

Fifteen minutes later, though, visibility had progressively worsened, to the point where there was very little to see at all. A car on the opposite side of the road passed, hardly more than a shadowy outline and two glowing orbs of headlights.

Skye almost rubbed her eyes to check they were working. 'Did I miss something? It's like we went through a wardrobe into another world, only this one's consumed by fog rather than blanketed in snow.'

Bear leaned forwards over the steering wheel. 'I like to think I'd have noticed a large bit of bedroom furniture in the way.'

'Mind you, given this is Scotland, who knows what might happen. The weather, I mean. Not the wardrobe. It could clear in an hour.'

Bear's brows drew together once more. 'Sorry.'

'Why are you apologizing?'

Bear frowned fully. 'I had visions of a sunny road trip, ambling around those buildings and then having a picnic somewhere. The blanket in the back seems optimistic now. I don't want you to be disappointed.'

'Why would I be disappointed?'

'Well . . . You might. I mean . . .' He tailed off.

Skye turned around and saw a tartan rug folded up on the back seat. Her heart gave a twitch, but then she remembered that this wasn't a date. Nobody had mentioned the d-word. They were merely two strangers thrown together in a small town, who didn't know anyone else, whiling away spare time. And she was healing her poor, shattered heart.

'It would be nice to have company.' Those had been his words. Not 'It would be nice to have *your* company.' That said, did anyone say the latter? Did the first essentially mean the same as the second? Working at a law firm so long had made quibbling minor grammatical points second nature. She told herself once more that it didn't matter either way.

'We might strike it lucky,' she said. 'Get some sunshine. Besides, it's still a day trip, whatever the weather. And the blackhouse will still hold the same magic, right?'

'You got me.' He was suppressing a smile. 'I bet you're pinching yourself, wondering how you ended up hanging out with such an achingly cool individual.'

This trip they were on, she wouldn't have found herself on anything like this with Will. He liked five-star restaurants, and fashionable clubs and bars, which admittedly Skye wasn't completely immune to the charms of. But drives to isolated buildings would have been out of the question, unless they were five-star hotels or wilderness retreats featured in the pages of the Sunday supplements.

Skye exaggeratedly took a thumb and forefinger to the skin on her right arm, enough that Bear could see it out of the corner of his eye while he was driving.

'Huge pinch. And as soon as we get back to Wi-Fi, I'll get you a T-shirt made — *Keep on crucking*.'

At this, Bear let out a loud laugh. 'Reckon I'd be a proper babe magnet with something like that.'

'So you're not seeing anyone at the moment?'

It fell out of her mouth before she'd had a chance to think it over.

Bear's lip curled. 'I was in a relationship until last year. But not since.'

'Oh? And what happened?' Skye sat cross-legged, nestling into the scratchy seats of the old hatchback.

'She divorced me.'

Skye felt the slow fingers of discomfort creep across her chest.

'I'm so sorry,' she whispered.

Bear looked at her. 'It wasn't working. We weren't working.'

It was a brusque explanation, not that he owed her one. Skye looked out of the window and focused on the fog to give Bear space for a second — or at least as much space as you could get in a car that could barely seat two people. She wound down the window in an attempt to dispel the onset claustrophobia.

'I didn't mean to pry. Shall we talk about something else?'

Bear nodded. 'Why not tell me about all the summers you spent here when you were younger? You mentioned them at supper, but didn't go into detail.'

Skye, was used to censoring stories about her childhood, and focused on the positives. The beautiful scenery, swimming in the sea, being allowed to go on rounds with her uncle and visit remote farms, standing at the edges of barns and watching him treat the bigger animals, like cows and sheep. As she told it, it sounded idyllic. It *was* idyllic without the

102

backstories she was withholding. Borrowing money from your mum's purse to go to an illegal rave didn't bring on nostalgia in the same way newborn lambs did. Who knew what Bear would think of that level of shenanigans.

Bear, for his part, had spent his summers in Sweden, where his grandmother had a cottage on the coast, a few hours from Stockholm. Various family members would decamp, and spend the holidays fishing, hiking, and eating rye bread. Days bled into each other, because they were so far north the sun hardly set.

'The way you describe it, I can see those houses,' said Skye. 'That bold shade of red.'

'It's traditional,' said Bear. 'A lot of buildings are painted that same colour. It comes from copper by-products.'

'You're a mine of information.'

'Very good! Honestly though, and don't laugh, we once went to the actual mine the copper comes from. It was an hour inland, but my great-uncle had decided it would be a brilliant excursion.'

'And was it?'

'Come on,' he scoffed. 'Copper mines?'

Skye snorted. 'I don't know! You might have loved them. People enjoy all kinds of pursuits,' she said. 'Like cruck frames . . .'

'What's yours?' Bear asked.

'My niche pursuit? I'm not sure I have one,' Skye said, dredging her mind for a mark of individuality. 'And now I'm feeling bothered that I might be one of the crowd.'

The discomfort at this thought tried to anchor itself in her mind. She flicked the hair band on her wrist, to distract herself from it.

'Don't,' said Bear. 'We can't all collect vintage poison bottles, or enjoy taking part in battle re-enactments.'

'True. Although I think I'd look great in a suit of armour.'

She briefly wondered about telling Bear that she had once been part of a local girl gang who spent their spare time messing about in their local neighbourhood, but — like the details of tagging along to illegal raves — decided against it. Misspent youth wasn't the same thing as a present-day hobby. Instead, they went back to talking about the work at the farm.

Before long, they'd arrived at a gravelled patch of ground by the edge of the road that might be a car park. Bear turned the car off, and they got out. Skye checked the pin she had dropped in the map on her phone. 'I think this is it, don't you?'

Bear pointed ahead. 'Yes. There, past those trees. Hold this?'

He passed Skye a rucksack from the open boot, and a camera bag, then proceeded to swap his trainers for a pair of more suitable boots. Skye was glad she had worn wellies. She had also popped some midge spray in her bag, in case. She spritzed some over her arms and round her neck, before rubbing it in. She passed the bottle to Bear, who did the same.

They set off through the mizzle, the ground squelching underfoot. The air was heavy with that sweet, earthy smell that summer rains bring, but the sun was burning through, a hazy yellowness displacing the grey of the skies. Bear led with a determined pace, and Skye marched to keep up.

They stopped not far along the track, in front of a long, squat building. A flat-ish thatched roof rose out of chunky stone walls, on top of which grass was growing. The little house had a tiny door flanked by two windows. It looked primitive, but cosy.

'This is it,' said Bear. 'What do you think?'

Skye came and stood next to him. She could completely understand Bear's fascination with places like this, and found herself wondering who might have lived here all those years ago. It must have been a hard life, eking out an existence in such isolation, praying that you would get a decent yield from any crops, working yourself to the bone every day.

Her thoughts flickered to Will, whose own hands were kept soft by an expensive moisturizer. Someone who had once lived in a house like this wouldn't have had time to gallivant around with a bit on the side. They'd never have had time.

She took in the building once more. 'It's incredible. You have to marvel at how people used to live. But you're the one who wanted to see it. What do *you* think?' Skye didn't want him to feel underwhelmed. He had really wanted to come.

'What do I think,' he repeated, quietly.

'Yeah.' What if he wasn't that impressed by the rough-hewn building? A knot of anxiety formed in her stomach. 'You said in the car you didn't want me to be disappointed, but I don't want *you* to be disappointed.'

Bear shot her a grin, and the knot started to disappear.

'I'm not,' he said. 'Or rather, I won't be. Though it's a shame the light's not great. I was going to take a couple of photos.'

'Keeping a scrapbook?'

She came to stand next to him, and he looked down at her. 'Something like that. It's for a project I want to work on.'

'Yet more mystery. Is this the same project you're saving up for? Hold on . . . Are you saving up to build your own cruck house?'

'Not exactly.' A slight crease appeared on the bridge of his nose. 'Let's go inside.'

Skye followed him in. It stood to reason that there was nobody else visiting today. Weather aside, the building was in the middle of nowhere, surrounded by peaty bogs.

It felt like a hallowed space, and Skye felt the need to whisper. 'It's pretty amazing, isn't it.'

'You know you can talk at normal volume,' said Bear, doing just that.

'It's my voice of awe,' whispered Skye.

This raised a smile from Bear. 'Really? You might find this interesting. Come here, let me tell you about these rafters.'

Intrigued, she walked over to join him.

* * *

By lunchtime, the mist had nearly evaporated completely. On a picnic blanket, on higher ground away from the bogs, Bear

105

placed some paper plates, then laid out some Scotch eggs and a quiche, and opened a box of salad. Skye reached into the bag to help, retrieving a bottle of sparkling water and some glasses wrapped in kitchen roll.

'This is a step up from curling sandwiches and a leaking flask of squash,' she said.

'I've even borrowed some cutlery from the B&B.' He handed her a fork.

There was silence for a moment, as Bear sliced up the quiche, and put some on a plate for Skye. Her mouth watered, and when she took a bite, it didn't disappoint.

'Did you make this?' She looked up at Bear.

He made a face. 'I'd like to say yes, but this is slightly beyond my capabilities, even if I wasn't presently without a kitchen. When I popped into Auchintraid yesterday to check something, I mentioned this picnic to Chloe, and asked if the shop had things like quiches. Instead, she insisted I took one she had in the freezer. It's been defrosting in the mini-fridge in my B&B room overnight.'

Skye laughed. 'You're not a cook, then?'

Bear scratched his head. 'Not of quiche. I can do a roast, make decent versions of some of my granny's Swedish classics. You?'

'I can. I spent part of one of my gap years cheffing.'

'One of them? How many did you have?'

'A lady never tells.'

Skye, who had a mouth full of quiche, regretted attempting to talk while chewing. She swallowed a large piece, which then caught itself in her throat.

She tried to clear her throat again, feeling her face turning red. Her eyes widened and Bear, correctly reading her expression as imminent asphyxia, took it as a cue. He scrambled to his feet and pulled her up, and had just put his arms around her waist when the quiche moved, travelling painfully down her throat.

'I'm OK,' Skye gasped, heaving deep breaths of air. 'It's out. Or in. I'm not choking.'

Bear handed her a glass of water, and Skye took a grateful sip.

'Thought you were a goner for a second,' he said, still looking alarmed. 'Not least as I have no first-aid training.'

'I think I was fine. But thanks all the same.'

Skye let a smile cross her face. What would she have done if Bear had stayed that close to her. Conveniently she was removing the potential life or death Heimlich thing from the equation.

At least if she was preoccupied by thoughts of Bear, it was a step on from dwelling on Will. She caught herself. Because now was not the time to catch feelings for someone.

'Let's take a break before pudding. I don't want to trigger you by offering another plate straight away,' Bear said. Skye laughed. 'So you've moved into a castle. How does that work?'

'I've known Hamish forever,' she explained. 'Once, when I was here one summer, I got lost in the woods. I'd gone for a walk, and after a couple of hours of bathing myself in the rays of sunlight which sliced through the canopy—'

'This is very highbrow,' said Bear.

'Ha — fine. After getting lost and bricking it for about twenty minutes, I spotted Glenalmond at the edge of the trees. I ran like I was being pursued by bears, only to bump into Hamish, who was coming out of a side door to go for a ramble. Have you met Hamish yet?'

Bear shook his head. 'I know him by sight, but not to say hello to.'

Skye resumed her story. 'He's a top chap. By that point I was close to tears. I didn't have a phone with me, my parents had confiscated it, but when I explained who I was, Hamish nodded. I reckon I was fourteen or so, and Hamish eighteen or nineteen. He was at uni, back for the long summer break.

'For some reason, he took pity on me, and took me under his wing for the rest of that summer. Despite what was then a massive age gap, we became friends, and then every summer after we'd hang out.'

'And you and he . . . ?'

Skye looked at Bear. 'He and I what?'

'Were a couple?'

Skye let out a shriek of laughter. 'Good lord, no. I mean, Hamish is a prince among men — a laird, to be precise — but we're friends. Nothing ever happened. For a start, he was a good five years older than me. It would have been creepy.'

'True,' said Bear. 'But you never know. Holiday romances and all that.'

'Not what they're cracked up to be,' said Skye.

She'd had one briefly, only for the guy to lose his shine as fast as his tan once they were home.

Another of her mistakes, although not quite as idiotic as the one she made with Will. Why had she not known sooner that he had been a terrible idea? She realized her mind was wandering when Bear spoke and brought her back into the present.

'You're telling me. That's how I met my wife.' He ran a hand through his hair, which had become tousled by the damp air.

Skye felt her eyes widen. 'Oh. Really?'

'Yeah. At a bar in Ibiza. She was from Edinburgh too, and we got chatting, and found out we'd got loads in common. And we also drank a lot, and I woke up in her hotel room the next morning. I got ribbed by my mates, but it seemed worth it when we swapped numbers to meet up when we got back home.'

Bear didn't seem the type to entertain a one-night stand, albeit one which graduated to a relationship. Moreover, Skye couldn't picture him in Ibiza. He hadn't struck her as the type to go large.

'And then what?' she asked, intrigued.

'We dated for six months, and when the lease was up on her flat, she moved in with me, and I obviously thought it was going brilliantly. She works at an interior design company, knows all about buildings, loves them too. I mean, she was

108

perfect. Smart, and clever, and beautiful — all those things. So perfect that I asked her to marry me. I mean, we were young and in love.'

'That *is* the main reason to get married. The "in love" bit, I mean,' said Skye.

'Exactly. So we were married. We were happy. We planned to wait for a while before thinking about children. By this point, I was fully qualified, and started working at my mum's firm. I should add *that* wasn't my plan. When I was training, I'd imagined going to London, or abroad, at least at first. But my wife's job was in Edinburgh, and she didn't want to move, and seeing as Mum's practice is one of the best, she encouraged me to ask there. In fairness, it seemed stupid not to.'

'Makes sense,' said Skye.

'But I found myself drawn to certain projects, and not the big new buildings. My wife wanted me to work on Edinburgh's answer to the Shard, whereas I liked working on existing buildings, restoring or reshaping. For her, that seemed to be a lack of ambition. We once had an argument about money, and she said: "I thought you wanted more." And I was still only newly qualified, so I hadn't been earning that much either, which seemed a sticking point. I don't think she'd realized that not all architects get paid megabucks to design museum wings.'

Skye concentrated on a loose thread in the picnic blanket, not wanting Bear to feel as if all eyes were on him while he spoke.

'I've recently had a breakup too,' she admitted.

'Really?'

'Yeah. A short relationship, a guy from my office. I found out he was cheating. Which means I'm well shot of him.' Then, not wanting to dwell, she asked: 'What's her name?'

'Her name?'

'Your ex-wife. She does have one, doesn't she?'

Bear blinked. 'Did I not mention it?'

'Nope.' Skye shook her head. 'I mean, I get that you might want to try strategies to disassociate yourself from a painful part of your life, I totally do.'

'It *is* a period of my life I'd rather forget, the wedded years. But she does have a name.'

'Which you don't want to mention because it fills you with emotions you'd rather avoid? Sorrow, or regret, or hurt?'

'Actually, the main reason I hadn't mentioned her name was . . .'

He halted, and Skye wondered what on earth was holding him back. She gave him an encouraging look.

Bear put his hand on the back of his neck. 'It's weird, but I felt like you already knew. Like we'd already spoken all about her, and that I could go over events again without saying it.'

'That *is* weird.' And maybe it was flattering, too.

'And somehow, I think it's good that I haven't mentioned it. Not breathing unnecessary life into the story means I've moved on from it. I got past the stage where I woke up every day thinking about it, then past the stage where I was worried that it would hang over me forever, and now I think I'm in the stage where it's still a part of my life, but it's not my future. Does that make sense?'

'Total sense,' Skye said.

It was as if Bear had summed up Skye's teenage wasteland years with a succinctness that she had never quite managed. True, she'd not yet found complete closure. But even so, she smiled.

'I didn't think it was a happy story,' said Bear.

'I'm not smiling because it's happy. I'm smiling because it resonated. And it *is* a happy story. It was very positive in the end.'

'Maybe,' said Bear. 'Only I'm sure it's going to make me wary about pursuing new relationships.'

'I understand that.' Skye conceded she'd likely find it difficult to trust the next man she went out with. It was too early to be thinking about it though, and she could cross that bridge when she came to it. She should give herself enough time to patch herself before entertaining feelings for anyone. 'You still haven't told me her name, by the way.'

'Oh! Well. It doesn't seem so important now, but it's Georgia. You know, when I think about it, I can't believe I could ever have been so stupid.'

'Don't we all have experiences we put in that box? Filed under "F" for "effed up"? I've got a few of those, if you hadn't noticed.' More than she was letting on.

Bear leaned back on his elbows. 'Yeah. I'm glad I'm not the only one.'

'Me too,' said Skye. 'Me too. Say, is it time for pudding?'

Bear reached into the bag, and pulled out a greaseproof paper parcel. He handed it to Skye.

'Smells good,' she said, unwrapping it. 'What is it?'

'Ginger cake, from the café, this time. I got it yesterday, and I'm hoping it's so treacly that it can't have gone dry.' Bear held out a clean plate, and she carefully slid the cake on to it.

Skye watched as Bear retrieved a knife and cut two generous slices.

'Thanks, this looks delicious' she said, as he slid a piece on to her plate. 'Look, Bear . . .' She paused, wondering if bringing their first encounter back to the fore was sensible, when they had now reached a detente. She remembered how his face flared, how annoyed he had seemed at being caught. But he had discussed his ex-wife, and perhaps he was in the mood for openness.

'I sense you're about to ask me something personal.'

Skye put her plate down, and dusted the crumbs from her fingers. Given the stickiness of the cake, most of them stayed put.

'The other day, on my rock. *The* rocks, I mean. Why were you yelling?'

'Your rocks?'

Skye smiled. 'I've gone to the rocks ever since I was a teenager, whenever I visit my uncle. Somehow I claimed them as my own.'

Bear looked into her eyes. 'Did you now?'

'Yes. At the time. But the yelling? I ask because I used to go there and shout from them too.'

Bear gave her a contemplative look, with a hint of uncertainty. 'Did you really?'

'Absolutely. Scout's honour.'

Bear put his plate down too, and turned so he was looking directly at her. He placed his forearms on drawn up, open knees.

'When I was younger,' he said, 'I wasn't exactly trouble, but I would get all wound up, particularly about how I was doing at school. My parents placed a lot of importance on being academic, and I simply wasn't, and it bothered them — Mum especially. Drawing, or design — that came easily, but everything else was harder. Ask me to write a coherent sentence at fifteen and it would look like it had been written by a ten-year-old. They were constantly on about it. I don't blame them for their concern. They only wanted me to do well, and they're part of that generation for whom that meant good grades.'

Same generation as my parents, thought Skye.

'But that inability to get it right drove me to the edge. I didn't want anyone to know how hard I found it. Couldn't even tell my friends. I didn't think they would understand.

'Sometimes I was so frustrated I would want to break something. I did once — I threw a glass at the kitchen wall. But that didn't help. Instead, I started going on long walks without telling anyone where I was going. Disappear for a day. I would go and find a space to shout it all out. Like an abandoned building, or derelict house. I'd go and yell until I'd cooled off.'

'I get that,' said Skye, as he paused to draw breath.

He fixed his eyes to hers. 'You do?'

'Of course! I used to yell from the rock, didn't I.'

'And why did you go?'

Skye was about to eat another bite of cake, and paused, her mouth wide open. She put the cake back down on the plate. 'Similar reasons. Anger. Uncertainty. Sheer exasperation.'

Bear might have thrown a glass, but he had never stood guard while someone broke a window. Tagged an underpass.

Been the active participant in The Event To End All Events. There were degrees of bad behaviour, and Skye felt that the worst of hers were off the chart. She never told anyone about her past if she could help it.

Bear met her eyes, and his mouth curled into a half smile. 'In the end, it turned out it wasn't wasted time, either. I reckon while I was there, the cogs in my mind were turning about the architecture of those deserted places and what could be done with them.'

'Not everyone's cut out for school.' Skye shifted towards him a bit.

'*You* must have been.' Bear raised an eyebrow. 'What with your law career.'

'You'd think,' said Skye. 'But I wasn't a model pupil back in the day.'

Bear tilted his head as if this was unexpected. 'Really?'

'Not until later on. But back to you and school and the pressure and frustration . . .'

'Yeah, well, it turned out they'd missed my being dyslexic. It took ages until a teacher spotted it. Thank heavens someone did, and they found the right strategies to help me out. Turned out I wasn't too bad at school after that.'

Frowning at the memory, he took a sip of water from his flask. Skye shuffled a bit nearer again.

'No wonder you were feeling frustrated, though. But I'm glad you got there in the end. So why the therapeutic shouting session on Monday?'

Bear's eyebrows drew together. 'The project is really behind. And there was a delay processing the Historic Scotland forms. I was so angry because it's all beyond my control at the minute. It makes me look unprofessional. Right now, it's crucial that my reputation isn't compromised. And the costs will likely go up too, which is a bother for the clients. When I got back to the site on Monday I could feel this frustration rising, and so instead of firing off a handful of emails — something which generally takes me longer than it might — I went to yell at the sky. All I want is for this project to work. I need it to work.'

'And did it help?'

Skye wanted to reach out and put her arms round Bear. She sympathized with what he had said about his struggles when at school, and then beyond. She had long thought that, with a decent quantity of elbow grease, she could accomplish the security one might expect in adulthood. A rewarding career, for one thing, or a stable relationship. That the world would play ball.

Skye found she couldn't read his expression. His gaze searched her face, before he looked her right in the eye.

'It did. Until I saw you,' he said, softly.

Her heart gave an unexpected extra beat. *A flex*, she told herself. *The heart is a muscle and that's what muscles do.*

She reached for her flask, and took a sip, and looked over at the blackhouse. 'Oh,' she managed.

* * *

Sometime after, they got in the car. It was far later than Skye had planned, but post-lunch, they'd taken a footpath that continued along past the blackhouse, to a small reservoir. Bear now turned the engine on, and they began the drive back to Eastercraig.

By the time they reached the turning for Glenalmond, Skye was fighting off yawns.

'Keeping you up, am I?' asked Bear.

Skye giggled. 'Sorry! I'm not used to this much fresh air. I can't remember the last time I even walked up Arthur's Seat, can you?'

Skye thought about the large hill in Holyrood Park. It was a bit of a trek, but it offered an incredible panoramic view of Edinburgh. She didn't think she had gone up it for at least a year. She hadn't had time, in between work and seeing Will, who — and she now knew why — liked leaving the city at weekends.

Bear looked over at her. 'I went up last month. With a couple of mates who were staying.'

'Well, get you. Does that count though? When you're posing as tour guide?'

Bear raised an eyebrow. 'However I look at it, I think it counts. I definitely went up it and came back down. Is this a lawyer thing? Am I being cross-examined? If so, shouldn't you let me know? You might be trying to catch me out.' He shot her a grin, and Skye felt herself pinken.

She laughed. 'I wouldn't dream of it. Look, here we are.'

They rolled on to the driveway, the gravel crunching under Bear's wheels. In the late afternoon light, the granite looked silver.

'Nice place, isn't it,' said Bear. He put on the brakes, and leaning towards the windscreen together, they both stared up at it. 'I wonder how much one of these goes for.'

'I think if you find one in the middle of nowhere, in a state of disrepair, you could get one for less than a flat in New Town. Perhaps that's your next project,' said Skye.

'Maybe if you come in as consultant. With all your experience of living in one.' He nudged her on the shoulder, which sent a thrill shimmying its way through her body.

'I've only been here a night,' said Skye. 'Thanks for today, by the way. I really enjoyed it.'

She looked at Bear, who turned back from admiring the castle to face her. He had *such* great eyes. And, when he produced one, a winning smile.

'I should be thanking you,' said Bear. 'For agreeing to come with me. If you're free another time—'

'I'd love to!'

As she had cut him off, Skye had been able to hear the exclamation marks, and she felt a fluster rising at her overenthusiastic response. Moreover, she could have been agreeing to anything.

As if he'd read her mind, Bear teased, 'What would you have said if I'd asked you to come and help out on the building site?'

'I'd ask you to pass me a hard hat, and get stuck in,' she said. 'With that, I'll be off.'

She opened the door, and got out, then rounded the car to the driver's side. Bear rolled down the window all the way, and Skye ducked down, resting her arms on the window sill. 'I'll await my personal invitation to join your project team.'

She caught his eye, then looked down, feeling a smile tugging on her lips.

'In that case, I'll call you,' he said.

They were so close, Skye was sure she could feel his breath. She could hardly bring herself to look up. Instead, she stood up and took a step back, into the cool evening air, only able to meet his eyes once there was a good few feet between them.

'Night, Skye.' He lifted a hand as he spoke, clicking the key in the ignition with the other.

Skye gave a small wave as the engine started up. 'Night.'

CHAPTER 15

Down the steps from the terrace at Glenalmond, at the bottom of the vast lawn — which was roughly the same size as a public park in Edinburgh — burbled a river, which meandered lazily past the castle. Skye had dragged an exhausted Hamish to a bench that overlooked it, for a glass of wine and a bowl of olives, a sundowner to ease his bones after a hard day's graft on the estate.

Higher up the hills, the water had to force its way down the valley as a small burn, a narrow stream that bubbled and burst around corners. Here at the bottom of the valley, where the land flattened, it calmed down a bit, gradually widening out before it reached the sea.

It went on a journey, Skye reflected, that resembled her own. You started out with enormous energy, crashing about, trying to work out where you were going, somewhat all over the place. There were rocks, sheer drops, bits you left behind, but all the while you kept going. Then, eventually, you slowed down, no longer in a hurry. And then, finally . . .

'What do you think happens to us when we die?' she mused aloud.

Hamish was lying at her feet, on a giant blue rug on the grass, his eyes closed. 'Have you been speaking to your parents? Did your father tell you we all end up where we deserve again?'

Skye felt a shiver at this, and hastily brushed it off. 'No. I haven't even told them that I'm here. They'll only ask why.'

Hamish opened his eyes and rolled over. 'You've just been through a really rough time, and you haven't told them? It's been a whole week, Skye!'

'Of course I haven't,' said Skye. 'I don't want to panic them.'

'Yeah, yeah. You keep telling yourself that.'

You couldn't get much past Hamish. He might have claimed to find it easier to talk to the trees on the estate than other people, but Skye knew from when they were younger that he had more emotional intelligence than most.

Skye let out a huff of defeat. 'I like to present the positives as a fait accompli. I want them to think I'm a functioning person who has grabbed life by the horns, ridden it like the most bucking of broncos without falling off, and won the game of life.'

Hamish sat up. 'Ah, so you're afraid of them seeing any of your less successful moments?'

'Yeah. Now at least.'

Who didn't want to be successful? Skye had broken her back working to get so far, taking comfort in the path laid out in front of her. Only now it seemed like somewhere along the road she had taken a major wrong turn.

'I get that,' said Hamish. 'You did have that wee rough patch as a teenager.'

'You gloss over it so eloquently.'

'Yeah, but that's all it was. And it's behind you now. You've moved on. We all fall down. Nobody wins all the time.'

'By that logic, nobody loses all the time either, but you could still fail ninety-nine per cent of it. Oh God, I sound so dreary. Tell me about your date, Hamish. Perk me up.'

Hamish had been out with a man he had met on a dating app. They'd been over in Nairn the day before, for a stroll.

'It was fine,' he said, with a shrug. 'No long-term potential, but at the moment it's all about practise. I was with Daisy for so long, I've almost forgotten what it's like to put myself out there. Which, as you know, was never really my thing. I hate these dating apps. I'm more of an organic situation kinda guy.'

'Why don't you go out with Paolo? You were getting on like nobody's business at the Anchor last week.'

Hamish's cheeks became more ruddy than usual, and lines appeared on his forehead. 'I'm not sure about that.'

Trying not to spill her wine, Skye slid off the bench on to the rug, and leaned up close to him. 'I think I'm on to something. Like the Sherlock Holmes of the Highlands. Denial, blushing, a faraway look whenever I say the name "Paolo". It's elementary, my dear, Hame.'

Hamish shifted. 'You're taking up most of my personal space, Skye.'

'Yup. Open up and I promise to remove myself from it.'

That Skye had hit upon something was as clear as a long June day in Eastercraig.

Hamish let out a grumbling noise. 'I've not properly dated a guy for ages, not more than a casual app-enabled sober afternoon meetup. Before Daisy, there was Augusta, and Letitia. Don't laugh, I'm aware they're quite posh sounding. I live in a castle, it attracts a type . . . But no guys since uni, for no real reason other than I was dating girls. Well, that, and the fact James broke my heart, and I didn't want to go out with another guy after that.'

Skye took herself back in time. James had been one of Hamish's best friends, and when they had broken up Hamish had been devastated. That summer, when Skye had arrived, Hamish had spent most of the holidays moping. Skye in turn had spent hers desperately trying to stop him from getting in touch with James and getting hurt further.

'Then last year I had this connection with Paolo,' Hamish continued. 'But I was with Daisy.'

Skye found it reassuring that there were some principled men left in the world, ones who still thought going behind their partner's back was an act perpetrated by only the morally bankrupt.

'Anyway, there are many reasons I haven't gone for him. Primarily, I didn't want to rebound on Paolo only to get it wrong. What if I didn't like men anymore, and it was merely a passing feeling? I ought to check, rather than make a mistake with him. It's why I'm soft launching myself back out there. Hence meeting Barry for a drink. "Baz". Ugh.'

'That bad?'

Hamish gave a small smile. 'There won't be a second date, but I'm currently arranging a meetup with a chap called Steven, if that shuts you up.' He rolled his eyes.

'Oh, Hame! Sorry,' said Skye. She gave him a nudge. 'Keep trying? They won't all be that dismal. And, let it be known, I still think Paolo and you would be a perfect match. Why don't you let me intervene? Sprinkle some fairy dust on the two of you?'

'Och, Skye. I'm not sure.' Hamish ran his hand down his face.

Somebody deserved true love, even if it wasn't her, and nobody deserved it more than Hamish.

'I really don't want to mess Paolo about. Or risk getting hurt myself. I'm happy to stick to swimming. That way I can see him regularly, without having to make a big deal out of it.'

'That's not a winner's mentality,' Skye replied, borrowing from a workshop they'd had at the office about manifesting success. 'You like him, so you should make a big deal out of it.'

'So many reasons why it would be a bad idea.' Hamish rolled his eyes. 'Too many.'

Skye pushed a little. 'Try me.'

'Paolo isn't shy. He's confident and outgoing. He doesn't melt into the background, and I bet wants someone with similar energy, like his last boyfriend. Perhaps that's why things have gone quiet — we've been hanging at the pool, and he's realized I'm wrong for him. And if I'm not wrong for him, and if something did happen, what if it went tits up? I'd have to bump into him every other day in town. The only alternative would be to become an eccentric recluse who never leaves his ancestral pile. Like Beast, from *Beauty and the Beast*.'

'There was a happy ending with that, remember?' Skye felt compelled to point out.

Hamish paused, and Skye sensed that the touchpaper had been lit.

'I'll be very subtle about it . . . He won't even know a plan is afoot . . .' She left it with him for a long moment, making herself count to ten in her head, before saying: 'Please?'

Hamish let out a small growl. 'Maybe . . . och, fine. Go on. But I'll still see Steven. He seemed nice in his messages and I don't want to muck him about.'

Skye let out a squeal and threw herself on to Hamish, then sat back, laughing at Hamish's attempt to keep any excitement from his face. 'Thank you. I swear I won't do anything extreme. Pass me some olives?'

An affectionate, if wary smile crossing his face, Hamish handed them over, and Skye took one, sucking the brine out. They were the healthy end of snack food, she argued, taking a couple more. The last one she flicked up into the air, and craned her neck back to catch. Hamish gave her a shove, and it landed on her bare arm, leaving a trail of oil as it rolled down towards her elbow.

'What did you do that for?'

'Didn't you tell me Bear had stopped you from choking yesterday?'

'Sort of. Why?'

'Because olives can easily get lodged in your throat, especially when you're trying to catch them like a child impersonating a bird. Be less bird, and more human. Know your limitations.'

Skye knew hers, thank you very much. They lay somewhere between being able to correctly choose the right partner and safely chew quiche.

'He didn't actually have to Heimlich me,' said Skye. 'But perhaps it would have been nice if he had.'

'For you? You mean? You wanted him to save you?'

She had lain in bed the previous night, thinking of how Bear's strong arms had momentarily wrapped around her, pulled her tight against him.

Skye scrambled for the words. 'Yes . . . no. I don't know.'

'Jesus, Skye. It would also have been a real bummer if he'd tried and failed. And you'd be dead an' all.'

Skye snorted with laughter at the truth Hamish had laid before her. She closed her eyes for a second and tried to parse her thoughts.

No, she didn't want to be saved by Bear, or for Bear to save her. The only person who could save her was, as she well knew, herself. Or — her father's voice interrupted her thought process — a higher power. She would only take that as a last resort, though.

No. She didn't want to be given the Heimlich by Bear. What she thought she wanted was the aftermath — a positive one. To have shared the real relief with him, to have collapsed into his arms, and been held for a second longer than needed while she . . .

'Oh crap.' She looked at Hamish. 'I think I fancy Bear.'

CHAPTER 16

It was after work on Tuesday and, somewhat under duress, Paolo was out in Beauly, on a date. Holly and Chloe had threatened to steal his phone and begin swiping right on every other profile if he didn't get out and keep trying and, not wanting to whinge, he had agreed to arranging some meetups.

At least a visit to the town wasn't a hardship. Worst case scenario, he could visit the bookshop, the treasure trove antique sellers, and the traditional outfitters — Donaldsons, before they closed. Donaldson's kept its clothes in neat wooden drawers and dressers, and on arrival you were attended to by staff in tailored tweed and tartan outfits. It was like stepping back in time, and Paolo, who occasionally thought he had been born in the wrong era, relished a chance to soak up the atmosphere there.

Paolo had chosen his favourite bar as the venue, inside the small hotel. While it didn't have a beer garden, it made up for it by being furnished with shabby old red leather stools, and mismatched chairs. It also had one of Paolo's favourite lagers on tap. If you couldn't guarantee the quality of the date, you could at least get a decent pint in.

Rhuari was pretty good looking, but over the first drink he had told Paolo how he spent most of his money on football memorabilia. There was nothing wrong with that, not really, only Paolo wasn't sure how to reply.

'So where is it you're from? Aberdeen? There's a play on at the theatre there that's meant to be amazing. Do you ever go there?' Paolo ventured into territory he knew better.

'Och, no. Not my thing. I go to the cinema once in a while though. Love a blockbuster. Have you seen the one that came out last month?' Rhuari detailed the latest in a long-running series of action films.

Paolo had in fact endured it with Chloe and Holly. They had dragged him along to one of their film nights and had teased him mercilessly for not knowing any of the characters.

Paolo much preferred foreign arthouse cinema, films that really made you think and often made you cry. 'I recently saw that French one, which won the BAFTA.'

Rhuari shook his head. 'I cannae speak French.'

That's why there are subtitles, Paolo thought. He'd never understood that argument about foreign films.

'I actually speak Italian,' said Paolo trying again. 'My grandparents came over from a tiny village in Tuscany in the 1950s. They set up a restaurant here and my mum runs it now, with one of my sisters.'

'I've never been to Italy,' Rhuari said. 'Me and the wife like to go to Spain though. The in-laws have a villa down near Alicante and . . .'

'I'm sorry,' Paolo interrupted him at that. 'Your wife?'

'Oh, gosh. I thought you . . .' Rhuari glanced around the room, looking anywhere other than Paolo's face.

Paolo leaned over. 'You're married?'

Rhuari looked a little pale, and shifted in his seat. He was still facing Paolo, but refusing to look directly at him.

When he didn't respond, Paolo hissed, 'I thought you were looking to meet someone. That's what you said in your DMs. But a bit on the side? Am I supposed to be some dirty little secret?'

Rhuari concentrated on his beer mat. 'Actually, my wife knows I'm here. It's more that . . .' He hesitated, and after a noticeable, nervy bob of his Adam's apple, he added: 'We're looking for someone to be a throuple with. I thought I mentioned that . . .'

He tailed off again, and looked longingly at the exit. Paolo was stunned. Rhuari had definitely omitted that particular detail in their exchanges. He never would have agreed to meet if he'd known. A throuple might work for some, but he just wanted to be in a committed relationship with one person, thank you very much. Unless, in his haste to get Holly and Chloe off his back, he had skim read the messages and not noticed Rhuari's predilections.

'Thanks for the invitation,' said Paolo. 'But I'm afraid that's not really what I was here for. Perhaps we should go our separate ways.'

He gathered his jacket up from the bench, and — for dignity's sake — walked out into the evening sunshine.

Pulling out his sunglasses, he decided to head straight to Donaldsons — a spot of retail therapy might erase the thoughts of what else Rhuari might have been going to suggest from his mind.

Walking along the pavement, Paolo comforted himself with the knowledge that even though the date wasn't a success, it had at least been anecdotal. This system of categorizing his dates had served him well recently, stopping him from getting too depressed Some of his misadventures had left Chloe and Holly in stitches when he was recounting them over a coffee before the surgery opened. That had to count for something.

He stopped in his tracks. Over the other side of the road he spied a figure with a familiar gait. Hamish. He was about to call over when he realized that Hamish had wandered over to someone else, a man Paolo had never seen before. His stomach sank as he watched Hamish peck the man on the cheek.

Paolo leapt into the doorway of a nearby grocers as the pair crossed the road towards him. He wasn't sure he wanted Hamish to see him. The pair of them were heading for the bookshop. Lifting the glasses and squinting, Paolo couldn't help but notice that the stranger was gorgeous, smartly dressed in dark jeans and a shirt. To only deepen his horror, Paolo realized that Hamish was out of his usual khaki hues. He had made an effort for this man!

Paolo peered out from his hiding spot, only emerging when he was certain that Hamish and the man had gone into the bookshop. He stepped out feeling unnerved and slightly shaky.

So that was why Hamish didn't seem into him any more. Paolo *had* been barking up the wrong tree when he had been fretting about Skye. Hamish had found somebody else. Paolo turned on his heel and took a very circuitous route back to his car to avoid both being seen, and having to see them again.

Ten minutes later, back at the car, Paolo rested his head on the steering wheel. The wind had been knocked out of his sails properly. If he really were a boat, he would simply drift away, never to be seen again.

A vibrating in his pocket awoke him from his state of woe. Holly.

He really didn't want to tell her how the date had gone, but he picked up anyway. 'Hols?'

'Paolo? I hope your date's going well.' Paolo was about to reply but Holly continued. 'A rider came off their horse out towards Lowburn Farm. They're fine, but the horse isn't and I need an extra pair of hands. Can you bear to come back?'

'Sure,' said Paolo, grateful to have something else to focus on. 'I'll be there in about half an hour.'

CHAPTER 17

That night, Skye lay in bed, her thumb marking the page in her book, and thought about the last week.

From the pit of doom in which she had been entrenched at the start of the month, she had managed to claw her way out.

Silver linings were everywhere. You just had to know where to look.

She ran through them. For starters, she had been given a month off, without asking. She hadn't even had to manifest that one. Tanya had basically tied that gift up with a bow and handed it to her. There was bumping into Hamish, and reconnecting with him. Then he'd offered a wee job which meant she could feel useful. Not to mention the luck of falling in with the surgery crew, Paolo in particular.

And then — Skye poked her head out of the curtains of the four poster and did an enthusiastic inner victory dance for the hundredth time since she had arrived at Glenalmond — there was this bedroom. It was decorated to perfection, from the antique furniture to the sumptuous fabrics. This wasn't a little win, it was huge.

Though it was warm outside, the walls of the castle were thick, and inside was blissfully cool. You had to admit, builders of yore, or whatever you called them, knew what they were doing. The walls kept the heat in during winter, and kept it at bay come summer. Skye glanced around, wondering where the tapestries would have gone.

She shivered, and scooted back behind the drapes, pulling them shut. There was a flexible clip lamp within, which readers of yore would have loved as it was incredibly useful and had been on for the last hour as Skye turned the pages of *Wuthering Heights*. She picked up the book, and then closed it again, instead picking up her mobile. It was late, half eleven or so, but Bear might still be up, and Skye had the urge to text him.

I wish you could see what the inside of my current bedroom looks like!

Whoa! Too flirty. Skye hit the delete button and watched the caret eat up the words.

He had darted back to Edinburgh to work on another project and had texted her earlier in the day to say he would be back soon. She tried again.

Hi! How's your week going? Staying at this castle is like living in some century gone by. Have you been for a tour yet? With your love of historic buildings you'd be in your element. Hope you're well x

That was far better. She hovered her finger over the send button, but hesitated. Again, she held her finger down and let the caret erase that effort. Instead of a third attempt, Skye tugged the blanket around her and bustled out of the bed.

She walked to the window and gazed out at the Glenalmond estate in front of her. She could understand why tourists descended on the place like vultures between May and September, when the gardens were at their best. The manicured lawn, which Hamish's dad liked to keep trim with his ride-on mower, was impressive, and to one side Holly could see the quirky topiary which Hamish claimed had been there for over a century. His mum, as well as running tours, liked to tend the herb garden, set in a beautiful parterre hidden behind neatly clipped yews.

The scene was bathed in white moonlight, the river at the bottom of the garden shimmering silver. Then something moved. Skye froze, focusing her eyes on whoever or whatever it was. She quietly opened the window a couple of inches, careful not to let in any midges, but even though it was a still night, no sound carried over.

Then, as they came out into the open, Skye realized it was a herd of deer.

'Wow,' she whispered, as ten or twelve emerged from the trees that edged the castle and gardens.

They moved gracefully on to the grass, dipping their elegant necks to graze. Alongside their parents, there were a couple of fawns.

She marvelled at them. Hamish had told her they represented both strength and tenderness, and that the loss and regrowth of their antlers was a symbol of rebirth. He tried to convince her that it was important to manage their numbers, but Skye hated the fact that people came to shoot them. They were wild animals, and she wished they could be free to roam.

Skye was still holding her phone in her hand, and she lifted it up to take a picture. It was a gorgeous shot.

This was the message, of course it was. She uploaded it to WhatsApp, and added a caption.

Another reason why this place is heaven on earth.

She paused, thinking how such a phrase would wind her father up no end. She remembered how she used to fling such sentences around with abandon, just to infuriate him.

It wasn't something she did any more. Everyone had a right to their beliefs, including her father. Besides, when it came to verbal duelling she had run out of steam some time ago. She preferred to maintain a peaceable relationship with him these days, which meant minimizing drama.

It didn't matter now though. The text wasn't for him.

She added Bear's name to the address box, and pressed send. Then she placed the phone on the window ledge, and watched the herd browsing the grounds.

After fifteen minutes or so, Skye wandered back to bed. Stifling a yawn, she made to turn her phone off, when it vibrated.

Is this a ruse? If so, top marks. Presumably you're working with the Eastercraig tourist board?

Skye chuckled under her breath.

I promise they're the real deal. Living, breathing, in my back yard.

Her phone rang, a delicious tingle running down her spine. She pressed the green answer button.

'Aren't they amazing?' she said.

'I bet you're glad you managed to land yourself such a fantastic place to lodge for the next few weeks.'

She could have told him that it took a fountain of self-doubt to get her there, but kept that to herself.

'I'm *very* lucky,' she agreed. 'You're up late.'

'I'm working,' he said, his deep voice rumbled down the phone. 'I'm moving on to yet another project soon. A potential redevelopment in Leith. What are you up to? Other than communing with nature.'

'For me, that phrase conjures up images of dancing naked with sage sticks, pressing my cheeks against the bark of trees and listening to what they have to say.'

There was a pause. 'That's quite a picture you've painted.'

'Oh God.' Skye blushed, only just seeing it for herself. 'Well. I could also commune fully clothed in a bird hide.'

'Right. Well, I reckon either would be a good look,' said Bear, after a beat.

Skye felt herself turn a deep crimson, matching the red of the tartan blanket on the bed. She pictured his strong face, those eyes she could drown in, imagining his strong arms around her. She focused on the carved wooden detailing on the bedposts, reminding herself to slow herself down.

'Thank you.' She tried not to stammer.

'You're welcome,' said Bear, his voice playful.

Skye gulped, feeling flustered. She pushed the window open a little further to cool down.

'When are you back in Eastercraig?' she asked, returning to safer territory.

'I'm not sure. I want to get back though. If I can get everything done here, I'll be able to make it up at the end of the week. Are you around?'

'I'm not going to be anywhere else. Give me a call?'

'I will,' said Bear. 'Right. This tender isn't going to write itself. Send me more pictures, will you? Of Glenalmond, I mean.'

'Sure,' said Skye, feeling herself break into a grin.

They said their goodbyes, and Skye closed the window, then wriggled down into bed, wondering how early the next morning was too early to ping over a photo.

CHAPTER 18

Skye's body was so attuned to the working patterns of the Tilling and Browne machine, that she still found herself waking up at 6.30 a.m. every morning, despite having no work to rush to. Since she'd been at Glenalmond, she'd been joining Hamish for a walk on the estate before heading to the estate office. Hamish liked to go out for an hour first thing, conscientious ghillie as he was, to check the grounds. He tended to do the same in the evenings. Skye didn't join him then; for the first week of her stay at Glenalmond, she had taken to luxuriating in the bath before going downstairs to help make supper.

At 7 a.m. that hazy Thursday morning, they went on the quad bike, zooming up to look at the burn. The small stream ran through the higher hills at the edge of the estate, before widening out into a larger river at the bottom of the garden. The burn wound its way snakelike through the rugged landscape, a sliver of bluish-grey cutting through the brown moorland with its swathes of purple heather. They had walked down one side, then hopped over boulders that acted as stepping stones across the stream, and left themselves another twenty minutes to loop around and hike back up.

'You always were a proper little ghillie dhu,' Hamish said, as Skye splashed her face with water from the burn.

'I thought they were male sprites.' Skye patted her cheeks dry.

'Aye, but we're very forward thinking here at Glenalmond.'

'And thinking forward, I want you to know I've not forgotten you and Paolo.'

Hamish rolled his eyes. 'I see what you did there. Very smooth.'

She chuckled and rubbed her hands together in pantomime fashion. Hamish shook his head, a rueful look on his face. 'Thanks. But rest assured, I am concocting a plan. When I'm not doing the admin, that is.'

'I wish I could say I was looking forward to it,' said Hamish wryly.

'I've been thinking about lines for you. We can get him over, and while I busy myself with something, you can say "The moon is beautiful tonight", or something.'

'Or something. Let me know when you've polished that up a bit,' said Hamish, before leading them back up towards the quad.

Skye was still smiling about it as she shuffled unfiled papers on her desk. She was loving the outdoors. It was now nearly midday, and she planned to sort the estate paperwork properly after a quick sandwich. She made to leave when the phone rang. It was an old fashioned one with a rotary dial.

'Glenalmond Estate, Skye speaking,' she said.

'I was hoping I'd get you,' came a voice down the end of the line.

Bear. Skye felt the corners of her mouth hitch.

'To what do I owe the pleasure?'

She caught herself neatening her hair as if he was there in person. While he'd been in Edinburgh, Skye had found herself thinking about him in most of her spare moments. And the un-spare ones too.

They had messaged each other on and off during the week, and Skye had taken to pouncing on her phone the moment it vibrated, hoping that it was Bear. Aside from the deer, who had returned the next night, she had taken to texting him different parts of the castle, seeing if he could give her the correct architectural name for it. Bear, in turn, had been sending pictures of Edinburgh.

'Do you want to do something tomorrow? I'm back in town and wondered if you'd like to meet up.'

Skye grinned and stifled a giggle. 'What do you have in mind?'

'The pub. I don't really know what else there is.'

'You know what,' said Skye, looking out of her window on to the hills. 'I might have an idea. Come over here tomorrow evening, at seven?'

'Mysterious,' said Bear. 'I'll be there.'

They said their goodbyes and rang off, Skye's heartbeat tripping over itself.

Did it matter that she was moving on faster than she had expected? Will had no claim on her feelings, and what was wrong with a little fun? Nothing at all, Skye concluded, as she got up to make herself that sandwich.

* * *

After the surgery closed, Paolo went back to his flat. He was going to meet Graeme Innes from his book group for a pint or two later. Graeme had a toddler and a baby on the way, and was looking to get his nights out, before the upcoming arrival made its appearance.

Paolo wasn't sure he was up for it. He had already had to rearrange swimming with Hamish.

It had been an especially hard afternoon. A family's pet labrador had been hit by a car, after scooting out the front door and on to the main road. The emergency surgery needed to fix the poor creature had taken over an hour. Then there was a last-minute farm visit with Holly when a calf got stuck in a cattle grid. Overall, it had been a physical day. It almost made Paolo wish more of their animal clients were baby gerbils who needed nothing more than having their sex checked.

He got a beer from the fridge, an aperitif before he headed to the Anchor. It was still warm out and he took the bottle back downstairs to drink on the bench outside the ground-floor windows of the building.

The sash window behind him clanked open, and an older lady stuck her head out. 'Long day, was it, darlin'?'

Paolo turned his head around. 'Evening, Mrs Brown. How are you?'

'Och, nothing to report. My Sandra's wee bairn's had a terrible cough, so I've been over on the Black Isle today looking after him while she works. And you?'

Paolo stood up to look at his neighbour. She was a smiley woman, with a silver bob and tended to wear sherpa fleeces regardless of the season. When Paolo went on holiday, she looked after Ginger, and when she was away, he tended her window boxes and large collection of exotic houseplants. She could talk the hind leg off a donkey given the chance, but Paolo loved chatting with her. 'Busy day at the practice. Non-stop. Busy week, now I think about it.'

'Aye, you've been looking a bit peelie-wally last few times I've seen ye.'

'Have I?' said Paolo.

'Maybe you should all be lamenting Hughie's holiday. I ken you couldnae wait to see him out, but seems to be busier than normal. Holly OK?'

'Aye. She'll live.'

Mrs Brown disappeared for a second, then the front door clicked, and she appeared on the steps next to him, a tin of gin and tonic in hand.

'Mind if I join ye?' she said. Paolo shook his head. 'Now, and what with all this dashing about, have you had time to find yourself a nice young chap yet?'

Paolo shook his head. When he had first moved to Eastercraig, Hugh had warned Paolo that his downstairs neighbour considered herself the town matchmaker.

'Go on, whip yer phone out. Let's be having a look at what's on offer.'

Paolo couldn't help but laugh. 'I've never known such a nosy old woman in all my days.'

Mrs Brown chuckled, and Paolo reached into his pocket and pulled out his mobile.

'Here we go,' he said.

Together they scrolled through the list of potential matches. Mrs Brown grumbled over most of them, and then made a hooting noise as someone called Patrick came into view.

'Now that's a nice-looking laddie. Why not ask him? Look, he's not too far away, and really, Paolo, you don't want to be driving too far. Petrol's very dear, and you don't want to be wasting your money.'

Paolo moved the screen closer to his face. Mrs Brown was right. Patrick was easy on the eye. Together they studied his profile, agreeing that nothing was a red flag.

'Well, I'll think about it, Mrs B,' said Paolo.

He told Mrs Brown about Rhuari, unable to suppress his own smile when she shrieked with laughter.

'And I thought I'd heard it all! The right person will come along, darlin',' she said. 'Now, there's something on the telly I want to watch, so I'll be heading back in.'

'See you,' said Paolo.

After the Rhuari fiasco, the great unknown didn't thrill him. Instead of a wide pool of eligible men, Paolo saw only stormy waters ahead. He skimmed the phone again. Patrick. He wasn't sure about the wisdom of any of this.

CHAPTER 19

'There's nowhere like this, is there?' Bear said quietly. 'It's spectacular.'

Friday evening, the sky bright and cloudless, Skye found herself with a helmet on, speeding up the glen on a quad bike. Without Hamish, she wasn't confident enough to go off-piste. The bogs could take you by surprise. Instead, she took the track up to the Victorian hunting lodge a few miles from the castle where Hamish took visitors to the estate for rustic lunches.

Pulling up outside, she sat for a second, gazing at the view. Ahead of them, the glen peaked and fell like a colossal wave, in a deep, peaty green. Dotted all over were tufts of heather, huge clusters of them. There was a softness to their colour, like they weren't prickly at all, as if the spread of purple blooms was nothing more than a cashmere blanket.

She turned around and grinned at Bear on the back of the quad, his face reflecting back admiring wonder.

'We can either hang out here and take in the view or go for a wee hike,' said Skye. 'I've got some beers in the cooler, non-alcoholic ones for me, and a couple of regular for you. We could sit and drink, or wander down to the valley and walk there. I've also got a flask of tea and some biscuits in the rucksack.'

'All bases covered then.' Bear raised his eyebrows.

'I like to be prepared,' laughed Skye.

'Let's walk,' suggested Bear, with a smile. 'We'll both be back in the city before long, and I don't know about you, but after initial doubts, I'm really going to miss this sort of thing.'

Skye agreed. Bear climbed off the quad, unclipped his helmet with one hand and offered Skye the other to get down. She took it, gripping it slightly longer than necessary. He didn't seem in a hurry to let go either.

Bear ran a hand through his hair, flattened from the helmet, and roughed it up. In the evening light, she could see he had a bit of stubble on his normally clean-shaven jaw. Would it give her a rash if they kissed? she wondered, lingering on his lips. *Stop right there.*

'We can go this way,' she said briskly, and pointed to a rough path between clumps of heather. 'I came out here the other day with Hamish. He said it's a picturesque route and we can paddle in the burn.'

'I'll roll up my trousers for that,' said Bear.

Hamish had also suggested the location because it was secluded, and done so with a knowing look. Skye had told him that she and Bear weren't there yet, and that she had no desire to engage in a round of tick removal. All the same, the image of the two of them, alone in the glen, had made her heart beat a little quicker than normal.

Taking care on the uneven ground, Skye led the way, pulling her bob into a stumpy ponytail to stop it sticking to her neck. It wasn't exactly baking, but the walk was still strenuous. Bear had insisted on carrying the rucksack, which was a relief, because Skye was beginning to sweat.

'Do you think we'll see anyone else here?' came Bear's voice from behind her.

Skye shook her head. 'I doubt it. It's private land. There are footpaths, but you'd have to come a long way, and it's pretty late in the day. There was a group up here this morning, but otherwise nobody else is booked in until tomorrow.'

'And how are you enjoying working here?'

'Loving it,' said Skye. 'It's nice to be able to muck in. The family were so good to me when I was a teenager that it's nice to give back. Not that they'd want to see it that way. But I do.'

'What do you owe them for?'

'For being non-judgemental, kind and welcoming people.'

'A mysterious reference to your youth.'

Skye turned around. 'Not really. How was Edinburgh?'

The track widened out, and Bear came to walk next to her. Skye took him in through the corner of her eye. He was wearing scruffy trousers, and a worn T-shirt with a couple of holes in the hem. Will wouldn't be seen dead looking so scruffy, but Skye found his lack of self-consciousness refreshing. It also meant she felt comfortable about being totally bare-faced in front of him, and not caring that she had a good showing of roots, revealing her true colour — a light red.

She had a flashback to getting ready to go out with Will. Carefully putting on foundation, contouring if she felt she needed it, a few fake lashes to thicken up her pale red ones, and tons of eye make-up. The Skye she presented to the world when they were out together was very different to the Skye she was presenting right now. In fact, she wasn't presenting at all.

'Fine. Productive. I drove up here this morning.'

'What were you up to there?'

'Och, not a lot,' he said, swiftly.

'Ah, does that mean you were working on your top-secret project? Don't tell me you're a spook. I think you stand out too much.'

'Really?' Bear gave a small smile.

'Spies have to blend in. You're too tall and handsome,' she teased.

Skye wondered if she was being too overtly flirtatious, but Bear wore it lightly.

'How did James Bond manage?' he joked.

'I think being fictional helped. You're allowed far more flights of fancy if you don't exist outside the pages of a book. But really, what were you doing there? Am I any closer to wheedling out of you whatever it is you refuse to tell me? Come on, you can say.'

Bear raised an eyebrow. 'No. And don't think I'll accidentally forget that I'm not telling anyone about it.'

'So purposefully decide to. Go on, spill those beans.'

'Are you always this nosy?'

Skye turned around, and began walking backwards, so she could stare him out. 'When I'm interested, yes.'

What was she doing, being so openly brazen? It couldn't have been the heat, because it wasn't hot enough to melt your brain into an incoherent blob capable only of flirting. And it wasn't alcohol, as Skye wouldn't dream of going out on the quad having had anything to drink.

It wasn't down to lust, either. Skye didn't think she was being swept along on a tide of barely disguised desire, throwing out comments as if they were fishing bait, hoping to reel Bear in. She wasn't that far gone.

It was fascination, plain and simple. She wanted to know who Bear was. What made him tick — other than cruck frames of course — what his hopes were, and his fears. What his secret project was, to some extent, but that mattered far less than getting to know Bear the Person.

'I've never thought of myself as a person of interest,' he said.

Skye, who had herself nearly been a person of interest — in the technical sense of the term — at least one time in her life, felt her heart leap at the phrase, and promptly stumbled back over a tussock. Landing on her behind, hands splayed, it took a second of water seeping through her trousers for her to realize she'd gone into a boggy patch.

'Oh shite,' she managed. She put out her hands to get up, only to stick them in more water. 'I guess that's why you generally hike facing forwards.'

Bear put out a hand for her to take. He gave a laugh of surprise, but his brow was lined with concern. 'You're not hurt, are you?'

He pulled her up, and Skye slammed into his chest. She gasped involuntarily. His body was just taut beneath his sweater as she thought it would be. Her heart jolted at the thought of them being so close, a vision of their being skin to skin flashing through her mind. She let it play for a second longer than she should, and stepped back.

Skye raised what she hoped would pass for an amused eyebrow. 'Not from crashing into watery moorland, no.'

'There could have been stones or something.'

'Something? Like what?' she asked.

Bear shrugged, a smile playing across his face. 'Not entirely sure. But the great outdoors can be deadly. There could have been leeches.'

They stood for a second, idling.

'Don't scare me,' she said. 'It's like space. Out here, nobody can hear you scream.'

'I should have come here for my yelling session,' said Bear, looking across to a far peak, then back at Skye. 'Although then I wouldn't be here right now with you.'

Skye fought off a blush and stepped back. She thought back a fortnight to when she had first encountered Bear. Back then, he had seemed so chilly and unapproachable. What a difference two weeks and some probing conversations made.

'Did your parents know about your shouting?' asked Skye. She tried to adjust her damp trousers, which were sticking to her legs.

Bear shook his head. 'No. I never told them where I was going. Even now, I tend to deal with my problems alone.'

Maybe that was why everyone in Eastercraig had found him so disagreeable when they first met him. He was internalizing all the problems about the Auchintraid project. Closing himself away.

'It usually seems easier not to burden anyone else with my issues,' Bear concluded, and ran a hand through his hair.

Amen to that, thought Skye, thinking of her own parents again.

'What about when you were married? You should at least be able to talk to that person.'

Skye knew it was a difficult question, but Bear was talking so openly, and she felt that she was slowly unboxing his personality, and that he was happy for her to do so.

'I tried, but like I said the other day, we were on different planets. She thought my problems were trite. That my career trajectory was obvious. It was as if she never quite got the essence of me.' Bear clenched his jaw.

Skye stepped closer towards him again, closing the gap between them. She was near enough that she could see his heart beating through his shirt.

'I'm sorry,' she said. 'I know what it's like feeling out of place. And also what it's like feeling life's not going the way you'd hoped. If you want to talk about the project at Auchintraid at any time, you can. Or you could just borrow my rock again. I'm happy to share it.'

A smile danced across Bear's lips, making Skye's fingers tingle. She wanted to touch those lips. 'I'll bear that in mind.'

It didn't escape her notice that she was resisting sharing everything, but Skye wasn't ready to be unboxed. Or to unbox herself. *Could you unbox yourself?* And sharing didn't have to be of equal weight, not least when you were in the early stages of getting to know somebody.

They walked a little further, Skye letting her fingers run across the tips of the gorse It grew in great bushes that lined the side of the path they were on. Not much longer and they would reach the burn.

'You've *still* not told me what you were doing in Edinburgh,' said Skye, probing once more.

Bear halted and stiffened. 'Georgia called me.'

Skye felt her eyes widen. What would she want with Bear? She stopped and turned around. 'Oh?'

'Our cat got run over.'

'Oh,' said Skye, trying to sound neutral, because in reality she found herself relieved. Not about the cat — that was horrible. But relief because for a split second it had seemed, despite everything he had said about her, Bear might have returned home to reconcile with his ex-wife. 'I'm so sorry. Is it . . .'

'He. Is he dead? No. He'll live to fight another day, but it was touch and go.'

'He's OK, though?'

'Yes. His leg's in a splint, and he has to be housebound for a while to stop him getting into more trouble, but he's fine. Useful having nine lives, isn't it? Poor old Frank.'

'Frank?'

'It's short for Frank Lloyd Wright. I wanted to give him a long name he could shorten if he wanted,' he deadpanned.

'And the cat lives with Georgia?' Skye tucked a hair behind her ear.

'Yeah. I'm more of a dog person, myself. I always wanted a terrier or two. But Georgia wanted a cat, so we got a cat. I got to name him, as you might have guessed, to make up for the fact I'd not wanted one. I've missed him far more than I have her; even when we were still married, Frank never wanted me to be anyone other than myself, assuming I provided food and water and a soft bed.'

Being someone other than yourself? Skye knew that feeling. As she had stared at that wretched exam paper, a realization had finally surfaced, running in tandem to the devastation over Will. That in fact, quite possibly, it might turn out that as a corporate lawyer she was going to be a big old square peg, in a tiny round hole.

At least Bear had shown some backbone and got out of the situation before he'd become unrecognizable to himself. Skye would like to turn back time, though exactly where she would have to go back to sort this out remained unclear. Was it agreeing to a role in the corporate department? Taking the traineeship at Tilling and Browne? It couldn't be the law degree — that time had represented a pinnacle of happiness in Skye's life.

Skye brought herself back to the conversation. 'Poor wee mite. How awful for you all.'

Bear stuck his hands in his pockets, and made a face. 'It wasn't great. I'd hoped that after the divorce we could go our separate ways, and not see each other again. I mean, I'm over Georgia, and we manage to be civil on the whole — not that we've much cause to see each other.'

She had been referring to the cat's accident, but Bear mistook her concern, thinking Skye meant his relationship.

'We didn't get spiteful and petty, though,' he continued. 'But it doesn't mean I wasn't left bruised. But it's like . . . I see my life like a house. I let people in, I let them out. There are different rooms . . .'

Skye gave a small, encouraging nod, trying to picture what Bear was saying.

'Anyway, when Georgia left the house, I closed the door behind her. You know — you have to preserve heat and . . . your well-being, your mental health and all that.'

Skye allowed herself to smile. Trust an architect to use a building metaphor, then continue it into the insulation stage.

Bear continued, shifting on his feet. 'Sometimes, you want to close the door firmly on something or someone. You don't need to bolt it, as you pray it won't come to that, but leaving it open definitely isn't an option. But bloody Frank means that I've built a cat-flap in my door.'

'Ah yes. The famous emotional cat-flap theory.'

Bear grinned, the seriousness visibly leaving him as his body relaxed.

'Sorry. I went off on a tangent there,' he apologized.

'No worries. I'm pleased Frank's all right.' She took a step closer, reached out and put her hand on Bear's forearm.

'Me too — shall we carry on? Unless you're too wet through and don't fancy it.'

'No. I'm up for going on down to the burn. It'll be worth it, promise.'

She took her hand back, wondering if she had kept it there too long, turned and began to lead the way once more.

For a second Skye wished she had brought a cossie to change into so she could take a dip. Even though she would emerge from the icy water more livid pink lobster rather than Ursula Andress in *Dr No*, dreamy summer evenings like this were made for it.

CHAPTER 20

Ten minutes later, they reached the burn, the hills turning a warm bronze in the low evening light. The water was dark, gurgling, bubbles forming as the water wove round corners. Stones lined the bottom, the odd one breaking the surface. On balance, it wasn't quite as inviting as the sea, or a gentle pool, and Skye hesitated.

Bear, however, sat down next to the river, and started taking off his shoes and rolling up his trousers. 'I really fancy a paddle.'

Skye tried to stop her eyes from roving over his strong calves. She nodded. 'Me too. Although I might as well clamber in as is.'

'Why not take your trousers off?' Bear said, then he flushed properly, the first time Skye had seen him do so. 'Christ. That sounded . . . I meant in a totally innocent way. Because you're already— Och, jeez.'

Skye let out a cackle, a really unattractive hag-like noise. Bear put his face in his hands but she could tell he was laughing too.

'I was thinking it was a shame I hadn't brought my swimmers,' Skye said, wiping a stray tear of laughter from her cheek.

'If you want, I'll do the same. My trousers, I mean.'

'Feel free to take your top off too,' said Skye, regaining some control. 'Don't hold back on my account.'

'Fine,' said Bear, as if this was a challenge. 'I'll go first, shall I?'

Skye nodded. Bear unbuttoned his trousers, and dropped them to the floor. Skye, under the guise of ensuring he was keeping up his side of the bargain, looked right at him and gave a satisfied nod. He didn't need to know she was appraising him at the same time. Not that she was objectifying him. She was merely appreciating the fact he was a stand-out example of the human form.

The new knowledge of what was under his clothes was causing her to melt a little, though. Had Bear not been looking right at her, Skye would have been fanning her face furiously to cool herself down.

'You're up, Edmonds,' he said. 'Keks off.'

The reciprocal stage of the operation was enough to stop her from spiralling any further. What a relief she was wearing sensible black pants. Nothing white that would go see-through in the water, or lacy, which was basically see-through in the first place. She peeled off quickly, tamping down a peal of nervous giggles that was rising inside her at the thought of being barely clothed in front of him. She held the anxiety back, trying to look blasé about the whole thing.

'I might keep my T-shirt on,' she said, shivering. 'But like I said, you're free to abandon yours.'

'Well, seeing as this has turned into a tit-for-tat situation, I'll keep my tats under wraps, ta.'

'You've got tatts?'

Bear laughed. 'No. I was trying not to say "tits".'

'I didn't think you were the crude type.' Skye grinned. 'Ready to go in? It's going to be chilly.'

Bear gave her a look, then Skye watched him clench his jaw, trying not to screw up his face as he dipped a big toe in. Knowing there was light flirting to be had in gentle provocation, she quietly inhaled and took two decisive steps off the bank, ending up ankle deep.

'Wow,' she gasped, looking over her shoulder at Bear. 'Pretty fresh.'

Bear gave an unbothered look. 'I don't feel the need to assert my masculinity by diving into a freezing stream. I'm content to edge in, toe by toe.'

She held her arms out to balance, and took a couple more steps, until she was in up to her knees. It was icy, but Skye felt it was cleansing both inside and out. The burn wasn't deep enough to swim in, and the bed was stony, but if she could have submerged herself up to her neck she would have.

Instead, she settled for splashing some of the water on her face. Bear, who was now ankle deep, did the same.

'Do you think we could drink this?' he asked.

Skye shrugged. 'Hamish seems to think it's OK, although I'm not sure I would before boiling it. But it starts up there on the estate, so it's not as if it's got sewage being dumped in it.'

'Is there fishing?'

'Further down. I can ask Hamish if you want to have go. About the fishing in the river, that is, not drinking it.'

Bear shook his head. 'Nah. Not my thing. Yours?'

Skye laughed. 'Can you imagine me, corporate bod and all-round city type, in a pair of waders trying to land a trout?'

'Sure I can. I find it easier to picture you in waders than in a suit.'

Skye did feel happy in her outdoor gear, tramping about in the borrowed wax jacket Hamish had lent her in case it rained. Two weeks ago, she had been in her fitted blazer with its nipped-in waist. It was very flattering, but like Britain leaving the Schengen Zone, it restricted her freedom of movement.

Internally, Skye groaned. The more she considered it, the signs had been there all along, right down to the fact her work wardrobe was screaming at her that she wasn't comfortable. At least she had put some of her piercings back in this week. It helped her feel a bit more 'her'.

She turned her attention back to Bear. 'Really?' she asked, raising her eyebrows.

Bear moved his hands towards where his pockets would be, then appeared to remember he wasn't wearing any. He settled them on his hips. 'You seem very at ease in the Highlands. You know, at one with your surroundings.'

'Communing with nature, wasn't it,' Skye said, reminding him of his words the other night.

Their eyes locked for a moment and Skye felt her pulse start to race. If she was feeling more confident about herself right now, she would flick her hair and give her most dazzling smile, but she wasn't. She was in a river, in her pants, feeling like someone was looking into her soul. She looked down, and turned, ready to take another step.

There was an enormous splash. Skye, completely shocked, thought for a moment it was something like a stag bounding into the river or the world's largest salmon leaping upstream. But it had been her, she soon surmised, goosebumps forming all over her body.

Bear waded over, and helped haul her up. 'Spoke too soon.'

'What are you talking about? I meant to do this. I'm feeling so at one with nature, I wanted to immerse myself in it,' Skye quipped.

'Is that it?' Bear smirked. And yet, Skye realized, her heart beating again, he still hadn't let go of her hand, or taken his eyes off her.

He led her over to a boulder, three of which acted as stepping stones across the middle of the burn. They sat down on it, skin touching. Skye waited for the adrenaline to wear off, but realized it was still rushing through her body.

'Stay here for a second,' said Bear.

He got up and walked back over the stones to the bank of the river. Skye watched him go through the rucksack and pull out the thermos of hot tea she had brought. Yes, a bottle of beer on a warm summer's night went down a treat, but after going arse first into a chilly river, something warming *would* be nice. He then bent down, and Skye saw that he was reaching for his jumper.

Bear returned, and handed her the knit. Gratefully, she pulled it on, her heart rate gradually slowing. 'Thanks,' she said, as he poured out the tea. 'You're a gent.'

'Doing my best,' said Bear, now pouring them both cups of milky tea and handing one to Skye.

He took a sip of his, and Skye, watching him out of the corner of her eye, pressed her cup to her lips and started to drink.

He looked over at her, and all of a sudden Skye felt lighter than air, as if she could float off into the sky like an escaped helium balloon.

It was a good thing Bear had chosen to sit on the next boulder along, because if he had been next to her Skye might have been tempted to lean in, run her fingers through his hair, take his T-shirt in her fists and pull him close.

In the event, she did no such thing. She simply let the moment hold, wondering if Bear felt it too.

* * *

Eventually, as the sun had fallen behind the glen, draping the scene in front of them in pale shadow, they pulled their trousers back on. Had she not been freezing, Skye would have been reluctant to end the evening.

Instead, her teeth chattering, she agreed to Bear driving the quad back. She held on to the back, trying to stop herself from overtly breathing in the scent of his neck. He smelled faintly of pine, woodsy and delicious.

They pulled up on the gravel, and Skye hopped down, pulling her helmet off. Bear climbed off the front, did the same, and handed her the keys. They leaned up against the quad, edging closer so their hips touched.

'I enjoyed that,' he said, mussing his blond hair back up.

'You not driven one before?' Skye asked.

'Oh, what? You mean this thing?' He patted the bike behind them.

Skye tilted her head to one side. 'Yeah. What were you talking about?'

Bear met her eyes. 'This evening. I had a great night. I have to go back to Edinburgh for work next week, but perhaps we could do this again? Meet up, I mean. You could show me more of Eastercraig. Turns out there's lots to like about it.'

He scratched his head, a half-smile on his lips. Skye looked down at the ground. She could feel a haze envelop them, hiding them from the rest of the world.

'We could do that,' said Skye, glancing up at him, the air around her seeming to hum with anticipation. 'I've had the best time. And thank you for saving me.'

'You didn't need saving,' said Bear.

'Then thank you for hot tea and your jumper, and your helping hands pulling me back up again.'

Strong hands, at the end of strong arms, which Skye would happily let him wrap around her, and pull her closer.

'Then I'll call you. We can set it up,' said Bear. 'Shame I'm not back sooner.'

They'd moved nearer to each other somehow, without Skye realizing. She could count the freckles on his cheek she was so close. Were they about to . . . ? She felt blood surge through her veins.

If she just leaned in a little closer. She could feel his breath tickling her neck.

Bear's face was barely a centimetre from hers. 'I feel like I can talk to you about things, and you get it.'

'Same,' Skye said. The white lie tripping off her tongue as she realized how she had hardly revealed her own problems, those from her present or her past. But would she? She had told him about Will . . . kind of. But the rest of it? She couldn't. Bear knew himself. Skye didn't know how to reconcile past Skye with present Skye. She didn't know how to work out which one, if either, was really her.

151

With a ripple of panic, she realized how dishonest she was being. It did feel like dishonesty, not telling Bear more.

'Talking to you is so easy,' Bear continued. 'There are things I find hard to think about, let alone say aloud, but today I didn't find that at all.'

'I'm glad,' Skye managed. The ripple of panic grew larger, cutting off the words, leaving her unable to say more.

'You OK?' Bear frowned. 'You look far away.'

Skye nodded. 'Fine. Totally fine.'

She closed her eyes to stop her head from spinning. Her lungs felt constrained, unable to take in enough oxygen. With an effort, she slowed her breathing down and concentrated on the sound she made as she inhaled and exhaled.

A tiny line appeared on Bear's brow. 'Sure?'

Inside she felt torn in two by the desire to spend more time with Bear, and the knowledge that she was hardly in the right place to do so given she was hardly out of her relationship with Will. And what had *he* said at the blackhouse about being wary about starting new relationships? He wasn't in the right place either.

Registering the concern in his voice, Skye blinked, her head clearing, and put on her most convincing tone. 'Yes. Call me.'

She felt in control once more, although disappointment and shame coursed through her. She wondered how much he knew of what she was feeling?

They said their goodbyes, and Skye waved him off, watching as his car bounced down the drive and disappeared. A guttural groan escaped her mouth as she turned and walked over to the castle. How could she have let her anxiety escalate out of control like that?

Hamish appeared on the doorstep, closely followed by Wolfie, who padded over to Skye and leaned against her.

'Saw you from an upstairs window,' he said, in a mock casual tone.

'Did you now?' Skye scratched Wolfie between the ears.

'Skye, you guys were saying goodbye for way longer than necessary. You're wearing his jumper. Don't tell me nothing happened.'

'It didn't. I promise.'

It hadn't. And Skye had decided Bear deserved better. As much as she felt sparks so strong between them they could set the heather ablaze, he deserved more than her.

She felt a shiver down her spine, unsure if it was her thoughts or her cold, wet clothes.

'Can we go inside?' she said to Hamish. 'This jumper is the only fully dry thing I'm wearing.'

CHAPTER 21

A week and a bit had passed since Skye moved into Hamish's place. No, not a 'place'. Paolo's own flat was a 'place', as was any other normal-sized dwelling. Glenalmond was a bloody great castle, ancient and imposing, lacking nothing but a cast of characters from a fairytale to fill it.

Paolo could tell why Skye had moved in. If he lived there himself, he'd spend any spare moment he wasn't up in the library reading, pressing his face against the cool stone, wondering if the building would whisper him secrets. Or lying in bed for hours. He knew from Skye that she was now sleeping in a four-poster, complete with heavy drapes, thick, woven in deep reds, a leather wingback aged to perfection, and a nod to the family's heritage in the form of a blanket in the family tartan.

Paolo would move into Glenalmond in a flash, even if there was nothing between him and Hamish. They could likely co-exist there without ever having to run into each other. Paolo's entire flat was about the same size as the Glenalmond library where, last year, he had first felt that spark.

He went over that moment in the library again, picking at it, over-analysing it until it was nothing more than shreds of

154

unreliably recalled thoughts. Was that why he'd read the signals all wrong? The (mildly absurd) possibility that occurred to him today was that instead of fancying Hamish, perhaps he just fancied the library. The sheer quantity of leather-bound volumes *was* a turn on.

He rolled his eyes at himself. He was tying himself in knots. It was all he had been able to do since seeing Hamish in Beauly. He hadn't told Holly or Chloe about it, too devastated to withstand their pity.

With a last spritz of disinfectant, he wiped down the table in the consulting room once more for luck.

'Are you ready for the next patient?' Holly asked from the doorway. 'They're out the front waiting.'

'Guinea pig with a probable broken leg? Absolutely.'

As Holly went to get them, he chucked the wipes away, washed his hands and put on some gloves.

Holly reappeared with Ronnie MacLeod and her daughter Lou, who must have been about seven or eight. Lou looked worried, as Ronnie gently placed a large cardboard box on the table. Paolo leaned back against the cupboards, as Holly opened the box and took the guinea pig out. It emitted a high-pitched squeaking as she did, but calmed down once she had it firmly in her arms.

'Remind me of the name?' said Holly.

'Pickle,' said Ronnie. 'We had him out for a cuddle and he was wriggling to be put down. Lou says he practically jumped out of her arms into the hutch, and landed badly. He's not putting any weight on it, and hopping around.'

There was a whimper from Lou at this.

'Don't worry,' said Paolo gently. 'It happens. Guinea pigs can be very squirmy sometimes, but you have to hold on tightly, even if they're desperate to be let go.'

'Can you X-ray it?' asked Lou.

Paolo tilted his head towards Holly, who nodded. 'That'll be the first thing, if you're happy for me to. We can then also rule out its being something else, like infection,' said Holly.

'We'll need to put Pickle under general anaesthetic, so if it's OK, could you pop back to the waiting room for me, Lou? Chloe has some biscuits there, if you want one. Mrs MacLeod, wait here a second, please.'

After Lou had left, Holly explained to Ronnie the risks of the anaesthetic. There was no need, Paolo knew, to cause Lou to fret any more — she was clearly already upset. Ronnie, who Paolo knew taught up at the primary school, agreed to the procedure, and Paolo went to get a mask to administer the minuscule amount of gas needed to put the guinea pig under.

The X-ray showed a small fracture. As Holly examined it on the picture on the computer screen, Paolo picked the fuzzy guinea pig up from the table, wrapped him in a towel, and held him until he woke up. He gradually opened one eye, and looked around slowly. Paolo gave him a gentle stroke.

'There, there,' he whispered. 'What an ordeal for you, you poor wee beastie.'

Holly went to get Ronnie and Lou, and outlined the break. 'We could pin it back into place,' she said, detailing the way that would work. 'But he's a young guinea pig, and if you keep him isolated, so he can't run around too much or climb anything, it stands a good chance of healing itself. I can prescribe some painkillers.'

Ronnie and Lou looked to Paolo. It often happened, people turning to him for reassurance. He nodded. 'It would be a lot of surgery for one tiny guinea, plus it would be a few hundred pounds easy. Holly's right. And you can pop back in a fortnight if it's not getting better.'

Slowly, he handed the guinea pig back to Lou, who buried her face in Pickle's fur, softly telling him that everything was going to be OK, before putting him back into the box with the utmost care.

Paolo waved them off, Holly accompanying them to reception, and got to cleaning up again.

* * *

At the end of the day, having seen three dogs, a budgie with a broken wing, a cat with a mangled tail, and a limp-looking gerbil, it was time to go home. It had been non-stop in the surgery that day, and he needed to go to bed early as he and Holly were off to a farm about thirty miles away the following morning. It was a long drive, and they'd agreed with the farmer they'd arrive at 8 a.m., which meant leaving by 7 a.m. to ensure they got there on time.

He pulled his summer jacket, a neat cornflower-blue linen one with oversized pockets, from the hooks in the side room. Chloe bustled in behind him. Hugh, their old boss, would always wait outside until there was space available, the portrait of old-fashioned manners. Chloe, the opposite — generous with hugs and happy to be in close proximity to anyone she'd known for more than an hour — squeezed beside him.

'Plans for the evening?' she asked.

'None. It's a Monday night, so I'm thinking *Eastenders*, some Scotch rarebit, book and bed. You?'

'Nothing. Well, not nothing. I'm going to research cakes for Holly's birthday. Greg's asked me to make her one because he said he's not a baker and her birthday's next week.'

'Oh crap. Of course it is.' Paolo had completely forgotten, given his inability to think about anything other than Hamish (whose birthday, Paolo knew only too well, was in July).

'And then for supper I'm making this pea houmous, which I'm serving with halloumi and falafels. I'm introducing Angus to vegetarian options.'

'Can you bring in the leftovers for lunch tomorrow?' came Holly's voice.

Chloe mouthed, 'Do you think she heard about the cake?' Paolo shook his head.

'Sure,' Chloe said, brightly. 'If Angus leaves any. Doing anything tonight, Hols?'

Paolo and Chloe popped out of the side room into the relative roominess of the reception area. Holly, her blonde hair piled high on her head, gave a shrug. 'Greg and I might go for a run. The weather's meant to hold out the next week and then rain. We need to make the most of the sunshine.'

'The couple who runs together . . . runs together,' said Paolo, no better line occurring to him. Oh God, even his powers of speech were diminishing. Was nothing in his life safe?

They moved outside. He and Holly waved Chloe off on her bike.

'She's a nutter,' said Holly affectionately, watching her puff out of sight. 'The road out to Auchintraid is uphill for at least a mile.'

'Keeps her out of mischief,' joked Paolo. 'You can't concentrate on anything else with all those potholes on the loose.'

'You know, I'm just going to double check the kit in the bags for tomorrow,' Holly said and she disappeared back inside the surgery. 'See you in the morning.'

Paolo loitered and stared out at the bay. It was early evening, the sun still far from kissing the horizon. Holly's birthday landed on the solstice, when the night lasted no more than six hours in Eastercraig and the stars only started appearing long after it was time to go to bed.

If only he had someone to enjoy these long evenings with, but being alone was the quintessential Paolo, it would seem. Chloe and Holly would both be going back to their houses, their men, their lives, which were working out in that time-honoured tradition where the next stop was certainly marriage.

When was it going to be his time? Hamish, it seemed, was completely out of the question. Funny how he had got it so wrong.

He had genuinely feared, given what Hamish had said about Skye, that there might have been some backstory there, that they were an item waiting to happen. But having seen Hamish with that guy in Beauly, it appeared that it had been his paranoia levels working overtime. Unless Hamish was secretly rampant. It seemed unlikely, but life had a habit of springing surprises on you.

Then, realizing that he had been standing in the same place outside the surgery for the last few minutes, he decided he ought to move. He was suffering from general inertia it would seem, besides being stuck on the pavement, he was stuck to the idea of Hamish.

Paolo needed to shake this off. He needed to shrug off the failures, ramp up the dating, go once more unto the breech. Stiffen his sinews and summon up the blood and all that, banish the memory of Rhuari forever, writing him and the rest of them off as a bad lot.

Would the Bard have winced at the re-assigning of his war cry to some guy's urge to find a partner, five hundred years down the line? Paolo liked to think that Shakespeare had a sense of humour. He *had* written all those comedies after all.

'You still here?' asked Holly, re-emerging.

'Admiring the view,' said Paolo, neglecting to mention the rest.

Holly nodded. 'Amazing, isn't it. Well, I'll see you in the morning. We're off to Gorroway to see Lucia Kilbride's herd tomorrow, remember?'

'Don't remind me,' said Paolo.

He waved her off, contemplating Lucia Kilbride, who was a tricky customer at the best of times. She tended to be snappy, and he didn't relish the thought of spending the morning in her company.

He felt his forehead creasing, and ran his fingers over the deep crevasse which had begun to form between his brows. He started to walk the short distance home. Fabien, the last guy he had dated seriously, was a tweakments convert. He hedged his bets on the long-term damage caused by fillers with the same swagger he used when analysing stock prices and choosing what to buy. Fabien liked to take risks. It was why Fabien was not only rich, but had been unable to register surprise for the last ten years. Perhaps Paolo's constant ribbing about the latter had led to their breakup.

Maybe *he* needed Botox though. All the anxiety was changing the landscape of his face. He looked like the Grand Canyon. A wee injection of something to make him feel less like he was crumpling. *Och, listen to yourself, Paolo*, he chided himself. He'd been a bit of a grey cloud of late.

Paolo pulled his phone out, and scrolled through his text messages to his last exchange with Fabien. It had been Fabien's annual Christmas message, sent to everyone in his phone, around five thousand people, probably. It showed Fabien, at the top of a mountain somewhere in Switzerland — where he lived and worked — reclining on a bench with his skis propped next to him, sipping a cocktail. The scenery shone with an almost unnatural purity, much like Fabien's fillered cheeks. 'Après me' was the caption. Trust Fabien to pun. Their quick-fire banter had been one of the first things that had drawn them together. Paolo had half-heartedly sent a Christmas greeting in return.

Despite the shock of their breakup, Fabien still crossed his mind occasionally. Paolo had to admit, they'd had their share of good times. Not that he wanted to get back with him. Not at all.

Yes, Fabien was smooth — and he didn't simply mean Fabien's forehead or expensively moisturized skin — but he was also deadly. Paolo knew Fabien picked people up and dropped them because of the rate at which he posted photos of himself and new boyfriends. He reminded himself that when they had been going out, Fabien had insisted it remain a secret, because he hadn't officially come out in Eastercraig, and wasn't prepared to. Despite his misgivings, Paolo had gone along with this.

It had never oozed long-term potential, and Paolo wanted long term. He wanted passion that petered steadily into lasting friendship. To grow old with someone who, in thirty years' time, he didn't fantasize about feeding poisonous mushrooms to. Someone kind, and thoughtful, and . . . Basically, Hamish.

Reaching his front door, he shook his head, and heaved in a deep breath of the salty air which floated in on the light breeze.

Why was it so hard?

His phone beeped. Skye.

Me and Hamish are having drinks on the terrace at Glenalmond. Come and join us? Weather apparently due to turn.

It was pretty punchy for a Monday night, but he might pop his head round the door. It should at least shift him out of this funk.

CHAPTER 22

Paolo drove his Fiat 500 up the lane, listening to it grizzle loudly as he changed gear. He had bought it as a nod to his Italian heritage, and because his nonna complained loudly about other cars and he didn't want to give her a heart attack by arguing about it. He was its third owner, and it made suspicious clunking sounds as he flew in and out of potholes down the drive to Glenalmond.

He parked up and walked around the side of the castle, then up the steps to a sprawling terrace round the back of the building, a nineteenth-century addition with a stone balustrade and flower-filled urns. Beyond it the lawn sloped down to the river, and Paolo could hear the faint but calming babble of water.

'Drinks on the terrace, on a Monday night?' he asked, spotting Hamish and Skye sitting on a bench beneath a large window. 'And spritzes?' They were wrapped in blankets, holding huge cocktail glasses containing neon orange liquid, snuggled up together. Skye was absent-mindedly unknotting Hamish's hair with her free hand. 'Or is that iron bru?'

'Definitely not. It's aperitivo hour,' said Skye with a grin. 'On the terrace.'

'Crumbs,' Paolo said. 'A small one, please. Only I'm driving.'

Hamish reached down to a tray on the floor, and picked up a glass, pouring in a couple of inches of drink.

He got up, and moved over to Paolo, and passed it to him.

'I'm not sure about these,' he whispered. 'But Skye seemed keen. And I wanted to keep her happy.'

Paolo's stomach dropped a few inches, suspicions returning with force. 'You did?'

'Aye. She's had a rough time of it of late, so we're trying to enjoy ourselves. Your idea, this, wasn't it, Skye?'

Skye got up. She was wearing a floaty seventies' dress, and silver clogs, a mohair blanket around her shoulders. It was a look as glamorous as the negroni in Hamish's hand. She moved over and put an arm around Hamish's shoulder. 'Hamish was keen for a whisky, but I had a real craving for something sunny.'

Hamish nodded in confirmation. 'You know me. This fancy stuff isn't my usual bag.'

Paolo smiled. He would be equally happy with a negroni or a whisky, or anything else, if only he could drink it alone with Hamish. 'Sometimes you've got to go with the flow.'

Never was a more true word spoken. He lifted his glass.

'Cheers,' said Skye.

They clanked their glasses together.

'Salute,' said Hamish.

Paolo smiled at his terrible Italian accent.

'How's life as the admin assistant?' he asked.

He didn't want to think about the time Skye and Hamish were spending together. He'd prefer to hear about their time apart.

'Fantastic. So far I've spent half of it on the welcome desk, and troubleshooting. And I did all the filing. It was overflowing like a waterfall out of the in-tray,' she said, taking a sip of her drink.

'Aye. She's been a marvel. If I could keep you around for longer than the next two weeks, I would,' Hamish said, running a hand through his unruly hair. 'She's really done some excellent work. Want to move in permanently, Skye?'

'I'd stay if I could,' she said. 'My bedroom here is an absolute dream. Did I tell you there's a tub in it and everything? I've taken to soaking in it after a day's work, window open, looking out on to the river. It's so big you could easily fit two people in there.'

Hamish raised an eyebrow. 'Steady on.'

'Tubs in the bedroom?' Paolo managed.

He desperately fought to keep the image of Hamish and Skye frolicking in the bubbles from his mind. Hamish had never struck him as one of life's natural frolickers, but the unexpectedness of seeing him with a cocktail in hand had thrown Paolo.

'Aye,' said Hamish. 'Mum and Dad had these big claw foot tubs put in several of the guest bedrooms about four or five years ago. It's totally ridiculous. It's as if they were testing the water in the literal sense — they had this fleeting idea to turn the place into a country hotel.'

'They wouldn't, would they?'

'Nah. I don't think so. In the end they thought they could manage to eke out a living from the rest of the revenue. Those baths are a big white elephant, if you ask me.'

'Disagree,' said Skye, explaining that when she had been at Holly's, and upstairs looking for the bathroom, she had spied one in Holly's bedroom. She'd envied it immediately, picturing herself in it, with a Flake for good measure. 'I'll happily make sure you get cost per wear out of it. Or cost per bathe. I'd float around in it all day if I could. Talking of baths, I need the bathroom. Back in a mo.'

Skye put her glass back down on the bench, and shed the blanket next to it. Struggling with Skye's suggestive invitation to Hamish, Paolo took a large slug of spritz.

'So how's the week looking for you, Paolo?' asked Hamish.

'Och. Off to Gorroway tomorrow morning for a farm visit first thing. I don't want to stay for too much longer, as it's a really early start.'

That, and he wanted to get out of this hall of mirrors where everywhere he looked, he was confronted with visions of Skye and Hamish together.

And that other man, where did he fit into all this? Did Skye know? What if there was a menage à trois underfoot? Rhuari's talk of throuples rang in his ears. She did have a wild reputation, as Chloe had pointed out. Skye didn't really seem to live up to it now, but she hadn't dispelled it either when she'd described some of her youthful antics.

'You seem to be getting on well.' He was aiming for breezy, but it was coming out blustery. 'Skye seems very relaxed.'

'She feels at home here,' Hamish replied. 'Sorry — that wasn't meant to sound rude. I didn't mean that you failed to provide at your place. More that she knows me and my folks.'

'Aye,' said Paolo. 'She's a . . . nice lass.'

'She is. We've known each other so long, and you know how great it is when you reconnect with someone special from your past.'

Paolo's head spun. What if, after his near-death experience, Hamish was trying everything, in an effort to live life to the full? Personality transplants after moments like that were well-documented. Paolo gulped as he swallowed the remains of his spritz in one.

'I ought to go,' he said. 'I only ever planned to pop by to say hi. I'm suddenly aware that if I'm dead to the world tomorrow morning, Holly won't be impressed.'

Hamish laughed. 'Is she turning into Hugh?'

Paolo shook his head. 'Not quite. But she does like everything just so.'

'Are you not going to wait for Skye? The, um, moon is very bright tonight. Very, erm, low and big. And beautiful.'

'Erm, I guess so.' Paolo put his empty glass on the balustrade. 'Will you say goodbye for me? Send my apologies.'

Hamish scratched his head, and Paolo wondered if his departing with so little warning came across as manic. Although Hamish seemed a bit odd tonight too.

'Aye,' said Hamish. 'I mean, we've barely caught up. Perhaps we could do this again. This drinks on the terrasse malarky. With whisky, next time, though. I think I can feel my teeth dissolving.'

That was the Hamish Paolo knew and— he stopped himself before he completed that sentence.

Anyway, he didn't think he knew Hamish at all, not anymore.

'Mmm. Sure,' Paolo said. 'Sorry, Hamish. I should head off.'

* * *

Skye drifted back on to the warmth of the terrace, spritz in hand. This could be Italy, not the Highlands, with this ornate patio set-up and dayglo drinks. This was exactly the kind of fairy dust she had been talking about. Hopefully Hamish and Paolo would be deep in conversation, and she could exit swiftly and leave them to it.

Looking into the distance, though, it was abundantly clear from the purple heathers of the far-off hills, and the forbidding trees off to one side that this was not the Mediterranean. More importantly, they were also down their only Italian.

'Where's Paolo?' she asked, with a swell of panic. 'How long was I gone for? Is your loo a time warp or something?'

Hamish turned round from where he was standing up against the balustrade, surveying the lawns. He looked as confused as she felt. And sad.

'I don't know,' he said, giving a small shrug. 'He made some excuse about getting up early, and went. He couldn't get back to his car fast enough.'

'Did you try any of the lines?'

Hamish cringed visibly. 'I tried the one about the moon. Not brilliantly executed, though.'

'Oh, Hamish. I don't think that was the best one. God — it's my fault for suggesting it. Perhaps practising lines was too contrived, and I should have let you be more yourself.' It was advice she could take on too, she thought, as she stood there dishing it out. 'Oh, what a balls-up.'

A surge of disappointment ran through her. She knew how much Paolo meant to Hamish.

Skye came and stood next to him, leaning her head on his shoulder, and putting a sympathetic arm around his waist. 'I'm so sorry, Hame.'

'Don't apologize. It seemed like a good idea at the time,' said Hamish.

Skye screwed up her face. 'Really? It didn't exactly go off with a bang.'

'Of course! It was a solid plan. I know for a fact Paolo likes a good cocktail. There are pictures of him on Instagram where he's in actual Italy, bellini in hand, gazing out over Venice at sunset.' Hamish took a sip of his drink. 'These really aren't my thing, by the way. I'm trying, but I can't. I might grab a beer.'

'Hold the phone, mister. You're not going anywhere. You're on Instagram?'

'For work.'

'Yeah, right. As if I believe that.'

Hamish sat down on a stone bench and kicked out his legs. 'You've known me long enough to know that social media brings me out in hives. In fact, why don't you take that over for the next two weeks too? You're much more tech-savvy than me.'

'Happy to muck in. Anyway, I reckon Monday's a dud night for a date. End of a busy day. And if Paolo said himself he had an early start, he wouldn't have wanted a late one,' sighed Skye. 'My bad, Hamish.'

She sat down on the bench next to him, flung an arm around him and took a sip of her spritz. 'I'm the anti-Midas,' she continued. 'I really thought tonight would be a winner. I'm so sorry, Hamish. Everything I touch turns to crap, it always has.' She sighed deeply. 'I should stop drinking these actually. Was that just a tad dramatic and quite possibly over the top?'

'Perhaps you're being a bit over the top,' said Hamish. 'And yet, nothing ventured, nothing gained. Not that we made great gains this evening . . . What if with all my hesitation, Paolo no longer feels anything? What if whatever it was has stalled and it's like fireworks in a bucket? Fizzle, fizzle, sputter, sputter.' As he spoke, he began to look almost irreparably downcast.

'Now who's being over the top?' Skye replied. 'I think it's salvageable, if you want it to be. You do, don't you? From where I'm sitting, you *really* do.'

Hamish stared down the lawn. 'Aside from the unbearable fear, I do.'

She thought about her own reasons for holding back from Bear. That it was surely too soon to move on, and even if it wasn't, he would judge her if he knew the full extent of her youthful misdemeanours. She had barely considered the thought of what would happen if it went wrong. She supposed she never need see Bear again. It's not like she'd bump into him whenever she left the flat to buy milk.

She rolled her shoulders a couple of times, as if warming up for another round in the ring. 'We didn't go about it in the best way, is all. A misfire. I'll get you together if it's the last thing I do.'

'Sounds ominous.' Hamish turned to her, and raised an eyebrow. 'I'm going to become a victim of your own romantic confusion, aren't I? How are you feeling about Bear today, by the way? Not that it isn't obvious, seeing as every time I've popped into the office you've had a new text from him and insisted on reading it aloud to me.'

And running her response by him too, before hitting send. Most recently, he had sent her a picture of a shell of a house in Inverleith, with the caption *Ripe for renovation!* Skye could feel his excitement.

'I shouldn't let myself get carried away. I know rushing in was a mistake before with Will too. I'm not going to do this right now. No way. I'm intending to remain in romantic stasis.'

It was becoming increasingly clear to Skye though that she had never been in love with Will. Not given how her heart had begun to spin at the very thought of Bear. And this sensation, in turn, made her head spin. How had she got it so wrong with Will? These last few weeks had turned everything she believed she knew to be true upside down.

'Is that so?' Hamish looked sceptical.

Skye nodded fervently. 'Yes. I'll be experiencing my feelings but not acting on them.'

And it wouldn't be at all fair to bring someone else into her mess. She had to fix the problems in her life before opening the doors.

'We'll see how that goes.'

'Thanks,' said Skye, trying to shove the thoughts out, and giving Hamish a gentle elbow in the ribs. 'But I also feel like Bear and I are friends. Like we've been friends forever, and I already know exactly who he is.'

She wondered if he felt the same way, if he thought he knew who she was. How wild a teenager she had been. But, of course he didn't. That was the point. And a big reveal might put him right off. A tiny quiver run up her spine at the thought.

Hamish eyeballed her with a knowing look. Skye felt her cheeks go pink. 'Fine. So, I haven't told him everything about me, not the full extent of the teenage capers, and he'd never guess. But it doesn't mean to say I can't like him. *Really* like him. I'm going to sit on him, that's all. Sit on *it*, I mean. God, that's inarticulate.'

Inarticulate but accurate, and a bit Freudian too.

'You sound more serious that I thought you would,' said Hamish.

Skye shook her head, desperate not to spiral. 'There's nothing serious about it. I'm in Eastercraig to relax. I'm not here to snog anyone, or — worse — end up in bed with them.'

'You want to end up in bed with him?'

'No!' Skye shouted. 'Oh, Wolfie, thank God! Please say you've come to spare my blushes.'

So huge and hairy he might have been half yeti, Wolfie loped across the terrace from the back door. Had he killer instincts he would have been lethal. Thankfully, he wasn't, and Skye knew his favourite soft toy was a tiny cat which he needed in his basket every night to go to sleep. He panted heavily and came to lean against Skye, nearly toppling her.

Skye spoke firmly, for her benefit as much as Hamish's. 'I need distraction. Which is perfect. I can dedicate myself to fixing you up with Paolo.'

'God help us all,' muttered Hamish.

CHAPTER 23

Back at his flat, Paolo shrugged off his coat, and threw it on his chair. Normally it lived neatly on the hooks in the hallway, but today he was bypassing his usual shipshape system.

Without bothering to remove his shoes, he flung himself on to the blasted snuggler. So much marketing was aimed at people in couples, right down to the nomenclature of everyday items.

'Och, you,' he said, as Ginger wound his way around his ankles.

The cat sprang up on to the chair next to him, before picking his way on to Paolo's lap, where he curled up into a ball and gave a satisfied purr.

He had never had a cat like Ginger. None of the ones he'd had in Glasgow growing up had shown any affection or, indeed, basic level of interest in being part of the family. They probably heard the noise levels generated by four rowdy children and thought better of coming into the house for anything other than a bowl of food. Ginger, however, was more like a dog by nature, friendly and insistent on physical contact.

When he'd been dumped at the surgery, Ginger, with his matted hair, and gunky eyes had been timid, and terrified of being picked up. But after a gentle haircut, a course of anti-biotics, and a week at home, he had settled in nicely. Now he always overjoyed to see his new owner, who he associated with regular mealtimes and plenty of fussing. There was an old cat flap on the ground floor and Paolo got permission to put one in his door, and bought a load of feline paraphernalia to keep Ginger happy. Ginger roamed freely, although he seemed to have a sixth sense about when Paolo would come home.

The moment Paolo put the key in the lock, his familiar would slink through the hallway as if by magic, and jump up on the nearest surface to his owner, purring with happiness at being reunited after a long day.

'Am I imagining things?' Paolo asked Ginger. 'There was definitely something going on with Hamish and Skye. They were all over each other. Skye giving him all manner of looks. And Hamish with his fancy drinks. I swear he was trying to tell me something. Probably that he and Skye are now official.'

What would Holly and Chloe say? The benefit of having two very different women as friends meant you would almost certainly get two very different opinions. Holly would be practical: she'd tell him to pull his finger out and go and ask Hamish what was going on. Chloe, more cautious in her approach to everything other than vintage clothing and baking, would insist he wait and see how things unfolded.

Paolo felt that Holly's approach was better. It would give him results.

That said, he knew from experience that slow and steady won the race. Once in high school he'd dyed his own hair over the sink, and then spent a week looking like a prick before his mother coughed up the money for a hairdresser to fix it.

He scratched the cat's ears. 'Tell me what to do, Ginger. Come on, you're so wise. By the power of your nine lives, show me the way.'

Ginger let out a loud miaou, and bounded off Paolo's lap, tripping along the floor before coming to a graceful halt by her empty bowl.

'Yeah. OK. Better not formulate a plan on an empty stomach.'

He dug out a tin of food for Ginger and plonked a bowlful of it on the floor. Then an exploration of the pantry cupboard revealed a bag of pistachios and a jar of sundried tomatoes. Along with some fresh garlic and the extra virgin olive oil his nonna always insisted upon, he whipped up a pesto of sorts, then put on some pasta to boil.

As it simmered, Paolo checked his phone, scrolling mindlessly on social media to take his thoughts off Hamish. He didn't want to go to his dating app, and text Patrick, which he still couldn't face after the Rhuari nonsense.

Chloe had posted a plate of delicately iced cakes, his sister Francesca had put up some of herself looking glamorous on a night out. There was a slew of bookstagram posts, some pictures of exotic scenery. And a few of Fabien.

He flicked though. Fabien was in Edinburgh, for some reason — Paolo knew those beautiful streets anywhere.

If Fabien was in Scotland, he was almost certainly planning a trip to Eastercraig, where his family still lived. If this was so, Paolo might end up seeing him once more. His stomach gave an unexpected flip.

CHAPTER 24

Skye reached lazily for her phone, one eye still on the television. *Speed* was on, and she hadn't seen it in ages. It was Bear.

How's Eastercraig? I think I'm finally missing it.

Skye's heart skipped. Turned out that even though her mind had told her to slow down, her body had other ideas. She diverted her full attention to her mobile, quickly composing and firing off a reply.

Still sunny! How's Edinburgh? How was Portobello? x

Bear was in the city to investigate a new project, renovating a Georgian property on the Promenade which overlooked the Firth of Forth.

Skye wriggled her fingers, awaiting the response, when her phone rang. It buzzed twice, and after a deep breath, she picked up.

'Hi,' came the voice down the line. 'I thought I'd call. You're not in the middle of something, are you?'

'Watching *Speed*,' she replied. 'Hamish is up at the lodge overseeing a dinner and refused my offer of help, and Moira and David have gone to bed.'

'You chose a high-octane thriller to relax to? What channel is it on?'

Skye laughed. 'ITV, I think. Yeah, it's cut to an ad break.'

'I'll watch along. I've not seen it for ages,' said Bear. There was some rattling around his end. 'There. I've found it, got my feet up on the table. Och. I don't have snacks. Balls. This is a real popcorn film, isn't it.'

'I've got a family-sized slab of chocolate,' said Skye, popping some in her mouth. 'Not sure I'd share it, mind.'

'And there I was, willing to give you my last Rolo.'

Skye's heart gave an audible thud at that. 'Do those exist still? I've not seen them for a while.'

'Very much so. Next time I'm around I'll bring a pack up to prove it. So, how's working for Hamish going? Now you've settled in.'

Skye smiled to herself, and began telling Bear about what she had been up to. She had spent that morning interviewing for her replacement, and found two decent candidates from town, both in need of summer jobs. Hamish was meeting with them on Friday afternoon. Other than that, it had been straightforward admin, as well as mucking in with the cleaning, so that the castle was in order for tours. Plus, the occasional minute spent wondering how to help Hamish get together with Paolo.

'In all, I'm really enjoying it,' she concluded. 'It's good honest work. I think I was feeling a little burnt out at the firm. Unhappy,' she continued, and broke off another square of chocolate. 'It's nice to not work every hour God sends, then fill the rest socializing with people I'd rather not share a room with. Some of the people at my firm — not everyone, I should point out, but a few — they're all about the money. They always have to have the latest trend, or go to the hottest new place. And because you want to fit in, you start going along with it. Eventually that grasping greed starts to seem normal. It just kind of rubs off on you.'

She thought of the sort of cases the firm took on. They would say yes to cases with big businesses or individuals Skye wouldn't touch with a bargepole, if those cases filled the company coffers. It was fundamental in law that everyone deserved a fair trial, but on occasion, Skye found it a principle that was hard to get on board with. What if when she returned, she ended up working on one of those cases for one of those clients? How would she handle that right now?

That panic from the exam rose up afresh, clogging her throat, and she took a sip of chamomile tea to rid herself of it.

'That's corporate life, isn't it? I have to do events for work sometimes, and the schmooze doesn't come naturally to me.'

'No kidding,' said Skye. 'You could barely look at me the first couple of times we met.'

Bear scoffed. 'That doesn't count. I went somewhere remote for a private yell, only to be interrupted by a bonny lass, who then kept popping up everywhere I went.'

Skye felt her breath catch.

'And I'm sure it hasn't rubbed off on you,' said Bear.

In the midst of her law degree, when she still found time for activism, she had envisioned herself as an Erin Brockovich, a woman of integrity. And she didn't know if she could do that at Tilling and Browne. The corporate team might scour away any authenticity she had. 'If only it was the kind of dirt you could shower off at the end of the day. Life would be easy. Although life is never easy, is it.'

Bear gave a low growl. 'You've got that right. How do you think it'll be, going back in a week or so?'

Skye envisaged herself sitting in her office chair, hemmed in by her suit, boxed in by other cubicles, slowly being pulped by the weight of her cases, some of which she felt *very* conflicted about. A pit opened in her stomach.

'Fine.' She didn't want to burden Bear with her expanding case of existential angst. Involving him risked pulling them closer together. She wasn't meant to be doing that. *Distraction* . . .

She flicked her eyes over to the television, to the out-of-control bus careering around LA, Sandra Bullock at the wheel, looking panicked. There was a parallel to be drawn with her current situation, she thought. Was that why she had chosen to watch this?

'You don't need to worry,' said Bear. 'It'll be like riding a bike.'

'You've seen me struggling with the hills round here, right?'

'Don't do yourself down. They wouldn't have allowed you a whole month off if they didn't think you were worth it.'

They might not have allowed me a whole month off if they realized I was going to feel quite so dubious about going back.

'Oh!' Skye's eyes alighted on the screen. 'Look, they're getting off the bus! They're going to be rescued. Top marks, Keanu. And well driven, Sandra.'

'Whoa, Skye. It's not over yet. Oh, and it's ad break time again.' There was a shuffling, a click in the lock, and the echo of feet on stairs. 'I'm going to grab some chocolate too. Or some popcorn.'

'You're doing what? It's late!'

'My flat's two doors down from a tiny convenience shop. And, let me tell you, it's very convenient. I can be there and back before the ads end. Stay on the line, you can come with me.'

They chatted through Bear's options, pausing briefly as he made small talk with the shop owner. Conversing with him, Skye realized, had brought her pulse rate back down, calmed her.

As the film restarted, he was back on the sofa.

'When are you back in Eastercraig?' Skye asked, as they watched in unison.

'Next week. Turns out there are a few jobs here to get on with, and the foreman over at Auchintraid is in control of things for now. Wednesday, I reckon?'

'Want to meet up? Next week's my last week here.'

Skye tried to sound casual, but in fact, this phone call had only made her realize more than ever how much she wanted his company. She could still see him, even while she planned to keep her burgeoning emotions at bay, couldn't she?

'Sounds great,' said Bear.

Skye's pulse gave a little twitch.

CHAPTER 25

Lying in bed late was one of life's great pleasures, so anything that began before 8 a.m. on a weekend had better be good.

Which is why on the following Saturday morning Paolo was steering a paddleboard out of the harbour, while Holly sat at the front of the board, staring out to sea. They had been going out on to the water like this every weekend since Holly first arrived in Eastercraig. She had been keen for a friend to join her, and at the time Paolo had needed to leave his comfort zone. And as the surgery opened an hour later than normal on a Saturday, it was the perfect time to do it. Even if it did mean neither of them got to lie in.

'How are you feeling, Hols? Three weeks has passed without Hugh and you're still standing.' He put his shoulders into a sweeping stroke of the paddle, feeling his muscles working.

Holly still refused to admit she was overworking herself, despite the fact she'd spent the previous day yawning between appointments. She insisted they keep paddleboarding in the diary. Paolo didn't really want to cancel, but he was worried that Holly was heading for burn-out.

'Are you trying to be funny?' Holly asked. She didn't sound happy.

Paolo winced. He knew how important the surgery was to Holly — but he hadn't expected her to snap.

'No. I was trying to tell you how smoothly everything has been running, and that you seem totally on top of it all,' he said. Sometimes compliments were best left un-nuanced.

Holly shuffled round to face him. 'God! I'm sorry. I didn't mean to bite your head off. Do you think I'm becoming Hugh?'

Paolo shook his head. 'As far as I can tell, no. But I'll let you know if you shrink a foot and get short grey hair and begin cursing everything from fruit in salads to mobile parking apps.'

Holly laughed, her brow relaxing. She tied her long, blonde hair up in a ponytail.

'I haven't had a chance to let off much steam lately,' she admitted. 'Greg's been away so much, and I always seem to end up getting home late and stewing over things before eating a crap supper. And . . .' Her words died away.

'And what?' Paolo stopped paddling a second. 'Is everything OK with Greg?'

Holly trailed a hand through the water as she mulled the question over. 'It's all fine.' Paolo sensed the 'but' coming. 'But I miss him. I'd spent so long not wanting to be in a relationship, and now I am I've decided it's the best thing in the world. I wish I could see more of him, and at the moment it's not possible.'

Paolo shoulders dropped in relief. For a second he had feared she would say something worse. 'Och, I'm sorry, Holly. He won't be working away forever, though. Once this contract comes to an end he'll be back here more often, won't he?'

'Yes.' Holly nodded, firmly. 'He will. It's tough, but I'll manage. Like I am with the surgery. Anyway, the letting off steam bit . . .'

'Anything in mind. Want to go to an escape room? I heard about a place where you can throw axes.'

'Actually, I did have an idea.' Holly sounded more like her usual, positive self again. 'It's my birthday on Wednesday, and I want to do something. Last year it was you, me and Chloe in the pub, but I thought I might do something a bit bigger.'

'What? Chlo and I aren't enough?' Paolo joked, not letting on that Chloe had been testing cakes.

'Of course you are.' Holly grinned. 'But there are other people who need to be there. Greg, obviously, and Angus. And Hamish?'

She said the last name with a hint of mischief. Paolo felt his insides curdle, and clearly the expression on his face reflected this because Holly stared at him.

'What? Did *I* say something wrong now? Has something happened?'

Paolo told her about the other evening at Glenalmond and confessed to the spotting in Beauly. Holly listened as he recalled every last detail, all of which had been plaguing him. It was a relief to get it off his chest. He'd not told either of his friends, fearing that if they weren't bored to tears by the subject, they'd lecture him on it.

'I thought you'd been distracted this week. I've caught you with a faraway look more than once,' she said.

'Well? There's obviously something going on with Skye, isn't there. And this other guy.'

He thought once more about the suspect spritzes, the way Skye's arm draped over Hamish's shoulder so comfortably. He pictured the man in Beauly, how Hamish planted a kiss on his cheek.

'Want to steer us away from these rocks?' asked Holly casually. 'Any time's good.'

He had forgotten to paddle for the last few minutes. The Hamish thing was taking up too much space in his brain. They might well have drifted all the way to Norway if Holly hadn't been there to remind him to keep going.

'Between Skye and the date he was on? He's running wild. I mean, I wondered if now he's free from Daisy, and cheated death last year, he's playing the field.'

'Oh, Paolo. Why didn't you tell us all this before?' asked Holly.

'I didn't want to bore you. Like I've blatantly bored Hamish. I felt like a crisp new shirt that was briefly thrilling, but that's been stuffed at the back of a wardrobe.'

He'd reached a new level of descriptive melodrama.

'Paolo,' said Holly, sounding like she was about to be the rational one of the pair, 'Hamish liked you. I promise. Maybe you were both scared to start something.'

'Why would I be scared to start something?' said Paolo. 'I know no fear. I'm very manly, despite my antipathy towards weightlifting and fast cars.'

'The true gauges of masculinity.' Holly rolled her eyes. 'You tell me.'

How far back should he go? To his experience with Fabien? Or was it that until last year, Hamish hadn't dated a guy for a long time, and Paolo didn't want to push him? In truth, he was scared of being deserted again. Hearts were fragile, and needed to be treated with care.

'I don't know,' he said, not wanting to tell Holly how deep his worries went. 'Look, if this was a Richard Curtis film, I'd be the also-ran, the one the audience is led to believe has potential, but was nothing more than a decoy before the main event.'

'You're getting daft,' Holly interrupted. 'And carried away. Listen to yourself!'

'Even if I forget the Beauly guy, Skye's moved in with him,' said Paolo, hearing his voice reach a higher pitch. 'Into a bloody castle. Again, if this *was* a film, the credits would be rolling already.'

Holly shuffled backwards, and, after slowly coming to stand, reached for the oar. Paolo handed it to her, manoeuvred his way to the front of the board and flopped on to his back. The paddle board rocked gently from side to side, until he felt it moving forwards once more, smoothly gliding through the water. He stared at the sky, a crisp blue, the sun beating down on his face. Well, beating was a little extreme. This *was* Scotland.

Holly took a deep breath. 'Right. What's going to happen is this. Skye is going to leave for Edinburgh at the end of next week. As for her moving into Glenalmond, it was about convenience and comfort. You barely know her, and she was squeezed into your spare room, which is lovely, but you can't swing Ginger around in it. Glenalmond on the other hand? It's a no brainer. An old friend asks you to move into their castle? You'd leap on it, wouldn't you?'

Paolo sighed. 'Of course. So you're suggesting the following as a plan. I ignore the flagrant sexual tension between the two of them, and carry on as normal, and — once Skye is out of the picture — make a tentative move?'

'Exactly,' said Holly, as if it was that simple.

'But Beauly guy?'

'When a suitable moment presents itself, ask him how he's been finding the dating scene. You'll catch him out with that, and he's likely to confess. You'll get your answers, and be able to proceed accordingly. I think that sounds like the most pragmatic approach.'

She allowed no room for irrationality, did Holly. Paolo, however, generally liked to experience his romantic crises totally, with the full smorgasbord of emotions. But for her sake, and probably his own, he decided he'd take her approach.

'Let's discuss your birthday,' said Paolo. 'It'll take my mind off Hamish.'

'Invite him. It would be weird without him.'

'Inviting him to your party won't help with taking my mind off him, Hols,' he said.

Holly either hadn't heard him, or chose to ignore him. 'And — don't hate me — we ought to invite Skye too.'

Paolo tried to hide the reluctance in his voice. 'I guess Hugh would approve. Why don't we do a picnic? The forecast is set to change at the end of next week.'

'I saw.' Holly sounded dismayed. 'We've got all those farm visits in at the start of July. They've all come at once, like bloody buses. I've been finding them easier in the sun.'

'Sorry,' Paolo apologized for being the bearer of bad news. 'We could do it here. If you fancy it. And I don't mean a crap one with a rug and some shandy in a plastic bottle. I mean coordinating crockery and a menu card written in slanting cursive.'

Thanks to Holly's superior paddling skills, they had rounded the headland and were edging closer to Finnen Beach. Sitting up, Paolo surveyed the scene in front of him. The water became clear beneath them, the sand visible through the blue shallows. A crescent of white sand, with grasses beyond, it could have been somewhere in the Caribbean, not the north of Scotland.

'How do you tablescape a beach?' asked Holly. 'Look, there's no need to go crazy. It's not a special birthday or anything.'

Paolo craned his neck around. 'Yes, but I've got a creative streak.'

Holly raised an eyebrow. 'You're trying to impress Hamish, aren't you? I know it, Rossini. And Hamish won't be won over by that. You *know* he's not that guy. He'd far rather bond over a hike through the woods than an outing to a fancy schmancy restaurant.'

Paolo slid off the board and into the water, where he turned to face Holly. He narrowed his eyes.

'I merely think it'll be a nice thing to do for your birthday. You know, celebrate you, and midsummer, before the storms on the horizon hit.'

He took out his phone from the drypack, and snapped a photo of the beach, which, as always, looked flawless, ready to post — *hashtag no filter*.

* * *

Holly was already in the surgery when Paolo got there. How did she get dressed so fast? He held out a frothy-looking coffee from the café down the road. 'Cappuccino. For being a whinge-bag this morning. And because I didn't know if we'd fixed the thing in the kitchen.'

The coffee machine in the practice, which had been Hugh's, was temperamental, and for the last two days had spat out brown mud, which tasted more of burning circuit board than a decent brew.

Holly smiled. 'Thanks.'

Chloe, in a fifties-style sundress patterned with deck-chairs, bustled in behind him, and sat down at the desk.

'You're not meant to be in today, are you?' asked Paolo. Chloe didn't usually work on Saturdays, but perhaps she was getting forgetful, with all the added work and associated sub-tracted sleep up at Auchintraid. 'I'd have got you a latte if I knew you'd be here.'

'Nope.' Chloe smiled, sounding perky. 'But I want to get a bit of filing done. I need to start late on Monday because I've got the dentist. Remember? I asked last week.'

Holly groaned. 'You're not here on Monday morning?'

Paolo took a sip of his coffee. Paolo now remembered Holly had said OK to it, he had been there last week when Chloe had asked. Though why Holly would have said yes on a Monday, which was always the busiest day of the week, was beyond him.

'No. And I'm out Friday too. Oh. Is that no longer good?'

Holly took a measured sip of cappuccino. 'It'll be fine. As long as everything is lined up ready.'

The doorbell went and everyone turned to see who it was. There was another five minutes before opening.

A woman Paolo recognized from Eastercraig, but hadn't met in person before, appeared in the doorway, a box in her hands. 'There's something wrong with my rabbit,' she said, her eyes watering. 'Is there a chance you can fit me in?'

It was going to be one of those days. Paolo took another swift gulp of his flat white, before going over and taking the box from the woman.

'Shall we take this through to the back?' said Holly. 'I'll whack on some scrubs. Chloe, make a note and let the Russells know we'll be with them shortly.'

'Hi, Mrs Leary,' said Chloe, as they passed.

'Oh, hello, darlin',' said the woman. 'We're down the road from Chloe,' she added to Paolo and Holly, in a tone of somewhat frantic explanation.

In the consulting room, Holly took the box and placed it on the table. Inside, the doe — a female rabbit — was lying in a corner, panting. Peering closer, careful not to frighten it, Paolo and Holly eyed the corner of the box. Their eyes met, and Holly's lip twitched.

'Paolo, can you go and get me some more straw?' Holly asked.

Paolo jogged down the corridor, and to the cupboard out the back that contained a cornucopia of supplies. He pulled out a bag of straw from the bottom of a pile as if he was playing Jenga, and hurried back to the consulting room.

'How old is . . . ? Sorry, I didn't take a name,' Holly was asking.

'Aurelia,' said Mrs Leary. 'Is she OK?'

'She's fine. And how long have you had her?'

'She's about six months, I think. We've had her for two weeks — she came from a sanctuary near Inverness. What's wrong with her? Has she got some kind of virus.'

Not so much. 'Lean in, but not too far. See what's there with her?'

Mrs Leary moved closer, and took a tentative peek into the box, then stifled a gasp. She came back up and looked at Paolo and Holly with wide eyes.

'But we got two females! Aurelia and Octavia.'

'She may have been pregnant when you got her, but if not, I think Octavia might well be an Octavian,' said Paolo, with a grin.

Holly nodded. 'If you want to book an appointment before you leave, we can have Octavia checked and neutered, if she is indeed a she. In the meantime, let's keep Aurelia here. This is kindling — that's what we call it when rabbits give birth. It usually happens in the morning, and you can expect around six kits. We'll let her nest, and get her some food, and keep a bit of distance. Then you can come and collect her later. We can talk through next steps then.'

'Is there anything else I can do?'

Holly smiled. 'For now, you could run and get some of her favourite veg, if she has any. But leave her with us. She's in safe hands.'

Paolo showed Mrs Leary out to reception, quickly informing Chloe what had happened. Chloe gasped.

'Kits! How sweet! Och — there's nothing like a baby animal to brighten up an otherwise routine Saturday.'

Paolo would normally be inclined to agree. Only once they had finished clearing up and writing some notes down, he and Holly would be fifteen minutes behind schedule, and they hadn't even started yet. Holly would flip, although only once the surgery doors had closed at 1 p.m. Honestly, the woman needed a locum.

He and Chloe waved Mrs Leary goodbye, and Paolo opened the door for the Russells. Before he followed them to the consulting room, he felt a tug on his scrubs.

'You hold back,' said Chloe, in a near whisper.

Paolo smoothed down his scrubs. 'Be quick. Holly needs a second pair of hands for the next one.'

'You left your phone here.'

'And . . . ? I didn't have a chance to pop my stuff away.'

'Someone liked your post,' Chloe said, cryptically.

'Who?' said Paolo, taking the phone as Chloe passed it over. 'Oh. Crap.'

Fabien. Fabien, who had refrained from liking any of his posts since he had moved to Switzerland. More importantly, there was a message too. *Take me back.*

He looked up. Chloe was staring at him, and he felt his throat go dry.

Paolo gulped. 'Well, that's unexpected.'

He shoved the phone back at Chloe, who took it, and hurried to join Holly and the Russells.

CHAPTER 26

'Come on, you ridiculous thing,' Skye said to Wolfie, half-fondly, half-sternly.

It was Tuesday, mid-morning, and Skye pushed open the door to Anderson and MacDougall. The bell gave a little tinkle, a happy, welcoming sound, and Skye tugged Wolfie over the threshold.

Wolfie gave a feeble growl, then, limping slightly, followed her in, and lay down on the floor with a thump. Chloe looked up from the reception desk, and gave a wide smile.

'Och, what's the bugger done now? Something about a sore paw, wasn't it?'

Skye nodded. 'He was out yesterday afternoon, haring around up on the moorland with Hamish. At some point he refused to stand on it, and Hamish removed a thorn, but it hasn't got any better. None of us at the castle can tell if it's swollen much, or what.'

'Poor old chap,' Chloe said.

She came out from behind the desk, and crouched down to give Wolfie's ears a scratch. He wagged his tail weakly.

'I'll let Holly know you're here. In fact, because it's Wolfie, come with me now. Come on, boy,' she said to Wolfie. 'Up you get.'

Out the back, Wolfie sat on the ground next to the table. Holly lifted up his paw and Paolo came to help hold it while Holly leaned in to take a look.

'I can't see anything, so looks like whatever it was is already out, which is good news. It *is* swollen, though,' said Holly. 'Let me take his temperature, listen to his heart.'

Skye watched as she ran through her checks. She glanced at Paolo, who gave her a small, if odd smile. She hadn't seen him for over a week, not since he'd come over to Glenalmond.

'All normal,' Holly declared, giving Wolfie a pat, then standing up. 'But I'm going to give you a prescription for antibiotics. A short course, which will clear up any remaining infection. I love you, Wolfie, but trouble seems to come and find you, doesn't it?'

You and me both, thought Skye.

She opened the door to leave the room, when Holly called her back.

'Skye, are you doing anything tomorrow night? Only I'm having a small picnic down at Finnen Beach for my birthday. Nothing massive, really relaxed, right, Paolo?' Holly shot Paolo a look.

'Being low-key doesn't mean you have to lack all sophistication,' said Paolo. 'We'll not have any of those red plastic cups. We're not in a frat house.'

'So, come?' asked Holly. 'I sent Hamish a text this morning asking him, but he hasn't replied. Probably out with visitors, I guess. Sorry it's so short notice.'

'I'd love to,' said Skye. 'If you're sure. I mean, I've not been here that long.'

'I am,' said Holly. 'As for not being here long, Chloe's asked Bear too, and he's going to come.'

One trouble with being so pale was that there was no denying a blush. Skye tried to freeze her face, to mask the inner excitement she felt at the prospect of seeing Bear again, but she could feel a magenta hue crawling up her neck.

'Great.' She smiled, hoping it wasn't too obvious. 'I guess I'll go and square this with Chloe, then. Come on, Wolfie.'

'Bring Wolfie too, if you like,' said Holly. 'Sadie's coming, that's mine and Greg's dog. I think she was having a day over at Auchintraid when you first arrived. Fiona looks after her sometimes to make sure she gets the care and attention she needs.'

Skye allowed herself a smile as she walked back into reception. The thought of another night with Bear filled her with warmth, like drinking a hot drink while wrapped up in a blanket. More than warmth — heat. She shook herself.

Back out the front, Chloe did not look her usual together self. On the occasions that Skye had seen her, Chloe had projected nothing but neatness, from the perfectly styled fringe to her pretty pumps, all the way to her immaculate workspace.

'Are you OK?' Skye asked.

Chloe was bent down, fiddling with a cabinet. 'Yes,' she said. She sat up, smacking her head on the edge of the desk. 'No. That hurt.'

'I shouldn't have startled you,' Skye apologized.

'You didn't.' Chloe rubbed her head. 'The dratted roofers want to come on Friday. Not that they're dratted, because we need a roof and it all has to be special materials, and I'm sure they're really lovely guys, but the never-ending saga of the renovations are frying my brain. And I'd booked it off, but now I don't think I can do Friday — we've got a full diary here. Holly looked stressed when I reminded her. But I need to be at Auchintraid. Och, shite! I really can't miss the meeting with them. Paolo could duck in and out, but if he's busy, who'll answer the phones? Soothe owners? Remember the PC password?' Her voice had risen to a squeak.

'I will,' said Skye. 'If I can. Can I? I'm only part-time at Glenalmond, and can wiggle the hours a bit. I've basically lived in an office for the last few years, and I know my way around a desktop. And anything I get stuck on, I could leave you a note, or text if it's urgent. I used to help out here when I was a teenager, but I expect things have come on since then.'

Uncle Hugh had obviously upgraded a few things. They hadn't even had reliable internet back then, and Skye remembered noting everything in a large leather-bound book.

'Really? That would be great, thank you! I'll do a bit of a handover. Show you where everything is.'

Skye nodded vigorously. 'I'm sure Hamish will let me take Friday off, and a couple of hours out on Thursday for a handover. Especially if I make them up in the evening. There's nothing big in our diary that day, so he could man the office for a bit. He'd be more than happy, seeing as it's you guys. And I'd love to help out. It's the least I can do, given how kind you were to me when I got here. I owe you all, big time.'

'You really don't, but wow. Just wow.' Chloe beamed. 'You're a superstar, Skye. Thank you.'

Skye let herself be led out the door by Wolfie, feeling uplifted.

* * *

'Paolo, of course I'm going to invite her. She's lovely,' said Holly.

'For someone who claims to loathe drama, you're certainly inviting it. Not only is she getting her claws into Hamish, but she doesn't like Bear,' Paolo replied.

'Why wouldn't she like Bear?'

'Because . . .' said Paolo, as if it were the most obvious thing in the world. 'She's obviously having it off with Hamish.'

'We'll follow the plan tomorrow,' said Holly. 'Play it cool. And by that, I mean play it as close to normal as you can.'

Paolo raised an eyebrow. 'My love life's on the line, Holly. It's the one area of my life where I'm less than relaxed.'

'Pragmatic approach, Paolo. Remember? It's what we agreed on the board.'

Paolo nodded at Holly's coaching.

Pragmatism was a sensible option. The best option. He thought about Fabien's message again, trying to guess his ex's intentions, and wondered if replying to Fabien was pragmatic too.

CHAPTER 27

Dress to impress and pack your swimmers and a towel in case the mood takes you. Cocktails from 7.30 p.m. That had been the invitation to the party.

The sun was glaring, but there was something in the air which told Paolo that the weather was about to change. The breeze carried more salt than usual, there was a tang to it.

It was just as well that he'd brought a number of cotton throws and old mats though, because for now it was one hot day, and they'd be flopping on the sand. There were some wicker hampers containing most of the food and wine. The carrier bags and cool box were stowed away where they couldn't spoil the image. The vibe he was going for was *Picnic at Hanging Rock* meets *The Talented Mr Ripley*, the filmic versions, Riviera chic plus Edwardian frills. Everyone would lounge dreamily and sip cocktails, which he had bought some pre-mixed in a flask, a necessary thus excusable cheat.

It had been a lot to heft down, but Greg and Angus, the latter of whom was the definition of muscly, had helped. Angus had brought it all down the path in a box lashed on the back of a quad — the land belonged to Hamish, who had given them permission to drive up. The end result was a vision.

Having taken his own dress-code diktat seriously, Paolo was wearing neat canvas shorts, and an azure blue linen shirt, his curls tamed back. He could have passed for Dickie Greenleaf, the Jude Law character in *Ripley*, although maybe that was wishful thinking. He had wanted to look his best, though, to impress Hamish, despite knowing full well that if there was one thing Hamish was less interested in than Paolo, it was fashion.

Chloe was the first to arrive, with a freshened-up Angus. Seeing as over half of her wardrobe was vintage, Paolo wasn't surprised she had taken the brief and completely succeeded in meeting it. Angus, rarely out of overalls, looked smart too.

'This is so beautiful, Paolo. A triumph,' Chloe said, eyes sparkling at the scene in front of her. 'Is it all for Holly, or for you?'

'For Holly. I wanted to do something nice for her. Partly for me too,' he confessed.

'To keep your mind busy,' Chloe whispered, though Angus had gone to start working on the fire and was well out of earshot.

'And thanks for the cake, by the way.'

Chloe had provided a beautiful lemon and lavender sponge, decorated with buttercream and sugared lavender sprigs.

'Och, no worries. I've wanted to make that one for ages.'

Holly tapped him on the shoulder. 'Bravo! I think this is the best birthday I've ever had. Certainly the most beautiful.'

Greg, at her side, gave Paolo a mock frown. 'You've shown me up though. How am I ever going to live up to this? I'll have to do something spectacular next year.'

Paolo grinned. 'Don't make me blush. It's merely an outlet for my creative tendencies. Shall I pour out some cocktails?'

They wandered over to the mats and quilts, and sat down. Paolo was handing out the drinks when he spotted Hamish and Skye walking through the grasses towards them. He heard himself take a sharp breath.

Hamish, normally never out of his waterproofs, even in the hottest of summer months, was in a kilt — the family tartan — and a coordinating knitted jumper in a light teal. He had brushed his hair off his face, and shaved off his usual stubble.

Paolo then took in Skye, with her long flowing dress, a bewitching white maxi, which gave off midsummer vibes. His eyes flicked back to Hamish, who hadn't looked so good since he had been in a kilt at the Glenalmond Ball the previous year. Then a thought struck him. Not that Paolo wanted to throw shade on Hamish's fashion choices, but this was out of character.

It must have been Skye. He was dressing for her.

Paolo closed his eyes for a second. He couldn't go down this route. He mustn't.

'Well, this is fabulous,' came Hamish's voice. Hamish sat down next to him on one of the mats. 'Not that I'd expect anything else from Paolo Rossini. You've got the best taste of anyone I know. We ought to hire you to deck the halls at Glenalmond.'

Paolo turned slightly to face Hamish. Out of the corner of his eye he could see Holly, raising her eyebrows at him.

He cast around for words, surprised by the compliment. 'You like it?'

'Yeah. In fact, Skye had bumped into Chloe, and Chloe said I should make an effort. Skye helped me find this in that knitwear pop-up that's appeared at the old pottery shop.'

'You've been in there? I thought you hated clothes shopping.'

Hamish had once told him that he only ever bought clothes from the Donaldson's in Beauly, and that he went once a year to replace anything in his wardrobe that was beyond repair. Paolo admired the sentiment, even if he didn't share it himself.

'Aye. You know me well. But I want to support local businesses, and the father and son who are running it intend to stay here. It's all made with the softest cashmere. Go on, touch it.'

If Paolo didn't have his major suspicions about Skye and Hamish, not to mention Beauly Man, he would have immediately filed that invitation under 'come-ons, innuendo-led'. He reached out and gave Hamish's arm a stroke. 'God, it's like it was knitted by adorable bunny rabbits.'

'You'd really like it. They had a few things in a forest green colour I think would suit you.'

'Oh,' Paolo managed. Honestly, since when did Hamish have an opinion on clothing suiting him? Hamish's only requirement when choosing clothes was that they suited the activity they were designed for. 'How's Skye been doing?'

'She's a wee marvel, I'll tell you. The office looks fantastic. Shame it's her last week, and frankly, I'm a little disappointed that she's coming to join you lot all of Friday, but she wanted to muck in. Feels she owes you all. How are things, by the way? We barely caught up last week when you popped over.'

'At the surgery? All right. Holly's coping with the workload, I think, as are we. But there seems to be a lot happening at the moment.'

'And you? I meant with you. What have you been up to? Have you been dating? Any good ones recently?'

Paolo gulped. It was as he feared. Hamish was softening the blow. He was about to break the news about Skye. And or Beauly Man. It was time to save face.

'Aye. Well, a few.'

Hamish raised his eyebrows. 'And how are you getting on?'

Paolo sighed. Why lie? 'Peaks and troughs, if you want the truth.' He curled one side of his lip. 'There's been nobody I wanted to pursue. Even if they look anything like their photo — and I'm not saying it's all about looks, but nobody wants to be catfished — none of them seem to be looking for anything long term.'

'Who've you been going out with?'

'Anyone, to be honest. Do they have a face? I'll date them.' That said, he still hadn't contacted Patrick. He had decided to park that one for the time being.

Paolo's inner insecurities were brimming over. The cock-tails had been sweet but strong, and he had downed two of them already, and they had definitely kicked in. The honesty switch had been flicked.

Why had they all been such whopping duds? Was there something wrong with him? Was he so un-dateable? He did, like everyone he'd met through dating apps, have a face. And while he wasn't a matinee idol, he was all right to look at.

The weight of previous misfires pushed down on his shoulders, practically squeezing the anxiety out of him. People probably sensed it wafting through the air like a bad smell and decided not to call back.

'You're still looking around, then?' asked Hamish.

Paolo shrugged. If he didn't think that Hamish had hit the dating scene hard, this would have been the point at which he said "No. Because it's you, it's always been you." But it would have required a bucket-load of confidence which Paolo couldn't summon.

He was rescued from dwelling on it further as Bear appeared beside them.

'Thanks for inviting me,' he said, holding a small bag in one hand. 'I brought a present, but I see Holly's all the way down there.'

While Paolo and Hamish had been talking, the rest of the group had made their way down to the sea and had lost no time in hitching up skirts or rolling up trousers. Holly was in up to her knees, and Chloe had tucked her skirt up into her belt and was taking tentative steps, Skye next to her. They were engrossed in conversation, their laughs occasionally turning to shrieks as they got splashed by Angus and Greg, who appeared to be in competition as to who could drench the other brother more.

'Oh shite, I didn't get her anything,' said Paolo. He looked to Hamish. 'Did you?'

'I mean, I got her some game terrine,' said Hamish. 'Which I found in the pantry.'

'But what with arranging all this, I completely forgot to bring her a present,' said Paolo.

Bear looked puzzled. 'Isn't *this* your present?'

'I guess so,' said Paolo. 'But not bringing a tiny offering, wrapped up neatly with a ribbon or two. I feel like that's a major fail.'

'Yeah, you're so thoughtless,' chuckled Hamish. He put a hand on Paolo's arm. 'If you arranged something like this for me, I'd be blown away.'

Bear said he was going to wander down to the sea, and Hamish and Paolo nodded, Hamish adding that he'd come for a wade shortly.

'Are you OK?' asked Hamish, once Bear was out of earshot. 'You're not your usual self.'

Paolo looked at the scene in front of him. Perhaps he was still wound up from arranging it all, pulling the pieces together like a theatre production, until the beach looked like the most wonderfully dressed set. Or, most likely, it was sitting so close to Hamish, and feeling so very far away.

'I'm fine,' he fudged.

CHAPTER 28

Skye let the water numb her ankles, before hitching her skirt into her pants and edging deeper into the sea. A voice behind her called her name, and she turned around to see Bear.

She felt her lips split into an involuntary smile. 'How nice to see you in person.'

Until then, Skye had been standing at the edge of the group, every so often flicking an eye backwards, wondering what Hamish was saying to Paolo.

'Not going to fall in, are you?' said Bear.

He leaned over, put a hand around her shoulder and tugged her towards him to give her a kiss on the cheek. He pulled away, leaving his hand where it was, and Skye felt heat emanate from that spot.

'I'll try not to. How's your week been? How're things down on the farm?'

'They're OK,' he said, finally removing his hand, only to drag it down his chin. 'It's not been the farm that's the problem.'

'Have you started working on another project?' The thought left her feeling empty.

Deep down, Skye knew that Bear was going to have to return to Edinburgh at some point. In fact, she would be going back first. It made her feel like a Dalí painting come to life, time melting away and everything else around her distorted. Once they were home, would they see each other again?

'Not yet. It's more . . . I've got to have a conversation at work that I don't want to have,' said Bear. 'Let's not talk about it now. I don't want to bring the mood down at the party.'

Skye shook her head. 'You wouldn't be. Why not get it off your chest? That way you might be able to enjoy the atmosphere here.'

'I *am* enjoying it,' said Bear. 'Has there ever been a better advertisement for quitting the city and running off somewhere that feels like you're not even on the mainland any more?'

He waved his hand across the scene before him, and Skye followed his gaze. He was right.

'I'm glad you've finally been converted, though I'm not sure either of us would be happy here, knowing we have to untangle problems at home,' said Skye. 'Come on, out with it.'

Bear sighed. 'You've worn me down . . . I need to have a conversation with my mother. Not in her capacity as a parent — that would be fine. But in her role as my boss. There's a manager above me, other people I report to, but what I want to do, I need to tell her first.'

'Ah. This is your secret project?' asked Skye.

It felt like a joke, how often they referred to it, and yet still Skye didn't know anything about it. Bear completely refused to divulge a single detail.

Bear nodded. 'Indeed.'

Skye smiled triumphantly. 'You've given away a huge clue. It's a work thing. You're quitting?'

She'd decided to guess big, but Bear didn't reply. He turned and looked at the sea.

'You want to leave?' she cried, so that Holly and Chloe, who were stood nearest them, looked around. She lowered her voice, and side-stepped closer to him so their arms were touching. 'Am I right?'

Bear looked down at her. 'You *might* be on to something. Not straight away, though. But please, *please* don't say anything to anyone. If anyone up here found out about it, and it got back to my mother before I'd had a chance to go to her myself, it would be really unprofessional. And there's the double whammy that she would also take it personally.'

'She wouldn't, would she?'

'Telling her I don't think my vision fits with that of the firm? *Her* firm? I think it would come as a massive slap in the face.'

'But you're not rejecting her as your mother, just as a boss.'

'I would hate to upset her though. I would like her to be proud of what I'm doing, but she might see it as me throwing all the opportunities she gave me back in her face.'

As Bear contemplated the ramifications of quitting, Skye mused how so much of *her* life had been spent trying to make things right with her parents. Trying to show them that she was forging a path of her own, after the enormous blip of her teens.

She still hadn't called them. The previous day she had fobbed them off with a text, skirting around the fact that she wasn't on the holiday they thought she was. Remorse wended its way through her at how she was pushing them away, shutting herself off. But how would they react, her father in particular — with his ethos of redemption through acts of service — to the fact she was endangering all those years of hard graft?

Bear sighed. 'All I can see is that she gave me a chance, at one of the best architectural firms in the country — I mean, the place is globally recognized; they get commissions from Chicago to Chennai — and I'm chucking it away.'

She understood him, she really did. But he was going on to bigger and better things. His mother would appreciate that. By comparison, Skye was going nowhere, backwards even, which was all her parents might see.

Skye looked at him. 'You're not beholden to your parents,' she said. 'It's their job to try to give you the best start in life . . .'

Skye's parents had tried to, in their own ways, even though it led to blows. It must be hard to know, as a mother or father, the correct way to raise your child.

A chill breeze flickered across the beach, and the lapping waves splashed up Skye's legs.

'. . . You're your own person,' she concluded. 'You'll have earned her respect.'

For some time, that had been Skye's aim with her parents, but she was starting out from a very different baseline. It was harder to gain someone's respect when you'd lost it and had to earn it back.

'Why not tell me where you've got to with Auchintraid,' she said, keen to change the subject. 'Wow, my feet are really chilly.'

'Aye. Mine are cold and all. Mind you, after the burn, I'd have thought you were OK with it. You risked coming fully clothed.'

'I'm intending to stay dry, thank you,' said Skye, meeting Bear's eye.

'Your track record isn't great,' he said with a roguish grin. 'Not that I minded.'

Skye raised her eyebrows. 'I'd argue you've seen enough of my bare flesh to last you a lifetime.'

A comeback was on the tip of his tongue — Skye felt a frisson run up her spine as she imagined a protest against her last statement — when there was a roar. Greg and Angus, down to trunks, had run into the ocean. Leaving the water immediately, and shaking themselves off like wet dogs, the Dunbar brothers walked up the beach, Holly and Chloe keeping a distance.

'Shall we follow them up?' said Skye, resigned to the fact the moment they'd been sharing was over.

Bear nodded. 'Let's.'

Smoky air floated on the breeze. The bonfire was now burning brightly, making Paolo's scene look almost pagan, and as they walked, Skye felt herself bumping shoulders with Bear every so often. The sand formed uneven ridges beneath

CHAPTER 29

Holly came and threw an arm around Paolo, and Chloe skipped over, putting one of hers round his other side.

'Bravo, Paolo. This was fantastic,' said Holly, giving him a kiss on the cheek. 'I've never been to such a gorgeous party. And it was for me!'

Chloe, who Paolo knew couldn't resist the allure of a cocktail, rested her head on his shoulder. 'She's right,' Chloe slurred. 'And . . . I don't think Hamish is with Skye.'

'How would you know? You're totally plastered.' Chloe poked her tongue out, and Paolo turned to Holly. 'Talking of which. If you're here, who's on call?'

'Me!' grinned Holly. 'Don't worry, I had a mere sip of cocktail.'

Paolo frowned at her. 'I totally forgot you couldn't drink. I'm such an idiot.'

'No, you're not,' said Holly, firmly. 'You're far from it. You're amazing. Besides, I ate about half the canapes.'

'Seriously amazing.' Chloe beamed. 'I think I need Angus to take me home. ANGUS!'

Paolo and Holly stared after her as she meandered along the sand towards Angus, who held out his arms. She tripped before she got there, only to stand up and announce to everyone, 'I'm OK! Nothing to see here.'

'Have you taken some pictures?' asked Holly. 'I'm not the social media type, but isn't this a hashtag no filter scenario? Hang on, Greg's calling me over.'

'I've already posted them,' said Paolo. 'See you in a sec.'

He had taken a few before they arrived, of the perfect mise-en-scene, then more at the bonfire, plus some close-ups of the cocktails and canapes he'd made. It was a good thing he had, seeing as the sky was now a charcoal grey, the remaining blue patches disappearing fast. As Holly walked over to Greg, Paolo looked at his phone again. There was a single bar of reception, but enough to let his account register a number of likes to his earlier posts. His sister, Francesca, his mum, some uni friends and . . . Fabien.

Paolo clapped his hand over his mouth. He scrolled down to the comments section.

Fabien: *Is this a mirage, or is this beauty for real? Shame I only hit town this weekend — looks like I've missed a lush evening.*

Paolo's stomach jolted.

Fabien was back. Because nobody had known they had ever gone out, save for Chloe, Holly, Hamish and a few others who had guessed, there would be no passionate moment where they might reunite on the front. *Heck!* Where had that thought come from.

He was spared further rumination by a drop of rain falling on his nose, then another two. He started to gather the mats and chuck them into giant carrier bags to heft back up to the quad.

* * *

It was incredible, the speed at which the weather could change. Only yesterday, Eastercraig had basked in sunshine, the line of pastel-coloured cottages on the front appearing a shade stronger than normal in the fierce light. Now, the clouds were tumbling over one another like waves. In the distance, Skye heard a faint rumble of thunder. She let the first few drops of rain fall on her face, and closed her eyes.

When she opened them, Bear was next to her. 'What is it they say in the shipping forecast? "Thundery showers. Good, occasionally poor later". Makes me glad I'm not a fisherman.'

He was toting a massive bag in one hand, a cool box in the other.

'Is there more to come up?' Skye asked. 'Angus was going to bring them, but he's having to carry Chloe.'

Behind them, Holly laughed. 'A few more things, yeah. Wow — you don't often see Chloe like this. I wonder if the stress of working and managing everything at the farm is getting to her more than she admits. Aren't you coming in tomorrow for a handover?'

Skye nodded. 'Yes. Dipping in for an hour to see how the bookings system works.'

'I really appreciate it, Skye. You didn't need to,' said Holly. 'Oh, shoot. I'm getting a call.'

Skye knew how it was working long hours, but at least when she got home, she was home. Poor Holly didn't seem to be able to catch a break at the moment; sick animals didn't work to a timetable and didn't break for birthdays either. Skye made a plan to buy some bath salts she had seen at the counter in the knitwear pop-up, and drop them to Holly tomorrow with a bar of chocolate.

'You go,' said Skye. 'We'll finish up here.'

Holly tried to smile through her sigh. 'Thanks. I have to go and tend to a dog with breathing difficulties. Think that's nearly everything.'

Holly plonked what she had been carrying into a crate that had been lashed to the back of the quad bike. She threw her arms around Greg and kissed him goodbye, waved to the rest and jogged down the hill to the town.

Paolo had already gone home, dispatched by the others who thought he shouldn't have to tidy, and Hamish had gone to the pub to ask Mhairi about having a group visit the Anchor later in the week.

Bear dropped his bags in the crate too. 'I'll go back and get the last few bits,' he said.

'Keep you company?' asked Skye.

She'd barely spent enough time with him that evening. Nowhere near as much as she would have liked, which was, she realized, a lot.

'Sure.' Bear smiled.

They retraced their steps back down the path, passing Angus — who was piggybacking Chloe — on the way. At the top of the dunes, they pulled off their sandals to walk back through the grasses on the beach. The sand had darkened with the rain and was sticky beneath their feet. The bonfire, which less than thirty minutes ago had blazed like a beacon, was now letting off the occasional twisting whorl of smoke, the once-glowing embers all but dead.

'I'll double-check there's nothing left,' said Bear.

He paced around the bonfire, scooping up the last of the mats, making sure they left Finnen the way they found it. Hamish had promised to come in the morning and deal with the remains of charred wood. As Bear did so, Skye took the other side, scanning for even the smallest bit of rubbish, before meeting him in front of the sea, the rain now coming down in big drops.

'Looks to be all of it,' he said. 'Come on, you'll catch your death.'

'The midsummer night's dream is over,' said Skye sadly, taking a couple of the mats from him, and tucking them under her arm.

She was stood right in front of him now, barely an inch between them. The rain pattered on loudly, leaving droplets on Skye's bare shoulders and arms. Neither of them moved, and Skye tried to slow her breathing, aware her heart was beginning to race.

'It needn't be,' said Bear, his voice dipping. 'If you don't want it to be. We could go to the pub for a warmer. Or . . .'

He leant in further, and she could feel his breath on her neck. 'There's an honesty bar at the B&B. If you want to come back for a nightcap. I could lend you a shirt or something.'

She thought about how she had secretly been wearing Bear's jumper all last week, ever since their night by the burn. She pondered the idea of hurling herself into whatever this was that was happening between them.

'You don't have to,' said Bear, still close. 'But the night is young.'

How would she get back afterwards? The taxi service in Eastercraig consisted of Fred Kilbright, who Skye knew from experience preferred to be booked a week in advance, and Terry, who didn't have a surname or a valid MOT.

She wouldn't get back. Was that the point? He might have been imagining a nightcap and nothing further. But this was the twenty-first century, and in Skye's experience, being invited back to someone's place — a permanent abode or no — meant the full works.

'That sounds really nice,' she said, stepping towards him.

Bear took her free hand, and Skye, feeling like her entire body was being flooded by an unabashed heat, took it. She squeezed it tightly, and he gripped it back.

They began walking back towards the dunes in silence. Skye looked down, noticing that the rain was turning her dress transparent. They moved slowly at first but then faster and faster, as if they couldn't get back to the B&B fast enough. She had a sense that Bear was feeling the same way she was. It wasn't only a nightcap on the menu after all.

He would make her tea in the morning, want to spend the day together. But then . . . ?

She was probably never going to see Bear again after this month. Sure, they both lived in Edinburgh, and while it wasn't a sprawling metropolis like London or New York, where you could go for years without ever bumping into someone you knew, it was still a big city. A city where they had their own lives to return to.

Halfway up the path, Skye ground to a halt completely. She turned to face Bear, let her hand slip from his, and swept her wet fringe out of her eyes, and wiped raindrops from her cheeks, her neck, her collarbone.

Bear looked at her. 'Are you OK? It's like you've run out of petrol. Want me to carry you the rest of the way or . . . Oh. You're thinking this might not be such a good idea.'

Skye shook her head. It wasn't that she didn't want to go back, but she didn't want to start whatever this was, only for it to fizzle out in a matter of days. She wanted more than just one night.

When she failed to answer, Bear continued. 'If you don't want to come back, I totally understand. It's completely up to you. If you'd rather keep things to daylight hours, we could do something Saturday.'

'I do want to come back,' she said, shooting him a look. It was always risky, being straight with someone. You could put your heart on the line only to get it smashed to pieces. But it needed to be done. 'Only I leave for Edinburgh at the end of the week.'

The implication that she didn't want a brief fling hung in the air. She looked to Bear, hoping he'd understood her.

'I'll be back in Edinburgh too, once I've finished at Auchintraid,' said Bear, his eyes dancing.

Skye began to feel her heart drumming in her chest, the rhythm quickening. She shot him a shy smile at the realization that they were on the same page. Bear gave a soft laugh which Skye felt travel through her whole body.

They began walking again, next to each other, moving quickly over the lumpy slabs that forged a path through the khaki grass. Bear placed his hand on the small of her back, and Skye felt electricity race through her body.

Almost at the brow of the hill, in her haste, she stumbled slightly, and Bear reached out and grabbed her hand. She realized she was holding it more tightly than before. This was it, she thought. This was a shot at true happiness.

She sped her pace up, Bear following suit, and Eastercraig came into view, as did the quad, which was perched on top of the hill.

Angus was making a call, and Chloe was sitting side-saddle on the seat, although she was looking far from her usual presentable self. Her head was resting in her hands. She spied Skye and Bear, an impish grin on her face.

'Well! If it isn't Hurricane Skye,' Chloe cried.

Bear turned to Skye, an amused look on his face. 'An old nickname?'

'Not really,' lied Skye, letting go of Bear's hand.

'Oh yes, it is. It's what she used to be called when she was up to all sorts of mischief when she was a youngster. She was a dreadful cheeky wee sprite. Not . . .' said Chloe, backtracking like a true drunk who's realized they might be saying the wrong thing. 'Not that she is any more, mind. She's going to be a top-flight lawyer. You mark my words. She's a reformed woman.'

Skye felt her stomach lurch, winded by Chloe's words. If only they were true. For all her efforts, she had made bad choices — Will, her career, and then running away from it all — mirroring all the blunders of her past. Either history was repeating itself, or Skye had never truly changed in the first place. She snuck a glance at Bear, who looked back at her, puzzled.

Angus hung up the phone and dragged a wet hand through his hair. 'I've had to ring Hamish to come up and drive the quad back,' he explained. 'There's nobody else sober enough to do it. I can't let Chloe hold on to the back, even with a helmet. She'll be off in a second.'

'He's being seriously overprotective. I'd be fine,' said Chloe, sounding like she would be anything but.

'Can we help?' asked Bear. 'We could walk Chloe back down to town.'

Skye was glad the focus had shifted from her for the moment. In an ideal world, Bear would forget everything

Chloe had said. She prayed for localized amnesia that would wipe Chloe's words from his mind.

'That's kind of you, but Hamish is coming back up now,' Angus replied. 'He'd only got as far as the harbourmaster's so it's no trouble. In fact, here he is.'

Hamish came striding back up the hillside with a mac on, his Land Rover awaiting at the bottom, the rain beating down with increasing force. Angus gently pulled Chloe up and held her to him.

Skye placed the mats she'd been carrying in the box, and helped cover it all with a tarpaulin.

'Chloe, what happened?' Hamish asked. 'You're going to need a couple of paracetamol when you get home. I'll drop the box at Holly's and then when you and Angus get to the bottom of the hill I'll drive you back. Then you and I can come back and get the quad, Angus.'

'Thanks, mate,' said Angus. 'We owe you one. Don't we, Chloe.'

Chloe smiled in a squinty sort of way. 'Thanks, darling Hamish.'

'And you, Skye?' Hamish looked at Skye and Bear, and hastily added, 'Call me if you need a lift back later, or something.'

There was a brief, awkward silence, before Chloe broke it with a yawn. Angus rolled his eyes. 'Come on, Chlo. Let's get you home. I'll run you a bath.'

Angus might have sounded wearied by the prospect of having to get Chloe home, but it was sweet seeing the love with which he pulled her to his side, helping her to navigate the hill back down to the town. It was obviously a relationship with strong foundations. None of which could be said for any of hers. She glanced up at Bear, who was still looking at her curiously.

Oh God, what was she thinking? Moments ago, they had acknowledged that going back to the B&B wasn't a one off, but a beginning. But Bear deserved more than to be dragged into her confusion. After all he had been through with his ex-wife, he didn't need anything or anyone else holding him back. And that's what she would do.

At once she felt guilty she hadn't told him more before-hand, and simultaneously paralysed by the fear that if she did, he might change his mind. That perhaps he *should* change his mind.

There was a great clap of thunder, closer now than it had been before. The rain was coming down in sheets. Hamish said his goodbyes, and drove the quad away, leaving her and Bear alone at the top of the hill.

'We ought to go back,' she said to Bear, shouting to make herself heard over the noise of the weather. She wiped her wet hair off her forehead. 'Come on.'

She started at a run, overtaking Chloe and Angus, who were not far from the bottom. Bear followed close behind her.

At the bottom, she took temporary refuge in the bus shelter. It smelled faintly of smoke, and Skye imagined some of the town kids had been smoking there before they realized the rain was more than a passing shower.

Sitting down, she tried to catch her breath, and order her thoughts at the same time. Chloe's words had shattered the happy illusion she'd formed of her and Bear's future back at the beach and she saw it for what it was — a rash move on her part.

There was no logic to it, no real thought process where she had tallied up the pros and cons of going back home with Bear. Whatever her reasons for going with him, it was a mistake.

'What's going on, Skye?' asked Bear. He came and sat down on the bench next to Skye.

She had to tell him the truth.

'I'm not really the person you think I am,' she said, wondering if she would regret this.

Her palms felt sticky, and her breath caught. She closed her eyes to focus, to try and push all the panic away.

'You're not Skye Edmonds?' Bear asked. 'Who are you then? And don't break my heart by telling me you're not into cruck frames.'

211

Skye turned to face him. 'If you'd asked me a few weeks ago, I'd probably had told you I wasn't. But as luck would have it, I find them fascinating. Your enthusiasm is infectious.'

'But what I really enjoyed about the trip was hanging out with you. There, at the burn, over the phone. I really like you, Skye. I think you're great.'

Which was where he was wrong. Her heart should have leapt at his words. Instead, it was thudding in her throat, making her nauseous.

Holding back on him had not been in the spirit of honesty, and wasn't honesty the keystone of a good relationship? How could she be that person, knowing how she had been floored by Will's dishonesty, only a few weeks ago.

'I've not been entirely truthful about why I'm here. Why I'm here this time.'

'Do you want to tell me now?'

'No,' said Skye. She had to stave off the panic, and a bus shelter confessional wasn't going to help. 'Not especially.'

'Is it about the guy you were seeing? Too soon?'

Skye held her lips tight. She didn't want to tell him about the past, about Hurricane Skye, and how it had turned her parents lives inside out, how it had somehow led her into this corner she didn't know how to get out of. She didn't want to tell him that she was still lost, even at this age. She couldn't share these fears, even as they made her dizzy.

'Yes. No. I don't know.'

Bear took a breath. 'Do you want to change your mind about things?'

Skye didn't. She really, really didn't. In fact, she would give anything to be at the B&B, sipping a nice glass of wine, or a whisky, warming up in one of Bear's sweaters, taking it off. But it wasn't the right thing to do. She felt tainted with the shame of pretending to be someone she wasn't.

Seemed Hurricane Skye could wreak as much havoc as ever.

'I'm not sure.' She could hardly look at Bear. 'Maybe it's not such a great idea after all.'

Despite best-laid plans, she had let him get close. So much for arm's length. She didn't want to go further without him knowing everything about her, but right now she still didn't think she knew her own mind enough to tell him.

Bear suddenly became very interested in a tanker drifting across the horizon, little more than a shadowy outline, almost completely hidden by the curtain of rain.

'That's OK. You do what you need to do.'

If only she knew what that was. Skye fought back a sob which rose in her throat.

'I reckon I ought to go back to Glenalmond,' she said, hoping to keep the waver in her voice to a minimum. 'Sorry. I didn't mean to lead you on.'

Bear shook his head. She could see the muscles in his jaw tightening. 'You didn't. I'm not sure what's just happened, though. Do you want to tell me?'

He wouldn't like it. Not the long and short of it. Not the truth of it. Skye didn't, so why would anybody else?

She shook her head. 'I can't.'

Bear got up, and nodded, his face set. He looked her in the eye, his expression unreadable. 'I'll see you around, Skye.'

He headed down the front, and Skye watched his back as he walked away from her. She hoped he would look back over his shoulder, but he didn't. She shivered, her body feeling empty all of a sudden.

June had been so warm, and now she could see her breath in the air in front of her. It was like watching her hopes escape.

* * *

Paolo looked out of his window at the rain. Aside from the weather, he'd managed a good party, and — he reminded himself — he wasn't responsible for the downpour.

From where he sat, in the small armchair, he had seen Bear going back to the B&B alone, running through the rain. And then, coming back a second time, Hamish's Land Rover.

213

He could make out Hamish, now in his big waterproof, as he hopped out of the car, and disappeared into the bus shelter. Paolo lifted his binoculars off the table by the window, and twizzled the knob until he could focus it where he wanted. It made him feel a little voyeuristic, but he couldn't help it.

Paolo watched as Hamish came out of the bus shelter, an arm around Skye, who was now wearing the waterproof. Hamish opened the car door for her, then ran to the driver's side.

He sat back. Skye had spent most of the night talking to Bear. She probably knew that he didn't know anyone and was being kind. And maybe Hamish had warned her away for the evening, not wanting anyone to know what was happening between them, fearing gossip.

Paolo sunk back into the chair and closed his eyes. Whichever way you looked at it, Hamish was taken.

Paolo pulled out his phone to call Chloe or Holly, then remembered that Holly was on a call and Chloe was likely passed out on the sofa. Instead, open his social media and found Fabien.

Paolo: *You're coming to town? I'm sure I can rustle up some more of my dangerous margs if you wanted one. Can't promise the weather tho* x

The response was almost immediate.

Fabien: *I'll call you when I arrive. Saturday some time. WLTM (retro acronym, I know)* x

Paolo thought his heart had stopped for a second, and he paused, only exhaling when he realized it was still beating. What if Fabien still liked him? He *had* been forced to go to Geneva with work, and the stress of long-distance did have a habit of breaking up the strongest of partnerships. They'd had some fun times. They *had* been a great couple.

Maybe this wasn't such a bad idea after all.

CHAPTER 30

Skye's fingers flew across the keyboard at lightning speed, as she tried her hardest to put Bear out of her mind. She needed to create distractions so as not to dwell on the night before; so alongside learning how to work the diary, she told Chloe she could update the website for them.

That morning, she had already been up when her phone had beeped, bearing a message from Chloe.

Hi, Skye! The earlier the better for going over cover duties. Will crash before long and Angus can drive me in first thing. Chloe x

'Thank the Lord he could ferry me down. I was utterly steaming last night. I wouldn't be surprised if I'm still over the limit,' Chloe had groaned when she let the pair of them into the surgery at 8 a.m.

Skye had spent the night fretting, her mind noisy with overcrowded voices, and had been up since dawn with them jabbering around in her head without cease. The text from Chloe had come as a welcome relief, and Skye had hopped on her bike, and cycled into town.

After twenty minutes, it was clear Chloe's initial burst of energy was wearing off. She had taken up residence on one of the armchairs, resembling a ragdoll devoid of its stuffing.

'When did you last take a paracetamol?' asked Skye, looking over the diary, which wasn't too unlike the calendar set-up at her law firm. She snuck a glance above the screen, to make sure Chloe hadn't hit the floor.

'An hour ago. And I had some ibuprofen. I think I need an espresso. A triple.'

Skye grimaced. 'I'd go easy if I were you,' she advised, scooting the chair around the desk. Working at her law firm meant engaging with the drinking culture on a regular basis, and Skye had suffered many a hangover that had to be shed while desk bound. 'Your heart'll race and you'll feel terrible all over again. When someone else gets here, I'll nip to the chemist and get you some rehydration powder, which *does* work. They open in about ten minutes.'

Chloe made a noise which sounded like 'uuuuuurgh' and closed her eyes.

Skye shimmied the chair back and flicked her eyes to the PC. She minimized the diary, and went back to the website, where she was adding a news page which Chloe could easily update.

'Paolo was a bit funny with me last night.' Skye tried to sound casual as she clicked her way around the screen. 'I'm worried I did something to upset him. He's been chilly with me since I moved in with Hamish. Do you think he's offended that I ditched his place and moved into Glenalmond?'

'Oh, now this I can gather my faculties for,' Chloe said, albeit with some effort. 'Ah, and here is Paolo himself. Let's ask him. Horse's mouth and all that.'

'No need for that,' Skye squeaked, leaping up. 'We can ignore it for—'

'Paolo?' said Chloe, genuinely seeming to have perked up, as if she'd had a caffeine injection.

'You made it then, Chloe?' said Paolo. 'Oh, good morning, Skye. I thought you were in later.'

Where he had practically chirped like a happy chick to Chloe, on seeing Skye his tone flattened. The wisdom of offering to cover Chloe, and therefore spend an entire day in his company suddenly felt like a very foolish idea indeed.

'Change of plan,' Skye explained, looking at Chloe as if she was about to launch a grenade.

'Paolo,' said Chloe, with the superior tone of someone who is in possession of significant knowledge. 'You can drop the grumpy act. There is nothing going on between Hamish and Skye.'

She swept her arm theatrically to point at Skye, who felt her eyes pop out of her head.

'Between me and who?' Skye asked. She was glad she wasn't holding her cup of tea. If she had been, she would have thrown it over herself, and it was way too early for third degree burns.

'But—' Paolo turned and stared at Chloe, then looked back to Skye, confused. '*What?*'

'Did you think . . .' Skye blinked. 'You thought me and Hamish were . . . But that's totally crackers.'

'But you and him. All cosy and touchy-feely and living together.'

'He's my friend. We've known each other since we were teenagers,' said Skye. 'Why on earth would I . . . ?'

Chloe let out a throaty chuckle.

'How do you know all this?' Paolo narrowed his eyes at Chloe. 'And why are you only telling us now? Have you been sitting on this for ages, watching me get worked up?'

Chloe smiled beatifically. 'I vaguely remember trying to say this last night. Are you going to tell him, Skye, or am I?'

Skye hesitated, which was a mistake, because Chloe rolled her eyes and said: 'I saw her holding hands with Bear.'

Paolo spun back to Skye. 'You and *Bear?*'

Skye's breath hitched, the truth catching in her throat. 'There is no me and Bear.'

It was pretty final, being invited back to his B&B, only to reject him. Bear's pride was likely wounded.

'Wait. I'm confused,' said Chloe. 'The air was burning with passion between you last night.'

'It's a wonder you could tell anything, Chlo, the state you were in,' Paolo interjected.

'Exactly,' said Chloe. 'The tension was so great that only a complete idiot could have missed it. I could actually see it.'

Paolo raised his eyebrows at Skye. 'What happened then?'

She caught a breath, her heart aching from her confession, and looked at Chloe and Paolo. 'Before I tell you, Paolo, I ought to apologize. I never meant to cause any upset with you and Hamish. Quite the opposite.'

'Water under the bridge,' said Paolo. The easy demeanour he'd had the first time they met had returned, to Skye's joy. It was simply about Hamish? 'Think nothing more of it. Or we can revisit later. But the Bear thing? If you want to tell us, that is.'

She told Paolo and Chloe what had happened. How she had been getting closer and closer to Bear, how he had made his move and how she had panicked and thrown it all back at him. How she had then gone back to Glenalmond feeling like she was falling apart all over again.

'But I don't understand,' said Paolo. 'Why didn't you go back with him? I mean, if you like him and he likes you. I'm all for taking things slowly, but if it feels right you can grab the bull by the horns, or the Bear by the ears, or . . .'

Skye shook her head. 'Bear's a great guy. Yes, he came off all cold when we first met him, but he's not like that at all. He's lovely. And more than that, I've felt a genuine connection to him. But ' she drew a breath — 'he deserves better. It's as easy as that.'

Paolo looked at her, puzzled. 'What are you talking about? You're a catch.'

'A moment ago you hated my guts,' Skye reminded him.

'Yeah, but that was before it turned out I was making assumptions based on nothing. Now I know you're not making moves on Hamish, I can go back to thinking you're not half bad.'

His words hit home. 'And half bad is the problem. You know when I moved in with you, I hinted at all the trouble I'd been in. Chloe mentioned it last night. You referred to me as being mischievous, reminding me that all those times I used to come here, it was because I'd screwed up. Because I was in a real state. Hurricane Skye.

'And look where I am now. Back in Eastercraig. Only three weeks ago I puked on your shoes, Paolo. That is not the behaviour of a woman who's got her shit together . . . I mean . . . I thought I'd left that messed up stuff in the past, but it turns out I'm still prone to doing stupid things. I've made so many crap decisions in this life that I'll be reincarnated as a bird poo in the next one.'

Skye sat down, slumped back in the chair, and reclined so she was looking at the ceiling, not wanting to make eye contact with the other two.

'I don't think you can come back as something that isn't technically alive,' Chloe piped up. 'All the same, nobody can have done anything *that* bad. And what's past is past, isn't it?'

Skye sighed. 'I don't know if it is past. I don't think the present is right either. All I know is that I don't think I should be with someone as nice as Bear. Not for life, and therefore not for one night either. I don't want to muck anyone about, especially Bear.

'Bear's a consenting adult,' said Paolo. 'I'm sure he could have handled whatever might have happened like a grown-up.'

'Pshhh,' Skye said. 'It doesn't matter. It would have been a mistake.'

'You were holding hands,' protested Chloe. 'It was sweet and tender and . . .'

'Chloe is a romantic,' Paolo interrupted her. 'And while I'm inclined to be a realist, Bear doesn't look like the type to race into things without due consideration.'

'No offence, but Chloe doesn't look like the type to drink all the cocktails on a work night? You can never judge a book by its cover,' said Skye. 'Not that I think you're wrong about Bear, by the way. But that makes us chalk and cheese. He's well-rounded. He knows himself. I can't stop ballsing up. I did when I was younger, and I've been doing plenty more recently.'

'We all make mistakes,' said Chloe. 'Like I did by consuming my body weight in cocktails last night.'

It didn't come close to what Skye was talking about.

'Bear has been so open with me. Those brooding eyes make him look fierce, but underneath he's this amazing person, full of passion. And he knows who is his, and where he's headed. I don't know if I'm coming or going. I think he deserves more than that. I can only drag him down with my scruples about my own career, and my own choices. And my past choices.'

'Hurricane Skye?' said Paolo.

'Not the bits like the rainbow hair, the drinking, the raving, but the very worst bits of her.' Skye puffed out her cheeks. 'I try to tell myself it was a silly phase, that I was so confused back then. And pursuing this career at Tilling and Browne felt like atonement. Thing is, while at times I've loved it, I'm worried it's not the job for me.'

'Och Skye,' said Chloe. 'You poor thing.'

Skye hesitated. 'It doesn't matter. Bringing Bear into my life would be extra havoc. And he really doesn't deserve all that I bring right now. God, why do I still feel like such a screw-up?'

'I can assure you, you're not.' Chloe came and sat next to her.

Paolo nodded. 'You're a qualified lawyer, Skye, with friends and family who love you. Whatever worries you have, you're doing fine.'

Skye gave a wiggle of her head. 'Maybe. Can we move on to something else? Something less dispiriting?'

Paolo gave Skye a sympathetic look, and the slightest of nods, before he turned to Chloe. Skye breathed an inner sigh of relief that he'd realized it was time to change the subject.

'Let's examine what happened with you, Chlo,' he said. 'Did you spike your own punch? Or did you have pre-drinks at the pub? There was a nice-looking rhubarb gin and tonic I spotted the other week.'

The mere thought of more alcohol clearly agreed with Chloe as much as the remaining alcohol in her system. She'd gone a shade of green. 'I had another wee spat with Fiona. She seems to think the building work, and all the chaos it's generating, is down to me. I wasn't the one who came up with the idea — it was Angus and Greg, but I think because I moved over to the farm at the same time she associates it all with me.'

'She's probably worrying about your moving in too,' said Paolo. 'She had lived there with the boys for ages, doing all the farm jobs, looking after Angus.'

'She's known me forever,' Chloe protested. 'And she knows how much I love Angus. I'm not the enemy. And I work here, it's not like I've made her redundant. There's tons to do up at Auchintraid that I can't manage.'

'What if she's feeling sidelined?' Skye suggested. 'Greg went off into the world, but she got to mother Angus, you know, make him supper, bake him cakes. You know all those clichés about mothers and their sons. And now you've come along and are doing all those things instead?'

Paolo nodded. 'Yeah. She might have moaned about having to look after him, but both of them living in that farmhouse together was a huge part of her life.'

'And I suppose she feels like she's being shunted into a granny annex,' said Chloe.

'You're not about to make her one . . . are you?' said Paolo, looking at her suspiciously.

'No!' shrieked Chloe. 'I'm not about to make her a granny. This sickness is genuinely all margaritas. But *she* was the one who suggested moving out, to give us more space. So when the boys came up with the plans, one idea was to convert a building for her to be in.'

'It's one thing deciding you're going to do something, and another thing entirely as to whether it all works out,' Skye offered.

It was one of life's truths that it was so much simpler to try to solve someone else's problems than it was your own.

'Confront it head on,' said Paolo. 'Go and talk to her. Get it over with.'

'I don't want to confront anything head on,' said Chloe. 'I already feel like I've confronted a truck head on. I've never felt this bad.'

'Not today,' said Skye. 'I don't recommend a difficult conversation when you're hungover. But don't let problems linger. They only get worse the longer you leave them.'

She could do with taking a dose of her own medicine. Where was a spoonful of sugar when you needed one?

'Do it tomorrow, when you're feeling better,' Paolo said, placing a gentle hand on Chloe's shoulder.

Chloe let out a low moan.

'You know what,' said Skye. 'Why don't I cover you today *and* tomorrow. There was a cancellation of a guided hiking day up at the castle because of the weather, and I'm sure Hamish would let me off.'

CHAPTER 31

Before Paolo finished for the day, he and Holly had gone over to Mandy Lewis's farm to look at some of her newly acquired donkeys. Mandy, whose frequent acquisitions Hugh had always ranted about, and who Holly diplomatically referred to as 'well-intentioned', had recently got two from a sanctuary that was closing down. Her smallholding, a few miles out of town, verged on chaotic, but Paolo knew her, and despite her habit of jumping into things, she was deeply devoted to all of her animals.

'This is Winnie, and the browner one is Freddie,' Mandy said, as he and Holly walked through the gate to the field.

The two donkeys began to plod over, coming to say hello to them. They paused, and one came and stood right next to Paolo. He scratched it behind the ears. He was reminded of Wolfie because they were roughly the same size.

'They're still young, then,' said Holly, eyeing them. 'They'll eventually get to here or so.' She lifted her hand up a couple of feet so it hovered by her chin, to indicate the height of an adult donkey.

Mandy beamed. 'I know. They're soppy things, aren't they. Very happy to come and have a cuddle, especially when I bring them a carrot.'

'Which is the one with the teeth problem?' asked Holly.

Mandy pointed at the one leaning against Paolo. 'Freddie. She's been drooling like anything these last few days. I cannae get my hand in far enough to see what it is.'

Paolo looked down. Sure enough, the donkey was dribbling all over his clothes.

Holly frowned. 'OK. Me and Paolo will have a go.'

Paolo gave Freddie a pat. 'Come on, wee lass. Why don't you come over to the stable and we'll tie you up and Holly can check you out.'

'Cup of tea for you both?' asked Mandy.

Paolo and Holly thanked her, then Paolo led Freddie back across the field and to the stable. The donkey followed him inside, contentedly, as Holly located the switch and turned on the light.

'She likes you,' she said, rooting a headtorch out of her bag, and fastening it around her head.

'Mandy or Freddie?' Paolo asked, giving the donkey another stroke.

'Both, but Freddie is the one pressed up against you again. She's clearly very happy in your company. Hopefully she won't hate me after this. I'll suggest to Mandy I give Winnie a quick look over too. They've not had a general health check yet.'

Holly opened the donkey's mouth, and put a gag in. 'Can you keep her calm while I look?'

Paolo kept a hand on the donkey, talking to it in a low, gentle voice. For a young animal, she seemed surprisingly relaxed.

'Here it is,' Holly muttered. 'It looks like some overgrown back teeth. Let me get the file, and we'll sort them out. I can't see any infection or anything else, so no need to remove any.'

Holly was, as was often the case, only half talking to Paolo. 'Want me to do anything?'

'Nope. Keep holding her still, and I'll file them quickly.'

It didn't take Holly long. At one point, Mandy appeared in the doorway, and Paolo held up his fingers to say 'five minutes', assuming Holly would find it easier to continue without Mandy around. Mandy had a tendency to fuss, and it might put Holly off her game. When they were done, Paolo motioned to a hovering Mandy to come in.

'She's been a star,' he said.

As if she was fluent in human, Freddie shifted herself back towards Paolo and gave a great grin. Paolo knew she was really just sniffing the air, but he liked to think she was simply very happy in his company.

'You will, however, need to have six-monthly checkups for them both. Donkey dentistry needs to be taken seriously. Keep an eye out for these signs . . .' Holly rattled off a list, as she packed her equipment away. 'You'll also need the farrier in regularly. Do you know one? If not, call the surgery — Chloe has a list of useful numbers. Otherwise, she seems very healthy. Can I check Winnie too, before we go?'

* * *

Twenty minutes later, Paolo and Holly were headed back towards the car, Paolo looking around him as they went. Mandy's farm was far more remote than Auchintraid, but somehow seemed cosier. It was the dinky stone cottage with flowers in window boxes, or Mandy's extensive vegetable patch which did it. The ever-growing collection of adorable animals probably helped too.

Auchintraid always seemed more lonely, windswept, and — in the depths of winter — harsh. He hoped that Chloe's meeting tomorrow with the architects went well. It was an ambitious project, and he feared that in moving over to the farm at the same time that building works had gotten under-way, she had bitten off more than she could chew.

Thank heavens for Skye, mucking in at the last minute. He chuckled to himself.

'Something funny?' asked Holly, giving him a look.

'Aye. Well, I was thinking how grateful we should be for Skye being at the surgery today, what with Chloe struggling with everything. And then I thought how last night I was cursing her very existence, thinking she and Hamish were together.'

'I did wonder if you'd lost the plot a bit,' said Holly. 'There was clearly never anything going on between them.'

Paolo gave an exaggerated sigh. 'Hindsight. The pinnacle of smuggery.'

Holly laughed. 'Yup. That it is. With hindsight, I would have hired a locum. And no I-told-you-sos, please.'

Paolo gave her a sympathetic look. 'God, when you're stuck in a hole, it's hard to know what to do, isn't it? Plus, even if you do, the fear of failure can hold you back.'

'But you live and you learn,' said Holly.

Paolo's most recent interactions with anyone he found remotely attractive flickered through his mind, and he wondered if they could be categorized as lessons rather than dumpster fires.

'Fail upwards,' agreed Paolo.

He had been hoping that with Fabien's arrival, such improvement might come his way. Not that he would tell Holly, or Chloe, or anyone else. They would all be shocked that Paolo had agreed to meet up with him.

* * *

Four hours later, Paolo was in the pub, enjoying a red wine. Holly, next to him was sipping a lime and soda, and Skye a G&T. Before they'd had a chance to dissect the day, Chloe came bounding in.

'I'm alive,' she said, breathlessly.

'Barely. You're wearing jogging bottoms,' said Paolo, his eyebrows raised.

'Nice to see you too, P,' she said, pulling over a spare stool from the next table. 'How was the rest of the day? And those rehydration sachets worked a treat, Skye. Thanks for the tip, not that I'll ever be drinking that much again.'

The three of them filled Chloe in on the day, and she, in turn, told them about her day spent on the farm: after her hangover subsided, she had a long talk with her mother-in-law about the building work and had — hopefully — cleared the air.

'So it wasn't an entirely wasted afternoon,' Chloe concluded. 'And you, Skye? Everything OK on reception?'

Skye nodded. 'I think so. Plenty of cute animals, no major mishaps, and the website's all sorted. All you need now is some news to put on it. Nice necklace, by the way.'

Paolo looked over at the three seed pearls on a gold chain which hung around Chloe's neck.

'Thanks!' Chloe replied. 'I got one for my sixteenth, one for my eighteenth and one for my twenty-first. Which was great, because before the third one arrived, I spent three years looking like I was wearing mouse testicles around my neck.'

'What a delightful image,' said Paolo. 'I got this for mine.' He held up his wrist and showed off an antique gold watch.

'Very nice. And more than I could ever dream of,' said Holly. 'I got a tenner each time to go to the pub.'

'All three times? The legal drinking age is eighteen!' said Chloe.

'Oh yes,' said Holly. 'What about you, Skye? What gifts did your parents bestow on you for the milestones?'

'Seeing as we undoubtedly all know about my turbulent teen years by now, I guess I can be honest and tell you they gave me some hefty advice about straightening myself out, plus funds to access when I was more responsible. Which I was eventually allowed when I was working for the law firm and needed it for a flat.'

'How are you feeling about going back to work, by the way?' Chloe asked.

Skye looked doubtful. 'So-so, although a case of Sunday-night blues is heading my way. Anyway. Let's talk about something positive. Paolo, now I'm no longer in the way of you and Hamish — not that I ever was — I want to say I think you'd be great together.'

Paolo looked at her. Skye clearly didn't know about Beauly Man. Hamish had been keeping it on the quiet. 'Och, well, that's kind of you to say.'

Skye continued vigorously. 'He's the nicest guy in the world. And you're not too bad either. You'd make a great couple.'

'Thanks,' he said again, not wanting to make it awkward.

He took his phone out of his pocket, and put it on the table. 'Can I get another round in?'

'Lemonade, please,' said Holly. 'God, I can't wait until I'm no longer permanently on call.'

Chloe snatched the phone up. 'Hold up. Paolo . . . have you been in touch with Fabien? Actively contacted him?'

Paolo felt his stomach sink. 'No. Why?'

'You ought to change your notification settings, you big fibber. It's here in front of my very eyes. Fabien's slid into your DMs — I *think* that's the correct phrase, isn't it?' Chloe flicked him a look of suspicion, then read from the screen. '*Weather on Saturday looking up. Perfect for spicy margs on the beach? x.* Paolo, why's that bastard saying that?'

The room had gone fuzzy. Paolo blinked, trying to bring everyone back into focus. He didn't want to tell them that there was a chance he still had a foothold in Fabien's heart, because they'd all refute that with gusto. Nor did he want to say that he felt compelled to take chances when they came his way, seeing as Hamish wasn't as available as everyone thought.

'Who's Fabien?' asked Skye.

'Paolo's ex. The only reason we vaguely tolerate him is because he's my landlord,' Holly answered. 'Anybody there, Paolo? What on earth is going on?'

'Fabien's the kind of guy with two phones,' Chloe explained further. 'Super-hot, but very bad news.'

'He liked my pictures from the other night,' said Paolo. He scratched his head. 'I'd liked one or two of his, recently. He said he was in town, I tested the water. It was boredom. And the obscene jealousy that Hamish seemed to be shacked up with Skye.'

228

'He's bad news. You can't see him, Paolo,' Chloe said, with a warning tone.

'But I can't not,' he replied. 'It would be impolite. He's in town for one weekend. He probably wants a catch-up.'

The excuses were coming out faster than he could stop them. True, he could see why they thought Fabien was bad news, as Chloe had put it. Heck, Fabien had barely arrived in Switzerland two years ago when he started posting photos of himself with a stream of attractive guys. Not that there was necessarily an overlap, but he had barely broken up with Paolo.

Perhaps Paolo ought to have moved on, and eliminated all thoughts of Fabien from his mind. But when a break-up wasn't on your terms, when you still wanted them long after you became nothing more to them than a fading memory, a little part of you could hold out hope for longer than was strictly sensible. Maybe Fabien had his reasons for moving on so fast. Long distance was a struggle, maybe Fabien was putting himself out there in an effort to get over Paolo.

And here Fabien was, back in Paolo's life and, nobody holding him back, other than his overly cautious friends. He wanted to see what Fabien had to say. You never knew what might happen. Even if Skye was no longer an obstacle standing between him and Hamish, there were others, Paolo's fear being the most glaring.

Chloe thrust her phone under Skye's nose, and he watched as Skye was scrolled through Fabien's social media posts, which Paolo knew were exclusively filtered and, without exception, depicted a life being lived to the full.

'He's devastatingly good looking,' Skye said. 'But it's a bit style over substance.'

'Like I say, two phones,' Chloe said, and folded her arms. 'At least. How he juggles all his dating apps I do not know. Bet he gets his secretary to do it.'

'It's very curated,' Holly pointed out, reading his thoughts. 'And don't tell me that's what gallerists do, Paolo.

Fabien might think himself an aesthete, but I'd say it applies mainly to his face rather than any deeper artistic instincts.'

'Ouch,' said Skye. 'That's painful.'

'Can we stop tearing the guy apart?' said Paolo. 'Only all the attacks on him are like proxy attacks on me.'

The comments were making his skin prickle, as was the situation in general.

'Fine,' Chloe said. 'Fabien is a lot of fun, I'll give you that. His thirtieth party was Boogie Nights-themed, and the glitter roller skates he arrived on were amazing. But you're way more fun than he is.'

'Yeah. Holly's party was incredible,' Skye chimed in. 'Easily the most stunning set-up of any I've attended. And the best cocktails.'

'Don't mention the cocktails,' Chloe said, closing her eyes. 'Delicious but deadly. Say no more.'

'Can we say no more about Fabien too, then?' Paolo snapped. 'Why shouldn't he have a second chance?'

He shoved his phone back in his pocket, his face burning somewhat under the three pairs of eyes suddenly staring at him.

'I'm off home, guys. I'm not in the mood.'

CHAPTER 32

By the time Skye arrived back at Glenalmond, she had missed supper. David and Moira tended to eat lightly in the evenings, and early too. Then they either went for walks, or watched soaps on television, a binary approach to activities that Skye imagined was good for their health.

She walked into the cavernous hallway and hung her jacket up in the cupboard — which itself was the size of the bedroom in her Edinburgh flat — and sighed.

Paolo had been in a right twist at the pub. The arrival of Fabien's message turned him into a completely different person. Having been able to discount his behaviour over the last couple of weeks, the misunderstanding over Hamish explaining it away, she was able to put him back in the pile of positive people, the type you ought to surround yourself with.

His reaction to the Fabien conversation had, therefore, come as a shock. Paolo had been on edge, reluctant to talk. And while he might have snapped at them, he'd done so with his shoulders hunched.

Footsteps sounded in the corridor, a heavy tread, accompanied by multiple, rapid thuds. Hamish and Wolfie. 'Hi, honeys, I'm home,' Skye called.

Not only had she failed to get Paolo and Hamish together, but her plan looked to be scuppered by Fabien's arrival.

Hamish emerged from the corridor. 'Heard your car pull up. How was work? I'm assuming the trip to the pub with everyone means you survived, and toughed it out with Paolo.'

'About that . . .' said Skye. 'We need to discuss.'

'I've got some pea soup and fresh sourdough in the kitchen. Come and tell me over that.'

While Skye batted away a nosy Wolfie, who was angling for a slice of bread, she explained the entire misunderstanding to Hamish — after Paolo had left, Holly had told her and Chloe about the guy from Beauly too.

'I know he's been dating, but he was into you. Still is. Properly,' Skye insisted. 'Really, Hamish, you should go for it.'

Hamish looked at the ceiling. 'I'm not that guy. I don't make moves. I'm not a Ham of action.'

Wolfie's ears pricked up at the mention of his favourite snack, and Skye patted his head. 'No, Wolfie. Honestly, he's got a special sensor. But, Hame, there's more . . .'

She told him about Fabien coming back, and watched as Hamish's face fell. Hamish dragged his hands down his cheeks and over his mouth.

He groaned. 'You know about him and Paolo?'

Skye recounted, word for defamatory word, what Holly and Chloe had said. And how this had upset Paolo. 'He seems to think there's still something there. And Fabien sounds like a real snake. You have to get there first, Hamish.'

Hamish didn't reply. He leaned down, and scratched Wolfie on the head. Experiencing a pang of anguish at Hamish's reluctance, Skye broke the remains of her sourdough in two, spread one half with butter, then shoved it into her mouth in frustration.

Hamish finally spoke. 'I think they need to sort things out first. If Paolo still has feelings for him, I don't want to go throwing myself in there. Fabien was always a bit flash for my liking, but he's dead charming. And I know Paolo was hung up on him for some time after Fabien left.'

'People move on!' said Skye, a pang of exasperation passing through her. 'I don't get it, Hame. You've said how well you get on with Paolo. I've seen it!'

'You know the reason, Skye! I've dated friends before,' said Hamish. 'And losing James was harder than losing anyone else. I'd lost a best friend too. I mourned that friendship for ages.'

'Oh.' Skye looked at the floor, embarrassed by the fact this hadn't occurred to her sooner. She raised her head, met his eyes, then reached over the table and put her hand on his. 'You're worried the same will happen with Paolo.'

Hamish's shoulders drooped. 'What I said before, it being a small town? I'd never escape him. You can't hide here. There's one pub, one café, and I'm at the bloody vets all the time. It would be excruciating.'

'Nothing ventured, nothing gained. It's a phrase you love to use. It could be some kind of wonderful, Hame.'

There was a pause. She stared Hamish out. He was arguing with himself, she could see that, chewing the inside of his cheek as he tried to reach a decision.

'If it worked, it would be. Och, Christ, Skye. Maybe it's like getting into the water at the pool. Every week, before I jump in, I have to close my eyes, hold my breath, and remind myself I'll survive. And I always do.' Hamish's voice was louder than before. 'Maybe I tell him.'

He stood up, and put both hands on the table, like a general about to go into battle. Skye punched the air, sharing his exhilaration. If you really liked someone, you should let nothing get in your way, not somebody else, or worse, your own fears.

'Yes! Tell him how you feel!' she said, matching his volume.

An automatic reflex then caused *her* to groan and put her head in her hands. Here she was, doling out advice which could be applied to her own situation as much as Hamish's.

'Is it that bad an idea?' Hamish asked. Skye looked up. 'Och, it's Bear. I've held off asking you about him but considering your return to Glenalmond last night, and refusal to talk, I'm guessing you're in some kind of Bear-related anguish.'

Skye rolled her eyes. 'We're talking about you, Hamish.'

'And now we're talking about you. We can return to me in a bit. Besides, you know I hate being centre of attention. Come on. You went to bed without telling me what happened.'

Skye told him about her epic meltdown the previous night. 'Not only did I reject his advances, which I would have liked to accept, but I didn't cover myself in glory doing it.'

'Yeah. You went a bit scorched earth there, didn't you.'

Skye managed a faint smile. 'Isn't it ironic that I've been trying to set you up, trying to encourage you to have a braver approach to relationships, and here I am, unable to start one with the man I think might be perfect for me.'

'Why do you think that is?' Hamish put his fingertips together.

Skye considered her answer. 'I've been lying to him the whole time. I might not be Hurricane Skye anymore, but I'm also not me. I'm a fraud. And as well as Bear, I've been lying to my friends, my family. God, I mean, about everything. I've still not told Mum and Dad that I'm here. They think I'm on holiday — I was meant to be on one right now. Not this one, obviously.'

'That I understand. We can't all be blessed with easy-going wonder-parents like mine. You can't choose your family, can you.'

You most definitely couldn't. How would her firebrand father react when she told him? Would he pull a verse from the Bible, or give her the silent treatment? Her mum would be upset Skye hadn't turned to them with her concerns, but Skye didn't want her mum to feel like she had to put on a happy face, search for words of comfort, or play the peacemaker. The guilt nicked at her synapses, making her head ache.

Skye let out a moan. It occurred to her that to sort all this trouble out, she had to go back to where it started.

'You know,' she said, 'I'm going to park the Bear thing. Seeing as I've irrevocably ballsed it up, I might as well. Instead, I think I need to talk to my parents. Try and get rid of this feeling I have that they always think I'm a massive failure. Or, if not, confirm that they think I'm said failure and move on. I ought to talk to them face to face.'

'Oh? Really?' Hamish raised an eyebrow.

'You sound, and look, very uncertain.'

Hamish had drawn back from the table, wearing a sceptical look that reached every last line on his forehead.

'You have an explosive relationship with your father. Not that I think it's a bad idea, but do you think going back to talk to them when you're at such a low ebb is a good one?'

'I doubt I can get any lower. Maybe I'll go tomorrow, after work. I think I can drive down in the evening, spend the night at my flat, and get back early Saturday morning and spend a last couple of days here with you, if that's OK.'

'More than OK. *Me casa es su casa*. Always.'

'Isn't that *me* castle *es su* castle?' Skye joked, faintly. 'Appreciate it though. I've always wanted one.'

She gave Hamish a hug, grateful that after she faced the challenge she had set herself, she would have somewhere to come back to, a place that felt far away, where she could cocoon herself for a few hours longer.

It was imperative she did this though. If she didn't like the person she was, how could she expect anyone else to like her?

235

CHAPTER 33

Skye drummed her fingers on the steering wheel. She had barely gone past the rocks on the side of the road that marked the boundary to Eastercraig, and already her nerves were beginning to fail her.

It was raining again. A couple of drops splattered on the windscreen, then it was as though someone had tipped an enormous bucket on top of the car, then filled it up and done it again.

Was this a sign?

'No, do *not* go down that route,' said Skye aloud. '*You* are responsible for all your choices, Skye. Don't go looking to the universe for advice.'

It wasn't a sign. It wasn't even a coincidence. If she had bothered to check the weather forecast, she would have known it was coming.

No, this was *not* an omen. Nothing was telling her to go back. It wasn't great, driving a car for three hours in these conditions, but she could do it. She had committed herself to this drive, and what lay at the end of it. No flaking.

Skye slowed into a tight bend, then slammed her foot on the brake as she came out of it. In front of her was a car, barely tucked in by the side of the road, its hazards flashing. She pulled up behind and, coat above her head, ran out into the rain to see if she could help.

Water immediately flooded her trainers, raindrops bouncing off the ground like rubber balls. Before she had got halfway she realized she knew who the car belonged to. A sinking feeling in her stomach started to spin the moral compass which had directed her to lend a hand. Still, no flaking.

'Bear? Bear!' She banged on the window, which was completely steamed up.

Bear wound down the window, frowned, and pointed to the phone he was holding up to his ear. He tilted his head to the other side, and Skye ran to the passenger door and hopped in.

'You can't get here any sooner?' he asked into the phone, pinching the bridge of his nose. There was a pause while the other person confirmed what was clearly bad news. 'In that case, I'll call back in a bit. I need to think what to do.'

He hung up, and looked at Skye. 'Hey,' he said, his face fixed.

Skye tried not to take his expression personally. He was stuck here, and the first person to turn up was her. She held up a cautious hand of friendship. 'Hi,' she said. 'Broken down? Sorry — stating the obvious is as much good as a chocolate teapot.'

Bear raised his eyes to the roof of his car. 'I was trying to get to Edinburgh,' he said.

Skye swivelled in her seat. '*I'm* going to Edinburgh,' she said.

It was a chance to make things right. This *was* a sign. Oh — no, she was done with all that, remember? But this one was ideal! It would be such a missed opportunity. Maybe, just maybe, you could pick and choose when you wanted signage to apply.

'You are?'

Skye nodded. 'If you like, I could drive you. We can push the car off the road a bit so it's not a danger, and I can let Hamish know it's here. Both sides of the road are part of the estate.'

'Really? You want to be in a car together. You don't think it might be a tad awkward?' His teeth were slightly gritted.

Skye drew her chin back. 'I guess yes, it *could* be awkward, but aside from it being a practical solution to your problem, there's an environmental argument for sharing a car, isn't there? And we can put the radio on the whole way. There's no pressure to utter a word. Although I'd prefer it if you didn't do any primal screaming, because I don't need the unexpected scares.'

Bear contemplated this, without smiling. 'I think I can live with that. Any other conditions?'

Skye shook her head. 'None.'

'Thanks. I appreciate it. And I'll pay you for petrol.'

'You don't have to do that.'

'Well, I'd like to.'

Skye sighed. 'We'll sort it out later. For now, shall we get this thing further off the road?'

'Fine, I'll push,' said Bear. He slammed the door behind him and stalked out into the rain, as she scabbled into the driver's seat and wondered if this was a good idea.

On the one, pessimistic hand, she was about to be stuck in the car with Bear Sinclair, who hated her guts so much he would like to feed them to the crows. His acceptance of the offer of a lift-share equalled three hours of the silent treatment, which the radio would struggle to mask.

On the other hand, which had its fingers tightly crossed, there was the chance to make things right between them.

She wound the window down, and stuck her head out. 'Are you ready?'

Bear was nearly hidden behind sheets of rain. 'Take off the handbrake, and I'll push on three. One, two, three.'

Skye hauled the steering wheel towards the verge, as if it was a juggernaut, rather than a tiny, old manual hatchback. The car juddered over the grass, the front wheel coming to rest in a hole — but it was well and truly off-road now. Skye jerked the gearstick back into neutral, and whacked the handbrake back on.

'I've got a pen in my handbag. Shall I leave a note?' Skye said, as Bear got back in next to her.

Bear nodded. He was soaked through, his light brown trousers now two shades darker thanks to the rain.

Broken down. Will collect later. Landowner informed.

Skye scribbled it all down on a page in her diary, tore it out, and placed the paper on the dashboard.

* * *

The snaking roads out of the Highlands could have been mistaken for rivers. Every so often they would go through a particularly deep patch of water. Skye had never aquaplaned before, there was a strong chance today was going to be the day.

She and Bear kept up an impressive silence for the first few miles. After about twenty minutes had passed though, Skye was beginning to feel discomfited by it. Her ears itched to hear something other than her own thoughts. She had got into a car with someone who didn't especially like her, to go and see her parents. Heck, she might as well go and see Will, make a day of it.

'Do you want the radio on?'

Skye asked the question as brightly as possible, giving a forced smile to add extra cheer to her voice.

'Sure,' Bear replied.

He reached down and turned it on and static fuzz erupted forth. He wound down the volume, pressing the buttons only to find crackly, interrupted stations.

'It's either the weather or the landscape,' he said. 'Signal's totally fouled up either way.'

Skye switched it off. 'Fine. Silence it is.'

Out of the corner of her eye, she sensed Bear's lip twitching. She snuck a glance at him, her eyes darting to his mouth. 'Are you smiling?'

Bear looked at her. 'No.'

She flicked him a look, before placing her eyes firmly back on the road in front.

'Then what's so funny?'

'You're regretting your decision to offer me a lift.'

'Psssh. I was doing what anyone else would do. So, what takes you back to Edinburgh?'

'The rain,' said Bear. 'A meeting I had at was cancelled, so I'm heading back to the city.'

'The one with the roofers? I heard about that,' Skye nodded. 'I was supposed to cover Chloe at the surgery this morning because she was going to be at it too. But she called first thing and told me not to worry cos she could work after all.

'Ah,' said Bear. 'Anyway, I thought I would go down to Edinburgh, drop into the office to do some paperwork.'

'Will your mum be there?'

Bear frowned. 'I imagine so.'

'You know you said you and your mum didn't get on at work from time to time? Does that ever make for an uncomfortable few hours at the table, when you have your Sunday lunches?' Skye asked.

'Yeah. There'll be a joint in the oven, neeps and tatties regardless of the season, which ought to be heaven. But the conversation is salted with unsubtle comments about how I ought to be powering on up through the company, and how she's given me a chance. It can be excruciating.'

Skye couldn't help herself. 'You know that theory about men going for women like their mothers? Do you reckon that's why you ended up with Georgia? You needed someone to nitpick, and push you about your lack of ambition? Something Oedipal embedded in your psyche.'

Bear didn't respond immediately, and Skye began to feel her face growing hot. She might win an award for insensitivity with that one. She was about to apologize when Bear let out a laugh. Not an enormous one — but it *was* a laugh.

'Yeah? Or perhaps *I* thought I had a lack of ambition,' said Bear. 'And I needed to find someone to push me.'

'Yeah, but there's a difference between encouraging someone to be the best person they can be, and shoving them into a box they don't want to be in.'

'Wise words.'

Skye smiled. 'Sometimes I manage to pull some out of the bag.'

Bear took a deep breath. 'Today's trip is also to visit the bank manager. I got a last-minute appointment, and I'm going to apply for a loan for my project. The full shebang. If they say yes, I'll have enough. I'll be one step closer to branching out.'

'Wow.' she gasped. 'If you've got all the cash, that really *is* the whole shebang.'

As far as Skye could tell, architecture suited Bear down to the ground. She didn't think she had seen anyone in their element as much as Bear wandering around the old blackhouse, establishing how it had been put together. His project had to be something to do with restoration work.

'You want to work on historic properties, right? You know more about old buildings than anyone I know.'

Bear laughed. 'How many people have you met who know anything about old buildings, other than what they've read in the guidebooks?'

'OK,' Skye admitted. 'It's not like it was a wide field. But still . . . You know all about old building techniques, and I think you've found the work at Auchintraid fascinating, even when it was difficult. You knew loads about the architectural style of Glenalmond too. I never managed to take you on a proper tour of the place. I wish I'd had the time — you'd have loved it. God, I'm going to miss you, Bear.'

As the words tumbled out of her mouth, she wished he would jump in and tell her he forgave her, and wanted her after all. Now would be the time, with the eleventh-hour vibes this journey had.

'Miss me? We're not going to see each other again?' asked Bear.

It wasn't the outpouring of emotion she had hoped for, but Skye thought she heard some disappointment in his voice as he said it. She tried to tally it with the tone of detachment that Bear had forced through a clenched jaw for much of the journey so far.

'I could understand why you wouldn't want to,' she said going for explanation. 'You must feel like I've led you up the garden path, around the houses — which, by the way are cruck-framed ones — and on a merry dance.'

'It's fine. You've got some stuff to sort out,' said Bear. He was cool once more. Skye felt a punch that they were so close, and yet so far away. 'Clearly.'

'Exactly,' said Skye. 'Which is why *I'm* going to Edinburgh.'

For some reason, this managed to kill the conversation entirely. Given the radio was still not functioning, silence reigned supreme.

After a while, they finally joined a larger road, one which was less prone to puddles so deep they might as well have been lochs. They drove along, still not exchanging any words, until Skye spotted a petrol station, and pulled in, swinging the wheel round like a rally driver.

'Wee and chocolate stop,' she explained, opening the door and leaping out.

And, more importantly, a chance to have time out from the oppressive atmosphere inside the car.

'I'll get the chocolate, shall I? Do you need me to pay for some fuel, too?' Bear got out and stretched his arms above his head. Skye looked away from the sliver of exposed taut stomach.

Skye shook her head. 'No, thanks. I've got a nearly full tank.'

They were underneath the awning, but the rain was coming in sideways as they ran towards the glass door of the main building.

Nipping to the loo, Skye sat down in the cubicle and tapped her feet on the floor. She closed her eyes. Sometimes you had so much you wanted to say, except you didn't know how to say it or seemed only capable of saying the wrong thing. She sighed. There was still a long way to go down to Edinburgh. She wished she had a delete button for some of the things she had already come out with.

She took a minute more than she needed to wash her hands, and to fluff her hair — the red roots were really showing now — before making her way back to the car.

Collapsing in her seat, she clicked the belt in, and put the key in the ignition. The windows were steamed up. She turned on the heat, and waited for the windscreen to clear. Bear, who had got back first, had bought a bag of chocolates and a collection of sweets, including the ones that came in tins with a dusting of icing sugar. She had forgotten about the snacks, given that she had not really needed them in the first place.

'You're sure you don't need to top up? Who knows when we might get to the next station,' he said, putting the tin under her nose.

'Are you mansplaining petrol to me?' she asked, more sharply than she intended.

'No,' said Bear levelly. 'I want to pay my way.'

'I was going to Edinburgh anyway, remember?'

Skye took a sweet and popped it in her mouth. Each interaction seemed to be more uncomfortable than the last, ending in an awkward silence. Everything Skye said was wrong.

'So, go on. What are you going back to do?' Bear asked, finally.

A question was an olive branch, of sorts, but Skye wasn't sure she trusted herself to speak articulately yet.

'You first,' she said, sensing his gaze on her. 'We never got to the bottom of it, did we.'

She wanted to be open with Bear, she did. But she wanted him to know he could be open with her too. Needed him to be.

'You can trust me,' she added, more quietly. 'I won't think it's stupid, whatever it is. I'm not a Georgia.'

'I know,' said Bear.

'And believe me, Hurricane Skye can top anything for shock value and sheer idiocy.'

Bear hesitated for a second, then spoke. 'You were right, earlier. My project . . . I want to start my own business. Architecture, still, but restoring older buildings. Either taking them back to their original states, or to make them more modern, but still in keeping.'

'The firm does that at the moment, though, doesn't it? You're doing that for the Dunbars.'

'As a favour. Dad and Greg Dunbar know each other somehow, and they talked about it, and the firm agreed to take it on. But it's not normally what they do, or where they do it. They're primarily into creating more modern buildings. It was also why I was in Portobello the other week; the Georgian building that could be a potential project. I was never looking at it for the firm, it was for my new venture.'

Skye looked over to him quickly, a wide smile across her face. 'Well, that's fantastic. You'd be brilliant at it.'

From the pictures he had sent of derelict and uncared for buildings, she knew how skilled he was at seeing potential in the most unlikely places. She wondered if it was a knack he might transfer to her, if she could find it in herself to tell him everything she had held back on.

'You think so?' said Bear.

'I know so. You're clearly passionate about it, and you've got an enviable portfolio. And that Georgian place over at Portobello in mind as a leaping off point. Would you set up alone, or with a team?'

'It would be just me to start off with. I've made enough contacts that I could get a team together for early projects. Eventually, though, I'd want there to be a few of us.'

She could hear the idea gaining momentum as he spoke about it.

'Why haven't you done this sooner? Or is that what you were saving up for?'

'Nail on head,' he said. 'I'm hoping it won't be too long before projects come in, but even though I'll hopefully have a loan from the bank, I need a float to see me through. I'll have notice to give, and it's daft to think that much'll get done over a Scottish winter. Plenty of building projects don't get going until the spring. It's only sensible to have a cushion.'

'You said Georgia didn't think you were ambitious enough, but this is *hugely* ambitious.'

'Ambitious, yes, but in terms of salary I wouldn't earn as much as I would in a bigger firm.'

'You'd have enough, though, right? To pay the mortgage and bills?'

'Aye,' Bear said. 'Enough to save each month, enjoy a meal out, and travel a bit. I'll never be a millionaire, but it's a decent salary, assuming it gets off the ground.'

'She was an idiot,' Skye said.

'Thanks,' said Bear. 'So's the guy who screwed you over.'

'You think so?'

'I know so,' he said, quietly.

He put a hand on her arm, and Skye felt goosebumps prickling up all over her body in response.

'Thanks.' Skye warmed a little, as if a tiny fire had been lit inside her. 'You know, I was sure I'd miss Will, that I'd spend my month in Eastercraig pining for him, weeping over my broken heart, but I barely gave him a second thought. Which, given he was cheating on me, is the best possible outcome.'

'It's good you feel that way. So, you had a whirlwind relationship that went bad. It's not the end of the world.' Bear sounded sanguine, as he removed his hand. 'I don't mean to belittle the experience, by the way. What I'm trying to say is that you're allowed to move on. But . . . I thought he was the reason you didn't want to come back the other night.'

Skye groaned inwardly. She had let Bear think it was Will who was holding her back.

'He wasn't the reason. Not really, though he was one of the latest in a line of terrible decisions I've made. I ought to

245

have known by now that it's best to pause before racing head-long into something. Fools rush in, after all.'

'What other terrible decisions have you made?' Bear asked. 'Only if you've stolen this car, that'll *really* impact your legal career.'

Skye gave a strangled laugh. If only he knew how close to home that comment was. 'It's mine, I promise.'

'Then what?'

How to tell Bear. It wasn't that she didn't want to. She did. If she was hoping for a last-minute reprieve for the two of them, this would scupper their chances. Blow them to smithereens. But if she was going to be honest about things, she had to take the plunge. An image of Bear yelling into the ether, the outlines sharp and clear, the colours bold and bright. He knew what it was like, struggling to navigate the world around him.

All the same, reluctance stuck its claws into her. 'If I tell you, you might think badly of me.'

Bear's voice dropped. 'Is this about when you were younger? I didn't have an easy time growing-up either, remember. If anyone could understand, it would be me.'

Skye recalled his stories and swallowed a bubble of shame. She had allowed the slightest sliver of a fear that he might judge her to catch hold. Still, little could compete with The Event To End All Events.

But she had to tell him. She owed it to them both to do so. If she couldn't tell Bear, she couldn't tell anyone. She had to be honest.

Bear waited, and Skye took a deep breath, and began.

'I was pretty wild as a teenager. Actually, that doesn't really do it justice. I was almost out-of-control. Some of the things I did . . . If I had a daughter who carried on the way I did, I'd have been pulling my hair out.

'It started when I moved school, to Lady Mary Sutherland's. My father was the headteacher, and he thought it would be best to keep me close. I'd already started doing things he didn't like, like sneaking out to parties and getting my eyebrow pierced.'

'That's hardly bad,' Bear said.

'And my belly button, and my nose.'

'Still not bad.'

'No. I didn't think so. And I still don't. But Dad was worried and he wanted more control. It completely backfired.

'Instead of making me more compliant, I hated that he'd dragged me away from my friends — who he thought were bad influences — and was trying to tell me who to be. Instead of miraculously becoming saintly, I threw it back in his face.'

'Being a teenage rebel is hardly shocking,' said Bear.

He didn't sound appalled, or shocked. But there was plenty more to confess. 'I was quite extreme. Sometimes I did things which I thought were important, but a lot of the time I was sticking two fingers up at Dad. Hurricane Skye was born out of a sense of self-righteousness.'

'Go on, then.'

Skye hadn't told anyone this much. Not any of her gap year or uni friends, or anyone on her law course, not the boyfriend she had before Will, not Will himself, not Houda. If written down, the list of misdemeanours could fill reams of paper.

'Why don't I give you my top three,' she said. 'Or we could be here forever.'

'Go for it,' said Bear. 'I promise I won't bat an eyelid.'

Skye hoped he was right, but she doubted it.

'I got a tattoo when I was fifteen, as a dare from my friend Janet, when we were skipping school. Fake ID, worked every time. An enormous long snake that coiled around my upper arm, over my shoulder and down to my ribcage. I had it removed during my gap year — which cost a bloody fortune. It wasn't really my thing.'

'Not so bad. I had one too,' said Bear. 'Georgia's name. Proof you're not the only one with regrettable body art. I had mine removed too.'

'Fist bump,' said Skye.

Bear obliged. Skye felt bolstered by the gesture of solidarity, but . . . She took a deep breath.

'One morning, Me and Janet leapt out of the window in the science block — ground floor, I should add — and with the spare keys I'd pinched from his bedside cabinet, we unlocked Dad's car. We managed to get it out of the car park, and then we drove from Edinburgh to Glasgow. Well, Janet drove, because her brother had taught her. We were going to a Greener Earth protest, and the trains were down. Oh, and she didn't have a licence, neither of us did. It was a hairy drive.'

Bear let out a low chuckle. 'Christ, Skye. That's wild. And kind-of ballsy.' His tone was lighter than she had expected.

Skye gulped. 'Yeah, well, that done, we drove back, and we were going to put the car right back to where it had been, only Janet crashed it into a bollard while getting het up about being caught. Hard. I got whiplash, we both had concussion from the airbags. The front of the car was ruined.'

'Jesus, Skye.' Bear could hardly hide his shock now.

'I got excluded for a week, as did Janet. There were talks with the police, and a social worker. But Dad didn't press charges, and it never went to court.'

'Your dad would never have done that, would he?'

'To teach me a lesson? And to demonstrate he was in control of his own family? He might well have done. I often wonder if he should have done.'

'You were OK in the end though?'

Skye nodded, explaining that after a week off school, most of which had been spent recovering from the concussion, she had been allowed to return.

She glanced at him and Bear gave a smile. 'Fine,' he said. 'So that's a bit worse. Props for ingenuity though.'

'Those infractions aside, I changed my hair colour by the week, which I was often sent home for. I had the multiple piercings — many of which Janet did with a safety pin — I wore outfits and makeup that made even my laid-back mum's hair stand on end. I'd go out all weekend, partying, causing trouble, only popping back for lunch.

'I began to loathe my father's principles. It all seemed so old-fashioned, so in league with the powers that be, so anti-progress. His values seemed to have come from the Bible — which was like contradictory fiction — and I'd read all manner of philosophy to rile him at the dinner table. Nietzsche was my hero.'

'Don't we all go through these stages?'

'Do we? Did you?'

Skye glanced over at Bear. He looked back at her expectantly, waiting for her to keep going. She hesitated for a second, because she knew that even if everyone did go through these stages, few people could hold a candle.

'Sometimes I felt like I was a warrior, like when I'd go on protests for things I really did believe in. I once disappeared for a whole weekend to join a march in London that I knew went against my father's own, very traditional, political beliefs; he's very conservative, small "c" and big "C", which is all in alignment with his very religious views. I sent my mum a text about it, but otherwise didn't see them until I rocked up on Sunday night. But it had been a cause I was passionate about. I had to fight the injustice that was everywhere I looked.'

Skye remembered the blood pumping through her veins, the excitement of standing up for what she believed in, standing shoulder to shoulder with thousands of other protesters.

'But that's great,' said Bear. 'You had purpose.'

'Occasionally. Other times I was playing games with my father, but I hardly cared. And it was exhausting, too. I had all this furious energy waiting to break out, but once it was spent I'd be left shattered. It's why I loved coming up to Eastercraig. No father to argue with, no mother to stress out. Nowhere to sneak out to other than the rocks, which Uncle Hugh encouraged anyway. I could still hold my beliefs, but there was no need to express them so . . .'

'Fervidly? When did you stop? When did Hurricane Skye become just Skye.'

It had taken a long time, and the mother of all incidents to make her realize she had to stop. The last of her top three. The Event To End All Events. Skye felt her insides clench as she recalled it.

'I went a step too far. Can we take a pause? I hate thinking about it.'

Bear put a hand on her shoulder, gave it a comforting squeeze.

'Then tell me what happened after it,' he suggested.

Honestly? The shock of The Event had been a wake-up call. Once she had left school, and left home, Skye thought she might be free of it all. This she told Bear, after crunching through another car sweet. She could leave the city and leave it all behind. Her mum had cried, and Skye struck an uneasy truce with her father, temping in an office to raise money before first joining a catering course for want of any better ideas, then going off and volunteering at a school in rural Argentina.

Far away from Edinburgh, she could be herself, be the girl she wanted to be. She read books, she hiked, she went to see sights she had on her list of places to go. Her one-year gap year became a two-year gap year, including another stint of volunteering at the school in Patagonia that she had loved so much, and by the time she got to uni, she wasn't Skye the teenage rebel with an almost-rap sheet, but a law undergrad on a mission to succeed. Then, after beating a hundred applicants to the job at Tilling and Browne — which she had never expected to get, and felt she would be a fool to refuse — she had been reborn as Skye Edmonds, the hard-working, positive joiner, a team-member who people liked to chat to in the kitchen.

'Look at you now,' said Bear. 'World at your feet. About to head back into the office, retake your exam and become the lawyer you want to be.'

Skye heaved a great breath. 'That's the problem, Bear. I'm not that person. I've become a corporate sell-out. All the raving, the partying, the general disobedience, I'm happy to have left that behind. But I've left behind my principles, my beliefs.'

'How do you mean?'

Skye thought back. The feeling she was in the wrong place would strike her from time to time, but rarely enough to put her off course from her well-paid job in a high-profile firm. She had all the trappings of success. Nobody who knew Skye from school could say she hadn't come out the other side of her stormy period, and left it well behind.

'From the outside, it looks like I made up for my mistakes. But I've gone and made a bigger one. I went from raging against the machine to greasing the cogs of it. My boyfriend, the one I broke up with, he would never have appealed to me once. And as I sat in the exam, thinking about how he betrayed me, I realized I'd betrayed myself.'

What was she doing, working for that firm, taking on those cases which made her question her choices? Ten years ago, she would have been appalled if she had known it was where she would end up.

'I was so idealistic back then. I thought I'd be helping solve hunger, or poverty, or climate change, and I'm miles from that now. And in the midst of sitting that paper, after learning the truth about Will, it all fell into place. I had a massive panic attack.'

Bear put a hand on her shoulder. 'I'm so sorry, Skye.'

She put her hand over her mouth for a second, recalling that moment almost a month ago. Bear reached over and took it, and held it in his own.

'So you see, I couldn't go back with you the other night.' Skye took her hand back and returned it to wheel as she turned a bend. 'I was in such a state, the anxiety coming for me. I was fretting about who I was, Hurricane Skye, and who I am now. And . . . I don't know who I am. It's why I'm going home. I have to talk to my parents. If I carry on like this, working in a job I don't believe in, I'm letting myself down. But if I quit

251

this theoretically amazing role at Tilling and Browne, I'll feel like I'm letting them down.'

Bear coughed, and she snuck a look, seeing that his eyes were on her. 'If it helps, *I* like who you are, even if you aren't clear on it.'

A laugh bubbled up, as her insides did pirouettes. 'Thanks. I thought I'd be more together by now. It's a bit embarrassing, really.'

'It shouldn't be. I've seen you during some of what might be considered un-together moments — crying on a bench with bird poo down your back. I didn't think any less of you for it, and probably liked you more. You saw me at a low point, the first time we met, and I like to think you haven't held it against me. Have you?'

Skye considered this. 'No,' she said. 'I probably like you more for that, too.'

'Good,' said Bear. 'Glad that's settled. And when you go back to work, go and have a wee word with HR.'

'You make it sound easy.'

'I don't mean to. I know it isn't. After I broke up with Georgia, I wasn't who I wanted to be. It's taken time and effort and some tricky choices — quitting my job included — to get to where I want to be. But none of that uncertainty ever made me a bad person. What you've just said? You're not one. And, Skye, your past doesn't define you either.'

Skye shot him a glance. 'You weren't horrified by my high jinks?'

'What do you want me to say? You're a wee scoundrel who deserves to be punished? You had a rough time, but you're obviously not a bad person.'

'You don't think so?'

She braked at a set of traffic lights, and Bear gave her a firm look. Skye searched his face for insincerity, but found none. Instead, all she could see was the faith he had in her. A wave of heat surged through her.

'No, not at all. You're kind and thoughtful, and supportive and positive and . . . Look — if this is you, thinking

252

you're a mess, for what's it's worth you're awesome. Maybe your rebellious streak was your superpower, and you never knew it . . .'

Bear tailed off. As she pulled away from the lights, Skye snuck a glimpse of him, noting his cheeks were pinkening. He'd seen her at what she considered her absolute worst. Well, almost worst. She hadn't managed to tell him about The Event To End All Events. But, that aside, her almost-worst was good enough.

'Thanks,' she said, a smile threatening to break out. 'It's nice to know you believe in me.'

Bear shrugged. 'I do. Have some confidence in yourself. You really ought to.'

It was true. The only thing holding her back was herself.

Inside, Skye's every cell was leaping. Bear was in her corner, and with him behind her, she was ready to go.

CHAPTER 34

Edinburgh always looked wonderful, even in the rain. The dark stone of the city, and the castle watching over it all from its seat in the centre, was never anything less than magical.

The last hour of the journey had passed rapidly, as they talked about Bear's business plan and Skye's nerves about her parents, stemming from her fractured relationship with her father. Now, her car chugged through the centre, and she enjoyed the scenic route they were taking. That conversation had returned to gentler topics probably contributed to the fact her fight-or-flight response was calming down. That, and once again feeling at one in Bear's company.

'It must have been amazing growing up in the middle of the city,' said Skye, who roughly knew her way through the one-way system towards the New Town. 'Although I imagined you guys in a glassy conceptual number out towards the Firth, with a pied-à-terre here.'

'Same,' said Bear. 'But they bought the house when I was a baby. It needed a lot of work and Mum wanted a project on maternity leave. I think they planned to sell, but the draw of the city proved too much.'

'You seem so at home in the countryside.'

'Aye, well, we did have a place by the water too. It's got quite a lot of glass.' Bear gave a sheepish smile.

'I *knew* it! I can see it now — all space and light. Bet it has soft-close kitchen cupboards too.' She gave him a light poke in the arm, and he gave one back.

She stopped at a zebra crossing, and turned to look at Bear, who was looking down, a smile on his face.

'Yeah. It's beautiful. I'd love to show it to you. I hate to brag, but it was nominated for a national award.'

'Best use of soft-close cupboards in a Scottish kitchen overlooking the Firth of Forth?'

'Something like that, though I think the use of light and space swung it.'

She gave another poke, and he gave her two more in return.

The people crossing the road reached the pavement, and Skye pulled away. She could sense Bear grinning, and she allowed herself a chuckle as he gave directions for the last mile. It felt like they were back to the way they were. No, better than that. It felt like the way they ought to be — happy together — and Skye's veins fizzed.

They pulled up in a Georgian crescent, the terraced houses tall and imposing. Skye, not immune to property porn when it presented itself, allowed herself to drool over the perfect proportions of the buildings.

'This is where I leave you,' she said.

'Are you going to be OK?' Bear put a hand on her shoulder, and Skye felt her body bend towards him.

'Is Iron Bru that colour naturally? It's doubtful, but there's a very slim chance.'

She pulled the key from the ignition, and looked over to the houses. She wondered if Bear's flat was in the one with the soft pink door. It reminded her of the colour of the bathroom walls in her own, tiny flat, which wasn't too far from here. She did miss it, even if there was plenty about the city that she hadn't pined for over the last month. If everything went wrong with her parents, she could drown her sorrows in a bar with Houda, then run back there, hole up for the rest of the night under her quilt, before heading back to Eastercraig on Saturday, for one last weekend.

Bear turned to her. 'Give me a ring if you want backup.' He sounded sincere.

'Likewise,' she replied.

Bear leaned over and kissed her on the cheek. Skye closed her eyes, wishing he'd gone an inch or two further to the left.

'And you'll call me to let me know it's all OK?'

'I'm going to have tea with my parents,' said Skye. 'I'm not going in for major surgery.'

That said, major surgery would be preferable. She felt a pang of guilt, knowing how messed up that was. Sure, not everyone had good relationships with family, but wasn't it what people aspired to? Close-knit, comforting, forgiving, phone-calling parents, perhaps a supportive sibling or cousin. Thank heavens she'd had Uncle Hugh.

'You're acting as if it is. You've been saying no to sweets for the last hour, like you're about to have anaesthetic.'

Skye swivelled in her seat, and looked straight at Bear, wanting to search his eyes for signs he was telling the truth as he answered her next question. 'Can I call you? Really? Even if it goes horribly wrong?'

He leaned back towards her, the proximity causing her breathing to turn shallow. 'Of course. If you need to. I'd like you to. Skye, did something else happen with you and your parents that you feel they'll never forgive you for? Or your dad, at least.'

Skye giggled, a maniacal one which brought a tear to one eye. Then the other. With a careful thumb Bear wiped a tear that had rolled down to her jaw. But if anyone was going to understand her, it was Bear, wasn't it? And if she was going to tell anyone about it, she wanted it to be him.

'This was the third thing I didn't get round to telling you earlier. The Event To End All Events.' There was a tremor in her voice. 'I didn't stop attending protests, even after the car incident. I just took the train instead, or hitched lifts with people I met through online noticeboards. My parents tried to keep a close watch on me, but I was well-versed in sneaking out and couldn't care less about the consequences. Anyway, at one protest, a huge one, I threw a brick through a window,' she said, half-laughing, half-weeping.

The thought of it sent waves of anxiety through her, trying to pull her under. As her heart began to pound, she wondered if she was about to have another panic attack.

'You what?'

'You heard me,' Skye wiped a tear from her cheek. 'It was an oil exploration company's building. It was bad, I knew it, but the energy in the protest was turning from peaceful to angry, and I got caught up in it. Other people were doing it too. A guy had the bricks in his backpack, and handed them out. So I took one and just hurled it at the building.

'With my brick, the window shattered completely. For a second it was electrifying. Then a young woman with a lanyard round her neck came out, a red mark on her cheek from being hit by the brick, blood all down her face, dripping on to her white shirt. She pulled a shard of glass from her wrist, which was also bleeding, and then fainted on the street in front of us. The exhilaration turned to horror. I was appalled at myself.

'I might have hated that company, but now I look back and realize how scary it must have been for people working there, especially that woman, and feel such shame for putting them through that.'

'Did you get charged?'

Skye hung her head. 'No. I was never caught. The police began to swarm. An older guy I was with was throwing things too, and took the blame; he said I was too young for a criminal record. I ran. The police asked for witnesses, though, and it was all over the news. But I never owned up. The guilt from it, and for him taking the rap, has followed me my whole life.

'I could have ended up going to court. Honestly. I should have done. The whole episode scared me out of my wits.'

'Does anyone else know?'

'My parents,' said Skye.

When she had got home that day, pale and shaking, she told her mum, then confessed to her father. He had gone white with anger, but said he wouldn't tell anyone, that the onus was on Skye to confess. She never had. Another rip in the already weak fabric of their relationship, and she hated that her parents had ended up complicit in this hideous secret, and the shame that came with it.

Skye wondered if she had gone too far, telling Bear all this. She felt her throat thicken, the air sticking as she breathed in.

'Do you think I'm a terrible person, now you've heard the whole story? Like a hurricane I tore up everything in my path, been literally destructive. Ever since, I've tried to shed any connection to this person who caused so much devastation.'

With dread, she turned in her seat to face Bear. He was looking into the footwell, focusing on a speck of dirt. Skye felt her stomach dip, but after a second he shook his head.

'No. I don't. Not at all. It was stupid, dangerous, reckless, but not premeditated. And you were a kid, Skye. Really, I kinda think you're brave to have told me.' He straightened up and looked her in the eye.

Skye exhaled. 'I'd understand if you'd rather I didn't call you when I'm done at my parents' place though. Not everyone wants to hang out with a someone who ought to have done time.'

'I'll take that risk,' said Bear. 'I'll answer.'

Skye threw her arms around Bear. He wrapped her in a hug, and pulled her closer towards him, and Skye buried her face in his shoulder, breathing in the woods-y pine smell of his jacket.

Bear didn't pull away, he only held her tighter against his chest.

'You're going to be OK,' he said, softly in her ear. 'You already are OK.'

'I'm not sure I am,' said Skye. 'I'm a royal mess.'

'Only you think that. Nobody else does. I don't.'

Skye pulled back and looked away, praying she could staunch the tears threatening to burst forth. It would be like a dam breaking. She would drown them both.

He rested his hand on her shoulder, patiently waiting for her to raise her eyes to meet — and then hold — his gaze. The sincerity, and the concern in his eyes. 'I'll talk to you later. I promise. If you promise to call me.'

'Promise,' whispered Skye.

CHAPTER 35

Did everyone have the tendency to make crazy decisions when they were frustrated? When your feelings were simmering away, and then the heat got turned up, the next stop was boiling point, wasn't it.

Neither Holly nor Chloe had brought up him storming out of the Anchor last night, and Paolo felt no burning desire to discuss it with either of them.

Hiding in the medicines cupboard, he read over the text Hamish had just sent him, feeling the strength which kept him standing ebbing away.

I'm so sorry. Can't do swimming. Tree weakened by storm has fallen down and need to prioritize getting it off the drive before the guests arrive — health and safety etc etc. Apologies again, H

That decided it. He might as well reply to the message from Fabien, which he had left unanswered up until that point.

It might be like inviting a vampire into your home, he thought, as he considered his response. Incredibly dangerous, but according to pop culture, also weirdly sexy.

Hi Fabien. Nice to hear from you. It would be lovely to meet up. Let me know when suits. P

He reread the message and immediately deleted it. He sounded so formal, so dour. That wasn't what Fabien liked. He liked flirty texts, full of innuendo and firm plans. Paolo paused — his thumbs hovering over the miniscule keyboard on the phone. Was his subconscious trying to steer him away by composing a reply that Fabien wouldn't be interested in?

And yet, he had to be decisive. Opportunities like this, ones where handsome men requested your company, didn't come your way every day. They didn't come Paolo's on a yearly basis.

I've got a bottle of tequila in the cupboard, crying out to be used.

Christ, that was no better. The subclause was a bit close to home, to be honest. He needed to seem more blasé to Fabien's appearance.

Sure. Can rustle up some more of my world famous margs. Meet you at Finnen at 7pm tomo? x

That was it. His heart gave a lurch as he watched the message disappear off into cyberspace. He shoved the phone deep into his pocket. On second thoughts, that was a terrible idea. He'd jump every time it buzzed against his leg, like a tiny taser of punishment. Instead, he popped it on the shelf, with the intention of only looking if he happened to be back getting drugs for any of the animals they had on the list for the rest of Friday afternoon.

'You look guilty,' said Chloe, looking up from behind the desk when he got back to reception. 'What have you been up to?'

'Nothing,' said Paolo, aware that he had slunk back into the room, eyes shifty.

'Come on,' said Holly, sticking her head out of the side room, then stepping out fully. 'Mrs Peters moved her appointment to next Monday. You've got ten minutes before the MacLewises arrive, I reckon.'

'You're here and all?' Paolo groaned, and went and stared out of the window, not wishing to look at either of them. 'Fine. I said I'd see Fabien. I want to feel wanted, is all. And Fabien wants me.'

'For—?' Chloe prompted.

'Not for anything serious.' Paolo cut across her before she could deliver a blow. 'I know. But it's nice feeling wanted. And I know he'll be here for a couple of days and then head back to Switzerland, but I don't think that matters. Please don't lay into me again.'

He leaned his forehead against the window, and breathed against it, a small circle of mist appearing in front of him, obscuring his view of the sea.

'It's OK for you two,' he continued. 'Loved up with someone to go home to at the end of the day. I don't have that. There is nobody there for me, and don't tell me Ginger counts, because he doesn't. A cat is not what I want for my happy ever after. I felt so drawn to Hamish, and he's off the cards. I think it might boost my confidence to see Fabien. A reminder that I'm not entirely undateable.'

He turned around to face his colleagues. Still in her chair behind reception, Chloe's eyebrows had merged with her hairline, and Holly looked like she was grinding her teeth, both hands on her hips. If he could choose who spoke first, he'd rather it was Chloe, who would happily mince her words so as not to offend.

'You were treated like rubbish by Fabien,' Chloe said. 'And now you're going to meet the guy for margaritas on the beach?'

So much for mincing her words.

'Maybe this is disappointing,' Paolo started.

'Disappointing?!' Holly cried. 'Try staggering! Come on, Paolo, you can do better than him. Tell him you've changed your mind.'

'It would be rude,' he replied. 'And, like I say, I want to see him. Chloe, anything else to add?'

Chloe shook her head. 'Don't think I've got the words, Paolo. Shall I make us all a cup of tea before Mr MacLewis comes? I know I could do with one. Oh, bummer, here he is already.'

Paolo plastered a smile on his face and held the door open to welcome Ivan MacLewis, the owner of the knitwear pop-up, who came in with his Scottish Terrier trotting obediently at his heels. He couldn't have arrived at a better time.

CHAPTER 36

Skye drove off down the road, simultaneously trying to recapture that heavenly scent of Bear's jacket and put him out of her mind. As she turned the corner on to the main road, she felt filled with strength from knowing that however badly it went, Bear would be there at the end of it. By the time she turned into her parents' street, however, this confidence had shrunk until it felt no larger than a pea.

She pulled into a space not far along from her parents' terraced house, which was unusual. A lucky omen, perhaps? She parked, then paused keys in hand, turned on the radio, and let herself disappear into the presenters' cheerful chatter for ten minutes. Finally preparing to get out, she checked her phone. A single message.

Bear. Her heart leapt.

Good luck, Skye. Not that you need it.

Skye tapped a reply.

I didn't go in yet. You at the bank?

The response came straight away.

Not yet. It's in an hour. Still at home. I made myself some soup, and now preparing.

Followed swiftly by another:

Have you been sat outside in your car the whole time?

Skye laughed.

You got me. I'll call you in a bit. Promise x

You'll be great x

Then, summoning up courage, she got out of the car.

She hadn't even thought about whether or not her parents would be home. They might have both retired, but they were out of the house most days. Her father spent a lot of time at the church, and her mum volunteered with community projects. Or they could be out enjoying lunch, or on a walk.

Pausing on the front step, Skye hesitated as she held the knocker up. Then, steeling herself, she let it drop, holding her breath as she awaited an answer.

Footsteps moved along the hallway — her mum's — and the door swung open.

'Skye! What on earth are you doing here? Aren't you meant to be on holiday?' Despite her surprise, her mum smiled, the creases around her eyes wrinkling up.

Skye made a face. 'I was, but now I'm not. Are you busy? Have I caught you at a bad time?'

'No, darling. I'm making a cake, and your dad's out weeding the garden. Come on in.'

Skye took her shoes off, and followed her mum down the corridor, into the kitchen. It had the same yellow cupboards that had been there since childhood. She was aware that most people would find such nostalgia comforting, but all she could remember was staring at those cupboard as she sat at the kitchen table waiting to be told off.

Her mum put the kettle on, and Skye stuck her head out of the side door, raised her hand in a half wave.

'Hi, Dad,' she said, in the hesitant way she always did.

Perhaps it was because it had been his job, but whenever she saw him, she felt like a child being pulled into the headmaster's office. Which had been understandable, in his real office at school, years ago, but she shouldn't still be

265

approaching every space he occupied with tentative steps and small gestures.

Her father looked up from where he was battling dandelions. 'Hello,' he said, gruffly. 'We weren't expecting you.'

'It's OK that I'm here though, right? You're not *too* busy, are you?'

'I was gardening. But it can wait, if you need to see us.'

The cool response was typical of her father, but Skye had come to expect it.

'I do, actually,' said Skye, as firmly as she could.

'Tea's ready,' said her mum, beside her. 'Shall we take it in here, or the sitting room, or the garden?'

'I'm planning to keep going out here,' said her father. 'Bring it out.'

'I thought we could sit,' said Skye. 'In the sitting room. All of us?'

The sitting room was closest to the front door. One of the first rules of staying safe was knowing your exits in case of a fire. Thank you Tilling and Browne corporate safety briefing for that one. This conversation had the potential to be incendiary.

Her father let out an audible huff, but threw down his gloves all the same. Skye and her mum made their way to the sitting room, and Skye sat on the armchair. She felt it gave her an air of gravitas that she wouldn't be able to manage if she being sucked in by the chintzy quicksand of the sofa cushions next to her mum. Her father appeared a minute later, wearing his indoor slippers and drying his hands.

'Now what's all this about, love?' her mum asked, gently.

'Do I need a reason to come over?' said Skye.

She had immediately gone on the defensive, a knee-jerk reaction. Her father didn't reply. As per usual, it was her mum.

'Of course not. But I know that look. It's a look I recognize.'

'From me?'

'From anyone,' her mum said, calmly.

Her mum had a soothing voice, which she applied like a balm.

'I've not been at work for the last month.' Skye dived in. 'Not just because I had booked annual leave, either. It was mainly because I ruined my chances with my exam.'

She told them about Will, about how she had thought she loved him and how he had let her down. About the light bulb moment that had made her realize that she was in the wrong place. About the sensation like a boa constrictor wrapping itself around her body and refusing to let go. How she had got up without completing the paper and walked out of the exam room.

'I thought I had got to where I needed to be, but it turns out I still can't get life right,' she said. 'I had a full-blown panic attack outside the exam centre. However hard I try, I'm still that fuck-up. I always will be.'

Her father's reaction was conspicuous in its absence. Not a flinch or a frown, not even at the swear word.

Her mum lifted eyebrows but quickly regained her usual composure and took a deep breath.

'Why do you think you're a . . . I can't use the f-word, sorry,' said her mum. 'You feel free to, though, we're all grown-ups.'

'I don't feel like one though. I'm back here on the sofa, at home, telling my parents I've ballsed it all up again.'

'What do you mean, *again*?' said her mum.

Skye pushed herself into the back of the armchair for support.

'I always make a mess of everything.'

'Well, that's simply not true,' said her father, his deep low voice cutting the air between them.

Skye felt her eyes widen, and she turned to him. He had his hands on his knees, presumably to prevent them balling into fists.

'I know *you* don't think that for a start,' she said.

Their eyes met. Skye knew she couldn't realistically conduct this conversation with her mum alone but still, it made her nerves twitch when her father weighed in. Yes, he had said something positive, but there was no telling when he'd switch to gruffness and suppressed anger.

'It's not, though. Yes, you went through a very difficult phase as a teenager, and yes, I struggled to accept it, but you emerged the other side,' he said.

'You've never felt that, though. I've always been a disappointment. I permanently blotted my copybook with you, and I get why you'd never forgive me. But I've spent the rest of my life trying to be a better person. Only I've ended up in the wrong place.'

Skye unpicked the decisions she had made after she had left university, which had resulted in her ending up at Tilling and Browne. 'I wanted so badly to show you that I was no longer the disaster I was as a teenager. Wanted to show myself, too. I know I caused a lot of damage, and I wanted you to be proud of me. I didn't think words would be enough, not after so many broken promises that I'd never step out of line again. I knew had to earn your trust, because I never thought you'd completely have faith in me again, especially after . . .'

She stopped, not wanting to talk about the brick. They never talked about the brick. Much like politics and finance, there were some topics best avoided.

'It all lined up perfectly: I could go into law, use my degree, do a job that mattered, become financially independent — comfortable, even — making all of us happy. When I was offered the job at Tilling and Browne, I thought I should take it.' Skye paused to catch her breath. 'If I could show you I was a good person, everything would be OK between us.'

'I have often wondered if your career choices were about that,' said her mum. 'Trying to appease your father and me.'

Them, and her conscience.

'But Skye, we knew it wasn't you,' her father interrupted.

Skye felt knots form in her stomach, her heart, her throat. Would you be able to tell if your kidneys were tying themselves together?

'You knew what wasn't me?' she whispered, after swallowing a gulp.

There was a pause, before her father spoke.

'The job,' he said. 'I'm not saying you're not capable of it. You could put your mind to anything you want and succeed. You proved as much when you got all those top marks in your Highers having barely spent any time in a classroom.'

Skye goggled. 'Why didn't you ever tell me this? I thought you thought I was a total screw-up.'

Her father shifted, looking surprised. 'It seemed better to let bygones be bygones. I thought you were keen to forget it, but maybe I was wrong. Then, before I knew it, you'd flown the nest. And when you came back to Edinburgh, you were ready to take on the world.'

'But work? You thought Tilling and Browne wasn't the best place for me?'

'We were surprised you chose to go there, but it's not for us to tell you what to do. Not anymore. And not that you ever listened when we tried.' He chuckled. 'Your mother and I had our suspicions, but any decisions about your career ought to come from you. Anyway, you were always terrible for reverse psychology. If we told you not to go out, you'd shin down the drainpipe. If we'd told you we didn't think a big, corporate job was for you, you would have certainly taken it.'

'Why exactly don't you want to work there?' Her mum asked the question Skye had spent the last four weeks trying to answer.

Skye looked at them. 'I spent all my youth trying to stick it to The Man, and now I am The Man. And . . . I was in a relationship with a man who was The Man. I'm doing myself an injustice.

'I work for this huge company, fighting cases I hate. A lot of the time I think I'm on the wrong side. I hate working for greenwashers, and businesses who don't treat their employees fairly, or who are involved in things that, well, that I'm bound by a confidentiality clause not to discuss.

'I've become the person I never wanted to be.'

There was a silence. Skye's tea had cooled, a milky film formed on the top. She drank it anyway, gulping it indelicately.

She looked from her father to her mum. Her mum looked as zen as ever, her expression entirely neutral. Unexpectedly, her father also appeared calm.

'I'm sorry,' said Skye. 'That I pushed the boundaries too far when I was younger. Way too far.'

'And I'm sorry that I didn't know what to do with you. All the growing-up stuff was beyond me,' her father replied.

'Can we take a second to reflect on the fact you were a head teacher? Growing-up stuff was high up the job description.'

'Aye, but it's different with your own flesh and blood, somehow. And sometimes I didn't know what to do with you either, Skye,' said her mum. 'And I thought after all my experience as a school nurse I'd seen it all. But it doesn't matter now, does it?'

Her mum looked to her father and raised her eyebrows.

He shook his head. 'Not at all.'

Skye felt tears prickling her eyes.

'Want fresh one?' Mum got up and took the cup, slipping out of the room before Skye had a chance to answer.

Skye looked at her father, taking him in. His face seemed to have changed over the course of the conversation, his skin more lined, his hair receding, he seemed slightly jowlier despite his otherwise slim build, cuddlier. The stern look had softened.

'I really am sorry, you know, for being the source of so much grief. I always thought I knew best, but I didn't then, like I don't now.'

Her father swatted her confession away. 'Teenagers are hardwired to rebel, and it takes all manner of forms. One might slam a door, another might take up smoking, others might play truant and graffiti the nearest underpass. Or all of the above.'

Skye felt herself blanch. 'Did you know about *everything*?'

Her father's eyebrows pulled together. 'I highly doubt it, and I probably don't want to either. No need to give me a coronary.' They relaxed again. 'Even *I* tried to show my parents

I knew better, many years ago. I remember telling my mother I refused to sing in the church choir. She was most upset, but I hated the itchy ruffs we had to wear. And the thought I might not hit a high note. Then my voice broke, and it was the last straw.'

'Not quite the same level, Dad,' said Skye, and they shared a smile.

A creak on the floorboards outside the room made her look up. There was nobody in the doorway, but the receding footsteps of her mum disappeared back up the corridor.

'All I'm trying to say is that you were not the first teenager to rebel, or last,' he said.

'You didn't hate me?'

The words flew from her mouth. All this talk of the past, and fears that normally skulked at the far back of her mind had surged to the front, vying to get out.

'No, of course I didn't hate you. Like our saviour, I preach and practise forgiveness, however challenging it might be. As I was saying, you're also not the first or last fully grown adult to wind up in the wrong job. And you won't be the first or last to change direction. Have you had any thoughts on what you'll do about it?'

The few ideas Skye had were still swirling around in her brain, like a galaxy in its infancy. She heaved a sigh. 'I've a few thoughts, but I don't want to risk getting it wrong again.'

'Now . . .' Her father paused. 'You might not want to take advice from a man with whom you haven't always seen eye to eye, but I'm going to give it anyway. You can take it or leave it. But we all make mistakes and what shows our mettle is how we deal with them. You might get it wrong again, but if you do, it's not the end of the world. And for what it's worth, I think you'll be fine, whatever happens. Though I won't insult you by suggesting I say a prayer for you at church, because I know how you feel about religion.'

'Well,' said Skye, scarcely able to believe this turn of events, 'it can't do any harm, can it?'

One side of her father's mouth twitched. 'Certainly not. Should I call in your mother? She is the bringer of sage advice.'

'If you like. But I think I've had the sensible advice from you.' Skye finally smiled.

'We all make mistakes. We just have to make them right. Proverbs twenty-eight, thirteen.'

'Remind me of that one?'

'*He who covers his sins will not prosper, but whoever confesses and forsakes them will have mercy.*'

Once, Skye would have rolled her eyes at her father's recital of chapter and verse. She kept her mouth shut though. Her father was entitled to his opinion.

'Our father forgives,' she said, unable to help herself.

'Thankfully, yes. Don't tell your mother, but I've just uprooted one of her favourite peonies.' Her father chuckled. 'Hopefully she forgives too.'

They were still laughing as her mum shuffled back into the room with a tray.

'I've got some more tea. It took me a really long time to make it,' said her mum. 'I got distracted by something in the kitchen and then realized time had passed. Are you wanting to stay for a late lunch, darling? I was going to do sausages for dinner but we can have them now.'

'Thanks, but I think I might head back to Eastercraig.'

'Back to Eastercraig? You've been there all this time?' Her mum's eyes widened for a second, as she passed Skye a fresh brew. 'But Hugh's on a cruise! Where on earth have you been staying?'

'Glenalmond mostly.' Skye took a sip of the tea.

A dreamy look crossed her mum's face. 'That beautiful castle? Oh, you always did like it there. And that nice boy, Hamish. How's he getting on? I'm guessing he's a man now.'

'He is, but aside from that he hasn't changed a bit,' Skye replied. She told them all about the estate and what they'd been up to.

'I'll tell you all about the rest when I get back,' she said, ten minutes later. 'There's something else I need to do.'

She still needed to fix things between Hamish and Paolo. Skye bid her parents goodbye. This time, her father gripped her in a tight embrace. She couldn't remember the last time he had held her like that.

Sitting outside in the car, Skye pulled out her phone, and read her messages.

There was one from Hamish:

When are you back? I'm assuming you're here this weekend and you didn't just ghost me x

Nothing from Bear, but he would be either on his way to the bank, or in his meeting. Though he might be already done there.

She picked up the phone, her heart in her mouth, and dialled him, hoping he was free.

'Skye,' came a relieved tone. 'I was beginning to worry about you.'

Play it smooth, Edmonds. 'You were beginning to worry about me?'

The question flew out with such delight she cringed.

Bear's voice reassured. 'Yes. It was a big thing, going and talking to your parents like that. Did it go OK?'

'Yes, and allayed some fears, and got everything out in the open. It really helped.'

That was the trouble with emotional baggage. You had to work out where you could unpack it all, and stow it safely when you had sorted through it. Today she had properly made some headway.

'Sounds great,' said Bear.

Skye smiled. 'It was. I'm heading back to Eastercraig now. Do you want me to pick you up?'

Bear took a sharp breath, and there was a pause. It shouldn't have taken any time at all, given all it required was a simple yes or no answer.

'I'd say yes, but actually, something's come up,' he said. 'Sorry, I'll be down here longer than I thought.'

'I can wait.'

'No. No, it's fine.' His voice sounded cooler, detached. 'You go ahead. I'll be in touch.'

They said goodbye, and Skye dropped the phone on to the passenger seat. She repeated his words, considered his tone. Why had he been hesitant, sounded uncertain? Was the thought of being in a car with Skye for another three hours so unappealing?

Or . . . Skye thought about everything she had confessed on the drive down. She groaned.

He hadn't changed his mind about a ride home. He had changed his mind about her. He'd have had a chance to think about all she'd told him. What man in his right mind would want anything to do with her?

Ice ran through her veins as she recalled telling him about the giant tattoo, the car theft, the brick. Sure, those things took place years ago, but she was still the human embodiment of a red flag.

CHAPTER 37

Skye drove down Princes Street, still trying to shake the last words she had exchanged with Bear. A song she liked came on and she sang along, the distraction a relief, and before she realized, she was going past the salad bar she went to in her lunchbreak.

She was a stone's throw from her office.

It was as if Skye had been struck by a bolt of lightning. All thoughts of Bear left her, as an electric feeling of clarity came over her. She knew what she had to do, and she felt supercharged. Why put off until tomorrow — or Monday — what you could do today?

Swinging into the underground car park, she rolled down the ramp and reversed into the first space she could find, glad her car was small enough to fit next to the SUVs and Range Rovers that otherwise populated it.

She walked past them, recognizing Will's black-windowed SUV, all the better for hiding clandestine activity. Skye shuddered.

Jogging up the ramp, she rounded the corner, and stood and stared at the glass building in which for the last few years she had spent most of her waking hours.

The last time she was here, Skye had been cursing her idiocy, about to run away. She had worried that she would feel sick at the prospect of standing there once more, but it wasn't as daunting as it had been in her imagination.

'Skye? It is you!' came a voice. Skye looked round. It was Tanya Green. 'You look completely different when you're not in a suit. Even your face seems more relaxed. And is that your natural colour peeking out there? It's gorgeous.'

Skye looked at her outfit. She was in scruffy jeans, a white tank, and a cardi that she had worn three days running, and all her ear piercings. And her hair — she'd forgotten about her hair — the red escaping at the parting.

'It is,' Skye said. 'Me. Skye. In the flesh. Right here before your very eyes.'

Having intended to go into the office, Tanya's appearance on the pavement had put her off her game, and she cursed her babbling. Tanya, to her credit, didn't blink. *So as not to wreck her false lashes.* Skye chided herself for that — Tanya *had* given her a month off.

'Thinking of popping in?' Tanya asked. 'On your last day of freedom?'

Skye nodded. 'I was planning to see if you were free. I stopped by on the off-chance.'

Tanya raised an eyebrow. 'You've caught me on my lunch break. Why not come with me? I'm going to get a panini. Have you eaten?'

Skye's stomach gave an audible rumble. 'I'm fine.'

'Not sure your belly agrees,' said Tanya. 'I'm off to Moretti's. Do you ever go there?'

'Sometimes,' said Skye. 'There, or to the salad bar, or I bring in leftovers.'

'Well done, you,' said Tanya. 'I barely have the time to make supper, let alone think ahead to making my own lunch. You, however, are the kind of person who is organized, who gets things done. It's why you're such a great fit at the firm. I'm looking forward to having you back in on Monday.'

'About that . . .'

Tanya grabbed Skye's arm, a desperate look across her face. She then let go with a contemplative, this-could-be-construed-badly look. Instead, she rounded on Skye and held her hands up, and Skye knew she was about to pre-empt her confession, beg her to stay.

'You're brilliant at what you do. I know you had a bit of a panic at the end of last month — I'd figured as much — but that doesn't define you, you know that? And, Skye . . . Considering you only did half a paper, you did incredibly. Jamie MacKenzie, one of the senior partners, said he'd never seen such skill. He also said it was a damn fine shame you didn't complete it, but still. You don't have to re-sit. Might not have been flying colours, but you passed.'

Skye couldn't find the words. 'You're kidding. But—'

Tanya shook her head. 'I am not a kidder. Come on. Let's go into Moretti's. Whatever it is you're about to say, I get the sense that it's better if I'm not hangry.'

Tanya marched around the corner, Skye almost jogging to keep up. They stepped into the tiny café, and Tanya said, 'The usual, please, Giovanni.' Skye ordered a breakfast sandwich, then Tanya steered her to one of the aged Formica tables at the back. On the way, she picked them each a cup of water from a tray on the counter.

They sat, and Tanya banged the cups down on the table, water slopping over the sides. 'Out with it, then.'

This was the Tanya she knew and loved, sharp tongued and one-track minded. It was oddly comforting.

Skye took a sip of water to steady herself.

'I don't think I'm right for Tilling and Browne,' she said.

'Is this about Will Tomlinson?'

Skye almost spat out her mouthful. Had she been the subject of office gossip? Had somebody spotted her and Will out together and reported them?

Skye swallowed. 'Can I check, is everything I say here confidential? *Totally* off-record, if that's possible.'

'Of course.' Tanya narrowed her eyes. 'Go on . . .'

Skye proceeded to tell her about Will. About the relationship and how he had told her not to report the relationship until they were entirely ready, and how he had been seeing someone else too. That Will was the catalyst for her skipping town.

'How did you find out about it?'

A waiter plonked two plates down in front of them, both their choices accompanied by a handful of crisps and a tomato garnish.

Tanya picked up her panini and took a bite. She chewed rapidly and swallowed, before dabbing her mouth with a paper serviette. 'He came to see me.'

Skye felt the air depart her lungs as she slumped over. 'The bastard.'

Tanya looked at her. 'It's something I wanted to address when you're back on Monday, but I might as well give you a heads up. He alleges that you came on to him . . .'

Skye's eyes widened, her back straightening as if an invisible string had pulled her upright. 'He what?'

'Let me finish. Now this is strictly off the record, but he came into my office to speak with me. Norah was next door, but she could still hear everything. After he left, Norah said she overheard him ask you out, after the Christmas party.'

'That's true,' said Skye, her nerves in tatters. 'He asked me out.'

'Norah said he asked her out two years ago. She said no, because she felt that working in HR and dating a staff member was a recipe for disaster. Which of course it would be.'

'Oh.' Skye felt herself redden.

'Eat your sandwich, Skye. It'll be revolting when it's congealed.'

Skye obeyed and took a nibble of her sandwich, praying she didn't bring it back up.

'I called him back into my office,' Tanya continued. 'And had another off-the-record conversation with him. If you don't want to pursue it, he won't either. Are you sure it's finished?'

'Oh, I'm very much done with him,' said Skye, with a burst of catharsis that made her muscles relax. Now for the hard part.

'The other thing, Tanya. I'm going to hand in my notice on Monday.'

Skye's eyes filled with tears as she said it. It was a universal truth that making the right decision wasn't always easy, but you hoped you could do it without turning on the waterworks. Tilling and Browne had taken her on, believed in her. And here was Tanya, who Skye had considered a dragon not to be prodded, taking her for lunch and offering an ear.

Tanya let out a sigh and put her panini down. She closed her eyes as she finished the mouthful she had just taken. Then she looked at Skye and gave her a hint of a smile.

'It was at the back of my mind, when I offered you that time off — and this, by the way, will make a complete mockery of my staff wellbeing scheme — but I've feared this moment might come.' She sounded tired, rather than angry.

'Really?' asked Skye. She blinked and wiped her cheeks with the cuff of her cardigan.

'Last year, there was a meeting on the Gordon case. I tucked my head around the door, and I could see you looking at the client, fighting to keep a look of disgust from your face. But your eyes were burning.'

'He was revolting.' Skye shuddered at the memory of the man.

'I'm not at liberty to comment,' said Tanya.

'How did you know? I didn't think I was that easy to read.'

'I do my job because I find people fascinating. I love all the personalities in the firm, most of them at least, and take joy in working out what everyone's like. Not to blow my own trumpet, but I'm bloody good at it too.' Tanya winked at her. 'Although you managed to keep the Will business very under

279

the radar. Had I known, I'd have warned you off him.' She picked up her panini, and took a large mouthful.

'I feel guilty letting you down. Especially after you gave me this time off, although I think the scheme is a fantastic idea for wellbeing. In all, it's been a difficult decision to make,' said Skye. Tanya looked unconvinced. 'Fine. It wasn't that hard. But it'll be a wrench. The firm has taught me so much and could have taught me so much more. It's opened up all kinds of doors.'

'And set you up financially,' said Tanya.

'Sure. But it would have been ill-gotten, in some cases. For me, anyway. I couldn't go on working on briefs that had me sitting at my desk trying to find a way to recuse myself from them.'

Tanya nodded. Skye took a proper bite of her sandwich. Amazingly, the egg hadn't set, and the yolk spilled out, satisfyingly soaking the floury bap.

'What'll you do next?' asked Tanya.

Skye put the sandwich down and gave the ideas that had tried to take hold space to grow. 'I'm going to look at charities and NGOs looking for legal counsel. I've got the right experience, and I'd go in at junior level.'

She would also, she thought, go to the nearest police station and confess to throwing the brick all those years ago. Do the right thing and hope for the best, and put it to bed once and for all.

Tanya nodded. 'It will pain me to do so, but I'll write you an excellent reference. I'll be sad to see you go, as will a lot of the staff.'

'Thanks, Tanya. That's really kind of you.' Skye's words were heartfelt. 'An irony, but maybe I should feel grateful to Will for setting off the whole train of events that made me realize '

'If I was you, I'd not thank him for anything,' Tanya interrupted.

Skye laughed.

'Well,' sighed Tanya. 'In that case, on Monday morning, why don't you come to my office. I don't need a long letter of resignation. A short one will do.'

Skye nodded. Maybe she wasn't going to have those Sunday night blues after all.

* * *

Skye's phone buzzed, an alert coming up over the top of the satnav. Houda. She ignored it. Seconds later, it buzzed again. Chloe. She could tell the text was in all caps, but didn't dare look any more closely. She was back to the hairpin bends.

'Zaza, read text messages,' she said, taking a second to marvel at the technology.

A robotic voice came in over the car's speaker.

You cow! You came by the office and you didn't tell me. Tanya said she saw you and that you looked wonderful. Call me. Miss you. H x

Skye smiled. She was looking forward to catching Houda up with all her news. She waited as the phone read the next message.

PAOLO IS GOING TO MEET UP WITH FABIEN. WE NEED TO SORT SOMETHING. HELP! C xxx.

Skye's ears almost stung from the alarm ringing in her brain. She had intended to sort out Hamish and Paolo as soon as she had returned from the city. All other thoughts — including those of a particular architect — left her head.

'Zaza. Put Hamish on speaker. This is urgent.'

281

CHAPTER 38

The rain had finally subsided, and as Paolo locked up the surgery, he was grateful for it. If he was going to have a good time with Fabien tomorrow, he wanted the sun out, so they could be over at Finnen beach, enjoying those margaritas against the perfect backdrop.

However, no matter how many times he told himself he was looking forward to seeing Fabien, Paolo had felt doubt drip through his body ever since he'd suggested meeting on the beach. Maybe he was forcing it, this idea of potential bliss. Fabian had, Paolo reminded himself, been a little toxic on occasion. Perhaps he ought to call it all off.

He walked back to the flat, the scales in his mind refusing to balance. Kneeling on the bench outside their building, and fiddling with her window boxes, was Mrs Brown.

'Flowers are looking pretty,' he said, admiring the box which overflowed with colour.

'You need a spiller, a filler and a thriller,' she replied, pulling out some dead leaves. 'Talking of thrillers, how was Patrick?'

'Och, I never bothered,' said Paolo.

Mrs Brown stood up, arms folded.

'Now, Paolo, I won't see you left on the shelf. Do you need me to intervene?'

'No,' said Paolo, fearing what form that intervention might take. 'Mrs B, when you met Mr B, how did you know he was the one?'

Mrs Brown had been married to her husband for forty years. Until he died of a stroke three years ago, they had been a famously devoted pair of lovebirds, according to Chloe. If anyone had the recipe for success, it was her.

'I felt so utterly happy with him. He made even the darkest day seem bearable. You know, *I* proposed to *him*. He was a shy man. I did most of the talking, and it only seemed right. Why do you ask?' Mrs Brown narrowed his eyes. 'Is there somebody you have in mind?'

He thought back to Fabien, their time together. He forced himself to be brutally honest. Fabien's refusal to fully commit, the fights, the texts that went unanswered, that feeling of angst as Paolo wondered what he had done wrong. He remembered running his fears by Chloe, who would try to be sympathetic, even though she must have thought he was mad to be trying to keep the relationship going.

Then he considered Hamish, quiet, pensive, rational. Who — when Paolo wasn't fretting about them — made Paolo feel like his own skin fitted perfectly. He was the type of man, as Mrs Brown had put it, who could make the darkest days seem bearable.

'I do,' said Paolo. 'I've got to make a call, Mrs B. Hold on.'

He made to reach into his pocket to call Hamish. He was going to make a date with him. A real one. But before his fingers touched it, his mobile started to vibrate against his leg.

Paolo felt his heart sink into his stomach. What if it was Fabien? If it was, he'd let it go to voicemail, sort it out later.

He looked at the screen. *Hamish?* Paolo gulped and picked up.

CHAPTER 39

Were it not for the debris from the storm scattered across the tarmac as she entered Eastercraig, Skye could have been forgiven for thinking it had been another blissful summer's day at the seaside. The sun was happy in a cloudless sky, as if it had never been away.

Locals were sitting outside the Anchor, or walking up and down the front, catching some rays. Some underage-looking teenagers were on the rocks drinking from bottles that looked suspiciously alcoholic. At least they weren't chucking bricks through windows, Skye thought, as she pulled into a space on the front.

She jumped out and jogged down the slipway, on to the harbour beach, and made her way towards a couple of large rocks that sprang from the sand, where Holly, Chloe and Paolo were nursing drinks.

'Got you a gin and tonic,' said Chloe, holding out a glass. 'Hope that's OK. We decided whatever's going on might call for it.'

Skye took it. 'Thanks. I'm beginning to wonder what kind of event we've turned up for.'

She had called Hamish to warn him of Paolo's intention to meet Fabien, and to gee him up, and after a few seconds of silent contemplation, Hamish had told Skye to meet him at the beach near the Anchor. He would handle the rest. She was completely in the dark.

She craned her neck round to face Paolo. He was tapping his foot, clutching his glass. He caught Skye's eye and gave a small smile.

'He didn't say? He cancelled our usual lesson at the pool earlier, then he called me and explicitly said I'm not needed in the water this week but to come here. I'm a little anxious,' he said. 'He can manage a length of the pool, but this? He said he's going to swim from here to the Anchor!'

'It's not that far,' said Skye. 'Three hundred metres?'

'Not for you, but for Hamish it's massive,' said Chloe. She sounded as concerned as she looked. 'When I say Hamish can't swim, I mean . . . He's like a boulder, with arms and legs which he can't coordinate.'

Holly, who had twisted round to watch out for Hamish, pointed over to the footpath that ran along the front. 'Look, here he is. He's got a float, at least. Not that it's deep when the tide's half out.'

Hamish, his face set, was walking towards them, in a red-and-black wetsuit, a large orange safety float under one arm. He swung himself over the railings, jumped off the wall and strode over, then jammed the float upright in the sand, and stood with his hands on his hips.

'I thought you had a tree come down,' said Paolo. 'And guests arriving.'

'Aye. I did, but the tree's sorted. Even so, I have limited time in which to do this. I have an absurdly large party at the castle, who need serving dinner at the hunting lodge at eight.' He frowned.

Skye looked at her watch. 'It's coming up to six, Hamish! You're cutting it fine.'

'But I need to do this. And I need to have a word with you, Paolo if that's OK. About what's going to happen.'

Paolo raised an eyebrow, and went over to Hamish. Skye watched the two of them walk down to the water's edge, then stand side by side, a good foot between them.

'Why does he have to do this?' Chloe mused, taking a sip of her drink. 'Couldn't he tell Paolo he liked him and be done with it? Why does he have to give this whole display of machismo? Hamish has never been one for peacocking.'

'When you told me that Paolo was going to meet Fabien, I called Hamish straightaway. I've met guys like Fabien,' Skye replied. 'They should come with a health warning. And I've been trying to get them together but only made things worse. I told Hamish he needed to be honest. To say what he wanted and go for it. This is what he came up with . . . I just wish I'd known how bad his swimming was.'

* * *

Down by the water, Paolo thought that the twelve inches between them was more like a yard, if not two. Hamish had been talking about technique, and whether the float might be held on to if his arms got tired and he had to switch to legs only.

'I've not even thought about cramp,' Hamish muttered. 'But I don't plan on being above shoulder height. It's not like last year, either. The sea is calm, there are no rainclouds visible, and I left Wolfie at home so he wouldn't attract any seals.'

Paolo pulled a hand down his face, feeling his cheeks stretch, then turned to Hamish.

'I'm glad to support you in this, but . . . could you tell me exactly why you're doing it? Why you think it's a good idea?'

Hamish dragged his fingers through his unruly mop of hair, and made a small coughing sound. He shifted slightly. Paolo folded his arms.

'Skye told me you were going to meet up with Fabien this weekend,' said Hamish, rushing the words. 'And you're well within your rights to do so, but I don't think you should. He's a real piece of work, Paolo. He might stamp all over you in his Italian leather shoes and think nothing of it.'

'Aye,' said Paolo. 'He might.'

'And,' Hamish continued. 'I think I'd like to be the one you met up with instead. Although I'm working tomorrow, and Sunday's meant to be mizzling and I have a coach party coming then too. But I'd be free Sunday evening. What I'm saying is . . .'

Paolo felt his jaw drop, as he digested this. 'Why haven't you said this before? And why didn't Skye tell me this the other day, when we were in the pub? She said she thought we'd be a good couple, but not that you actually liked me.'

'Skye promised me she wouldn't explicitly say anything. And besides, you two didn't seem on best terms for a couple of weeks, and then latterly I don't think she wanted to interfere, especially after spritz-gate.'

'But what about Beauly Man?'

'Who's *that*?'

'The guy I saw you with the other week. On a date?'

'Och.' Hamish went cerise. 'You saw me? It doesn't sound brilliant, but I was seeing what dating men was like again. To make sure. I didn't want you to be my test case.'

'Christ,' said Paolo.

Hamish looked uncomfortable. 'Only, when Fabien became a very real prospect, Skye thought she ought to step in again, hence her ringing me earlier. And I realized I didn't want you to meet up with him, only for Fabien to be serious. He might have decided he wanted to settle down.'

'Fabien? Unlikely,' scoffed Paolo. 'You know, I don't think I really wanted to meet up with him. I cancelled it.'

Right before Hamish had called, Paolo had decided that if he wanted to be with the right person, he had to act like it. There was no wiggle room, no margin for regrettable errors. As soon as Hamish had hung up, he had called Fabien and told him gently that he didn't think margs on the beach was a good idea after all.

'I wanted to come and see you too,' Paolo added. 'Ask if you wanted to spend more time together than an hour a week at the leisure centre pool.'

'I like swimming,' protested Hamish. 'And I really want to improve. Not that I could get any worse. But spending more time together sounds great.'

'In that case . . .' Paolo paused, pushing his feet into the sand, trying to drive away the incipient nerves that he could feel creeping in. 'Want to hang out more? Not only at the pool? Not only as friends?'

'Yeah,' said Hamish. 'I'd like that. A lot.'

Paolo laughed, feeling a lightness flood his body. Knowing Hamish wasn't the kind for public displays of emotion, he leaned over, and gave Hamish a sideways nudge on the shoulder. Hamish returned it immediately.

Then, Hamish leaned in, and gave Paolo a kiss on the cheek. It wasn't tentative, but firm and confident, and Paolo was momentarily stunned.

'Oh my!' he managed.

'Too much?' asked Hamish.

'Not at all,' said Paolo, blinking slowly as he processed what had just happened. He felt a smile break out across his face as he turned and caught Hamish's eye. 'Just right.'

Somehow managing to stop beaming for a second, he kissed Hamish back. Knowing how big a step this public display of affection was for Hamish, he didn't go for a passionate snog, rather a tender kiss that landed close to his mouth. Close enough to make it clear what Hamish meant to him.

'Glad we got that cleared up,' Hamish said, slightly pink in the cheeks but smiling.

Paolo, only just realizing his heart was racing like the clappers, nodded fervently in agreement. 'Same. Now, are you going in, or what?'

CHAPTER 40

Skye whooped as Hamish ran into the water. She, Holly and Chloe left their seats on the rock, and ran the short distance to Paolo at the shore, all squealing and hugging him tightly in celebration of the moment they had just witnessed.

After the excitement died down a bit, Holly looked concerned. 'Is this a sensible idea? Could you not have just left it with the kiss?'

'Nope,' said Paolo. 'There was no stopping him.'

'I have a lifeguarding qualification,' said Skye. 'Well, had, from when I was nineteen. So while it's not valid any more, I can remember most of it.'

She dragged her eyes away from the sight of Hamish floundering into the bay. He was getting deeper, the water past his torso.

Holly raised an eyebrow. 'It's better than nothing, isn't it.'

There were many romantic places in the world — Paris, New York and even Finnen Beach — but the harbour, while wondering if your friend was about to drown himself attempting an ill-advised, if well-intentioned athletic feat wasn't necessarily one of them. She turned back to the water. Hamish appeared to have stalled.

'Oh gosh,' Skye said, wishing he could chivvy himself along a bit.

Hamish disappeared beneath the surface. His head emerged for a second, and then went back again.

'Hamish!' Chloe squealed. 'He's tangled up in the bloody float rope.'

'I'm fine,' Hamish yelled, his arms flailing as he attempted to tread water.

There was a brief pause, while they all watched Hamish bob up and down. It was no good. Skye couldn't watch him flap about. What if something serious happened? The whole reason for this swimming malarkey was that he'd nearly died the previous year.

Skye pulled off her trainers. 'I'll get him, I think.'

'No, it should be me,' said Paolo, quickly. 'Knight in shining armour and all that.'

Skye watched as Paolo took off his shoes and trousers, then ran into the water in his T-shirt and boxers.

'Crikey', said Chloe. 'This is more nail-biting than any box set I've watched all year.'

'I'll say,' said Holly, chewing her lip.

Paolo was chest height in water when he got to Hamish, by which point Hamish had righted himself.

Hamish spat out a mouthful of water. 'I'm OK,' he shouted, so that everyone on the shore could hear him. He blinked salt from his eyes, and pulled his hair from his face.

Skye watched as Paolo offered Hamish an arm for balance, which Hamish took as he wriggled his legs free from the float. Together they walked back through the water to the beach.

'You looked like you were struggling,' Skye said, when they got closer. 'Why's the cord on this float so long? They're meant to bob next to your waist.'

Hamish looked sheepish. 'I didn't have one, so I borrowed the one from the bottom of the lawns. We've always kept one there in case anyone fell into the river.'

'Good grief, Hamish,' Skye looked at him. 'Seriously?'

Hamish set his jaw. 'Right. You hold this. I'll continue. Paolo, maybe you could come in too. Follow at a slight distance in case?'

Hamish thrust the float Skye's way and, once in water that was only up to his hips, he started off again. Paolo waded along, five metres behind. In the end, Hamish swam about a hundred metres, with confidence, if not finesse. And the odd pause.

Eventually, he came to a full halt and stood up, his skin blotched with red spots of cold.

'Voila! I'm done! I think I've proved my point.' Hamish shouted.

Skye watched as Paolo went over and took Hamish's hand, gripped it, and raised it into the air in victory. It wasn't just a win for Hamish's sporting ability, she thought. It was one for love, too. Along with Holly and Chloe, she joined in with a round of applause.

All wide smiles, talking quietly to one another, Paolo and Hamish walked back towards the beach to a flurry of cheers from the group. As they reached the shallows, Paolo jogged over to the rocks and picked up a towel for Hamish.

'Well, Hame? How do you feel?' asked Holly.

Hamish stood in a power stance, the water lapping at his ankles. 'I feel like a champ,' he announced.

'You are,' said Skye, going and giving him a hug.

'He's a bloody idiot,' Paolo said fondly, and Skye stepped aside as he wrapped the towel around Hamish's shoulders.

'Drinks at the Anchor?' suggested Chloe. 'We ought to raise a glass to this momentous moment.'

'Och, it took longer than I'd planned, and I really ought to get back to Glenalmond,' Hamish said, looking disappointed at the thought. 'I've got that group there. And I still need to sort out the lodge for this dinner.'

'Why don't I come with you?' said Paolo. 'If you're behind, I can muck in. Come back and dry off in my flat quickly first?'

'And I can spare a couple of hours before Angus gets back. Supper's in the fridge and only needs reheating,' Chloe piped up. 'I'll come and help set up too.'

'Same,' said Holly. 'Assuming nobody calls. Hot drinks all round?'

'I'm in too,' said Skye, pulling her trainers back on. 'Let's do this.'

* * *

Five minutes later, Skye jogged over to Paolo who was walking towards her carrying a caddy of take-out cups from the café.

He handed a cup to Skye. 'Latte, wasn't it?'

Skye thanked him, and they walked the remaining distance to Paolo's flat together. A flock of razorbills squabbled through the air, landing in a cluster on the sea. You would never have guessed that the placid scene before them had, barely ten minutes ago, been the location of an absurd romantic gesture.

'I still can't believe he did that,' said Paolo, another laugh escaping him.

'The swim or the kiss?' asked Skye.

'Both,' Paolo smiled.

'Well, you know what they say,' said Skye. 'The course of true love never did run smooth. But now you've got a happy ever after to enjoy.'

'Aye,' said Paolo. 'But Hamish. Honestly, that man. Still can't barely swim, and off he goes into the sea. What a twazzock.'

Skye snorted. 'Well, goes to show that you can't help who you fall for. And that when it happens, instead of performing a high-risk stunt, you could simply tell the person how you feel.'

Skye halted, the coffee sloshing over the top of the cup. Paolo, a couple of steps ahead, realized she was no longer next to him and turned around.

'Forgotten how to walk, is it?'

Rooted to the spot, Skye shook her head. 'No. What I just said, about not being able to help who you fall for and telling them. I went down to Edinburgh with Bear, and . . . I thought he might come back up here with me, but he didn't. Paolo, I need to talk to him. I need to go.'

It had been a day of facing up to everything in her life which terrified her. She couldn't not tell Bear how she felt about him, even if the idea of doing so scared her to death.

Paolo tilted his head. 'Could you not call him?'

Skye shook her head. 'I have to see him in person.'

Paolo looked from one of his hands to the other, and let out a dismayed huff. 'If I wasn't holding my own coffee in one hand and this wretched, flimsy caddy in the other, I'd shake you. Haven't we just established that it's far simpler to use words than deeds?'

Skye took his point. 'OK, OK. I'll ring him.'

Juggling her bag and her coffee, she located her mobile, and dialled Bear's number. It went straight to voicemail. It was with a pang of yearning that she listened to his voice.

'No answer. And this *is* a sign,' she said. That habit was proving one which refused to budge. 'I have to go back.'

Skye had to. She had spent the entire day facing up to fears, settling scores, taking her life back into her own hands. Her sense of what was right and wrong might have landed her in trouble when she was younger, but perhaps, too, it *had* been her superpower. She had been fearless, and strong, and determined. And Bear had been the first person to see that.

Paolo rolled his eyes. 'For crying out loud.'

CHAPTER 41

The sun had chosen to only bless the coast with its rays. About twenty minutes inland, clouds had gathered and the skies were gunmetal grey and threatening. Above the grizzling radio, there was a deep rumble of thunder that echoed about the peaks and glens of the Highlands.

'Zaza, call Bear Sinclair,' said Skye.

'Cannot find Bear Sinclair,' came the monotone response.

'Oh! Idiot!' Skye slapped her forehead. 'Angry-handsome Man. I mean, Zaza, call Angry-handsome Man.'

If any of this went to plan, she was going to have to change his name in her contacts list.

The phone took a second to connect, but again, went straight to voicemail.

'Zaza, hang up,' Skye commanded.

She pulled a sweet from the glove compartment, wondering what she wanted to say to Bear. She pictured his face, his piercing blue eyes, and wondered if she would have to say anything at all. Maybe he knew how she felt all along. There was a thread between them, and over the last month it had tightened and tightened. For Skye, it was if all that time they had existed in the universe for one another, their finding one another pure kismet. Until that afternoon.

She recalled his tone, and bit her lip, asking herself if this was stupid.

'No,' she told herself. 'And even if he does say no, you've done the right thing. Not hidden away.'

A plop of rain hit the windscreen, then another. Skye glanced up. A flash of sheet lightning lit up the skies. Thirty seconds later, heavy drops started to rebound off the windscreen, the road ahead disappearing.

She slowed, clunking the gearstick back down. Driving in the city rarely stressed her out — you could only pick up so much speed, and when the weather was bad, you were never going far, the streets tidy and familiar, and straight.

Out here, though, there were surprising turns, hairpin bends. Concentration was key, even when the scenery tried to steal your gaze from the tarmac, especially in conditions like this.

Skye crossed a small bridge over the burn which ran through the Glenalmond estate, not far from where she and Bear had abandoned his car earlier that day.

'Zaza, call Angry-handsome Man,' she said, glancing over at the abandoned red hatchback as she passed.

Again, no answer. Skye growled in frustration.

She leaned forwards, trying to work out what was in front of her, the windscreen wipers struggling to keep up with the volume of water coming down. The visibility was down to zero. Driving in the pelting rain was feeling less safe by the second, and Skye's knuckles were white as they gripped the steering wheel. It would be sensible to pull over, but she didn't want to stop.

From around the corner, a car appeared, making her jump. It occurred to her that it was the first one she had seen since the downpour began. Most people would have decided it was a fool's errand, coming out in this.

Her phone buzzed. She could hardly take her eyes off the road, but she flicked them to the screen for a second. *Bear!*

'Zaza, pick up. Answer,' Skye said, quickly.

'I'm sorry. I didn't get that. Please try again.'

'Zaza, answer the bloody phone. Answer.' She heard her voice go up a pitch.

'Would you like me to accept the call?'

How could such a clever machine be so utterly useless? She had known pencils with more intelligence than Zaza.

'For crying out loud. Yes! Accept call!'

She practically shouted the last words, and there was a click as the connection was made. Skye inhaled sharply.

'Skye? Are you OK? You've been calling me.'

'Bear! I'm coming to see you. I couldn't get hold of you. I'm driving back to Edinburgh.'

Bear's voice faded, then reappeared. 'I missed all of that. Think it's my signal.'

It was hers. Between the storm and the mountains of the Highlands, she was surprised the phone had connected at all.

'I'm coming down to Edinburgh. I need to see you. I . . .'

She didn't have a chance to say any more.

Skye's eyes widened as she came out of the next bend. Ahead of her, a deer lay in the road, its fawn standing next to it. She swerved to miss it, the wheels losing contact with the ground below. The car skimmed across the water, spinning around at a right angle to the road.

In that brief instance, she couldn't remember what to do. Did you steer into it, or was that ice?

Time became very slow as she skated towards the edge of the road. She barely dared look and see what was next to her. Best case would be flat land, but there could be a ditch, or worse. Skye closed her eyes. And then slammed on the brakes.

With a series of bumps, the car ground to a halt. Skye's heart was pounding so fast she thought it might burst.

She stayed where she was, rigid in the seat, the seatbelt digging into her neck. Her eyes were still screwed up tightly. Despite knowing she was upright, she didn't dare open them.

'Skye? Skye? Are you there? What the hell was that noise?'

Bear! He was still on the line.

'What noise?'

'The squealing? Are you OK?'

The brakes. She hadn't registered them making a sound. 'Bear. You're there. I'm fine. I'm just . . .'

Skye opened her eyes, wound down her window and peered out of the window. Rain hit her face, splattering the door and the dash. The car had come to rest on a patch of grass, the front bumper crumpled up against a fence post. Beyond it was a field, which soared up into a high peak. The other side of the road was a cluster of pines. A couple of horses were padding over to say hello, there was nobody else in sight.

'Skye?' Bear sounded concerned.

'I've come off the road. I was about to hit a deer, and . . .' She turned the key in the ignition. The engine made a yowling sound, then died away. She tried again. 'Now my car's stuck. I'm what, half an hour from Eastercraig, somewhere.'

'I'm coming to get you,' said Bear.

'But you're in Edinburgh? I'm fine, really. I'll call road-side assistance, and then ring to get help from Hamish.'

'No. Skye, I'm on my way now. I've just passed the garage outside Kirkmuir. I'll be there in ten minutes.'

'What? You're where?'

'Stay in the car, Skye—' The phone cut out. 'I'll be there in '

Bear fell off the line. Skye reached out to take her mobile from the holder, only to find herself pinned to the seat by her seatbelt. Her neck felt sore. She unplugged the belt, leaned forwards and dialled again. She had no desire to employ Zaza again today.

Nothing. Bear must have disappeared into another signal dead zone. If he was where he had said, he wouldn't be long.

Skye grabbed her coat, and ran into the storm, back up to where the deer had been. Her legs felt as though her bones had been replaced by jelly, but she needed to know if the deer was dead, if the fawn was OK.

As she got closer, rain dripping off her nose, she realized it was breathing. She crouched down low over the deer. Its chest rose and fell rapidly, its body struggling with invisible wounds. There wasn't, as far as Skye could see, blood on the road.

She stood up, and squinted through the rain for the fawn. It was nowhere to be seen. Terrified by her car, it must have darted into the trees.

She got her phone, relieved this spot had signal, and called Hamish. The Glenalmond estate was so vast, it might sprawl this far. If not, he would know whose land it was. The first time, the phone went through to voicemail, but on the second attempt, Hamish picked up. Skye shuddered with relief.

'Skye? Aren't you on your way to Edinburgh?'

'I was, but I swerved to avoid a deer. I came off the road, and my car won't start. But Hame, there's an injured doe here, and her fawn has run into some trees. I'm somewhere past the turning to Ben Hendry, roughly ten minutes from Kirkmuir.' Skye wiped rain from her face.

'Stay put. Holly's still here, and she and I and Paolo will come out. And Chloe too. We're pretty much done, and Mum and Dad can hold the fort until I'm back.'

As they hung up, the heavens were lit up by another flash of lightning, silhouetting the towering peaks. A round of furious thunder rolled through the valley.

'You poor thing,' Skye whispered, getting back down on her haunches. 'Hold on, OK? You've got a little one to care for.'

Hardly audible above the roar of the storm, Skye heard a car. She looked up, and waved her arms, hoping that whoever it was wouldn't hit them. It pulled over by the side of the road, a swanky navy hybrid.

The window wound down, and Bear stuck his head out. Skye's heart leapt. She used a hand to beckon him over.

'What the heck are you doing? Get here now,' he yelled.

Skye frowned. 'I can't,' she cried. 'She's injured.'

'The storm is directly overhead, Skye. There's one cluster of trees. You're at risk of getting struck.'

A bolt of panic that felt as if she had been zapped by a stun gun hit her. Skye hadn't considered this.

She looked at the doe. 'Help's on its way,' she said.

Skye ran to the car. Bear opened the passenger door, and Skye threw herself in.

'I didn't think,' she gasped. With her sleeve, she tried to dry her face, but her cardigan was wet through.

The mountains were illuminated by another flash, accompanied by more thunder. Bear switched the headlights on, making sure other cars couldn't miss seeing the deer.

Bear looked at her, face full of concern. 'Come on, take that off, and grab a blanket. I'll turn the heating on. Oh, Skye, you're bleeding.'

Skye looked at him. 'What? Where?'

She raised a hand to her head, felt around, then examined her fingers.

'Where your seat belt was,' said Bear.

Skye wriggled out of her cardigan, and Bear took it and chucked it onto the back seat, then pulled a cashmere blanket through to the front. As she wrapped it around her shoulders, Bear produced a handkerchief from his pocket, another of his grandmother's, and held it gently to her neck.

'It's not too bad,' he said, quietly.

He was very close, and she could hear his voice reverberate through her body. It was making her pulse dance.

'Is this your mum's car?' said Skye, her eyes alighting on the cream leather interior, taking in how immaculate the vehicle was. 'From what you said she isn't going to be thrilled that I've dumped half a gallon of water over the upholstery.'

She was putting off the conversation she needed to have, she knew it but couldn't stop herself. She wanted to prolong the moment when she knew it really was all over between them, before it had even started.

'Aye,' said Bear. 'And aye, she'll be underwhelmed when I return it to her. Skye . . . I need to tell you something.'

It was time. The last truth had to out, and she couldn't put it off any longer. Whatever Bear was going to say, she needed to let him know how she felt. Skye swivelled round in her seat, and pulled her knees up under the blanket.

'Me first, please. Look, Bear, I told you everything about me, and perhaps it made you think twice, but I was driving back to tell you how much I like you. The last month has been amazing, and I can't handle the thought of never seeing you again.'

He didn't reply. Skye felt her blood zing around her veins as her fight-or-flight urge started to kick in. She closed her eyes, scared to look at him, terrified she had said too much and that she had misread the pull between them.

'Skye?' Bear sounded sincere. 'Skye?'

She opened her eyes and looked right at him. His face was set, those bright eyes waiting for hers to meet them.

'In that case . . .' he said, in a low voice. 'That makes two of us.'

Skye let out a gasp of shocked relief, a half-laugh, but Bear wore a serious expression and continued. 'I will warn you, however, as of this afternoon, I'm a guy without a current situation, but I *do* have prospects.'.'

'As if that matters,' said Skye, wanting to tell him her news. 'Because actually . . .'

She hesitated.

'What?' he asked. 'What is it?'

'I handed in my notice. I'm going to look for a role where I can be of more use to the world. I know it sounds idealistic, but somebody has to be, right?'

Bear nodded. 'The world needs people like you,' he said. 'I'm so proud of you, Skye. You've faced your fears today.'

Skye felt her heart grow stronger at his words, but she hadn't finished.

'I have to go back to being a person who stood up for what they believed in, although this time I'll go about it the right way. I have to be myself. Once I sorted that out, I realized that there was one last thing I had to be honest about — my feelings for you . . .' She paused. 'I hope that the real me is someone you might want to be with.'

300

It was as if Bear was looking into her soul, and Skye felt electricity in the air, nothing to do with the storm outside. It pulsed through her, her fingers and toes tingling. She could see crinkles forming in the corners of Bear's eyes, a smile forming. She felt the corners of her mouth turn up in response.

'What do you think?' said Bear. 'The real you is *exactly* the person I want to be with.'

Skye bit her lip, holding his gaze, then leaned in. Bear reached out, put his hands on her shoulders and pulled her closer. He moved with caution, taking care where she was hurt.

His lips finally met hers, and as they kissed Skye felt nothing but pure happiness radiate through her. More than happiness. She had never had a kiss like it, and she held tight to Bear, never wanting to let him go.

* * *

'So, why did you not want to come back with me earlier? You sounded so far away on the phone. I thought you were letting me down gently,' Skye said, pushing her back into her seat.

Bear looked at her as though she had put one and one together and made seventy-three. 'I would never do that.' He scratched his neck as he thought about it. 'Maybe it was this? The bank approved my loan.'

Skye squealed. 'That's what you meant about prospects! I'm such an idiot — I cut you off as you were telling me. I'm so sorry. And I can't believe I didn't ask you. Bear, that's amazing.' She threw her arms around him, then pulled back, still gripping his shoulders. 'That's brilliant.'

Bear grinned. 'Thanks. I had everything I needed, so I went to the office and resigned. In the same way you want to be you, I need to be me. It wasn't an easy conversation though, so perhaps that's why I sounded distracted. I'm sorry if I did. I had to psyche myself up for it.'

A rapture rushed through her, warming her body. They were like two halves which fitted together perfectly, lost to each other but now found. Without knowing, and like at so many other points in their lives, their actions today had mirrored one another's, each of them taking a risk to live the lives they wanted.

Skye let out a laugh of joy and relief.

'Don't apologize.' She flung her arms around him afresh, squeezing him tightly for a second, before moving back a little to speak. 'How did your mum take it?'

Bear grimaced. 'She was disappointed. But also upset that I'd not told her before. She can't be that annoyed, though, or she wouldn't have agreed to letting me borrow this to come back and see you.'

A kind of calm descended over Skye, as if the universe had found harmony once more. She leaned in, and kissed him once more.

'It's as well you did, really,' said Skye, when she could again think clearly. 'Seeing as I trashed my car and almost got struck by lightning as a result.'

A car pulled onto the road ahead, drawing Skye's attention. 'Oh, look! There's Holly, Hamish and Paolo. Oh, and Chloe too. Do you think it's safe to get out now?'

'The rain has eased off,' said Bear. 'So I'd imagine so. Hey, before you get out, where were you planning on staying tonight?'

Skye grinned. 'It'll be a shame not to enjoy my four-poster this weekend, but I think a B&B, don't you?'

She stopped, and squinted ahead. 'Oh my gosh! Terrible timing, but hold that thought.'

A fifth figure had got out of the car. With more white hair than when she had last seen him, and a very fine tan, Uncle Hugh stormed towards the car with intent.

Skye leapt out, and ran towards him. 'Uncle Hugh! I'm so glad you're here.'

He took his glasses off and eyeballed her. 'I get back from holidays, call Holly for an update on the surgery, and turns out all this is going on! Why didn't you try harder to get hold of me? If I'd known you were here I'd have come back immediately,' he said gruffly. Then he beamed. 'Come here.'

'For that exact reason,' said Skye. She threw her arms around him. 'But I've been very well looked after in your absence. And you know what? I've had a wee crisis, but I think everything's going to be OK.'

'Well, I'm very glad to hear it.' Hugh smiled.

She looked over to the doe, who was being treated by the roadside. 'Is the deer going to be OK?'

Hugh put a hand on her arm. 'We'll see, we'll see. I'll let Holly work her magic. And who is this?'

Hugh peered around Skye, who spun round to see Bear approaching.

'Ah,' said Skye. 'There's someone I'd like you to meet.'

EPILOGUE

The following morning, Skye yawned in a breath of salty air, and pushed her feet into the sand on the beach. The tide was out, and the harbour beach was empty, but for a tiny Jack Russell and his owner. Skye smiled, as it trotted along the sand, sniffing under rocks, and chasing the birds.

'One latte and a croissant,' came a voice from behind her.

Skye turned around, her heart swelling at the sight of Bear. He sat down on the rock next to her, presenting her with both, then unrolled his own paper bag.

'Maybe we have a low-key day today,' he suggested, giving her lips a soft kiss. 'After the excitement of yesterday. A trip to a distillery, or a hike. You can show me the bits of Eastercraig I've missed. Perhaps I can properly meet your uncle, unless you'd like some alone time to catch up with him.'

'No, I think he'd like you to come along,' said Skye. 'As would I. Yes, let's stay local today.'

Skye pondered a walk along the coast path, to where they had met at the start of the month. Their rock. They could continue further, along to the crumbling remains of Lowndes Castle. It was a romantic ruin, with an air of mystery that lured you in. Bear would love it, and it seemed a fitting expedition, starting from the point where this had all began.

Bear pulled a cinnamon bun out of its bag, and chewed contemplatively. He took a sip of his coffee, then tried another bite.

'Something not quite right?' asked Skye.

'Good, but not as good as my grandmother's. I remember saying I'd make you some. Once we're back in Edinburgh.'

Skye felt a flicker of excitement at all that his words entailed. She looked down at the ground, to hide her outsized grin.

'Do you think the doe will be OK?' he asked. 'Have you heard from anyone this morning?'

Skye looked up. 'The outlook is sunny! Hamish texted to say Holly took it back to the surgery, and bandaged its poor legs. He also said I'm a soppy lass, because he'd have shot it. The fawn's at someone called Mandy's smallholding, and the mum will join it later. And I spoke to the mechanic. He can sort both our cars by next weekend, and has a courtesy car that we can have in the meantime.'

'Grand. I don't know what your plans are for returning to Edinburgh, but if you wanted to drive back down with me on Sunday night, I thought I might go and look at office premises this week.'

'Are you looking for trendy, or trad? Or is that a daft question?'

'I think you know the answer. One thing I wanted to do, though, was make it dog-friendly. Looking at this chap has reminded me how I've always wanted a dog. Are you a dog person?'

'I am,' said Skye. 'I like dogs, cats, horses and deer, obviously. But I have a real thing for Bears.'

Bear looked down at her. 'Good. Glad that's sorted.'

THE END

ACKNOWLEDGEMENTS

They say it takes a village to raise a child. There are parallels to be drawn when it comes to writing books. There are lots of people who've helped this book on its way, and I'm supremely grateful to them all.

Huge thanks to Emma Grundy Haigh at Joffe Books, for bright ideas, endless patience, and knowing about gerunds. Also to Becky Slorach, Sarah Tranter and Elizabeth Hinks. And all the rest of the team at Joffe Books for all their hard work.

Thank you to Laura Macdougall at United Agents for all your support, and to Olivia Davies. Also, to Amy Mitchell, and the UA Foreign Rights department.

To my lovely friends without whose input I would have struggled. The James Street Girls and the Hens deserve a special shout out for eleventh hour brainstorming.

Gigantic thank you to Jake. You've been so supportive, patient and generally wonderful. I'm so glad I found you.

THE JOFFE BOOKS STORY

We began in 2014 when Jasper agreed to publish his mum's much-rejected romance novel and it became a bestseller.

Since then we've grown into the largest independent publisher in the UK. We're extremely proud to publish some of the very best writers in the world, including Joy Ellis, Faith Martin, Caro Ramsay, Helen Forrester, Simon Brett and Robert Goddard. Everyone at Joffe Books loves reading and we never forget that it all begins with the magic of an author telling a story.

We are proud to publish talented first-time authors, as well as established writers whose books we love introducing to a new generation of readers.

We won Trade Publisher of the Year at the Independent Publishing Awards in 2023. We have been shortlisted for Independent Publisher of the Year at the British Book Awards for the last four years, and were shortlisted for the Diversity and Inclusivity Award at the 2022 Independent Publishing Awards. In 2023 we were shortlisted for Publisher of the Year at the RNA Industry Awards.

We built this company with your help, and we love to hear from you, so please email us about absolutely anything bookish at feedback@joffebooks.com

If you want to receive free books every Friday and hear about all our new releases, join our mailing list: www.joffebooks.com/contact

And when you tell your friends about us, just remember: it's pronounced Joffe as in coffee or toffee!